The Sorcerer's Song and the Cat's Meow

By

A. A. Roberts

AN EVERWHEN BOOK

Printed in the United States of America

ISBN 978-1-84728-725-0

Published by

Everwhen Productions

Ashford, CT 06278

Contact: *marketing@genspace.com*

This book is dedicated to my editor, father and best friend

Dr. Arthur D. Roberts

and of course the angel I got to marry

Elizabeth

And all the other wonderful people who have assisted in my artistic enevours over the years.You know who you are and you will not be forgotten.

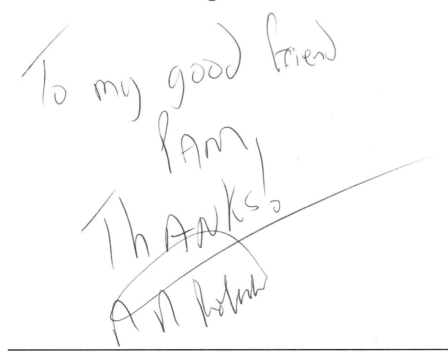

Place a

picture of

your cat

here

Pendella Purrfect

Contents

Of the Feline Pendella Purrfect

My name is Aikeem Abdul Jamal Yosaffa, and it is with a singular clarity that I recall my first encounter with the feline Pendella Purrfect—also known as Orc Slayer, but that is another story. I was in New York City in the late spring of 1980, and it was very early in the morning. I was walking the streets of the city, admiring its nocturnal essence, when I chanced upon a deserted alley. I heard a faint rummaging echoing from the dark at the other end of this place, and my curiosity got the better of me.

At the end of the alley, under a pile of discarded paper, a tail whipped back and forth. Some creature was having great fun with some garbage. My foot brushed an empty can, startling the creature, and out popped a cat.

I knew the instant she was in full view that this was no ordinary cat. If you looked just right and concentrated on the non-electromagnetic end of the spectrum, you could see an amber aura surrounding this feline of obvious prodigious talent.

"This," I thought, "is a creature of power," whereupon she gave me her most seductive kitty-eyes.

I am quite familiar with this unique, feline form of non-verbal communication. The cat in question, like others of its kind, will close its eyes halfway and in such a manner as to enthrall your spirit. If a human female were to do this to a man, his mind, body, and soul would become enslaved to her. Cats, being of a different species, are just looking to ensnare your heart, soul and the occasional fishy treat.

"It seems, dear lady," I said, for it was obvious to me she was female, "that I have caught you at play."

Imagine my surprise when the lady meowed and a wave of communication poured over me. It was more than telepathy and, at the same time, less. It was a million subtle movements intertwined with a look and a powerful thought that all translated into, "Play? I was sharpening my nails. There is adventure to be had this night." She watched me very carefully. I imagine she expected me to run screaming from the alley.

Did I mention I'm a bit of a traveler? I am not native to America or a New Yorker for that matter. I was born Egyptian, but I like to think of myself as a man of the Earth. I have seen many strange things during my travels, and believe it or not, having this cat talk to me was not among the strangest.

"Adventure, you say? Of what sort would that be, dear lady?"

I smiled at her perplexed look. It is not too often one sees a confused kitty. They are ever sure of themselves. She collected herself and came closer.

"Adventure in the name of the Thirteen of which I am a member."

Now it was my turn to be surprised. Did I mention I'm a bit of a historian? Let me tell you of the Thirteen. Each of the major species (except humans) has a Council of Thirteen whose charter is to protect its members from extinction and enemy forces (whatever form these forces may take). Most of the councils were created just before the Great Purge (yet another story), and every member is imbued with arcane powers.

Not all of the councils serve the best interests of the world, and some are harbingers of evil. You can guess who those might be: the rats, the snakes, the jackals, the bats, and particularly the three-toed sloths. They're very bitter about not having the other two toes.

Typically, the council members remain hidden and direct their charges from secret places. So it was much to my surprise that this feline had revealed herself to me.

"I know of the Thirteen, dear Lady. I am honored that you have disclosed yourself to me."

"I am Pendella Purrfect, and I am in need of a human this night. I think you'll do." With this the lady rubbed up against my leg and claimed me for herself.

I suppose most men would have been put off by the lady's assumption that I would simply acquiesce to her desires, but I have never been like most men. I picked the lady up and stroked her neck, and she let her motor go with a purr most profound.

After ten minutes of this, my fingers were becoming quite sore. I finally asked, "So what is the nature of this adventure, Pendella?"

Pendella shrugged herself out of my arms and jumped to the ground. "We go to battle the gutter folk. They are up to dark purposes this night. Come." And with the flick of a tail, we were off into the night.

Pendella led me across many side streets, down secret alleys, under little traveled bridges, and over seldom-used paths until we came to a manhole. She plumped her little arse down in front of the steel plate and began to lick her paws. "You may open it."

"Miss Purrfect, why is it you so quickly assume that I can open this steel portal?"

"Because I choose my humans well."

I suppose this was meant to be a compliment, but cats do have a way of making you feel inferior even when they are complimenting you. Of course, she was right.

Did I mention I'm a bit of an engineer? Not that one needs to be an engineer to open a manhole cover, but it does mean that I am given to carrying a minimal tool set in my trusty backpack, which I always have with me. After several seconds of rummaging through my pack, I withdrew my special pry bar. It is special because it was made for me by the great oriental craftsman Shang Sen Su. Besides being virtually unbreakable, its ends are ingeniously designed to serve several purposes, and it collapses to only ten inches in length. After only an instant, I had the cover off. Of course, this yielded a look of, "I told you so," from Miss Purrfect, but I ignored this dismissive gesture.

"What a delightful aroma you've discovered, Pendella. I assume we're to enter this dark place?"

Pendella wrinkled her nose at the stench wafting up from the nether regions and said, "That is a smell only a dog could love."

A faint tittering noise followed the stench, and I gave Pendella a sideways look. "How many gutter folk are to be expected?"

"It matters not, newly beloved. I will protect you," she said, and with this the lady jumped into the sewer. Now, I am not adverse to adventure. As a matter of fact, there are some who say I crave it. But I prefer my adventure in light airy spaces, not in dark, dank, smelly affairs. I pondered the black hole in front of me for a few seconds, and then sighed. I pulled a flashlight from my trusty knapsack, and clumsily dropped through the hole. I knew I wasn't going to like this.

Pendella waited for me on the narrow, stone curb that lined this very old sewer. She was dry. I was not.

Pendella marched off into the gloom, and I followed. "Are you going to enlighten me as to why we are pursuing the gutter folk? I hope it is for more than a late night snack on your part."

"Unlike some of my canine acquaintances, I do not think with my stomach."

"I'm surprised you have any contact with dogs at all. I thought you felines hated them."

"Not at all. Some of my best friends are dogs. Rodents, on the other hand, are an entirely different story. One of our informants has suggested that the foul Lord Dark Seer is going to try and raise one of the nameless ones tonight."

I stopped in horror. "One of the nameless dark gods?!?"

"It's true."

"Is this Dark Seer insane? Does it not know what horrors these creatures are capable of committing? Does it not know that these vile beasts destroy all life without exception?"

Pendella shrugged. "Rats are like that."

I followed her in amazement. I could not comprehend any creature being so craven as to risk creation, and its own immortal soul, by releasing one of these nameless horrors upon the world. Rats do have a tough go of it, being near the bottom of the food chain and all, but surely things weren't that bad?

We traveled for what seemed an interminably long time. The farther we went, the louder the tittering became, and the more foul the stench. Eventually, I pulled a bandanna from my pack and covered my nose. My olfactory system was close to overload, and I imagined in my mind's eye that my nose was turning gray and falling off my face.

The sides of the sewer were caked with a thick, brown sludge. Here and there a sickly green, gelatinous substance bubbled up from the heart of the brown sludge. Occasionally, a snake-sized worm or a cockroach of prodigious size would wriggle out of said sludge.

Eventually, I was able to turn off my flashlight. Whatever the fungus on the ceiling of this dank place was, it gave off a green glow that cast an evil, but visible pallor to this subterranean nightmare. Pendella stopped immediately, as did my heart.

"What is it?" I asked in a barely audible whisper.

She was gone in a flash, and for the first time, I began to feel fear.

I waited a few minutes. Finally, I could not contain myself. "Oh, Miss Pendella. Where have you gone?"

There was a splash behind me, and I spun with a start. Pendella dropped the carcass of a monstrous dead rat into the putrid water. "Must you make so much noise? We are in the heart of the gutter folks' lair. A bit more caution is advised."

"Well, excuse me, but I thought you had abandoned me!"

"I told you I would protect you. I was merely removing their sentries."

"Plural? There are more of this size?" I asked incredulously.

"Ten, actually, but now there are no more. Come."

My eyes must have been as wide as saucers. "Ten! I don't even like the one! It's awfully large."

Pendella ignored me and continued her trek through the slimy place. A little farther on the sewer began to widen. After a few hundred feet, it opened into an immense concrete cavern filled with ankle-deep, gray-colored, fetid water. In the center of that cavern was a sight to send shivers up the spine of the stoutest of heart.

Thousands of rats circled a clearing wherein thirteen upright, man-sized rats circled a very small pool of slime. The thirteen rats wore rags that were formed into long, dirty robes. Two of them held staffs made from some poor creature's bones. These wizard rats—for that is what they had to be—swayed back and forth and tittered loudly, waving vicious looking upraised claws. The pool of slime before them must have been about a foot in diameter, and it glowed with an eerie green light.

For some strange reason, my horror turned to humor, and I laughed quietly. I turned to Pendella and said, "I thought you said they were trying to raise a nameless one? It looks more like they're trying to raise a pool of slime. Why? Because rats are like that."

Pendella looked at me askew, obviously uncertain of my mental condition. There was a crack of thunder and a bolt of black lightning that deafened my senses. The rats all began to titter in unison. My humor changed back to horror as I watched a huge glob of slime rise up out of the pool and instantly become a quivering mass of putrid flesh the size of five elephants.

The wizard rats all scampered away, but some of their slower fellows were not so lucky and were consumed in the growing mass of corrupted, green flesh. A black maw of torn cartilage and broken teeth opened on one side of the creature and issued a scream that causes me shivers to this day.

"Really Pendella, we weren't invited to this party. Maybe we should leave."

Pendella gave me a sideways glance and returned her attention to the monstrosity before us. "We're a bit late."

"And I forgot my Nameless Horror Be Gone Spray," I quipped.

"If only I had thought to bring some salt with me," Pendella lamented.

I looked at Pendella and wondered where she would keep salt even if she had it. "Salt?"

"It has been my experience that creatures of this configuration do not react kindly to salt. It tends to melt them."

"And how much salt would be required to do the job?"

"A ton."

"A ton! Lady, we do not have time to conscript a salt merchant and a dump truck!"

"Well, we could get by on only a handful if it was lobbed into the creature's mouth."

The creature screamed again, and its maw, which was on the other side of a sea of blood thirsty rats, was easily the size of a small room.

"And being the only member of this party with the necessary appendages capable of throwing salt into said mouth, that task would fall to me?"

"If we had salt."

I will not repeat what I grumbled as I began to dig into my trusty backpack, which of course contained not one, but two handfuls of salt. Did I mention I'm a bit of a gourmet chef?

I swear that cat was smiling when she said, "I told you I choose my humans well."

It was just about that moment that the two of us noticed several thousand beady, feral, red glowing eyes staring at us.

"My that's unnerving. Any ideas your Highness? I'm feeling a bit outnumbered."

"I told you I would protect you," and with this Pendella's aura began to burn more brightly.

Oh, it was a sight to behold. That amber light wrapped around her like an ethereal cloak. Her coat began to take on a metallic sheen. The rats that had begun to advance stopped. Pendella crouched low, and her tail whipped about like a razor lash. Her entire body seemed to have tripled in size, and her canines (or would that be felines?) quadrupled in size.

One of the wizard rats at the other end of the cavern screamed at its cohorts and pointed its bone staff at Pendella and me. That's when they charged.

The screams of the rats were deafening, but they were nothing compared to the roar that issued from Pendella. She met the rodent's front head on, and I was reminded of an ambulatory meat grinder. Rat bits flew all about as Pendella opened up a red path through the sea of rodents before me. Without hesitation—well, maybe a little bit—I followed Pendella into the sea of vermin.

I swung my backpack about with one hand and clutched the salt with the other. The wizard rat closest to the slime god aimed his staff at me, and I ducked none too soon. A dark ray of black light shot forth and blasted apart the sewer wall behind me. Great chunks of the concrete fell into the ankle deep water and crushed the rats who were slow to move.

The slime god reared up on its hind sludge and screamed from that horrific mouth. It then made for us in an undulating motion that I found quite disturbing.

Pendella's momentum had been halted, although she managed to keep the rats at bay. At our feet, just under the water, were the bones of what must have been homeless people who had been unfortunate enough to discover the secret of the gutter folk.

One of the other wizard rats raised his staff in our direction and began to chant in a rodent-squeak voice. Its staff glowed with an evil, purple light. I decided this was intolerable, so I picked up a splintered femur at my feet and hurled it at the rodent. It made a most delightful squeal when the skeletal spear pierced its heart.

This activity served to inspire Pendella once more, and she regained her momentum toward the slime beast that was, in turn, headed toward us. I resumed swinging my backpack and crushing more than one vermin skull until we were within but a few feet of the nameless slime god.

It was ugly, but even worse, it smelled like death and sewage combined. Great green gobs of greasy, grimy, gobs of rotten, malodorous, fibrous… well you get the idea, were falling off it. It screamed again, and I could not shield my ears from this nerve shattering noise. I hurled my plastic-wrapped handful of salt into that vent of noxious smells, and for the first time the blasted creature went completely silent.

Now it's hard to say that anything with no discernable features got a funny look, but somehow that's precisely what happened. The rats all ceased their attack and the wizard rats lowered their staves, which were in the process of powering up. The slime god began to shake and pulsate.

Pendella turned to me. She was quite out of breath and had a very concerned expression on her face. "I think it's time to go," and with that she turned and ran.

The rats all began backing away from their dark creation, and the wizard rats were suddenly nowhere to be found. That's when it occurred to me to run like hell.

I was just at the entrance to the cavern when the thing blew. It didn't blow up into bits; it blew out into an ever-increasing blob of disgusting slime. The rats screamed as they were swept up in this tidal wave of puke green, nameless god chowder spewed from the cesspools of hell.

I was about fifty yards in front of the mess when it hit the sewer I was in. I ran as fast as I had ever run in my life. I even caught up to Pendella who had reverted to her normal feline form.

"You didn't tell me it was going to turn into a river of goo!"

Pendella leapt up on to my backpack as I ran past her, and as she hung on for dear life she simply replied, "Run faster!"

The mess was only a dozen yards behind us when I leapt to the highest rung I could reach below the open manhole cover. I scurried up the rest of the rungs, and Pendella leapt from my backpack out through the opening. I lofted myself over the edge as the goo bubbled up from below me, but I was too late… my brand new shoes were ruined.

I threw the manhole cover back over the open pit and sat down against a pile of discarded boxes. Pendella came over next to me and sat on her haunches.

"You did well human. I would have your name."

I smiled, realizing I had never given the lady my name. "I am Aikeem Abdul Jamal Yosaffa, dear lady, and when you promise adventure, you do not lie."

"Cats never lie, Aikeem; that is a human construct."

"That may be lady, but I've known a few given to exaggeration."

I saw the smile in Pendella's eyes, and she replied by jumping into my lap and rolling on her back. I stroked her neck and belly, and she began to purr loudly.

"You are a fine human. I'm so glad I selected you."

"Me too, Pendella Purrfect."

And that was how I met and became Pendella's companion for many, many years. We've had innumerable adventures, and I'm sure we will have many more. Did I mention I'm immortal?

Of the Human Aikeem Abdul Jamal Yosaffa

My name is Pendella Purrfect, and I am very important. I am the tenth in the Circle of Thirteen, and I am often given the most dangerous tasks to fulfill in the name of felinity. I am not particularly big or strong, but I am exceptionally beautiful. I try not to trade on my beauty, but humans can't help themselves in my presence. One must be tolerant of humans, for in most cases they mean well, and they do give such wonderful massages. Puuuuuuuurrrrrrrrrrrr.

Only last season, I acquired a new human. He proved himself to be worthy of my association, and since his initiation, we have had many adventures together. I was pleased to discover that not only is his lap very warm and his hands soft and skilled, but he also has considerable talents in areas that most humans do not know exist. Let me tell you of our most recent adventure.

My human's name is Aikeem Abdul Jamal Yosaffa. Our journey through the world brought us to the edge of a great desert that Aikeem called the Sahara. Personally, I'm not fond of deserts. I prefer lands that are green and moist. Aikeem seems to have sand in his blood.

As we trekked across the great expanse of sand, I could hear Aikeem grumbling about having to carry us both. I was within the confines of his wonderful knapsack. His knapsack is wonderful because Aikeem has laid magics on it that control the atmosphere inside. I was as cool as a kitten. He was not.

We were headed to a place Aikeem called Qar. Aikeem told me that in its day it was a splendid city, but the sands had long since claimed Qar for their own. Personally, I had no desire to go to this place, but I could see that it called to Aikeem. Actually, it had been calling to him for a few weeks, although he refused to admit it. I could tell by his agitated sleep that something was wrong. Finally, I became impatient with him—he kept rolling about, and he knocked me off the bed on more than one occasion—and I entered his dream.

Typically, I'll only enter a human's dream to protect them from shadow creatures and nightmares, but this was something else. I trotted behind Aikeem as he walked through the ethereal mirror of the once mighty Qar. Humans in long robes haggled with each other in a lively market. Gaily dressed women in fine gold jewelry and fancy feather headdresses hid from the noonday sun under palm and bamboo parasols. Children played tag about the various kiosks, much to the dismay of the merchants. And, of course, there was the occasional canine munching on some disgusting, smelly bit of garbage. Sigh… Aikeem did not dream up even a single cat, and I didn't count because I was there of my own accord.

At any rate we moved through this market in what seemed like slow motion. No one seemed to notice us as Aikeem looked for something. He stopped, and I followed his gaze. She was breathtaking. I am quite capable of recognizing a beautiful human, and this woman fairly glowed beauty. Her waist-long, straight, black hair blinded me with its intense, radiant sheen. Her dark brown chocolate eyes were wide, but decidedly feline. Her angular face still held soft edges, and her lustrous brown skin cried out to be touched, much like my own beautiful multi-colored fur.

At once, I realized Aikeem knew this woman. When he saw her, his expression transformed into one of pure bliss. The woman turned to Aikeem, and her expression mirrored Aikeem's. Instantly they started for each other. Their arms were stretched out to one another as they ran to embrace. And then the skies became angry.

I found it quite disconcerting, even if it was the Dreamscape, that the skies should so quickly turn to an evil, inky-black, boiling, roiling mess. Aikeem and this woman still ran to each other oblivious of the environment. Lightning blasted out of the heavens, and struck down one of the city's towers. A face began to take form in the clouds. Wild winds whipped up, and the merchants and children ran for their lives. Still Aikeem and this woman moved toward each other.

The face in the clouds formed into a most vile human apparition. This man was decidedly evil. He was mostly hidden within the folds of his black cotton ghutrah, but his dark, burning eyes spoke of profound hatred. This was most intolerable, so I did what any self-respecting dream warrior would do. I leapt on Aikeem's back and bit his ear to wake him from this terrible nightmare. My reward? He kicked me off the bed. Sigh…

It was our second night in the desert when Aikeem finally decided to tell me of his dream. Aikeem had stopped our march, and had laid out a comfy fire. The desert night was crisp and cool, and the sky was gloriously lit by a million brilliant stars. I lay on my lover's lap, and Aikeem stroked my fur with sensitive but firm hands. Puuuuuuuuuurrrrrrrrrrrr.

"Tell me of the woman in your dreams, Aikeem. She was very beautiful."

Aikeem became melancholic. At first his expression was a little sad, but it turned into a smile when he spoke. "Jamila. Her name was Jamila. At one point in my life, she was my very reason for living."

"What happened to her?"

"She was taken from me."

"By the man in the black cotton ghutrah?"

The light of realization illuminated Aikeem's eyes, and he looked down at me with a most incredulous expression. "That was you in my dream so many weeks ago! What were you doing there?"

"Protecting you, of course. Like most humans you can be most careless on the Dreamscape."

Aikeem's gentle laughter rolled across the desert. "And you dear lady can be most presumptuous, although this time I thank you for waking me. Yes, it was that vile wizard Farjule that took my beloved Jamila from me. I have loved since then, but never as passionately. Jamila had a light about her that could redeem the damned. Everything about her bespoke beauty, and I was proud that she chose me as her lover."

"What did this wizard do?"

Aikeem stretched out before the fire, and I was forced to lie down next to him. He stared intently at the fire as he told me his story.

"I was unaware of my immortality when I entered the city of Qar over five thousand years ago. At the time, I was only in my forties. That was old back then, but I thought nothing of it at the time for I was still young looking and strong. Jamila was young. She had only just turned twenty, but it scandalized the city's populace that she had not taken a husband. Her father doted on her, and would not force her to marry. Qar was strong with a standing army that no potentate dared challenge. So, Shah Romalla could afford to dispense with the necessity of a political marriage. As I said, he doted on Jamila.

"In my early days, before I discovered my true nature, I was a warrior of notable talents. Few dared tempt my scimitar. I came to Qar with the intent of enlisting in the Shah's army. I had become tired of roaming the various city-states of the desert, and I desired to settle down for a time. I was given an audience with the Shah based upon recommendations from my former employers. He offered me a position of captain, if I could best ten of his most skilled warriors."

Aikeem smiled with vivid memory. "I was so brash. I asked the Shah what weapons his warriors would wield in that I did not wish to kill anyone in his service. The Shah explained to me that this would be a non-lethal test and that his warriors would swing only wooden swords. He was gracious enough to extend the invitation of a wooden sword to me. I declined and asked only for a small tin cup. The Shah had a most curious expression on his face when I asked for this innocuous item, but he was too dignified to ask what I might do with it.

"His soldiers circled me and I stuck the cup in my sash. They were good, but I was much, much better. I danced among them like... well, a cat."

"Oh, then you must have been very good," I observed.

"Much to their dismay. Within a few short minutes I had made a neat pile of them at the Shah's feet. At that point I whipped out my cup and asked for a victory drink. I do believe they heard the Shah laughing in the next city over."

"Aikeem you truly are crazy some times."

"Thank you, my lady. I take that as a compliment. At any rate, it was at this point that the princess Jamila revealed herself to me. When our eyes met, the entire palace seemed to disappear. It was just two of us locked in an embrace that seemed to span the throne room. I remember that the Shah cleared his throat to snap us back to reality, and I noticed a smile at the corner of his lips. I think he had finally spied a husband for his beloved Jamila."

"Obviously you were hired as captain."

"I was made captain of the Princess's Guard. The Shah REALLY wanted a husband for his daughter. Our courtship lasted only a month before we were engaged. If only I had known about Farjule, the Shah's wizard, before it became too late, things might have been different. You see, I came to find out later that he too had vied for Jamila's attentions."

"Human jealousy, I've seen it before."

"And Farjule's was caustic. At first he suffered in silence, but the week before we were to be wed, he cornered me in one of the palace gardens. He threatened to feed my soul to the sand demons if I did not abandon my Jamila."

"Sand demons are most annoying."

"And thankfully extinct. At any rate, I laughed in the wizard's face and told him if he so much as blinked in either my or Jamila's direction, I would cut out his heart. I should have killed him then and there."

"What did he do?"

"Now I must tell you of the Jewel of Qar. In the center of the city, under a fountain in a strong room, rested the Jewel of Qar. Jamila showed it to me early on, and it was magnificent. This was no ordinary gem. It was a fiery red ruby that glowed from within, and it almost seemed to emit delicate music that played at the edge of your consciousness. Qar derived its strength from this gem, or so they said anyway. In retrospect, I believe it was true."

"It was an artifact of power?"

"I believe this to be so. After all, Qar was in the middle of the desert, but for miles around the city the land was verdant. It made no sense until one saw this gem. It was Jamila's job by tradition and as a princess to care for the Jewel, and she was always polishing the stone."

"Humans love such baubles."

"You seem to be quite fond of the silk, jeweled collar I got you."

"That's different."

"Of course. Anyway, three days before we were to be wed, Jamila, the Jewel of Qar, and Farjule all disappeared."

"He stole the ruby and the Princess?"

"Who else could have? Besides, Farjule, Jamila, the Shah and myself, no one had access to the strong room. The Shah was distraught. He knew of Farjule's infatuation for his daughter, and he knew of the man's vile temper. He begged me to return both his daughter and the gem to him. It was not as if I needed to be asked.

"I took fifty men with me. We knew that he had fled the city for the desert so we headed out into the sands. The wizard threw everything he could at us, sand demons, rocs, a fire jinn, but in the end nothing could defeat my fury. I was down to only three men when finally we tracked him down. He used the last of his magic to send a fierce sandstorm to hide his path, but it was to no avail. Our scimitars made love amid howling winds and biting grit. My last three soldiers watched with grim expressions as Farjule and I danced the dance of death. Eventually, I beat his sword from his hand."

"Did you cut off his head?"

Aikeem laughed a mirthless laugh. "Oh, no lady, I did much worse. Farjule did much more than steal my woman and the city's bauble; he showed me my true path. I bid one of the soldiers to bring me one of his dark tomes from the packs on his steed. We staked him out in the sands and bade him tell us where he hid the lady and the stone. He swore he had taken neither and had run simply because he knew he would be blamed. I knew in my heart he was a liar. The storm disappeared and the blistering sun showed itself to Farjule. While it baked him, I studied his book of dark magic. Still he did not speak the truth. I leaned close to him and whispered in his ear. 'Tell me where my lady is, Farjule, or your ghost will roam this desert forever.'

"I could see the fear in his eyes as he realized which section of his book I had been studying. Then he cried and pleaded with me, but he would not tell the truth."

"What did you do to him?"

"I cursed him as he died. I cursed him with the charm of specter. My soldiers did not have the gift of the sight so they did not see what I did. As the sun baked the life out of him, his spirit rose up and was denied passage to the next world because of my curse. I'll never forget the look of hatred he gave me. His parting sneer should have warned me of things to come. Finally his ghost fled across the sands and we burned his body."

"Remind me to never make you angry."

Aikeem smiled at me and gave me a most delightful rub under the chin. "You could never make me that angry lady. I returned to Qar with my remaining men, but the city was gone."

"Gone!?"

"Farjule must have laid some curse upon the city while we battled. The city and its inhabitants had disappeared into the desert sand. Everything I held dear was lost to me. It would be centuries before I could love again."

"And now the city calls to you again."

"So it would seem. You've seen one dream. There have been others. Someone calls to me and asks for forgiveness and protection. I do not understand, for the words come in many voices, and as one voice. Some of these voices are familiar."

"Do you think the city will be revealed to you?"

"The voice of voices says this is true."

"How long until we are there?"

"Another day's journey, lady. Now let us rest, for one of us has a lot of marching to do."

"I don't understand why we didn't take one of your human conveyances."

"There is dark magic afoot here lady, and these conveyances can be turned against you."

With this Aikeem laid his head down and was soon asleep. I pondered his words for a short while and then joined him on the Dreamscape.

We continued our trek across the desert very early the next morning. After a few hours the pillow-lined compartment I was in began to shake and spin violently. I ran out of the room and scampered out of the portal to pop out of Aikeem's knapsack. I found him on his hands and knees coughing up a foul smelling effluent.

"Do you have a fur ball?"

After a few gags, he managed to compose himself, and he turned to me.

"No lady. Evidently we are heading in the wrong direction."

"I don't understand Aikeem."

"Since we entered the Sahara, I've been guided to Qar by my stomach. If I head in the wrong direction I become nauseated. When I tumbled down that last dune it was in the wrong direction, and, thus, I was forced to my knees and the Technicolor yawn."

"Really, Aikeem, you must be more careful. Being tossed about like that in your pack is quite disconcerting." With that, I returned to my comfy room in Aikeem's wonderful knapsack. I won't repeat what I heard him grumble as we resumed our trek.

We rested again during the heat of the day under a broad white tarpaulin Aikeem kept in his pack. Toward evening we resumed our travels. A few minutes before dusk, we topped a large dune, and Aikeem set his backpack down. I scampered out of the pack to find a broad, empty sand field before us. I sat on my haunches next to Aikeem as the fiery desert sun melted behind a dune. The beauty of the sunset was not lost on me.

"We are here beloved furball."

"I see naught but sand. Where is this Qar?"

Aikeem seemed upset by this observation and scratched his chin. "I do not know lady. This is confusing to me because in my heart of heart I know this to be the place. Not to mention that my stomach no longer troubles me."

"Maybe you need to speak a charm or cast a spell or offer a sacrifice?"

"I know of no charms or spells to raise a city. Perhaps a sacrifice, but I'd prefer not to."

"Why?"

Aikeem smiled a devilish smile. "Because in Qar it was the practice to offer up cats to the gods."

I imagine my total look of horror was quite amusing to Aikeem, for he laughed quite loudly. "Jesting, my princess, just jesting."

"I didn't find that particularly funny."

A smiling Aikeem began to unpack the camp accoutrement. "We'll camp here for the night. The winds seem calm, and this spot affords us a good vantage point."

The chill night air came quickly. Aikeem and I were soon cuddled up next to a comfy fire, and after a brief, but satisfying meal, Aikeem was on the Dreamscape. Once again I chose to follow him there.

Aikeem's dreaming inserted us in the Shah's palace. I trotted just behind Aikeem as we made our way through the royal quarters. Aikeem looked quite dashing in his white silk captain's uniform with a broad red sash, tall black boots, and a scimitar stuck smartly into the sash. I found the feather festooned turban a bit trite, however.

The palace was eerily quiet. After a few moments, it was evident that the place was deserted. Further inspection revealed a thick layer of dust on everything and piles of sand where sand shouldn't be. Aikeem's expression betrayed concern.

After a minute of walking, we entered the throne room. It was splendid and silent. Marble floors were graced with colorful but dusty rugs. Ornate gilded refinements adorned much of the furniture, and the throne itself was comprised mostly of gold. It too was dusty.

Energy coalesced about the throne and a form began to take shape there. My claws extended, but I did not call forth my beast as I felt no immediate danger. The form was decidedly human, but it seemed to be many humans at once. After a few seconds the dominant form became the princess Jamila.

Aikeem's heart nearly melted before my beautiful eyes. I felt for him. He obviously still loved Jamila very much. She reached out to him and in a ghostly voice that was predominately hers, but also many voices, she said simply, "Forgive me…"

With that the Dreamscape shattered, and both Aikeem and I were ejected into deep sleep.

Our sleep was broken apart by a deep rumbling that emanated from the ground beneath us. Aikeem struggled to his feet, but was quickly knocked to his knees. Although I stirred, I was not shaken to the ground. Four paws have their advantages.

The sun blasted through the dawn behind us, and Qar rose from the sands. I have beheld many impressive sights in my long life but few rivaled the image of Qar slowing rising from the sands. Majestic but time worn towers pierced through the earth first. Many tons of sand spilled out of the way as the city walls rose. Onion domed temples, the city's palace, and the rest of the dwellings that comprised Qar soon followed.

At the apex of the city's rising, a fierce wind blew up behind Aikeem and me. Aikeem dived onto his backpack and bedroll to the scream of the winds. I dived on Aikeem's leg and dug in my claws; otherwise, I surely would have been blown away.

The screaming wind raced down the dune into the city and swirled away the sand piled in its streets. This went on for a short time until all of the sand was blown from the city. Finally, the wind ceased as quickly as it began but the screaming remained.

"Laddddddddyyyyyyy!!!!!!! PPPPPllllllleeeeeeaaassseeeeeee!!!!!!"

I retracted my claws and leapt from Aikeem's bloodied leg. "Sorry."

"I am not a scratching post Pendella!"

"You saved me from being taken by the wind Aikeem. Thank you."

I will not repeat what Aikeem grumbled under his breath as he dabbed at the wounds on his leg.

"I assume it is safe to say that this is Qar?"

Aikeem turned back to the city and smiled. "Yes. I have not seen it for five thousand years. It is still beautiful."

Aikeem did not exaggerate. Although I prefer nature's architecture, humanity, on occasion, does produce some fine sculpture. Qar was one of these. The morning sun radiated off the various towers, onion domes and rooftops with a glorious light that boasted of the splendor in which this city once bathed.

Aikeem packed what was left of his belongings into his backpack and hoisted it onto his broad shoulders. He placed me on the backpack and across one shoulder.

"These are strong magics Aikeem. We must proceed with caution."

"This is true lady, and so it shall be done." And with that, we descended the dune and into the city.

We entered through the main gate into the silent place. City banners still hung limply from the walls. They were torn in places but otherwise well preserved. As we walked through this dead metropolis, we noticed most everything was as it was prior to the city's disappearance. A beggar's cane lay against one wall. Clay pots surrounded a merchant's stall. Brightly colored rugs hung from windows. A child's string ball sat unattended.

"It's as if the people just ceased to exist," I observed.

Aikeem remained silent and continued on until we reached the marketplace. The silence was deafening, well, disconcerting anyway. I leapt to the ground as Aikeem surveyed the plaza.

My fur stood on its ends with shock as a hundred ghosts suddenly filled the place. Aikeem started and lurched back against a wall. I ran behind his legs to protect his rear.

In seconds we realized these apparitions did not even seem to know we were there. They went about their business, which evidently had not changed in five thousand years. Merchants haggled with their customers and the children played about the stalls. I looked up at Aikeem, and he simply shrugged, being as confused as I.

Aikeem took two steps into the marketplace, and the ghosts ceased their mundane pursuits. Everyone turned to stare at us. Their expressions went blank.

"My that's unnerving," I observed.

"Hush lady. We do not want to anger them."

They slowly began to surround us. It was hard to tell if they meant us harm, but they all began to raise their fingers and point at Aikeem. Aikeem stepped back against the wall. "I really don't like this."

In one voice all the ghosts said, "Forgive me," and then disappeared.

Aikeem looked down at me, and I shrugged. "It would seem they are in need of redemption. Did they slight you in some way once upon a time?"

"I don't understand lady. I don't know most of these people. It was a large city. I couldn't know everyone."

Aikeem and I almost jumped out of our skins as a nerve-shattering scream pierced the silence.

"Now what?"

"I don't know Aikeem, but I prefer a calm *forgive me* to that."

"You!"

Aikeem tumbled back over me, stepping on my tail I might add!. Towering over us, hands on hips, his dark face revealed, the profoundly hate-filled wizard Farjule glowered at Aikeem.

"Oh, sweet day! You who have cursed me have returned! How long I have waited for this revenge!"

For a second terror filled Aikeem's eyes, but my man was always given to control, and the fear was instantly replaced with self-assurance.

"Farjule, you're looking well. How have you been?"

Farjule's hate was somewhat disarmed by Aikeem's calm manner. "How do you think I am? I've been naught but a listless spirit forced to roam this desert for five thousand years! Do you have any idea how tired I am of sand and scorpions?"

"Really Farjule, you might have considered a hobby."

Farjule squinted with loathing. "You make jokes Aikeem about the curse YOU laid upon me! Now I will have my vengeance! Soon I will be free and the tortures I have planned for you will last centuries."

Aikeem picked himself up off the ground and smiled. "What are you going to do Farjule? Assault me with foul language? Flit annoyingly about my head? You're still just a ghost."

Now it was Farjule's turn to smile. A nerve-killing shriek pierced the air behind us. Aikeem and I spun around to find the source of Farjule's mirth.

The wizard's venomous hiss informed us. "But I have an ally."

"Sand demon," Aikeem yelled.

"I thought you said they were extinct."

This seven-foot horrific apparition staggered toward us. Its skin, if it could be called that, undulated and shifted of its own accord. The creature's face continually changed shape although its dry, runny, dark maw remained in place.

Burning red eyes moved about the top of its head and radiated hate from under a furrowed brow.

The creature staggered toward us, and I began to summon my beast.

"Do not bother lady. Metal claws and a whiptail are no match for this beast. You can not cut sand."

The creature approached, and I ceased my summons. "Then what to do?"

Aikeem spun on a heel and was gone.

"RRRRRRUUUUUUUUNNNNNNN!!!!!"

The creature took a swipe at my tail, but I was already gone. I quickly caught up to Aikeem, who took a quick left down a dark alley. After a few twists and turns, we ended up at a dead-end capped by the city walls. That cursed shriek echoed behind us.

"Really Aikeem! I thought you knew where you were going."

"Lady, I haven't been here for five thousand years! Give me a break!"

"AAAAAAAAAAAAAAIIIIIIIIIIIIIIIIIIIIIIIIIIIEEEEEEEEEEEEEEEEEEEE EE," screamed the demon.

I leapt into Aikeem's arms in what appeared to be fear but was really an attempt to guard his chest. Aikeem backed up against the city wall. The creature appeared at the opposite end of the alley and began to shamble toward us.

"Maybe you could throw some water on it," I speculated.

"Then we would be fighting a wet sand demon."

"Well, then, how does one defeat a sand demon?"

"A fierce wind will disperse it, or you can knock it into a lake or summon a deluge. Unfortunately, I'm prepared for none of these."

Aikeem threw me back to the ground and charged the demon. My man is most brave if not always terribly smart. He flew through the air and launched a vicious flying sidekick at the monster. He made a thud as the kick connected. He passed through the monster and landed on the ground behind it. The demon spun around, grabbed Aikeem's head, and pulled him into its stomach.

It was quite disconcerting to watch my man flail about, suffocating within the gut of that dusty demon. I did what any self-respecting feline warrior would do when confronted with a mobile sandbox of this magnitude. I leapt to the creature's head and peed on it.

Its head began to melt and smell badly before I leapt off. The creature let Aikeem go and fell backwards clutching at its head and reacting to the noxious ammonia odor. Personally, I felt it was overreacting. My pee doesn't smell THAT bad.

"Come Aikeem!"

A dazed Aikeem stumbled after me as he spit sand from his mouth. "What did you do?"

"There is an expression I've often heard you use. I really pissed him off."

"How?"

"I used him as a litter box."

Aikeem burst into laughter as we rounded the corner into the main street. The sand demon screamed and once again gave pursuit. Aikeem scooped me up and began to run down the street. I was placed on the top of Aikeem's backpack as he flew by the silent buildings that lined the streets.

After a few seconds, a huffing Aikeem ran into a central plaza. In the center of the place stood a glorious stone fountain.

"Too bad it no longer spouts water. We could have pushed our granular silica opponent into it," I observed. The creature screamed again from nearby.

"It is getting closer lady. I can't keep this up all day. I swear I'll always bring a wind spell with me when I go into the desert from now on."

With that, the plaza filled with ghosts. This time they seemed intent on doing us harm. Aikeem backed up toward the fountain as hundreds of obviously angry apparitions started toward us.

"This is not going well at all," Aikeem said, just as a stone section of the fountain dropped out behind him and we tumbled over backward. I managed to leap off the backpack to keep from getting crushed, but I too fell down the dark hole into the stone chamber below. At least I landed on my feet.

Poor Aikeem was covered with scrapes and bruises. Blood trickled from a cut over one eye, and I rushed to lick the hurt clean.

"Lady please!"

"I only mean to tend to your wounds."

Aikeem dabbed at the cut with a rag from his pocket. "Thank you lady, but you have a tongue that is akin to sandpaper."

Aikeem groaned and stood to survey the stone chamber around us. With a snap of his fingers, a glow ball appeared over our heads.

"I see you remembered to bring a light spell, not that I have any use for that."

The sand demon screamed from somewhere above and began to pound on the thick stone trap door that had sealed behind us.

"Persistent devil, isn't he? This place looks familiar to me. Let's go that way," Aikeem said as he pointed to an open corridor.

The corridors we traveled were all carved out of rough stone. Iron brackets were intermittently placed on the walls for torches, but no torches had burned there for several millennia. After spending at least half an hour roaming this tomb, we entered a large room with a circular dais in the center.

"By the one God! This is it!"

"And what would that be beloved?"

"This is the Temple of the Jewel! This is the secret chamber where the Jewel of Qar was kept!"

Aikeem approached the dais in silent awe. His light went out. We were cast into a darkness so complete that even I could see nothing. The dais began to radiate a warm, gold light that filled the room. An apparition took form in the center of the dais. At first it seemed to be just a singular human, but then it became many all in the one space.

In a hushed tone I asked, "What is it Aikeem?"

"I do not know lady, but it does not seem hostile."

Aikeem's heart nearly stopped as the shimmering, ethereal image of Jamila formed in the center of the dais.

"Jamila!" Aikeem exclaimed as he ran up the dais. He grabbed the lady's hand, which seemed to be one but many at the same time.

"We are Jamila, Aikeem, but not."

"What are you talking about? What has happened to you my love? What strange magics are these?" Aikeem was desperate to hold her, but she withdrew her hand.

"It is the power of the Jewel, Aikeem. I am Jamila, but I am not. Forgive me."

"I don't understand Jamila. You never wronged me."

"The day we/I disappeared… it was my/our fault not Farjule's."

"What?"

"I/we had taken the jewel back to my room to study it. I/we were foolish. I/we opened a portal to its center and were sucked in."

"You are trapped in the jewel?" Aikeem was most incredulous.

"At first. I/we were desperate to escape. I/we knew so little of the arts but enough to cause great trouble."

Aikeem leapt back from the apparition that instantly transmorphed into Shah Ramalla. "After you left, Aikeem, she unleashed a great power from the jewel. All of the city's inhabitants without exception were drawn into the jewel and made as one."

The apparition changed into one of the city guards. "We are one, but many, Aikeem. We are bound with the jewel."

"Bring Jamila back to me!" Aikeem demanded.

Jamila coalesced from the apparition of the guard. "I am no longer Jamila, Aikeem. You must understand that. I am something more."

"I can bring you back Jamila. It has been many years. I am a great wizard in my own right now."

"No!"

Aikeem was knocked down the steps by the force of that command. He picked himself up, and Jamila smiled down upon him. "You must understand Aikeem. We are something new. We are not what we once were. We have been this way for thousands of years. If you were to separate us, you would kill what we have become."

"A most interesting dilemma. If you free your lady love, you kill the super being she's become."

"Hush lady! I need to think." Aikeem's brow furrowed. He typically does not talk to me like this, but he was quite distracted.

Eventually, Aikeem slumped. He seemed resigned to the fact that his beloved Jamila truly was no more. "You break my heart again Jamila. Why did you summon me here after all of these years? Why do you cause me this pain? I don't know that I can bear to lose you again."

Jamila smiled a sad smile, and the love that was once there was still evident. "I/we still love you Aikeem. Never forget that. I/we would never purposefully cause you pain."

"Then why have you summoned me?"

Jamila's expression turned to one of concern. "Farjule has found Qar. Even now he searches for the Jewel. If he finds it, he will use its power to free himself from the curse you laid upon him. If he does that, the power required of the jewel will separate us and I/we will die. You must forgive us Aikeem and lift the curse from Farjule. He was not to blame for what has happened."

Aikeem slumped to the ground in realization of what he had done. My man was quite distressed. I felt very badly for him, but there was nothing I could do. The weight placed upon his shoulders was ultimately of his own doing.

Aikeem stood and looked into his once beloved's eyes. She smiled and then so did he. "I will always love you Jamila, and, of course, I forgive you."

A bass note rang out from the ground below our feet along with a rumble that must have caused the city to shake. In counter point to this was the ear-shattering scream of the sand demon as it entered the room opposite us. Farjule's malevolent spirit followed close behind.

"Farjule! Would you shut that blasted creature up! It's giving me a headache!"

"It is going to do more than that in a second, Aikeem. It is going to rend you into bloody little bits!"

"Farjule, I never liked you, but now that I have learned the truth, I have come to realize I have done you a great wrong."

Farjule spied Jamila on the dais, but his expression did not soften. "Oh, so the sorceress-wanna-be filled you in on her first and only spell, eh?" Farjule grew even angrier, and he screamed at the many Jamila. "That's why magic requires adult supervision!"

Aikeem frowned. "She has already professed her sorrow to me Farjule, and I have forgiven her. I hope you can forgive me."

Farjule smiled an evil smile as the demon slowly made its way toward us. "Is that supposed to make me call off my demon? Do you honestly believe this pathetic attempt at an apology will let me forget five thousand years of suffering? Do you honestly think that her sudden revelations mean one thing to me? I will have her power and I will be free!"

"No Farjule. You will simply be free. I cursed you, and now I release you." With this Aikeem waved his hands in the air to form an ancient runic gesture. A flash of light filled the air, and Farjule screamed in terror as he realized the curse was broken. Farjule dissolved into the air like so much smoke. An instant later his demon lost cohesiveness and fell into a pile of sand on the floor.

"You have saved us, Aikeem. We will be eternally grateful," the many Jamila said with the most loving of smiles.

"I would die for you Jamila. You know that. Even if you are more than what you once were."

"I am more than what I once was, Aikeem, and I am more for having known you. You must go now for the city must return to the sands. As you travel through the world, Aikeem, know that you are always loved by us and may this in some way sustain you." With that the lady was gone.

Aikeem said nothing as we left the city. I did not attempt to break his silence. I could see he had a very heavy heart. We made our way back to the dune from which we had seen Qar rise. As the sun set opposite us in rosy splendor, Qar sank back into the sands from whence it came. A few tears rolled down Aikeem's cheek, but I pretended not to notice.

I learned from this adventure just how special my man is. He is not given to discussing his emotions with me, so sometimes it is hard for me to understand his truer nature. However, I have seen that he is capable of great humility, forgiveness, and love, and I am proud to say that he has saved some of this love for me. Well, most of this love for me. After all, I am Pendella of the Thirteen. Puuuuurrrrrrrrrrrrrrrrrrr.

A Vanity of Digits

Tony Milano just knew he was one tough kid. Of course, that was before he got lost in New York City. Boy Scout Troop 56 was taking a day trip to see *The Lion King*, and he managed to slip away from the theater. He was so cool. He'd get to see the real New York, not that wussy junk that Disney had on display.

At first it was a lot of fun. He checked out all the new electronics at the circus-like gadget stores that lined Times Square. He shared a butt with a street guy who was playing guitar for the passersby. Some guy even gave him a flyer about a girlie show, but he didn't go to see that. You don't want to be too cool all at once. Besides, he didn't much like girls anyway, never mind with their clothes off. Yuk!

Time flew by, and Tony realized he'd had too much fun. He was lost. All of a sudden, he didn't feel so cool anymore. Everything that moments before seemed new and exciting was now large and menacing. He was afraid to ask for directions. This part of town was rougher than Times Square, and he was scared by what they might do to him if they knew he was lost. He'd heard stories about kids being taken into the sewers and fed to the alligators. He used to laugh at that story. He wasn't laughing anymore.

He turned a corner into a dark, smelly, garbage strewn alley and stopped. There was no way he was going in there. He turned back and a shiver ran down his spine. There were two scary guys staring at him from across the street. They wore long black trench coats and stood about six feet tall. You couldn't see their faces because they were hidden under big floppy hats. Tony could have sworn beady red eyes glowed under those hats.

Tony bolted down the alley. He was sure it connected to the main street on the other side. He was wrong. A rusty chain link fence blocked his way. Tony spun. He looked for a place to hide, but he saw hundreds of beady little eyes peering out at him from under the garbage. Rats!

Tony felt like crying. He felt like a little baby. Those two big men with the floppy hats came for him out of the gloom of the alley. He swore he'd never smoke another cigarette or drink another bottle of beer and that he'd be trustworthy, loyal, helpful, friendly, and the rest of that Boy Scout stuff if he could just escape from this place.

He backed up against the chain-link fence that blocked his escape. He sucked in a lung full of air to scream for help, but the word never came. A foul smelling, furry claw clamped down over his mouth. Tony was snatched up under one arm. He struggled but quickly fell unconscious. Tony wasn't going to make it home tonight.

***

Bechhart Schulman was a mess. His normally perfectly pressed suit was wrinkled. His dirty blonde hair hadn't seen mousse for days and was in wild disarray. Bechhart's normally beautiful blue eyes were red-rimmed and tear-stained. Bechhart's little girl was missing.

Inga was Bechhart's universe. Everything he did he did for his little girl. When she smiled, his life lit up, and when she laughed, Mozart would have been jealous of the music created by her joy. But now she was gone. She had disappeared from the park four days ago while there with Gertrude, Bechhart's wife.

Gertrude immediately went to the police, but so far they had found nothing. Bechhart had not slept for the past two days, and this had not gone unnoticed by his employer. On top of his personal tragedy, he was being called into the boss's office.

Some said that Bennington Wadsworth Sloman III, the Chairman and CEO of Global Finance Corp (GFC), had no soul. Some said he had a computer for a brain and a hard drive for a heart. Bechhart was the CIO of Mr. Sloman's financial conglomerate, and he was not allowed to perform his work at anything less than perfection.

"To hell with the job," Bechhart whispered to himself.

"You may go in now Mr. Schulman," Mr. Sloman's personal secretary said to Bechhart.

With no small amount of trepidation, Bechhart rose from the plush leather seat in the waiting room and opened one of the two large mahogany doors that sheltered Mr. Sloman from the rest of the world. Some said he never came out of this place.

Bechhart had only been in this room a few times before. Contrary to what one might expect, it was filled with fauna from all over South America. This veritable jungle was home to a few tropical birds that flitted about the place. One section of the office even had a small garden with a lawn and a meandering path. For all this foliage, it was still a dark place.

In stark contrast to this natural environment, there stood a mahogany desk with a very powerful computer on it. Looming behind that desk and in the shadows cast by the trees behind him was Mr. Sloman.

"Come Bechhart. Sit." Mr. Sloman pointed to an empty leather chair in front of his desk. Bechhart jumped at the squawk of a parrot from somewhere in the room. Bechhart complied with Mr. Sloman's request.

"Mr. Sloman, I know my performance of late—"

Mr. Sloman held up a gloved hand and silenced Bechhart. "I know of your daughter's disappearance, Bechhart." Mr. Sloman eyed Bechhart from the shadows, sizing him up.

"I also know that the commonly held belief is that I am a heartless monster. I have cultivated this myth myself so as to keep my competitors off balance, but the fact of the matter is that it's not true Bechhart. I want you to take whatever time off you need to attend to this situation. There will be no effect on your position at this company. If there is anything you need from me, just ask."

Bechhart was shocked by Mr. Sloman's offer. After a moment of silence he blurted out. "Mr. Sloman, I don't know what to say. Thank you so much!"

Bechhart may have detected a smile, but it was hard to see much of Mr. Sloman's face, which always seemed to be lost in the shadows.

"I can't have my employees distracted to the point of incapacitation now can I?"

"No sir," Bechhart replied. He still could not summon up a smile, even with Mr. Sloman's good news.

"Go home and attend to your wife, Bechhart. Let the police do their job. They'll find your daughter, and you will come through this all right."

"Thank you, sir. I'll do that."

With this Bechhart left the cavernous office/jungle. Somewhere in Mr. Sloman's office, a parrot squawked and a snake hissed.

***

Keith Barnnet finished off the last of the Thunderbird with a gut wrenching swig. He belched a cloud of sickly sweet alcohol-breath and then tossed the bottle in a pile of garbage across the alley. It crashed against the wall in a shower of glass. Several somethings scampered away under the garbage.

"Damn rats," Keith mumbled to himself. Keith searched through the pockets of his dirty wool coat, but he couldn't find any more cigarettes. He coughed a rheumy cough and began to pick himself up. After three bottles of Thunderbird that was a bit of a task, but following a couple of false starts, he was finally able to stand up straight.

Keith stumbled back in surprise. Two tall, well-dressed men in black trench coats and big floppy hats stood in front of him.

"Where'd cha come frum?"

One of the men growled, "Show us your hands."

"What?"

The other one pointed at Keith's dirty, scarred old hands. "Show us your hands!"

Keith figured these two to be cops and complied. He wiggled his fingers and smiled. "See? No guns, no knives. I'm just a homeless guy."

The taller of the two men in black lashed out with his fist and Keith's head snapped back. The poor old drunk collapsed into a pathetic pile on the ground.

"A homeless man with all of his fingers," growled the shorter of the two men. They grabbed Keith by his hands and feet and took him to the trunk of a limousine that was parked at the end of the alley. As they drove away, one could barely hear the gleeful tittering of the rats hiding under the garbage.

***

Aikeem gently placed his knapsack on the park bench and spread out in the early spring sun. He sighed a sigh of perfect contentment. The birds chirped. The children played. The pretty girls sunned themselves, and a delicious quantity of sun beamed down on Aikeem. Pendella pushed up the flap to Aikeem's knapsack, climbed out, and took a seat next to him.

"What a lovely day, eh princess?"

"Very nice," she replied in a distracted tone. Aikeem noticed she was eyeing a nearby flock of pigeons.

"I hope you're not thinking of lunch."

Pendella looked up at her man with a look of total disgust. "City pigeons, my dear Aikeem, are dirty, smelly, and stupid. They are the rodents of the avian world. I would no sooner eat one of them than I would their ground based cousins."

Aikeem smiled at his soul mate's disdain. "I've seen you kill quite a few rodents in my day."

"Kill yes. Eat no. One must have standards," Pendella replied.

Aikeem's attention was snatched by the beastly growl of a Doberman Pinscher. Fifty yards off, a red-faced, portly gentleman clutched an empty leash and ran toward Aikeem and Pendella. The Doberman circled to face Pendella head on. It barked and then growled most menacingly. Aikeem was obviously apprehensive. Pendella cleaned a paw with her sandpaper tongue.

"He seems a most disagreeable sort," Aikeem observed.

"He's trying to impress me with his ferocity," Pendella yawned. "I'm just soooooo impressed."

Of course, this set the Doberman to barking even more ferociously. Bits of salvia and foam formed on its lips as it came closer.

"Shoo!" Aikeem snapped at the clamorous canine. The Doberman turned his attentions to Aikeem, which forced him to back up on the bench. Pendella reached into her soul and drew a glimpse of her beast out for the Doberman. For a split second her eyes pulsed with a dark amber glow. The Doberman yelped in terror and ran back to its master who was staggering up to the bench, close to a heart attack. The confused gentleman leashed his pet and walked away, admonishing the beast the entire time.

"Thank you Lady. The only defensive spell I'm carrying causes your attacker's head to explode, and I'm somewhat reluctant to use that in such a public place and for such a small offense."

"Really Aikeem, that kind of spell seems a bit overdone."

"Well, ever since we ran into that nameless horror here in New York City, not to mention the debacle with the sand demon, I've tried to be more prepared."

"You worry too much Aikeem. We destroyed both beasts and the rats have learned their lesson. Our spies report no movement among the gutter folk. Besides…the goopy one didn't really have a head."

Aikeem chuckled and stretched out in the sun. He closed his eyes and smiled a most satisfying smile. "Not anymore. That's for certain… and that's a good thing."

Pendella started as a little girl plumped down on the bench next to her. "That is a very pretty cat. May I pet her?"

Aikeem opened one eye to give the little girl a once over. He smiled at the seven-year-old blonde, blue-eyed picture of perfection. This little girl was sure to break many a heart in the years to come.

"May she pet you Pendella?"

"Well, she obviously has an eye for beauty. I give her permission."

"She would love your attentions young lady," and with that Pendella sidled up to the little girl who immediately began to stroke Her Highness.

"She's very beautiful. You said her name is Pendella?"

"Pendella Purrfect," Aikeem replied, which immediately inspired a giggle from the little girl.

"Why is it my name always elicits this response from your kind?"

"Why ask why dear heart?"

"Excuse me?"

"I'm sorry. I was talking to Pendella." Aikeem held out a hand to the little girl. "I am Aikeem Abdul Jamal Yosaffa and you are?"

"I'm Cassandra Dolan, and I live over there," Cassandra pointed to the Upper West Side.

"Really? Well, Pendella and I live just across town from you then."

"Casey!"

"Uh-oh, there's my mother," Cassandra pointed at a very attractive woman in her mid-thirties running toward them. Aikeem stood for the lady as she collected her daughter.

"Casey, how many times have I told you not to run off? You nearly gave me a heart attack!"

"I assure you dear lady that she is well protected in this company. My cat Pendella would fight to the death to defend Miss Cassandra." Aikeem bowed for the little girl's mother. The lady was caught off guard by Aikeem's charm and could not help but smile. She held out a hand to Aikeem, which he took and shook in a most gentlemanly fashion.

"Hi, I'm Mary Dolan. I see you've already met Casey. She can be a handful."

"I can say the same about Pendella."

Pendella gave Aikeem a sideways look. "I could say the same about you."

"Oh, that's so cute," observed Mary. "Look at her. It's almost like she understands what we're saying."

"I hope Casey has her father's brains," jibed Pendella.

Aikeem shot Pendella a dirty look but ignored the remark. "She's a very intelligent sort… almost to the point of precocity."

"Precocious? Moi?" purred Pendella.

"Well, she certainly is beautiful," Mary observed.

"Oh, there's definitely hope for this one," Pendella opined.

Aikeem stifled a chuckle while Mary grabbed her child's hand. "Say goodbye Casey. We have to go now. Nice meeting you Aikeem."

"It was my honor lady." Aikeem bowed for the favor of a most delightful smile from Mary. Aikeem returned to his place on the bench. Pendella snuggled up next to her man, and the two basked in the noonday sun. Puuuuurrrrrrrrr.

Across the park, under a trashcan, and hidden behind some garbage, a pair of beady red eyes stared at Aikeem and Pendella. With the flash of a rat-tail, the creature disappeared down a nearby hole.

***

Keith moaned and slowly came to. He was being dragged by the arms and shoulders over a rough stone surface. He managed to open an eye and spied black boots and the hem of a black trench coat. The bile of fear began to rise at the back of his throat.

Keith was thrown on to a chrome steel table. He tried to struggle, but rough furry hands threw him back against the hard metal surface. In seconds leather straps bound his feet and arms to the table.

"Let me go! I got rights!"

Keith reeled in horror. A furry face with beady red eyes thrust itself in his face and hissed. "Not in here human."

Another tall man hidden behind a white surgical mask approached Keith's table. This "doctor" was dressed in the light green garb of a surgeon. There was something odd about his face too, but Keith could not quite put his finger on it. The doctor withdrew a monstrous syringe from behind his back. It was filled with a glowing green liquid that seemed to have a life of its own. Keith screamed and struggled against his bonds.

"Hold his arm still," hissed the Doctor.

Keith screamed as the man drove the needle home and pumped the old alcoholic full of his vile concoction. After a few seconds his eyes glazed over, and he relaxed.

One of the men in black addressed the doctor. "You need any more?"

The doctor surveyed his little chamber of horrors. Six other tables contained victims as wretched as Keith. "No, this should do. We're very close. In days I'll have the combination correct, and then we can begin the harvest."

The men in black shrugged uncaring shoulders and left. The doctor returned to his experiments.

Keith moaned from the effects of the serum that had been pumped into his veins. Through his fog shrouded mind he swore he could hear the sound of children sobbing.

***

Pendella waited patiently while she watched the humans in the box-of-fools that Aikeem kept in his living room. She found most of the images that played on the front of the box annoying and stupid. These images were primarily about humans and their ridiculous exploits, which held no interest for her. Although she noted that Aikeem never acted like the humans in the box. However, on occasion there would be very short stories about her brethren coaxing yet another free meal from their humans.

She was very fond of a male named Morris who was a master at dealing with his humans. Unfortunately, she had not seen him for a number of years. She also found the story about a dog that confused some faux human concoction for bacon strips hysterically funny. "Bacon! Bacon! Gotta have Bacon!" Dogs were sooooo stupid.

The VCR remote stood nearby. Aikeem had shown her how to work it, and she had a tape of her own that contained a collection of short stories. Her patience had paid off and she pounced on the remote. The VCR began to record her favorite! The singing cats doing a new rendition of her favorite song. Meow, meow, meow, meow that just about says it all!

Pendella began to sing along as the VCR recorded, and the houseplants in the room began to shrivel from the feline cacophony. As with all of these short stories, it ended too soon and Pendella fell silent. Something Aikeem called "The News" replaced Pendella's short story, and she turned away in boredom.

Pendella leapt up to the plush leather couch behind her and burrowed underneath her blanket. Only her eyes were visible as she began to lick herself to perfection. Pendella stopped what she was doing and watched the box-of-fools intently. She called to her man.

Aikeem strolled into the room, and after a few seconds found his mate under the blanket. "What is it lady? I'm trying to do my finances."

"I have… oh, bother, how do you say it, made memories of the box of fools on my tape."

Aikeem smiled at Pendella's struggle with human context. "Recorded. You recorded to the tape."

"Yes, yes," she said impatiently. "There is something there you should see."

Aikeem picked up the remote from the floor and rewound the tape. He punched the play button and rolled his eyes. "Yes, lady the singing cats are very nice, but—"

"No, not this bit. Be patient."

Aikeem watched the frolicking cats for the hundredth time. He started at the news story that replaced the crazy cats. "Casey!"

"It is the little girl from the park. What is it they're saying? I have trouble enough understanding human speak, never mind from out of this blasted box."

"She has disappeared. Shortly after she left the park with her mother. Oh my!"

"Why is your image on the box Aikeem?"

A pencil drawing that was a very close rendition of Aikeem played across the screen. Aikeem hit the pause button and stared at the police artist's interpretation of him.

"Because, my dear lady, they believe that I had something to do with Casey's disappearance. My nose is not that big!"

"Make the pictures move again."

Aikeem hit the play button and the story continued. The camera cut to an image of an empty park bench.

"Stop it!" exclaimed Pendella and Aikeem complied. "That is where we were today."

"Yes. The reporter just said that's where you and I were last seen with Casey."

"Surely, they don't think I had anything to do with the disappearance of this girl?"

Aikeem smiled at Pendella. "No lady, they hold me entirely suspect."

Pendella raised a paw and pointed at the trash can that sat opposite the bench across the park. "Look under that garbage container Aikeem."

"It's very small, lady. It's too small. I don't see anything."

Pendella began to lick a paw. "You don't see two pairs of rats' eyes reflecting the light?"

Aikeem squinted. After a few seconds he could barely make out four pixels that most assuredly were rats' eyes.

"Very good, lady. Yes, now I see them. What of it? Do you think the rats had something to do with this?"

"I merely observe that they are there, in the middle of the day, and in a very public place. Not very rat-like behavior, is it?"

Aikeem pondered this for a minute. "We need to retire to the Room-of-See."

"Agreed. We must find this little human. She's already quite talented in attending to feline massages and will make a fine mate for a cat someday."

Aikeem smiled and gathered up Pendella and placed her across his shoulders. "Of course, your Highness."

***

"Idiots!"

The two men in the black trench coats and floppy hats shrunk from the caustic abuse of Bennington Wadsworth Sloman III. Mr. Sloman stood and pounded his desk with a misshapen gloved hand. His computer beeped in protest.

"Not only did you take the child of one of *my* employees, you chose the daughter of one of my vice presidents! Why don't you just stick a sign out on the front of the building? Police! Please start your investigation here!"

"It was an accident Great One. She was alone. No parents were evident. She was close to us, and there was no one to observe her disappearance," one of the men whined.

Mr. Sloman glared at the pair and sat down. "You had better be right or I'll have a rug made of your hides." The two men shivered because they knew that Mr. Sloman was not waxing metaphorical.

"You snatched the last donor yesterday, correct?"

"Yes my lord. She has been placed with the other twelve."

"And how about Striped Seer? Has he perfected the process?"

"He has finished the growth serum, my lord, but not the perfection of digits."

"He's sure the serum will work? Has he tested it?"

"He tested it on three of the little ones until he had it perfected. They are not so little anymore." The other dark man hissed in laughter at this observation.

"How long did he say it would be until the perfection of digits is complete?"

"Three days my lord. In three days you will have all that you need to claim the world." The men in black wrung their hands in anticipation of that thought.

"Double the guards around the laboratory and see that Striped Seer has all that he needs," Mr. Sloman ordered. "I will suffer no more mistakes." With that Mr. Sloman dismissed the men in black, and they withdrew from the room. Mr. Sloman closed his eyes and retreated to the place from which he did all of his planning.

***

Aikeem entered the Room of See. Seven torches about the room instantly sprang to life. Aikeem's footsteps echoed along the marble floor covering the mostly empty room. A blue domed ceiling centered the room over a marble pedestal, which supported a large dark blue crystal. A gold pentagram several yards in length was inlayed around the center of the room. At the base of the pedestal rested a roll of paper towels and a bottle of Windex. Aikeem was a very fastidious sorcerer.

Aikeem stopped before the crystal, and Pendella leapt from his shoulders to the floor. Aikeem picked up the glass cleaner and began to polish the Stone of Summons.

"Are you going to do glow balls, eyeballs, demonettes or flying lizards?" Pendella queried.

"I was leaning toward glow balls, lady."

"Oh, do lizards! They're so much more fun to watch," the excited feline purred.

Aikeem smiled. "And so it shall be lady."

Aikeem closed his eyes and began to mumble. The crystal began to glow. Pendella began to attend to the fur between two of her claws. The domed ceiling began to luminesce of its own accord. A column of light formed between the crystal and the ceiling. Aikeem's words became more audible as the force of his spell became more adamant. An ectophasic, subquantum delirium began to weave between the light. A star burst, and seven flying lizards popped into our realm.

The little green reptiles, which looked very much like tiny dragons, began to flit about the room. Pendella was entranced as she watched them fly. One brave little soul zipped in front of Pendella and hovered before her nose for a few seconds before flying off.

"I love their aerial acrobatics," Pendella observed.

"Attention dragons! To me!" Aikeem exclaimed along with a magical gesture.

The lizards circled Aikeem and hovered around him. Aikeem gestured and a ghostly, three-dimensional image of Casey formed in midair.

"This is Casey. She is the little girl you are to look for." Aikeem traced a rectangle in the air and a map of the Upper West Side of New York coalesced from the ether. Aikeem drew a route on the ghostly map.

Aikeem pointed to an X. "This is where the girl lives in apartment 1900. You can gather her scent there." Aikeem gestured again and a semi-transparent image of the park faded into view. "And this is where we saw her last. Any questions?"

In a very high-pitched voice that was just audible to human hearing, the closest and largest lizard asked. "Squeak?"

"Just find her location and bring it back to me. We'll take it from there. No heroics dear friends. There may be danger here."

The little dragon saluted Aikeem with a fore claw and squeaked again. The little dragons followed their spokes-lizard and zipped off toward the ceiling. In a flash of subphasic endomagic, they disappeared through the ceiling.

"I love it when they do that. The lights are pretty," Pendella observed.

"Let us hope they find her soon lady. I can do little from behind the walls of a prison cell."

"Tonight we need to go to a dark place downtown. I have arranged to meet with one of our informers in the rat population."

"Really? Who would that be?"

"His name is Conniving Blitherskites. He used to be one of the Thirteen of High Rats until he ran afoul of Lord Dark Seer."

"And you believe he can be of assistance to us?"

"If the rats in this city are up to something, he'll know." With that Pendella turned tail and left the Room of See. A thoughtful Aikeem put out the torches and soon followed.

***

"Enter," boomed Mr. Sloman's voice from within his jungle room.

A timid and still depressed Bechhart entered holding a gaily-wrapped box.

"Bechhart!" A genuinely surprised Mr. Sloman exclaimed. "What are you doing here?"

Bechhart placed the package before Mr. Sloman. "My wife wanted me to bring this to you. It's just a small token of our appreciation for your generosity. We can't begin to tell you how grateful we are."

Mr. Sloman waved Bechhart off. "It's nothing, Bechhart. You are one of my most valued employees. How could I not do this for you?"

Mr. Sloman began to open the package. "Have you had any news?"

"The police haven't found anything yet. Another little girl was abducted yesterday. They're afraid some sick group is responsible."

"That's terrible! Oh, scotch. How nice."

"It's Laphroggs. I was told you really like scotch, and this is some of the best."

"You're very thoughtful Bechhart; thank you. Of course, the greatest gift will be the return of your daughter."

"Thank you, sir. We pray this will come true."

"It will. It will. Now go back home to your wife and keep her company," Mr. Sloman said as he motioned Bechhart to the door.

"Thank you again, sir," and with that, Bechhart left the room.

Mr. Sloman rolled up his nose at the sight of the bottle of Scotch. "Alcohol! Yuk! Whoever starts these rumors?" Mr. Sloman pushed the bottle off to the side and returned to his nap.

***

Pendella preceded Aikeem down the dark alley. A flickering fluorescent light cast a deathly pale at the other end of this dismal place. A short, fat man of no more than five feet in height waited for them at the other end. The hood wore typical gangster fare from some bad '50s mobster movie. He was constantly in motion, burning off nervous energy with his fidgeting. Pendella and Aikeem stopped before the man.

"All right you dirty cats! I ain't done nothin' see! I wasn't even there see! You ain't gonna pin this rap on me see!"

"I thought you said he was a rat, Pendella? He seems like a bad mimic to me."

"He is a rat," Pendella waved a paw and a burst of amber light blew away Blitherskite's magical façade. A large, fat rat replaced what once looked human.

"My… he's a big one," observed Aikeem.

Blitherskites jabbed a dirty claw in Aikeem's direction. "One of the biggest see! You don't want to mess with me see! I'm the roughest! I'm the toughest, I'm the—"

"Blitherskites will you shut up?" exclaimed an impatient Pendella. The rat clammed up and withered at Pendella's command.

"Several children have disappeared in the past two weeks. What do you know about it?"

"It wasn't us! We rats don't go near kids ever since that Pied Piper thing."

Aikeem looked perplexed. "What's that got to do with you? It was the Piper's fault."

Blitherskites became even more animated. "Oh, that's what you humans all say on the outside, but we know what you're really thinking. Oh! If the rats hadn't been there in the first place, the Piper never would have showed up and stolen our kids!"

"I think you're being a tad insecure," Aikeem mused.

Pendella snickered, "Rats are like that."

Blitherskites's rat eyes closed half way, and he leaned conspiratorially forward. "It wasn't us rats what took 'dem kids see. But it weren't no humans either."

Pendella sat on her haunches and extended her razor sharp claws. She began to lick them clean as she spoke. "What do you know Blitherskites? And tell us the truth."

Blitherskites warily eyed Pendella's claws as he spoke. "I don't know much. All I know is the buzz is there's some members from another Thirteen in town, and they're snatching humans."

"Another council!" Aikeem exclaimed. "Here in the city!?"

"That's what I'm sayin'," Blitherskites jabbed a claw at Aikeem.

"Which clan, Blitherskites?" Pendella inspected the point of one claw.

"I…I…I…don't know. No one's saying," Blitherskites jammered.

Pendella placed both paws on the pavement, squinted her eyes and leaned forward. "Are you sure?"

Blitherskites tried to hide under his arms and backed up against the wall away from Pendella. "Don't hurt me! I'm tellin' ya the truth. I don't know!"

"We need to take care lady; if it's the snakes, we could be in for a fight."

Pendella gave Blitherskites one more withering glare. "You had better be telling me the truth Blitherskites. If this is some intrigue to get you back on the Thirteen, then I'll turn you into a rat burger."

Blitherskites almost seemed to turn pale. "I'm tellin' ya Pendella. It's the truth!"

Pendella pondered the shivering rodent for a few seconds. She turned and left the alley. Aikeem smiled and followed his iron mistress out of this dark place.

***

One of the big men in the dark floppy hats carried a stack of dog bowls filled with chopped meat through the Striped Seer's chamber of horrors. He stopped before a dark dank cell that was sealed off with iron bars. Three pairs of furry, dirty arms shot through the bars and grabbed at the bowls. Guttural, bestial screams accompanied the attempts to snatch the food.

"Patience my pets. All in good time," soothed the dark man in the big floppy hat. He placed the bowls on the floor and kicked them to the creatures in the cell. He laughed at their desperate struggles to feed themselves. His hollow laughter echoed along the halls as he returned from whence he came.

In the cell next to the feeding creatures, huddled up in terror against the opposite wall sat Tony Milano, Inga Schulman, and Casey Dolan. The three children clung to each other and shivered at the sounds of the feeding beasts.

"We're never gonna get out of here," Tony sobbed. "They're gonna turn us into big monsters too!"

Inga sobbed at this thought, and Casey admonished Tony. "Oh, hush! You're scaring Inga. Someone will come for us."

Tony started to say something but stifled his argument. Inside he hoped Casey was right. Casey turned away from Tony. For a brief instant she could have sworn she saw a tiny dragon hovering in midair in the empty cell across from them. There was a small flash of light and then it was gone.

***

Aikeem set his wonderful knapsack down in the alley behind the Global Financial Corp. building. Pendella popped out of the backpack and rubbed up against Aikeem's leg. She purred in anticipation of the night's activities.

"There is adventure to be had this night, Aikeem."

"Yes lady. Let us hope it is an adventure and not a grave that awaits us."

"Oh, pooh! You worry too much."

"I may be ageless lady and immune to disease and poison, but I can still be killed. Cut off my head or remove my heart and…"

"I'll protect you."

Aikeem smiled. "Please do."

"How many spells have you prepared?"

"Seven."

"Seven? That's all?"

"I'm not an endless font of energy, lady. Seven spells are just about my limit. I can do ten on a very good day."

"They say Elderond Bundermage could store twenty."

Aikeem frowned. "Elderond was a hack… and dead I'll remind you."

Aikeem pulled off his long black coat and placed it next to his knapsack. He began to rummage through the knapsack.

"Are you bringing a boom stick?"

Aikeem sighed. "Yes lady. I'm loath to use them, but in this day and age if you don't bring along a gun you run the risk of being overwhelmed by firepower. Spells are simply not enough in these modern times."

Aikeem withdrew a twelve-gauge, pump action shotgun with pistol grips and a sling that was filled with ammunition. He strapped the weapon across his back and sighed. "It seems so unwizardly."

"Will you bring Moonwind?"

"Oh, most assuredly," Aikeem replied. He pulled a three and a half-foot katana from his knapsack. "Here it is."

Aikeem loosed the blade Moonwind from its scabbard and with a few deft flicks sliced the night air. "No beast, be it hell born or otherwise, can resist the kiss of this blade."

Aikeem strapped the scabbard across his back next to the shotgun and then put his coat back on. With a few deft, movements he transformed his backpack into a butt pack and placed it on his hips.

"There we go. All ready for battle and the honor of my lady," Aikeem bowed to Pendella.

"Oh, you look most dashing, Aikeem… for a human."

Aikeem smiled at the off-hand compliment and turned to the metal door nearest them.

"Did you bring a sound spell?" Pendella mewed.

"You're so spoiled lady. You must have theme music every time we go into battle these days," Aikeem observed.

"It confuses our enemies and fires my beast."

"What would you like? Something energetic obviously. Rock and roll? Heavy metal? Techno?"

Pendella rubbed up against her man's leg again and replied, "Something loud and exciting?"

"Well, then, we'll need some hybrid mayhem… with a beat," and with this Aikeem began to gesture in the air. Murmuring accompanied the gestures and soon a pulsing rhythm began to emanate in surround sound from everywhere and nowhere. A lone guitar screamed out the opening battle cry, and Pendella began to purr.

"Oh, that's very nice. Let's go kill something."

Aikeem turned his attentions to the metal portal in front of him. "First we must attend to the door lady."

***

One of the men in a large floppy hat pulled two 9mm handguns and ran down the cement corridor to the stairs that led to the alley. His keen hearing picked up the sound of music just outside the metal door that sealed off this place. Everyone was on high alert, and this was most assuredly a security violation.

The guard in the floppy hat mounted the metal stairs that preceded the doorway. He stopped on the landing and flipped on the monitor that was electronically attached to the camera just outside the door. There was a man and a cat just outside, and the man was gesturing wildly in the air.

***

Aikeem finished the spell by thrusting outwards and the door blew inward with a sonorous bang. Man and cat rushed through the opening. Aikeem drew Moonwind as they entered.

They stomped over the fallen door and did not notice the body underneath. Pendella sniffed something familiar as she rushed over the fallen guard but paid it no mind. A torn floppy hat lay against a wall. A dark furry snout was barely evident under the door, one that belonged to a creature whose magical façade was gone and that would breathe no more.

***

"Did you hear that?" Casey exclaimed. "Someone's come for us!"

Tony and Inga hugged each other in a corner. The light of hope ignited in their eyes. Casey strained to see past the bars. She saw a lot of men in big floppy hats with guns running around.

***

"Feel free to summon your beast whenever you like, lady."

Pendella peered around a corner. "As you said before, I am not an endless font of energy either. It is best to hold my beast until we really need her. Two approach and their weapons are lowered."

In time to the music, Aikeem leapt from around the corner into the center of the next corridor. He fired his shotgun as he did so. Two men in floppy hats were blown over backwards before Aikeem even landed. Aikeem followed Pendella who sprinted for the next adjoining corridor.

"This place reeks of foul magic," Pendella observed.

"Aye lady and did you notice the rat like appearance of those two brigands?"

"Yes, although it's hard to tell under those hats. Most curious."

***

Striped Seer began to scurry about furiously. Two of the men in floppy hats wheeled a sedated Keith Barnnet into the room. "Put him over there and then go assist your comrades. We've been breached!"

Striped Seer replaced his surgical mask and grabbed a meat cleaver. "This is terrible. This is not the way it was supposed to happen."

Striped Seer leaned into Keith's unconscious face. "I really don't want your digits. They're too old and corrupt. We were to grow the children and take theirs, but now there is no time."

He swabbed the thumb and pinky on both of Keith's hands with a glowing green ichor. He spoke the Spell of Transference, the Spell of Stasis, and then raised the cleaver high over his head. Fortunately Keith was unconscious.

🐾

Aikeem rounded a corner and immediately pulled back. A fusillade of bullets accompanied his retreat.

"Time for spell number three," Aikeem exclaimed and began to gesture. A ball of lightning six feet in diameter formed opposite him. With a metaphasic push, Aikeem sent the ball rolling down the corridor. The screams of men in big floppy hats resonated down the corridor.

Aikeem didn't need to waste a shell. The corridor was littered with smoking bodies.

"Come Princess! According to our reptilian spies we're almost to the prison."

***

"I don't care what the risks are! We have a wizard in the building! We've been found out, and we need to act now!"

Striped Seer withered under the admonishments of his dark lord. "Then do not hold me responsible for the outcome, my lord. This is the best I was able to do under these circumstances."

Striped Seer placed two blood soaked rags on Mr. Sloman's desk.

Mr. Sloman smiled in anticipation and began to remove his gloves. "Let us get on with it!"

***

Aikeem rounded a corner to find a corridor lined with prison cells. He rushed by each cell until he found the one with Casey in it. He did not notice the empty cell just next door.

"Aikeem!" a joyous Casey screamed.

Aikeem slung his shotgun and with a flourish bowed to Casey. "Sweetest princess, I have come to rescue you."

Casey clasped her hands to her heart while Tony and Inga looked quizzically at the strange man in the long black coat. "I should have known you would come for me Aikeem."

Tony's eyes went wide with terror. "Look out!"

Two long furry arms encircled Aikeem from behind and lifted him up off his feet. Aikeem flushed as the air was driven out of his lungs. A monstrous rat over six feet tall held Aikeem and breathed its fetid breath into his face.

Aikeem managed to squeak out, "Lady please!"

Pendella watched as two more man-sized rats charged out from behind Aikeem and his attacker. A furry claw slammed the ground where she was. Pendella leapt between the legs of one giant rat and tripped it up. The creature smashed into its fellow rat, and both creatures fell to the ground with a sickening crunch. Pendella leapt to the leg of the monster holding Aikeem and began to use its leg as a scratching post.

The giant rat screamed, dropped Aikeem, and went for Pendella. Pendella was gone. Aikeem leapt over the two monsters on the floor as he turned, raised his hands and fired his spell. The standing rat's head exploded. The children screamed; the two large rats on the floor screamed; Pendella laughed. The two remaining rats watched their comrade's headless body fall to the ground, and then the monstrous rodents ran off in absolute terror.

Aikeem turned to the cell. "Sorry about that children, but I was in a bit of a strait."

Tony began to throw up and was immediately joined by Inga. Aikeem gestured and all of the cells lining the corridor opened of their own accord. Aikeem turned to Pendella.

"Lady! Escort the children out of here to safety. I'll attend to whoever is in charge of this den of evil. Casey, you help Pendella."

"Take care Aikeem. You only have three spells left."

"I will lady," he said and was off.

Casey gathered up the remaining children from the other cells, and all fourteen followed Pendella out of the place.

"We're following the cat?" Tony asked.

"She's very smart," was Casey's reply.

"Yes, she'll make a very good companion to someone," Pendella thought. Pendella noticed that the men in the big floppy hats were not men at all, nor were they rats.

***

Aikeem entered Striped Seer's laboratory and found a bloodied, dazed Keith moaning on a gurney. Aikeem picked up the poor man's hand and winced at the sight of the missing digits.

"How rude," Aikeem observed. "I thought I'd need this healing spell for me. I guess you need it more."

Aikeem said the words of power and waved his fingers over Keith's hands. Had Keith been awake, he would have noticed a warm feeling as his fingers regenerated. Aikeem smiled at his handiwork and began to weave a locator spell. A three dimensional display of the GFC building formed up before him.

Aikeem spoke to the intelligent endoplasmic energy.

"From where in this building is the most magic power emanating?"

A bright red light danced around Mr. Sloman's office, and Aikeem smiled. He had only one spell left, and now he knew where he would spend it.

***

Aikeem burst into Mr. Sloman's office, but the financier was nowhere to be found. Aikeem leveled his shotgun at the empty desk and cautiously made his way into the room. A parrot squawked and Aikeem jumped.

"Curious décor," he said to himself.

Aikeem spun. He did not fire at the man in the surgeon's garb who escaped out the door.

Was that a furry body under that outfit and possibly a tail?

Aikeem passed the desk and headed toward an open lawn set up behind Sloman's office furniture. He looked into the foliage overhead, but nothing was evident. A chill slowly crept up his spine. Something was watching him. Aikeem walked up to the bush that lined the lawn and began to push it apart with the tip of his shotgun.

From an overhead branch Mr. Sloman lowered himself behind Aikeem. Aikeem felt the presence of the financier and spun. Mr. Sloman snatched the gun from Aikeem and slammed him in the face with the butt of his own weapon. Aikeem toppled backwards into the bush. Mr. Sloman dropped to the ground, grabbed Aikeem by the ankle, and hauled him out of the bush.

Dazed Aikeem focused on Mr. Sloman and cried in realization, "You're no rat!"

"Of course I'm not a rat! I'm a sloth you moron! You won't be needing this."

Mr. Sloman emptied Aikeem's shotgun of ammunition and then tossed it into the surrounding jungle. He smiled an evil smile and waved his fingers in Aikeem's face. "I used to be a three toed sloth. Now I have a full compliment of digits! Aren't they beautiful? Originally, they were supposed to be the fresh sweet fingers of an artificially enlarged child, but then you showed up and ruined my plans."

Aikeem was nonplussed. "You went through all of this just to grow a couple of fingers?"

"They were not grown. They were lifted... so to speak," Mr. Sloman said becoming more animated. "And now the Sloths shall ascend to their rightful place at the head of the animal kingdom!"

"I beg your pardon?"

"Your species has boggled up the earth quite enough. It is our turn to rule! We have spent many years planning on the Dreamscape, and with these extra digits we can finally weave the spells necessary to subordinate all other species!"

"It takes more than just five fingers to cast the kinds of spells you're talking about," Aikeem observed.

"So you say wizard, but I know otherwise. We have plotted from our treetop perches for millennia. We have conducted various experiments in the Dreamscape, and our spells always failed because these fingers were missing! And have you ever tried to fire a gun without an opposable thumb? You can just forget about chopsticks!" Mr. Sloman waved his new fingers in the air.

Mr. Sloman pounced on Aikeem and knocked him back. He reached behind Aikeem and drew Moonwind. "Nice sword. It feels very good in my full fingered hand."

Mr. Sloman began to wave the sword around in the air. "Soon my Thirteen will gather here and we will speak the Bayless Charm. A portal will open up to our special place in the Dreamscape, and our own Chitin army will march through and make the earth ours."

Aikeem began to crab walk away from the unreasonable sloth. Mr. Sloman turned his attentions from the sword to Aikeem. "There's just one thing we're missing... a human sacrifice. Are you free tonight?" Mr. Sloman laughed maniacally and moved toward Aikeem.

Aikeem bumped up against the desk, jumped to his feet, and desperately grabbed the first thing that came to hand. Aikeem hurled the bottle of scotch with all his might at Mr. Sloman's head, but the crazed sloth caught the bottle by the neck with his free hand.

"Really wizard. That was an act of desperation." Mr. Sloman's smile left his face as his hands dropped the sword he was carrying and began to open the bottle of scotch. "What!?"

Mr. Sloman was powerless to exert any will over the fingers stolen from an old drunk as they drove the bottle of single malt scotch back into his mouth, upended the glass container, and forced an entire quart of liquor down his throat.

A dumbfounded Aikeem watched as the horrified Mr. Sloman dropped the emptied bottle, looked up at him, hiccuped once, and then keeled over dead.

Pendella sauntered into the room and rubbed up against Aikeem's leg. "Did you use your last spell?"

"No lady. Evidently he stole the wrong set of fingers, and it seems he could not hold his liquor."

"Sloths are like that," Pendella observed.

Aikeem retrieved his sword and sheathed it. "I trust the children are safe?"

"I took them across the street, and they pressed the numbers of safety."

"911?"

"Yes, I believe that was it. The men in the cars with the flashing lights came for them. The children all seemed very happy about this and kept asking if they could make the siren work. That's when I left."

Aikeem transformed his butt pack back into a knapsack and put Moonwind and the shotgun back into it.

"Come lady, it is time for us to leave." Aikeem motioned to the opening in his pack, and Pendella jumped in. Aikeem left the aftermath for the police. He mused how their report would explain an alcohol-poisoned, man-sized sloth in a three-piece suit and the disappearance of Mr. Sloman.

Aikeem gestured and his last spell erased all traces of his being in this building. With this, he exited the GFC headquarters and hoped to never see another sloth again, except at the zoo.

***

Striped Seer cursed himself for listening to Sloman's promises. He knew this stupid plan would never work. All he wanted was an extra set of fingers so he could finally play poker without dropping the damn cards all over the place.

Striped Seer pushed the last of his belongings into his bag. He was returning to the forests of the Amazon and to his beloved cecropia tree. He was giving up his position of Seer for the Thirteen and was resigned to spending the rest of his life living as most normal sloths do... asleep.

Striped Seer turned to go. Terror transformed his face. Two magically enlarged, angry, man-sized rats emerged from the shadows. No one in the upper levels of the building heard Striped Seer's screams.

Warren the Prolific

My name is Warren, and I used to be King. I had it all: fancy digs, the best food, and thousands of sweet little bunnies available for my every desire. Life was good. Now I'm stuck in a cage between the guinea pigs and the freakin' ferrets, eating stale lettuce and drinking from a drip bottle. The salt block is nice, though.

It all started when I found the idol. At the time I didn't know it was an idol. At the time I didn't know much. Back then I was just another dumb bunny whose only concern in life was staying alive, eating and procreatin'. I do so love procreatin'.

One day I just got the urge to start digging. That ever happen to you? You're just hopping along and all of a sudden, WHAM! You just gotta dig? That's what happened to me under the lilac tree. Of course, being a creature of instinct at that time, I gave into my urge and started digging.

I must have tunneled two burrow lengths down and then BOOM! Well, actually it was more of a serious nudge when I came up against this rock. I thought it was a rock and then realized it was a hard place. I sniffed it a couple of times and then licked it—I gotta stop thinking with my tongue. It was wood!

This strange dark light oozed out of the wood and got all over me. That's when I got smart. The whole universe opened up to me. In a flash, I realized that there was more to the world than my tiny burrow, the little garden next to the house, and the occasional encounter with whatever female I chanced upon.

No! There was much more than this. There was the whole freakin' farm! There were huge tracts of land filled with carrots and cabbage! And bunnies? Oh baby! There's a whole farm filled with desirable, wanting, fertile sweeties just waiting for my...

I also got bigger. A lot bigger. My haunches swelled; my ears got longer; and my fur took on a healthy, yet manageable sheen. By the time the light returned into the wood thing, I was easily twice as big as I was before and easily half again larger than any rabbit I knew.

This was no ordinary wood. It called out to me. It whispered to me secret promises. It showed me the way to be king, but first it wanted to be dug out. So I got down to it and built this wonderful full sized burrow with lots of closet space all around the wood. When I was done I sat down on my haunches and stared at it.

It was beautiful. I didn't like the fact that it was basically shaped like an upright human—I don't care much for humans—but other than that, it was breathtaking. It appeared to be both male and female at the same time, which I found strange. It was smooth as a frog's skin, and its lines were subtle and delicate. Its color was a rich, deep, dark brown. It was at least three rabbits tall and extended from the floor of my new burrow right to the root-encrusted ceiling.

I don't know if I came up with the ideas or if it pumped them into my head, but all of a sudden I had a plan. All of a sudden I knew how to be king. I was tired of being chased by the stupid dog and hunted by the murderous cat and shot at by the crotchety farmer. I wanted the farm. Us rabbits were around a long time before man and his homicidal friends showed up. Yeah... things were gonna change.

***

The first thing I needed to do was set up a power base. At the time, Half-Ear and his mate, Shill, ran the warren. Half-Wit was more like it. This clown's idea of running things was kicking the crap out of anyone who got near his harem. Shill was sweet though. She had such a nice tight little tail that just cried out to be…

I used to hang out with these two guys, Alfredo and Jump-A-Lot. Alfredo was big, but really dumb, I mean even for a rabbit (not as stupid as these freakin' guinea pigs though). Alfredo's the only rabbit I know who ever charged the dog. The dog got so freaked out it took off. I asked him why he did it, and he said, "What dog? Did you see the really big carrot I found?" Sweet guy… not too smart.

Jump-A-Lot was real twitchy. Just the slightest noise set this guy off. He used to run away when the robins chirped. How embarrassing! The three of us were quite the team, Dumb, Scared, and Randy. Of course, that was before I found the idol, which I later came to find out was its name.

The idol gave me more than just smarts and a fine body. It also gave me the ability to pass on some of my abilities to my fellow rabbits. I hunted up Alfredo and Jump-A-Lot and found them where I usually did, munching on clover in the small field behind the farmhouse.

"Yo Alfredo! What's up rabbit?"

Alfredo gave me his usual doleful, vapid look. "What?"

Jump-A-Lot frenetically hopped over to our spot. "What? What? What?"

I loved these clowns, but conversation used to be really tough. I jumped on Alfredo, bit deep into his neck, and my magic ran into him. He struggled at first, but soon the light of intelligence sparked behind his eyes. "Rabbit! What it is! How'd you do that?"

I jumped off Alfredo who immediately stood up and began to see the world for the first time. "Woooooowwww. Check out all the colors."

Colors? I guess the power of the idol affected everyone differently. I gave him a few seconds to soak in my gift, and then I knocked him back to reality. "I'm taking over, Alfredo, and I want you to help me."

"Taking over what?"

"The warren, dumb bunny! What else?"

The thought was foreign to Alfredo, but eventually the stone wall that was his brain accepted the concept of leadership. "How we gonna do that?"

I remember feeling very satisfied with my newfound intelligence and big plan. "I'm gonna have a talk with Half-Wit."

Alfredo shrugged. I knew he didn't really understand, but it didn't make a difference. I knew he would take orders unconditionally. He was perfect.

I looked around, ready for step two. "Where's Jump-A-Lot?" Of course, he ran off after what I did to Alfredo.

I found him later that day and gave him my special kiss…

***

It's hard to hop with a swagger, but I did. I was feelin' mean, green and totally obscene. I was one bad bunny out to kick some tail. Just call me *lepus attitudiness.*

Half-Ear was munching down on some clover with his harem when the three of us hopped up. His eyes went wide when he saw the new larger me. "Who are you?"

"It's Warren, Half-Wit. Don't you recognize me?"

"My what strong haunches you have," observed Shill.

"Warren-The-Randy? How's this possible?"

"I've been sneaking into the spinach patch. Guess what?"

"What?"

I fairly glowered when I gave old Half-Ear the news. "I'm taking over."

Half-Ear dropped the clover shoved in his mouth and hunkered down for a battle leap. I pulled back my lips in the dreaded foul bunny sneer and all the sweeties split. Alfredo and Jump-A-Lot lined up on our flanks just in case any of Half-Ear's friends decided to interfere. We weren't too worried about that because, as far as I knew, Half-Ear didn't have any friends.

"I don't want to kill you Half-Ear. Just mess you up a bit."

I could see the fear in Half-Ear's eyes. I didn't really want to mess him up either. I'm a lover, not a fighter, but I was hoping to scare him into submission. Like I said before, he wasn't too smart. He leapt. I head butted him under the chin and flipped him over backwards. He bounced back up and took another leap at me. I head butted him under the chin again. Moron.

This went on for about a minute, and then Half-Ear began to stagger. I was getting a serious headache. "Give it up Half-Wit. Your small lepine brain is becoming addled."

"I am Half-Ear! Defender of the Down! I may wobble, but I won't fall down!"

What a putz. He surprised me by attacking exactly the same way again. This time I fell over backwards and kicked out as he landed on me. He went ten bunny lengths over my head and landed in a cow pie.

The three of us hopped over to the dumb bunny. He wasn't moving.

"I think you killed him, Warren," Alfredo observed.

I was beginning to feel pretty badly. I didn't like old Half-Ear much, but I didn't really want to kill him. Then he began to twitch and then finally a much humbler Half-Ear jumped up to his feet.

I got right in his nose. "I expect you'll start taking orders now, right Half-Ear? It's either that, or we feed you to the dog."

Half-Ear looked terrified at that prospect and Jump-A-Lot took off. Jump-A-Lot needed a lot of work.

"I will obey," was Half-Ear's only reply. He was one dejected rabbit when he hopped off. Now he knew what it felt like. That night Shill moved in with me.

***

The idol told me how to take over the farm. It said I needed an army of trustworthy soldiers and the only way to do that was to breed them myself; if you can't trust your own family, who can you trust? Procreating your own army. I liked that. That first year was real busy and probably the best year of my life.

After the first six months, the rest of the males were getting really jealous. I was keeping all the sweeties to myself, and only Alfredo and Jump-A-Lot had access to my harem. I figured I could take on any three rabbits at the same time, but not the whole clan. That's when I figured it was time for me to show them I deserved to be king. It was time to take out the dog.

We all hated the dog. I can't tell you how many friends I lost to that old Son of a B. Joe-The-Laggard, Slow-Foot, Half-Leg and Dizzy all got eaten by Yeller. He was pretty old by the time I came to power, but he was a crafty hunter. Poor old Stumble-A-Lot was the last to get it. Yeller was hiding in a bush and... well, suffice it to say the squeals were ugly.

I went over the plan with the idol, and it gave me some good ideas on how to proceed. Pretty soon every male bunny in the clan was happily digging for "The Cause." They were all so busy digging no one had time to worry about the sweeties. Of course, I was digging the sweeties.

It took about six moons, but finally D-Day arrived; that's Dog Day in case you didn't figure it out. Every night the farmer gave Yeller his bowl of dog food, and then Yeller would go lie down in his house.

We waited until he was fast asleep and then we did him. Five bunny lengths below him my rabbits were waiting. Right underneath his house, we'd dug a monstrous burrow. The ceiling was held in place by sticks that were in turn supported by two large branches. At three bunny-lengths down there were access tunnels that held loose dirt.

I gave the word and Alfredo and Jump-A-Lot kicked out the main supports. It worked like a charm. The ceiling caved in and Yeller crashed into the underground burrow. Yeller got tangled up in the sticks and dirt from the false floor and then Jackson, Butterlegs, Stomps-A-Lot and Frenzy kicked in the dirt before Yeller even knew what hit him. The farmer never even heard him yelp. Not a single rabbit cried when old Yeller died.

We spent the rest of the night filling in under his doghouse from the various access tunnels we had prepared for this purpose. After that the rabbits had a party for the next month, and I was the undisputed king.

***

A year later, the first of my army arrived. They were so cute. By the middle of that next year, I had one hundred bad bunny soldiers. The idol taught me the secret ways of fighting, not something at which rabbits typically excel. Above all, it whispered in my mind, I must continue to procreate. I must have a bigger army. Who was I to argue?

In turn I taught my offspring-army the shadow ways of Ninj, the secret rabbit fighting arts that the idol gave me. The other rabbits were all scared to death of my offspring, which was fine with me. Thanks to Ninj, I didn't lose a single soldier to the cat or farmer that year. To top it off we were taking whatever we wanted from the farm. We were rolling in carrots that year.

It was the end of that summer when my clan stumbled upon the forest clan of Jake Rabbit. As my army got bigger our down expanded past the boundaries of the farm and into the forest. It was there where my Ninj scouts ran into Jake.

Jake was one tough bunny. He was the first rabbit I ever met that'd been shot and survived. His clan was on the small side, but they were all tough as stones. Jake was big and tough, almost as big as me.

It was a hot summer day, late in the afternoon, when I hopped out to meet him. I brought Alfredo and Jump-A-Lot, and he brought along Blood-Smear and Stain. We met by the old tree at the edge of the cabbage field.

"So you're Warren the Prolific? I hear you took out the dog. Is that true?"

I squinted real evil like and smiled. "I came up with the plan. It was a group effort."

"I hear you're pretty smart. I hear you're talking about taking over the farm."

"That's the plan, rabbit. You want in?"

I could tell Jake was interested. His nose was twitching like he was sniffing cat. "What's in it for my clan?"

"We're gonna take out the farmer and the cat for starters. You like the farmer and the cat?"

Jake fairly spit at that, and Alfredo and Jump-A-Lot snickered. "What do you want us to do?"

"Follow my orders and maybe send some of your females my way."

I could see Jake didn't like that thought much, but I could also tell he wanted in. "No one in my clan is forced to mate with anyone else. But someone of your stature would probably get the pick of the warren if he crossed the black-way-of-death and survived."

Jump-A-Lot started to run, but I kicked him in the tail. Alfredo started to get the hops. I stared at Jake, and I could tell he was daring me.

I'd never actually seen the black-way-of-death, but I'd heard about it. Some said the humans made it; others said it was the creation of some evil demon. Many a bunny had lost its life to the metal monsters that cruised the black-way-of-death.

"What do you say, Warren? You cross the way and my clan will follow you. Anyone who takes out the dog and cheats the black-way-of-death has got to be a king."

I really wanted to talk this over with the idol, but obviously I couldn't leave without taking up the challenge. "All right! Let's do it."

Jake led the way as we followed him through the wood. I never realized how close the black-way was to the edge of the farm. My clan had heard too many stories about it, so we stayed away from it. The clear path of dirt connected the farm to the black way and we stayed away from that also. The farmer rode in one of those metal monsters too.

We stopped at the edge of the black way. Two long yellow stripes traveled its entire length, and it smelled bad. There were no metal monsters evident. The only noises we heard were the sounds of the grasshoppers and the birds. It was a beautiful day. I really didn't want to wreck it by being squished.

"Look over there," Jake motioned with his nose.

"Damn!" I observed. "The grass is greener on the other side!"

Jake smiled. "If you make it. The metal ones come up real fast, and you've heard about their eyes haven't you?"

"No."

"At night, and sometimes during the day, they glow and steal your mind. If you look into their eyes, you can't move because they lock your brain."

"Whoa!" I resolved not to look into the monster's eyes.

"You should be all right this time of day though. So... you gonna do it, rabbit?"

"You gonna follow my every order if I do?"

"You have my word."

I didn't even answer him. In a flash of tail I was gone with a super hop. It was only seconds, but it seemed like an eternity. I felt like I was running in slow motion through molasses. On the other side I bolted behind a small bush and panted mostly out of fear. I could see the other five bunnies were mightily impressed. While I was there I tried out some of the clover, and it was sweet. I even found some wild strawberries, but then it was time to go.

"Just do it," I thought to myself, so I did. I got half way across and froze. I made the mistake of looking up the road and I saw its eyes. The light! I saw the light! It was beautiful. It was so bright and it filled my entire brain as it got closer and closer and closer and...

"Run!" the idol screamed in my brain from nowhere and everywhere.

I felt the wind of the metal beast brush my tail as it made a terrible squeal. It tried to snatch me up, but I dove through the brush and slammed into my fellow rabbits. In a flash the entire pack of us had gone back into the woods.

Word got around both clans quickly about my cheating the black-way-of-death. There was no question from a single bunny about who was King. A few days later some females from Jake's clan showed up. Time to make the army.

***

Grumble-Hop was a legend, so much so that none of us believed that he really existed. As far back as rabbit memory went there was always Grumble-hop. There were those who believed that he was a member of the Lepus Council of Thirteen, but then none of us really believed in the Thirteen either. Imagine my surprise when he hopped into my burrow.

He was so old. His fur had as much gray and white in it as brown, and his eyes seemed to have a cloudy coating over them. His nose was wrinkled and faded, and his ears could no longer stand up on their own. When he hopped, it seemed each movement took profound effort. He stopped and looked past me at the idol.

"So this is the source of your power." I was shocked. None of the other bunnies had caught on to the wood. They all thought it was just a funky support for my burrow, but Grumble-Hop knew the truth.

"Do you know what it is, Warren?"

"Wood?"

"That's what it's made of. It is an idol. A human artifact of power left over from before the purge."

"Idol." I rolled the word around my tongue until it dribbled out my mouth and onto my fur.

"I'm not familiar with this one. It's not too powerful, but evidently powerful enough to control you."

"What do you mean control? Me? I'm the King around here, bunny! I do the controlling."

Grumble-Hop turned his attentions from the idol to me and gave me the once over. He said with a grin, "The rabbit who would be King."

"Who is King," I corrected him. "What do you want here Grumble-hop? Carrots? Cabbage? A mate? In deference to your being a legend and all, you can have whatever you want." I was feeling particularly generous having had such a good year.

"I came here to give you a warning, Warren."

"A warning?"

"There was a reason that magic was expurgated from the world. It is unruly, uncontrollable, and not meant for the likes of mortal creatures."

"Expurgated? Is that like fumigated, because there's a rumor going around that the farmer's gonna try and gas us."

"You're not listening to me."

I was trying to be respectful, but Grumble-Hop got my tail up. "Listen old bunny! We're finally on top around here! Even the cows and the chickens are startin' to swing our way. Now you're telling me to back off? I don't think so."

Grumble-Hop gave me that all-knowing stare of his and then wisely said, "We older rabbits have a saying: Power corrupts, and magical power corrupts magically."

I guess I was supposed to be impressed with that. I wasn't. I didn't even know what the hell he was talking about.

Grumble-Hop turned to go, but before he left he told me, "They say you intend to remove the cat. If you do that, it will be your undoing."

With that Grumble-Hop left my burrow. I pondered his words over a freshly dug carrot.

***

We rabbits have mixed feelings about humans. The farmer's offspring weren't bad. They pretty much left us alone, and on occasion they would feed us. Some say humans worshipped a great rabbit named Easter, but I think that's a lot of cow pie.

None of us liked the farmer at all. Over the years he'd shot many rabbits with his boom stick. I guess he didn't like us eating in the gardens and fields. I really wanted to get rid of the farmer, but the idol pointed out a very important fact. The farmer was the one who grew stuff. If we took him out, who would feed us? Rabbit can not live on clover alone. Well, actually we could, but who calls that living? What's a world without carrots?

The idol gave me some secret pictures in my mind. It told me what they meant and how they sounded in human speak. It directed me how to draw these pictures and how to make the farmer see them. Come the revolution the farmer would be educated with these pictures.

The next year I had over a thousand bunnies in my army, and we were ready to go. We had convinced the cow, the horse, and the chickens to join our rebellion. The pigs were being real stinkers and refused to sign on. The sheep were so freakin' dumb that the concept was beyond them.

We decided to do the cat and the farmer on the same day. There was much discussion about the cat since I made the mistake of telling my war council what Grumble-Hop had told me. In the end we decided to take the cat captive and decide its fate at a later time.

***

We spent a whole week prepping for VF day; that's Victory over the Farm day. The night before the rebellion, I led the horse, the cow, and the sheep around the field. I told the sheep we were looking for that Bo-Peep character they're always going on about (what's up with that?). After our exercise, we returned to get some sleep before the big day.

The farmer always let the cat out just after sunrise. The cat typically would head over to the barn to catch a mouse, and then out to the field to try and catch one of us. VF day was no exception. The cat got a poor little mousey. I felt badly. I should have included the mice in the revolution.

True to form, the cat headed over to the field after torturing the mouse. I was waiting for her when she sauntered over. "My you're a brave one. Have you decided to sacrifice yourself to me?"

"I've decided to kick your punk tail into next week. How's that Miss In-For-A-Big-Surprise?"

It's not often you get to see a surprised cat. The look on her face was perfect. She immediately responded by crouching for the kill. That's when five hundred of my Ninj soldiers jumped out of the cabbage. The cat's eyes went as wide as moons, and she took off. There was a column of rabbits and chickens waiting for her. She hissed the entire way as she was guided by rabbit kicks and chick pecks to the back of the barn.

Midway along the back of the barn, she fell into the camouflaged, straw-covered pit we'd dug the night before. Alfredo gave the word to the horse in his stall, and he kicked out. A good section of the barn wall went over the pit. The cat was trapped!

I hopped over the section of wall that now covered the pit and looked down through a knothole at the cat. "How does it feel to be a captive, cat?"

The cat's only reply was a pitiful rowl that echoed out over the farm. It was one of the most beautiful sounds I'd ever heard.

The farmer came running out of his house when he heard the barnyard commotion. My rabbits were waiting for him. He got several rabbit lengths outside of the door when my cadre of Ninj jumped out and surrounded him. You should have seen the look on his face when several hundred rabbit soldiers confronted him all sporting the dreadful foul bunny sneer.

Every time he moved we moved. A couple of times he looked like he'd try to make a break for the house, but we'd all start squealing and jumping and that shut him right down. Eventually the cows blocked all the entrances to the house by leaning up against the doors.

We rabbits parted, and the horse walked up to the farmer. It nudged him and then the horse led the farmer to the barn. At the barn, we rabbits and the chickens formed a column to the loft. The farmer got the idea and went up the stairs. We led him to the back of the loft where the open doors looked out over the field. His eyes grew wide when he saw the pictures we had drawn there.

The idol was right. The farmer looked at the pictures and said out loud what I already knew they meant. "Grow food or die."

Humans are typically a light brownish color. The farmer turned white. I thought that was hysterically funny. That was until he passed out and almost fell on top of me.

I had a hundred of my best bunnies surround him in a circle and when he woke up he passed out again. Sigh… Eventually the farmer became more stable, and we led him back outside.

Phase two of the plan was complete. The horse had gone inside and removed the farmer's boom stick. We watched with glee as the horse stomped it flat. The cows and the horse kicked and stomped the metal monster until we were sure it could move no more. Finally, we took out the lightning strings that tied the house to the main road. For some reason, the horse was sure the farmer could call for help over those strings. I was skeptical, but I wasn't taking any chances.

We imprisoned the farmer in the root cellar by having the cow sit on the door, and then we partied. It was Rabbit City at the farm and everyone was free. We went all through the farmhouse and took what we wanted.

The pigs put up a stink about the whole thing, but we told them to back off or we'd banish them to the black-way-of-death. One of them made a snide remark about some farm animals being more free than others, but we just ignored him.

The next day I woke up with one hell of a hangover. I overdid it on the carrot juice. I hopped out over behind the barn and found the cat hunkered down in her pit. I hissed with laughter at her state.

"Hey kitty! How do you like your new digs? Get it! Digs!"

The cat shot me a dirty look. "When the farmer finds me, he will set me free, and then I will come for you."

"Hate to ruin your world pussy cat, but the farmer's cooling his heels in the root cellar. From now on he goes nowhere without a bunny escort."

That shut the little pussy up. There's nothing quite as satisfying as the sight of a fearful kitty.

"What do you plan to do with me?"

"Personally I'd like the horse to kick your tail into the well, but he won't do it, so I'm still trying to come up with a plan."

"You have violated the laws of nature. Rabbit was not meant to rule. Rabbit was meant to be eaten."

"Says you furball. Things have changed around here, and you can get with the program, or you can get run over by it."

The cat sat up on its haunches. It squinted its eyes in a venomous stare. "I smell vile magic here."

"Magic? Yeah, well most of the sweeties feel that way about me," I mocked the cat.

She studied me for a bit and then said, "I have gone to the Dreamscape and summoned my Auntie. You will soon suffer the consequences of your breach of natural law."

"Your Auntie? Am I supposed to be impressed?"

"She is Pendella Purrfect and is the tenth of the Thirteen." I froze. Freakin' rabbit instincts. I hate 'em. After I got over my brain lock, I hopped away and left the cat to her hole.

I never thought about the cats having a Council of Thirteen. I always thought that whole Thirteen thing in general was a big lie to make rabbits feel better about being at the bottom of the food chain. If it were true, and if this Pendella was one of their Thirteen, then I knew we were in for big trouble.

I let my fellow rebels celebrate that next day, but then I let them know what the cat told me. Everyone was pretty depressed about it, but we decided to put up a fight. Someone pointed out that freedom's just another word for nothing left to lose, and what did we have to lose? Although, I did like being king.

***

We spent the next week prepping the farm for the arrival of the cat named Pendella. My soldiers and the horse kept the farmer in line. The cat didn't like the pit too much, but considering the way she'd treated us in the past, we took pretty good care of her. However, we did make her eat the dog's food. She wouldn't eat it at first, but there's nothing like hunger to humble you.

Finally PP-Day arrived—that's Pendella Purrfect day—and we were ready to fight for the farm. Around midday, a metal monster came down the clear path of dirt and a tall, dark human exited the beast. He held the door open and out strode Miss Pendella Purrfect.

You could tell she was special just by the way she walked. She didn't have to swagger. She had her own special personal force that seemed to drip off her tawny fur. Her jade green eyes were rich in color and vast in experience. This was definitely no ordinary cat, but then I was no ordinary rabbit.

Imagine our surprise when we heard the human talk under-speak to the cat (under-speak is the basic communication method of all animals). "Are you sure about this lady? I don't see any rabbits."

Pendella looked around the barnyard suspiciously. "Really Aikeem you are so nasally impaired. This place reeks of rabbit."

The human shut the door to his metal monster and slowly strolled toward the farm house. "Well, nothing seems amiss. Are you sure the encounter with your niece on the Dreamscape was nothing but a dream of the ordinary kind?"

Pendella looked up at her human with a most disdainful expression. "Aikeem, when it comes to the Dreamscape, I'm the expert."

The human replied with a smile. "Yes lady."

"Belindamor is very reliable and a great mouser. Although she is not one of the Thirteen, she has served us with distinction in the past. If she says there is magic afoot and that she is in trouble, then that is what is."

"And rabbits have taken over the farm," Aikeem broke into laughter.

Pendella frowned, "I know it seems unlikely."

"I guess it's not so unlikely. Jack-asses have been ruling mankind for centuries."

"You will not find me disputing that," Pendella replied.

The two stopped at the front door to the farmhouse. The one called Aikeem reached out to open the door.

"No!" Pendella screamed and launched herself at the human's leg. He stumbled back a bit, which probably saved his life. The door exploded outwards with a kick from the horse. The man flew over backwards and landed twenty bunny-lengths from the house on his back. Pendella managed to duck the debris and dove to one side.

My Ninj warriors streamed out of the house, and the horse went after the dazed human. In seconds we had Miss Pendella Purrfect surrounded. The cows circled up on the outside of our lines in case either of our enemies broke through.

Aikeem dodged just in time as the horse's hooves came down where his head had been. I directed my rabbits to attack Pendella. There were stories that members of the Thirteen were magical, but magic needs to be gathered. That much the idol told me. If we kept the pressure on the cat, then she would have no opportunity to summon her powers.

She was amazing. My rabbits launched fierce flying rabbit kicks that bowled her over several times, but she always got up. On occasion, she would spin and catch one of my hapless warriors in a deadly embrace. Her rear claws would rake and in an instant my poor soldier was finished.

The human was less skilled than his mistress. The horse chased him around the barnyard, and my soldiers attacked his legs. He fell down a dozen times, and each time narrowly missed getting crushed by either the horse or one of the cows. The horse backed him against the barn wall, and the chickens started pecking his legs.

The human kicked a couple of chickens over the fence and screamed. "Back you pugnacious peckerheads!"

The chickens and my soldiers split to give the horse some room. The horse reared. I was sure the human was about to become a lot flatter, and then he did the most amazing thing.

This Aikeem waved wildly in the air and with an outward gesture from both hands, lightning leapt from his fingertips. The bolts slammed the horse in the chest and leapt to the cows. They all fell over from the blast. They twitched a little bit and then became unconscious.

Blasted human! We had it sewed up until he started using magic. Cheat! I directed my Ninj to attack him head on. Their squeals were legendary and their assault never ending. My hope was this would keep the sorcerer from wielding anymore spells. Unfortunately, he had this big heavy backpack, which he unslung and began to swing about. He knocked the senses out of my soldiers.

I should have been paying more attention to the cat and not the human. She broke free from my soldiers and in one terrible leap she was on top of me. We rolled over and over in the dirt. Both of us were trying to get in position to rake the other one's stomach, but we were an even match in size and strength. We rolled up against one of the prone cows and Pendella managed to get to my back.

She closed her jaws around my neck and said, "Cwaw oooff urrr aabbootts!"

My body froze. Damn bunny instincts. After a second I managed to squeak. "What?"

Pendella wrapped an arm around my throat, hooked a razor sharp claw under my jugular, and let my neck go. "Call off your rabbits."

Her man went over backward under the onslaught of my Ninj, and they swarmed over the fallen human. "Laaaaaadddddddyyyyyyy Pllllleeeeaaasssssseeeee!"

I hesitated and she dug deeper with her razor sharp claw. "Then die."

"No!" I cried. I do like living even more than procreating. "Stop! Ninj warriors! Fall back."

My soldiers fell back and the wobbly human got up. He slowly rose as several hundred sneering, hissing rabbits looked on. He dusted himself off, and then strolled over to Pendella and me. He picked me up by the scruff of the neck and held me up.

"So this is their leader. Do you have a name rabbit?"

"Warren. What's it to you?" I tried to muster as much bravado as I could.

"It would seem my lady was right about you bunnies. Where's the farmer?"

"And Belindamor, you rapacious rabbit!" Pendella cried.

"The farmer is in the root cellar, and the cat is in a pit behind the barn."

"And where's the idol?" Pendella asked me.

My eyes went wide. "How'd you know about that?"

Aikeem looked down at his mistress. "What idol?"

"There is a rabbit named Grumble-Hop who also visited me on the Dreamscape. Warren has in his possession an artifact of power. It is the source of his power," Pendella shared with her man.

"Grumble-hop! That old Son of a B!"

Aikeem turned back to me. "You are not authorized to be in possession of such an item lepine one. Where is it?"

"I'm not saying!" I refused to give in so easily.

"It's been a long time since I've had rabbit stew. I'm willing to bet the farmer would be more than happy to share some with me."

I knew this human wasn't bluffing. "If I tell you where it is, I'm rabbit stew anyway."

"I give you my word. You will be spared."

"We can't let this one live, Aikeem. The idol has altered him. He has become more than your average bunny, as evidenced by the state of this farm."

"Nevertheless lady, if he tells us where the idol is, he will be spared. Well, bunny?"

***

Damn human! Damn cat! I had it all! I was King of the farm until they showed up.

I led them to the idol, and they took it. The human declared it was a fertility statue—duh! I could have told him that—left over from before the Great Purge. My Ninj warriors scattered after the idol was taken; its magic was broken.

They freed Pendella's niece, and the two cats celebrated by giving each other a bath. How disgusting! It took Aikeem an hour to get the unconscious cow off the door to the root cellar, but he finally got the farmer out.

The farmer was pretty crazy by the time Aikeem got to him, but the sorcerer said some words and made some magic that shut the farmer up. By the end of the day, the horse, the cows, the chickens, and everyone else were locked up again. Before they took me away, I saw a smiling Half-Ear watch us go.

Aikeem threw me into the belly of the metal beast and a few days later he took me to this place. He left me here in this cage between the guinea pigs and the freakin' ferrets. What is up with these guinea pigs? What is that freakin' noise they make?

One of these days I'll escape, and when I do, I'll find a new farm, one without a cat.

Hey! What's that human got? Oh, my maker! He's opening the lid! Look at those eyes! That fur! That nose! Those ears!

"Heeeeelllllllooooooo baby."

She looked at me coyly and said, "My what strong haunches you have."

Thomas Wondermore

Once on my special blanket, I sat down and gave myself a bath. Even the dimmest human knows that every feline bathes by licking one's self. This serves two purposes. One's coat is licked into a healthy, luxurious shine, and the statement we felines live by is physically reconfirmed: "I love me all over."

Aikeem wandered into the room. With a heavy sigh, he plunked down on the couch beside me. My poor man. I could tell that he was out of sorts. A cloud of gray seemed to hover over him, and I suspected he had a heavy heart.

"What's wrong lover?" I rose and rubbed against him. This always makes him feel good. He took me in his arms and stroked my back. I began to purr because I know this soothes his nerves.

"It is Celise. The woman vexes me. I swear by the one God she revels in my discomfort."

"Then why do you see her?"

Aikeem sighed again. "Because once again I've let my heart control my brain, and I've fallen in love with her."

I rolled over on my back and Aikeem stroked my stomach. That feels sooooo good. "I see. Human mating rituals. They're so strange. It's a wonder you're able to procreate at all."

Aikeem chuckled. "This isn't just about procreation dear lady. It's about affairs of the heart. Surely you've been in love before? With one of your own kind that is."

"Of course. Many times, for as you know I have lived a very long time. However, we felines do not need this lifelong monogamous connection. We prefer to move in and out of each other's lives, loving passionately when we intersect."

"I see. So you have never suffered a broken heart?"

I rolled back on to my stomach, and Aikeem rubbed around my neck. I sighed. "I wish that were true. Let me tell you of Thomas Wondermore. Maybe my story will make you feel better."

Aikeem settled himself into the couch, and I settled myself into Aikeem's lap. "Do tell lady."

***

After the Great Purge, and after the feline Council of Thirteen received its charter from the Administration, I was given to wandering the world. At first, I was searching for the dark ones that escaped the purge, especially the orcs and man-sized gutter folk. After a while I began to fancy travel. I've met many wonderful creatures on my journeys, and I have seen many amazing sights.

An age after the purge passed, I found myself in the jungles of what you call Africa. Back then the desert was much smaller, and the great jungle extended almost to the northern coast. As you know, I love the jungle, and at this point in my life, I had a great desire to explore all of its secret places.

When traveling through the jungle, one must keep every sense alert, for there are many creatures that are always hungry and not very discriminatory in their taste. Of course, having all the senses heightened in this fashion allows one to absorb every nuance of these moist, lush places.

Ahhhh, it is such an emerald green affair that fairly glows with life. The birds and arboreal creatures keep the canopy alive with their songs. The vegetation perfumes the air with a riot of scents that almost makes one dizzy and lightheaded. The insects keep the floor alive with their neverending motion and chirping, and the air is thick with moisture and heat. Many days, after I was done with my hunt, I would simply lie on a tree branch and soak in the world around me.

At that time, I made no particular place my home. I roamed through the undergrowth during the day and slept in the trees at night. Then one day I discovered an ancient human city. I immediately recognized it for what it was. A cloud of shadows was fixed over this place. This was one of the cursed realms.

I'm sure you've heard of them: Atlantis, Mu, Mo Cheng, and a host of others. Most were blasted from the face of the earth during the Great Purge. Some were flooded and others were burned. I suppose their method of destruction depended on the amount of evil they were steeped in. This was what was left of one of these places.

The remains of a wall surrounded the city. Great stone idols carved in the images of horrific, demonic creatures guarded what once must have been the main portal. The broken down, squat granite buildings lay demolished beyond this wall. The jungle had reclaimed most of the area, but this city still managed to scar the earth.

The fur along my spine picked up of its own accord, but I was determined to enter this place nevertheless. As the Tenth of the Thirteen, it was my duty to inspect such places to make sure they were not being used as a source of further mischief.

I cautiously entered the city and began to explore its twisted streets. The walls that remained were carved with depictions of unspeakable horrors. I'm always amazed at what one human will do to another. The people in this place evidently had no qualms about sacrificing their own to their nameless gods.

Eventually, I came to the center of the city where a small pyramid had been built. At the top of the structure, which was about ten cats high, was a stone table. All the stones on this edifice were still stained red from the thousands of victims that had died there. This was where these evil folk came for their entertainment. I shivered and left.

For the most part, the city was dead. I could feel remnants of evil in some of the darker places, but it seemed detached and unfocused. Of course, there was the occasional rat, bat, or snake, but these were just creatures native to the jungle that had taken up residence here.

At the far end of the city, I came to a mound of dirt that had been pushed up from below and had toppled one of the buildings. It struck me that it must have been an earthquake that had destroyed this place. In the center of that mound, something had carved out a tunnel that was at least two cats in circumference. I sniffed at its entrance and it smelled like snake to me.

"My you are a beautiful creature," hissed a voice from the burrow.

A pair of yellow eyes became apparent at the far end of the tunnel.

"How is it I have never seen you before, beauty?"

Its words were soothing, caressing, and its eyes were absolutely mesmerizing. I'm afraid my guard was down, and all I could do was reply, "I am new to this city. Who are you?"

"I am Skaaaa, Keeper of the Under-Burrow, Lord of the Lush Green Floor."

"Greetings Lord Skaaaa. I am Pendella Purrfect."

"A name that does you jussstice for truly you are perfect. I find ssssuch beauty inssspiring. If I had one ssssuch as you by my ssside, I would be given to moving the world!"

Oh, his words were so sweet and those eyes! I found myself moving forward just to be closer to the sweet things he was saying. He began to move closer to me too.

"Come clossser lovely. Might I have the pleasssure of an adoring kisssssss?" His eyes loomed from the dark, and although I should have been terrorized, I wanted nothing more than to take his gift.

A flash of green struck out at me and from nowhere came a flash of orange. A large ginger cat knocked the gaping jaws of the monstrous python away. My savior latched on to the neck of Lord Skaaaa with a terrific growl and raked the snake's back with his hind claws. One of the serpent's coils lashed out and knocked me against a wall. Lord Skaaaa tried desperately to wind his coils about the ginger, but this cat was too high up on his neck and too quick with his claws.

After much thrashing about, the ginger cat jumped out of the fray and screamed at me. "Come!"

I followed him around the winding streets of this dead city. Eventually we climbed a short, stout tree, and jumped onto one of the only intact roofs in this city.

I rubbed up against this brave male in thanks. "I can not thank you enough sir cat."

His wonderful, intelligent, yellow eyes fairly glowed. "You are more than welcome Mistress. I am Thomas Wondermore."

What an incredible feline he was. Thomas was very large. He was twice my size and had large almond shaped eyes. His fur was very clean and striped like a tiger's. He was not a creature of power, but he certainly was an outstanding representative of the species. Everything about him betrayed raw feline grace and energy.

"I am Pendella Purrfect," I rubbed up against him again, and he began to purr. "And I have never met a braver cat, other than myself that is."

Thomas laughed at this. "I have had more than one altercation with Lord Skaaaa. He seems to think that everything on this earth was placed here for his own personal dining pleasure. If you had had the time to notice, you'd have seen that his scales bear more than one scar from my claws."

"He's so big! It's amazing you've survived."

"He's big, but I am fast, and my claws are sharp."

I began to clean my paw. "How is it you are in this place, Thomas? Typically, we prefer the company of humans."

"My ancestors lived in this place, but there was a great cataclysm that destroyed this city of men. Since then we have lived in the jungle that surrounds this place. I am the last of my line."

"So you do not live in the city then?"

"Twelve moons ago a man came to this city. I adopted him as my own, and we moved into the city. He loathes snakes, and I keep them from him. In return he shares his food with me. How is it you come to this place?"

"I like to travel. I have wandered the jungle for some time, and now here I am."

Thomas pounced on me, and we began to roll around. He was wonderful, so strong and heartfelt. He had a purity of spirit about him that you very rarely find, except in children and truly gentle souls. We played for a time, and then we mated. I think he wanted me to bear him a litter, but I could not do this. Being the creature of power that I am, I have control over such things. I have only so many kittens in me, and the council had directed me to save those for some uncertain future. Regardless, we had a pleasurable time.

When we were done, Thomas invited me to meet his man. We traveled the streets of the dark city until we came to a building that was not as decrepit as the other structures. It was evident that someone had been at work here. The front of the building had been built up with tree limbs, and a rough thatch roof covered the stone walls. A smoke hole was open in the center of the roof and steam poured from it.

"I smell fish, Pendella! My man makes an excellent fish stew."

I followed Thomas past the broad leaf screen into the stone house. Perched over a crude clay pot was a tall, lanky human of the dark-skinned kind. He seemed older to me but not ancient. His face was painted with white stripes and a long thin bone was shoved through his septum. His hair was adorned with a multitude of brightly colored feathers. He was quite a handsome looking fellow, and I found his adornment gay but not ostentatious.

He turned to greet us and when our eyes met, I knew him to be a creature of some power. I instantly hid my true self and played the part of the ordinary house cat. When he saw me he smiled. "So Pumba! You have found yourself a friend."

I turned to Thomas. "Pumba?"

"That is what my man calls me. It is better than Stinky!"

We both had a laugh over this, and Thomas launched himself at me. I went over backwards and we clamped into a feline embrace. Thomas's man thought this was great fun and began to laugh deep bass guffaws.

"Come my pets! Have some fish stew with me."

I joined Thomas as he scampered to his feet. We shared a wooden bowl together. Thomas's man took a seat near the fire and ate from his own wooden bowl. He stared at me for some time, and then, to my surprise he began to communicate in under-speak. "So say the words of the world do I, Thomas's friend."

I pretended to be much less than I really am. I wanted to know him better before revealing my true nature. There were dark shadows that seemed to speak to this man.

"The stew is very nice."

The man saluted me with his spoon. "Enjoy. I am the shaman Shakar. How is it one of your kind is so far from the enclaves of man? Are you a feral cat?"

"I can be feral when it suits me."

Shakar thought this was very funny and entertained us with his sonorous bass laugh. "Me too lady, me too. Will you stay with us here in this place that was once called Lampor?"

Lampor? I had not heard of this city before. I looked over at Thomas who furiously attacked a bit of fish. "Thomas is a very handsome male."

Shakar laughed again. "Yes he is, and my dear friend, he has saved this old man's life more than once. He is quite adept at killing snakes. I have a dreadful fear of the blasted creatures. There is a particularly large serpent on the other side of the city who I think would like to make a meal of me, but Thomas keeps him at bay."

Shakar froze; his eyes went wide; and his hands began to tremble. I found this behavior most curious until I noticed what he was staring at. A small cobra was slithering toward his feet. Thomas was quite engaged in his fish and did not see the danger his man was in.

I pounced on the serpent. With one quick rip I tore its head off and dropped it at Shakar's feet. I returned to the stew. Shakar said nothing to me even after he'd regained his composure, but I knew that my place in his house was secured for a long time.

That night Thomas and I curled up together in a ball by the fire. Shakar rested on a fur-lined cot of wood and reed. I watched him through the fire as he drifted off to sleep.

Not long after Shakar fell asleep, I watched in horror as shadows distended from the dark corners of the room. They coalesced into tenuous human shapes and gathered around Shakar. They leaned close to him and whispered secrets.

I am a dream warrior. The council trained me for many years in this art, and I knew what these shadows were up to. They were infecting Shakar's dreams with their poison, and I knew this would come to no good. Unfortunately, I was powerless to do anything. If I jumped into Shakar's dream at that moment, those shadows and Shakar would have recognized me as a creature of power. All I could do was watch.

Eventually, the shadows retreated, and I pondered the shaman's still form. This poor man. I knew he had a good soul, for his love of Thomas was evident, and he had treated me well. However, I knew these shadows were corrupting his soul.

What should I do? I could not tell Thomas because I was sure he wouldn't believe me. Thomas was wonderful, but he did not have any of the gifts. He probably didn't even believe in the Thirteen; most of my kind didn't. If I were to tell him his man's soul may have been corrupted, he might become very angry with me. When we attach ourselves to a human, we come to love them unconditionally. It is our blessing but sometimes our curse.

I resolved to be patient and see what these shadows were up to. In the end, it would be up to Shakar to save himself from this kind of evil. It was apparent to me that these shadows had no hold over the physical world. At present, all they could do was shed whispers and prey on dreams. If Shakar was strong, all he would have to do was ignore them. I hoped he was strong.

Thomas showed me the city the next day. He instinctively avoided the pockets of evil that had pooled about this dead metropolis. He did not know these places for what they were as I did, but he knew enough to stay away from them. Other than these blemishes, Lampor was a wonderful city to hunt through. There were many nooks and crannies to explore. Outside the main wall of the city was a stream that was rich with fish, and on occasion, Thomas would snatch one from the running water. It was great fun.

The next few moons were some of the happiest days of my life. The darkness that pervaded Lampor seemed to slip away. Maybe I just got used to it or maybe it was because of the company I kept. At any rate, Thomas and I spent almost all of our time together. Sometimes we would spend the entire day just sleeping and giving each other a bath. We loved each other all over.

Unfortunately, Shakar began to become more distant. He was given to roaming about the city and poking through the ruins. I was sure he was looking for something, but for what I could not say. He also spent a great deal of time in a small structure that had a stone door on it. He would close that door to deny Thomas and me entrance. I did not want to go in there anyway. It was one of the dark places.

Every cat must occasionally have solitude, and it was on one of these occasions when I ran into Lord Skaaaa again. I was roaming the streets of Lampor alone with no particular destination in mind when I passed an open building. A familiar hiss issued forth.

"Lady Pendella, how niccce to sssee you. Come talk to me."

I turned to find His Majesty laid out in the sun on one wall of the building. Two bulges in his long body revealed a recent meal.

"I trust you will not try to eat me again, Lord Skaaaa?"

"My apologiesss, lady. Sssometimesss my ssstomach takesss over my brain, and I am given to rasssh activity. I would have been very sssad had I eaten you. It is sssoooo hard to find good converssssation in thisss placcce."

"That is not the only reason you would have been sad. I think you would have found me quite indigestible."

"Aaaaahhhh, ssso you are a creature of power then."

Lord Skaaaa caught me off guard, and I was shocked into silence. Lord Skaaaa knew more than he should of such things. "How is it you know this?"

"I have been in thisss placcce a long time, lady. The ssshadowsss usssed to talk to me. They usssed to tell me thingsss, teach me thingsss. They hoped that I could help them. Now that that cursssed man hasss come, they no longer talk to me."

"Who are the shadows?"

"They are the men that onccce ruled thisss placcce. They esssscaped the wrath of the one God by entering the other worldsss, but now they can not get back."

"So they have gone to Shakar for his help?" I asked.

"Thisss isss true. I have no handsss. One needsss handsss to weave the more complex ssspellsss."

I pondered Skaaaa's words and shivered at the prospect of these evil creatures returning to the world. This could not be allowed.

"Thank you for this information Lord Skaaaa. I must go now," and with that I left the large python to his wall. I had much to think about.

The next day I resolved to see what Shakar was up to. I left Thomas at the stream while he fished and I reentered the city. After an hour or so I found Shakar rummaging through the remains of a demolished building. After a while he jumped with glee and pulled a golden relic from the building.

It was a hideous thing of gold, and obviously an artifact of power. It was mostly a circle of twisting worms about one cat in circumference, which surrounded a glowing red ruby within its center. Shakar stowed it away in a large leather pouch and left this place.

As I expected, he traveled through the city until he came to the small structure with the stone door on it. He placed the covered artifact on the ground near the door and with a grunt opened the portal. When he went to retrieve the artifact, I snuck in the door behind him.

It was a terrible place, dark, dank and permeated with evil. The entire length of the stone corridor that led down into the bowels of the earth was carved with horrific pictures. Nameless Gods and vile demons battled among their human supplicants. War beasts of unspeakable confirmation tore each other apart. Blood was a central theme. I shivered as I ran through this place.

Shakar lit a torch at the entrance of this place and began to descend into the dark earth. I found a broken urn along one wall and hid behind it. I did not want to precede Shakar into this terrible scar in the earth. I was unsure of what horrors might lurk at its base.

I followed Shakar for some time until finally we came to an open chamber. The walls were engraved with arcane runes, the nature of which I could only guess. One wall sported a floor to ceiling metal mirror. Shakar had obviously polished it for hours because it reflected perfectly.

Before this mirror was laid out a number of objects. I recognized them all as artifacts of power. Shakar had been busy. He placed the circle of golden worms on the ground before the mirror and knelt before it.

He bowed his head, arms outstretched, and began to chant in some long forgotten tongue. Finally, he began to speak out loud in a language I could understand.

"Hear me great ones! I have brought the Worm's Eye as you have directed! Guide me now. What more do I need to bring you forth?"

Lord Skaaaa was right! This foolish human intended to bring the evil forebears of this place into our world. What a terrible realization this was for me, for Shakar was my friend.

The mirror was suffused with a dark light and voices as one issued forth. I do not know how Shakar could not have recognized these creatures for the evil that they were. Their hideous communication was oily and diseased. It almost made me sick to hear such vile sound.

"You have done well, Shakar, and soon we will bestow our gift upon you. You will have the powers we have promised. This configuration of artifacts is all that we need to escape this accursed prison. Now all that we need is time. Two days hence the moon will be full. You will speak the words and weave the charm we have given you. When this is done, the portal will be open and we will be free!"

Shakar bowed before his new masters and the light dissipated. He soon left this vile place with me close behind. He did not see me scamper by his legs as he turned to reseal the entranceway.

I ran for a long time through the city streets. I was very upset. What was I to do? Shakar was about to violate one of the most sacrosanct laws of the

Administration. It was my duty as one of the Thirteen to stop him. In the end, I decided to discuss my predicament with Lord Skaaaa. He knew these creatures. I thought maybe he could impart to me some information that might help me defeat the shadows' plans.

I hunted up Lord Skaaaa the next day and found him lazing in a tree. I kept my distance for there were no more bulges in his long body.

"Lady Pendella, what a pleasssant sssurprissse. To what do I owe thisss honor?"

"I have come to seek your council Lord Skaaaa."

"Then truly I am honored, lady. How may I asssisssst you?"

"The shadows have enlisted the aid of Shakar to free them from their self-made prison."

"Asss I have sssaid."

"They must be stopped."

"And why isss that lady?"

"They are evil, vile creatures who have been banished from this world. It is the law of the one God."

"I have heard of thisss one God before. He was very cruel to my ancesssstorsss. Something about a piece of fruit I'm told."

"I'm sure he would look kindly on any assistance you could give me in this matter."

Lord Skaaaa mulled this over. I could not tell what was going on behind those heavy-lidded eyes of his, but he was decidedly spinning a plan.

"When isss thisss man sssuppossssed to releassse the ssshadowsss?"

"Tomorrow night at the apex of the full moon."

"And he will be alone in the under burrow of the ssshadowsss?"

"Yes."

Lord Skaaaa thought on this and then said, "The ssshadowsss whissspered their plansss to me. Sssome of the artifactsss that that man hasss taken, I dug up. It isss a very tricky ssspell. The artifactsss mussst be laid out in precisssely the correct order. If they were to be dissssturbed, who knowsss what might happen?"

Joy filled my heart. Here was a way to foil the shadows' plans and save Shakar. I could steal one of the artifacts and close the portal. Shakar would be angry with me, but I could reveal myself to him and tell him the way of things. I believed that there was still enough good left in him that he would listen to me.

That night Shakar stayed in, and Thomas and I slept together by the fire. It was hard for me to sleep knowing what would transpire the following night. Thomas and I spent the next day together playing and hunting. I made it my business to tire him out so that I could place him out of harm's way.

That night Shakar left us early to go to the Chamber of Shadows. Thomas was fast asleep when I left him. I headed out after Shakar. Through the heavy foliage overhead, I could see the full moon making its journey to its apex.

I came to the surface entrance of the Chamber of Shadows and was surprised to find the door wide open. I should have expected this. Shakar intended to release a host of new creatures through this door into the world. I wondered if he really knew what they were. I wondered if he was so blinded by their secret whispers that he could not see their true nature. I hoped so; otherwise his immortal soul was in jeopardy. Fate does not look kindly on those who would sacrifice all in the lust for power.

I descended into this terrible place with no small amount of trepidation. I considered summoning my beast, but I was afraid to do so. Even after all these thousands of years, I have enough trouble controlling my elemental self. Back then I had even less control, and I was afraid what I might do to Shakar if I summoned up this form.

Shakar was prostrated before the mirror in a deep trance when I arrived. I should have struck then, but I could see the shadows at the edges of the mirror guarding the artifacts. At the very least, they would have alerted Shakar to my presence. All of the artifacts were large and heavy, and it would take some effort on my part to steal the smallest of them.

Shakar began to chant, and the mirror began to glow with the dark light. I decided upon a silver orb that was clutched in a black skeleton hand. The remains of the forearm still attached to the hand would give me something to grab onto with my teeth.

A low, gray mist rolled out of the base of the mirror. I knew the moon to be near its apex. Shakar chanted louder in the base tongue of these evil creatures. His arm gestured wildly as he began to weave the spell. I began to become desperate as no opportunity was affording itself. Should I just make a desperate grab for the artifact?

Lightning-charged energies flashed with a bang across the face of the mirror. The maniacal laughter of a thousand oily voices peeled forth from the mirror. The screams of the damned wailed from nowhere, perhaps the very pit of hell itself. Shakar screamed a death word, and the mirror became as gelatin.

In shock and horror I watched as a green flash split across the room and wound about Shakar. Lord Skaaaa! He had snuck in the open door to this place to take his revenge on Shakar and had betrayed me!

The voices behind the mirror screamed in rage and grotesque claws strove to reach through the gelatinous mirror. Shakar screamed in terror and fought to hold Skaaaa's gaping jaws from his face. Skaaaa wrapped around Shakar's entire body and one leg. The man was doing all he could to maintain his balance.

"No!" Thomas Wondermore screamed in a fit of rage.

In terror, I watched as my brave male raced down the stairs and launched himself at the head of the snake. All three toppled back into the mirror with the impact of Thomas's body against the unbalanced shaman. The craven hands dragged them in.

I was shocked to inaction, and then those vile creatures began to claw their way out. I had no choice. I could not allow them entrance. I rushed up to the skeleton orb and grabbed it. I yanked the disgusting thing and pulled it from its mystical configuration. There was an audible sickly pop as the spell was broken.

I could hear the shadows wail as they were forever damned, back to their self-made prison.

I dragged the orb out of that place and then ran from the city. I found a high tree branch and wailed at the moon. Cats seldom cry. That night I cried for what seemed like an eternity.

Eventually, I contacted the Thirteen, and they, in turn, contacted the Administration. What remained of Lampor was erased from the earth, and the shadows' fate was sealed.

***

Aikeem looked down at me with a profound sadness in his eyes. "I'm sorry Beloved. I can tell how much you loved Thomas."

"He is always in my heart. A finer cat there never was."

"And the point of this story is that as bad as things are with Celise and me, they could be worse."

"Precisely," I replied.

Aikeem smiled as he lay out on the couch. He pulled me close and we snuggled up together. I watched him with a purr as he drifted off to sleep. I imagined that somewhere in heaven Thomas looked down upon us with a smile.

The Weaver and the Needle

Lamar Johnson clawed at himself and screamed in abject terror as he ran down the corridor of the third story of his mansion.

"Get them off! Filthy Rats! Get them off! Get them off!"

He stumbled and spun on his way toward the floor-to-ceiling arched window, jerking about like some demented marionette. Lamar appeared to be pulling something off of his face as he crashed through the glass window into the cold night air, but there was nothing in his hands. He continued to rip at his clothes and bat away the vermin that infected his imagination. He never saw the ground coming in the instant before it caved in his skull.

***

Frederick Silverman III stepped out of his limo and thanked the driver. He didn't really give a damn about his driver, but it was important to make the help feel wanted. He made his way up the broad marble steps to his palatial estate. He was in no particular hurry. His time at home was time away from work and that depressed him a little.

Being CEO of Pharmican Global Pharmaceuticals was the core of his being. Everything else was mere distraction. He lifted the brass lion head handle on the massive carved oak door to let himself in. He caught movement out of the corner of one eye and sighed. The help was still here. He preferred them to be gone by the time he got home.

Migdalia gave Frederick a nervous smile as she hustled out the door. "Good evening, Mr. Silverman."

Frederick graced her with a wan smile. "Good night, Migdalia."

The older woman closed the door behind her, and Frederick sighed with relief. He had enough of people during the day, never mind having to deal with them at home. He placed his briefcase on the marble table next to the door and checked his tie in the mirror.

He was a handsome man in his late fifties. Silver streaked his dark black hair at the temples. A dark mustache and goatee gave him a leering quality that unbalanced his competitors. He was lean and tall and would not hesitate to use his height to intimidate those around him.

He stripped off his leather gloves and threw them on a table next to the briefcase. He made a mental note to order a new pair tomorrow. These were at least two weeks old. Although he enjoyed the smell of new leather, he was sure the gloves had to be dirty by now.

He wandered through the foyer and past the living room into his expansive dining room. He took the time to admire his collection of artwork on the way. He congratulated himself on his exceptional taste. There was no portraiture in this house. The work he collected was mostly architectural in nature. He'd managed to grab architectural drawings from all the greats, including I.M. Pei, Frank Loyd

Wright, and even a few sketches by Da Vinci. He sighed. That rat geek Gates had outbid him for the Codex dex Leicester, which was what he really wanted.

He found a warm lobster meal waiting for him on the room-length dining room table. He pulled off the silver cover of a side dish to find lemon asparagus in a dill sauce. The smell of fresh baked rolls permeated the air. A bottle of white wine sat in a bucket nearby on a sterling silver stand. He grabbed it and filled an empty glass. He sat down at the end of his empty table and reveled in his solitude.

He'd always been a loner, even as a child. He expected his iron-willed father had meant it to be that way. It was Frederick's ex-wife who really opened his eyes to his feelings about humanity. He wasn't really sure why he married her in the first place. It seemed like the thing to do at the time. Five years of hell proved to him that he was indeed capable of making grave mistakes. It also pointed out that the ultimate truth for him was that solitude was preferable to community of any sort.

He flipped out his napkin and laid it on his lap. He picked up his fork and speared part of the lobster's claw. He dipped the lobster in the butter and relished the contrast of the salty butter against the slightly sweet meat.

He was not so obsessed with his aversion to people that he could not control them. From his office atop the Pharmican building, he was very adept at manipulating an empire. People were his tools to gather power, and power was what he loved most. He absolutely thrived on orchestrating thousands of lives and successfully collecting even more power.

Many of his peers reveled in the acquisition of things. Their main purpose in life was to collect toys and show them off to their friends. Frederick scowled at the thought of this conspicuous consumption. He enjoyed his things, but it was the ability to control the world around him that was really important.

He finished the last of his meal and sat back with his glass of wine. He smiled and toasted the empty table before him. He would soon retire and have a warm dreamless sleep. The night could not pass fast enough for him. Tomorrow would begin another fascinating day of corporate intrigue, and that is where he most wanted to be.

***

Renee Lavalle stumbled on a root and cursed at a stubbed toe. This only served to fire her venomous anger even more. She ran through the jungle with a butcher knife in one hand and a large stick in the other. She could hear him about twenty yards in front of her crashing through the bush.

She swore to herself. "Cursed Caplata! When I catch you…"

Her breath was coming in ragged gasps now. She'd been chasing the Haitian shaman for ten minutes, but she would not give up. She was fired by the image of her daughter Marie's tear stained face. That evil worm had lured her into his shed, knocked her out with zombie dust, and taken advantage of her. Renee would not be denied her revenge.

She broke through a swampy clearing and found the shaman scrambling on his hands and knees. He'd fallen. She was on him in an instant. She leapt high in the air and smashed the stick across his back. He screamed in pain and spun around. He backed away from her crab style.

He mumbled something and then screamed at Renee, "If you kill me, woman, you will release a hex I've made. It will curse you and all your heirs with the dream death!"

Renee spit on the fallen shaman. "Just the words I'd expect from a coward."

She swung her stick and slammed Daagbo across the mouth. His head snapped to one side. He turned back, sneered, and started to rise. Renee dropped the stick and pounced. Daagbo wore a quizzical look as Renee backed away. He stared in disbelief at the knife in his heart.

"Oya avenge me," were Daagbo's last whispered words.

Renee stood over the dead man for a few seconds and shivered. She felt his spirit pass on to the next world. Her vengeance left her satisfied, but she feared what she might have released.

***

Nancy Etherton looked up over her book at the young man on the other side of the pool. She licked her ruby red lipstick and smiled. He nervously smiled back. He was probably only twenty-two, but she didn't care. He was a meal just waiting to be eaten.

Nancy was in her mid-thirties, but she bore the body of someone ten years younger. She was a fanatic in the gym. She went in for only an hour each day, but that hour was a firestorm of intensity. Her dark, beautifully sculpted face was home to a pair of chocolate brown eyes that would have made Cleopatra jealous, and as always her rich black hair was perfectly coifed.

Nancy returned to her book and quickly finished the last page. She closed the book and threw it into her bag. The young man was swimming now, and she watched him like a jungle cat studying a meal. She was having an on-again off-again affair with Edmond Jeffries, but she liked a little variety now and then. On occasion, this left a broken heart on her doorstep, but that was not her concern.

She picked up her bag, stuffed her towel in it, and rose to leave. She strutted out with a walk meant to capture the young man's attention. She left with a smile that told him to drop by some time. She was sure he'd show up that night.

It was the end of her day, so she took her time making her way back to her luxury apartment. Once inside, she threw the bag on her leather couch and headed to the kitchen to fix herself some tea.

While the tea brewed in the designer art-deco steam kettle she looked out the open kitchen into the living room. A fully complemented, electronic entertainment center filled one wall. She loved the ultramodern styling with its accent on chrome and leather, but she was beginning to wonder if it wasn't time to give Fabio a call to redecorate again.

Of course, that would mean taking time from her career, and that was something she couldn't afford to do. Besides, Frederick had taught her long ago that stuff was fun, but it was the accumulation of power that was important. She didn't really like Frederick that much as a person, but she absolutely adored him as a mentor. He had no hang-ups about her being a woman, and he never hesitated to give her opportunities.

She grabbed her tea and reclined in a plush leather chair that sat before the entertainment center. She punched a button on the remote and soft jazz began to surround the room. She sighed in contentment and relished the music.

She was in her glory. Her entire life had been under the shadow of her two brothers, Eric and George. Eric was a football jock and George was a genius. Her family had all the bases covered when it came to the boys, and Nancy was just so much decoration. Her parents expected she would just marry and produce even more Ethertons.

She had shown the entire clan. She was a top tier executive at Pharmican and the youngest ever to achieve such a position. She would even have a chance at the top spot if she played her cards right.

Success Magazine had just done a glowing article on her, and she sent copies to both of her siblings. Eric was the manager of a sporting goods store, and George was a programmer in a sea of programmers at Microsoft. They were both successful in their own ways, but in Nancy's eyes she had buried them both.

She spun her chair to look out over the New York cityscape through the expansive windows of her apartment. The sun was just going down, and the view was breathtaking.

"This is what it is all about," she thought, "and someday I'll be looking at this view from the top of the Pharmican building."

***

Pendella purred mightily in Celise Bellamore's lap. Aikeem sat next to the girls on the plush leather couch in the great room of his apartment. He stared with a contented smile into the fire burning in the hearth.

"Oh, yessssss, I like this human a lot. She has talented hands," Pendella mused through the rapture of a tummy rub.

"Your cat seems very happy, Aikeem," Celise observed.

"Unfortunately, she seems to be a master of the obvious," Pendella jibed.

Aikeem frowned at Pendella. "Hush."

"Excuse me?" an incredulous Celise replied.

Aikeem's expression turned to one of alarm. "Not you, my love. I was talking to Pendella."

"Oh, but I like her purring."

"See? She likes my purring, Aikeem; you hush!"

Aikeem stifled a grumble. Celise looked over at him and smiled. His heart melted. She was perfection. Her green almond eyes could seduce the hardest of souls. Her full red lips cried out to be kissed, which Aikeem did at every opportunity, and her creamy, coffee colored skin was the delightful gift of a Jamaican mother and a French father. Her perfectly sculpted features would have made a fashion model jealous, and her voluptuous body would have been the envy of any Hollywood starlet. Aikeem sighed just looking at her.

Celise took Aikeem's hand in her own and pressed it to her heart. "What's wrong my love?"

"Nothing, dear heart. I'm just basking in the glory of your beauty."

Celise smiled again. "You're so sweet, Aikeem. How did I ever get so lucky?"

"It is I who is the lucky one, lady."

Pendella rolled to her stomach. "You can tell her to work on my back now."

Aikeem smiled. "She likes her back rubbed too."

Celise turned her attentions to Pendella's back.

Aikeem returned to the glow of the flames and then remarked, "It occurs to me, Celise, that we have been seeing each other for three months, and I know absolutely nothing about your family."

Celise's smile quickly faded, and Aikeem noted the veil of sadness that replaced it. "My mother died when I was only five, and my father died when I was ten."

Aikeem placed an arm around her shoulders and gave her a delicate hug. "I'm sorry dearest."

"I remember my mother's wonderful, beautiful face always smiling at me."

"She must have been very beautiful to produce such glorious offspring."

Celise smiled at Aikeem's compliment. "My father was a famous chemist and biologist. He doted on me and when my mother passed on, he doted on me even more. After he was gone, there was a big vacuum in my life."

"I'm sorry, Celise."

"After that I was raised by governesses hired by my father's trust and put in various private schools. He was very rich and saw to my upbringing even after he was gone. I've enjoyed the freedom his estate has provided me, but I would have enjoyed his company more."

"I'm sure."

"And what of you, Aikeem? Tell me of your parents."

"Well, my parents have been gone for a very long time too, but they lived full, happy lives. My mother bore five of us, and I was the oldest. I was named after my father who was a merchant in the city that is now called Cairo."

"What was it called when you were there?"

Aikeem coughed at his temporal indiscretion. "Ah, Cairo. It just seems so long ago, and I've been in New York for so long."

"Oh," replied a somewhat confused Celise.

"At any rate, we were a very happy family, and my father was very successful. He wanted me to become a merchant also, and, indeed, I did sail some of his ships in my youth."

"Oh, he was in the shipping industry?"

Aikeem smiled. "He was a merchant. Eventually, I went with my heart and joined the army. My father was nervous about my career choice, but he was also very proud. There was much love in our family."

"That's so nice. I wish I could have experienced that kind of love."

Aikeem leaned forward and shared a passionate kiss with Celise. "There are all kinds of love, lady."

Pendella bounded out of Celise's lap and secured a comfy spot in front of the fireplace as her human became more entwined with his lady love. She continued to purr as they began to make love. Pendella was happy when her man was happy.

***

Edmond Jeffries carefully slid a razor down one perfectly sculpted cheek. He hated shaving. Every shave was a chance at nicking his beautiful face. He inspected the cheek and found it clean of wounds. He hated noisy electric razors even more, so he was forced into this adventure with a double steel blade every morning.

He slowly and deliberately finished his shave and was ecstatic when he completed the task without incident. He patted on some fresh smelling after-shave and began to mousse his perfect blonde hair. He sighed in the mirror as he did so. God, he was beautiful.

His body was lean and hard from hours on the treadmill and other exercise machines. He smoothed some body lotion across his chest and suddenly wished Nancy was here. He didn't want her out of any emotional desire, just pure animal lust. She was the only woman he knew who turned him on as much as he turned himself on.

Edmond strolled out of the bathroom into the bedroom. He began to don a gray silk suit in front of a floor to ceiling set of mirrors. He marveled at how beautiful his eyes were as he assembled his tie.

He checked his profile and sighed. "It's no wonder I'm such a success," he said to his reflection.

Edmond made his way to the kitchen and pulled a yogurt out of the refrigerator. He skimmed the morning's copy of the Wall Street Journal as he finished his breakfast. In a few moments he was done, and he tucked the newspaper under one arm. He grabbed his briefcase and headed for the door.

He stopped at the door and smiled at the portrait of his mother that was displayed on a side table. He sighed. She was so beautiful. In terms of looks, she was the polar opposite of Edmond. She was dark and mysterious. Edmond knew her to be the most passionate, strong-willed woman on the face of the earth.

Everything Edmond was, he owed to his mother. Not only had she borne him, but she had given him the confidence to oppose any who stood in his way. In the past, if anyone had gotten in his way, she knocked them down for him. Of course, he had to do that on his own now, but Mom had taught him well.

Edmond blew the portrait a kiss and exited his apartment. He wondered to himself what Nancy was up to tonight.

***

Now alone, Pendella lay in front of the fire in the great room. One eyebrow arched in surprise as she watched a cat walk through the wall. Pendella raised herself out of respect and sat back on her haunches. The ancient feline newcomer sat down in front of her. His body was very old, but his eyes were alive with life and energy.

"Greetings, Grizzle-Whiskers. To what do I owe this honor?"

The First of the feline Thirteen turned to soak in the heat from the burning fire. He was a gray tiger of prodigious size. He was twice again as big as Pendella and sported long, well-groomed fur. Bits of white tinged most of the fur about his face. The whiskers around his nose were very long, drooping halfway to the floor and were interspersed with short, stubbly hairs. He had a very broad face and equally broad green eyes that fairly radiated with power.

"There's trouble on the Dreamscape, Pendella Purrfect."

Pendella began to clean a paw. "And what is the nature of this trouble?"

"There is a Dream Weaver loose."

Pendella stopped licking her paw and looked up in shock. "A Weaver!"

"Aye, tiger mistress, and a talented one at that. The council believes whoever it is has been active for quite sometime mucking up the netherverse. We became aware of its presence only recently because of the manifestation of a profundity of rats. At first we thought Lord Dark Seer was up to his tricks again, but this was not so."

"Then who was it?"

"We do not know, but one of our dream scouts spied a human."

"A human! A Dream Weaver who is human? This is unprecedented."

"Truth. Methinks they do not know what they are up to. The Dreamscape roils from their presence, and chaos spews across an already entropic realm. Many children sleep restlessly these days."

"This is terrible!"

"We have traced the Weaver to this human city. Enlist the aid of your sorcerer human and terminate this Weaver."

"Yes, my lord."

"And one other thing."

"Yes, Lord Grizzle-Whiskers?"

"Do you have any tuna?"

Pendella smiled and led her mentor into the kitchen.

***

Nancy Etherton could not move her head, or for that matter, the rest of her body. She was strapped into a chrome steel chair that was bolted to the floor. Black nylon straps restrained her head and immobilized her wrists, ankles, elbows, knees and stomach.

A tall individual dressed entirely in a black surgical outfit loomed over her. Nancy's eyes filled with terror as this person drew a long sharp needle. She struggled against her bonds but could not move. Due to the androgynous nature of the dark person's outfit, Nancy could not tell if it was a man or woman. The dark one began to thread the needle with surgical thread. Nancy began to scream.

The dark person put a finger to Nancy's lips and she quieted. When the dark one spoke, the voice also seemed genderless. "Are you familiar with the phrase, be quiet or I'll sew your mouth shut?"

Nancy cautiously nodded in the affirmative.

"Guess what I'm going to do?"

Nancy began to scream again, this time in earnest. The dark person pinched her lips closed with thumb and forefinger and moved in with the needle.

***

Marie Lavalle placed her head in her mother's lap, and the older woman stroked her daughter's hair.

"I can't make you stay my dear. I know you love this man and want to be with him. But I fear for your safety. There is the curse…"

Marie smiled at her mother's superstition. "You always tell me of the curse Mother, but I have never seen or felt its sting."

"That is because I pray and sacrifice to Yemalla and Oshun. They look over you while we maintain their altar in this house. Will you make an altar for them in your new house?"

"I don't think they do such things in America, Mother. They will think me strange."

"Is it that or is it because of your new husband?"

Marie blushed. "He is a scientist, Mother. He has no use for vodoun or its gods."

"Maybe they have no use for his science."

Marie looked up at her mother. "Our love will protect us Mother. You must have faith in that love."

It was a sad Renee who looked into her daughter's eyes. "I have no doubt of your feelings for each other. I have peered into this man's soul, and he has a good heart, but there are dark forces that wish vengeance on our family. That Caplata bastard cursed us and we must protect ourselves."

Marie reached up and touched her mother's cheek. "Daagbo is gone mother. His only curse is the stain of his memory in our hearts. I'll never forget what you did for me."

Renee smiled and returned the caress. "No one hurts my daughter. The Lavalles take care of their own."

Marie returned to the comfort of her mother's lap. Renee stroked her daughter's hair, but the fear for Marie's destiny remained.

***

Edmond Jeffries bounced into Nancy Etherton's office with a grin that fairly glowed with self-satisfaction. When he saw Nancy, his grin slipped away.

"What the hell happened to you?

A very haggard looking Nancy looked up from the financial reports she was attempting to read. "I had a nightmare you wouldn't believe."

"Jesus! That must have been some nightmare. You look like crap."

Nancy grabbed a mug of coffee and took a sip of it. "Thank you so very much."

Edmond grabbed the chair in front of Nancy's desk and took a seat. "What was it about?"

"Some sick surgeon sewed my mouth shut. I felt every stitch."

"Ewwwwwww. Girl, you gotta stop eatin' jalapeno's before bedtime."

Nancy sat back in her chair and gave Edmond the once over. Nancy and Edmond had been on-again off-again lovers. The bottom line was that they were both married to their careers. Their affairs were more for convenience than romantic satisfaction.

"I didn't have anything to eat before I went to bed. I've never had a dream that was so real before."

"Oh, ducky. At least you could have had a realistic dream of mad passionate love making with me."

Nancy smiled a teasing smile. "The depth of your ego never ceases to amaze me."

Edmond shrugged his shoulders. "Hey! If you've got it, be happy with it."

Nancy sipped at her coffee again. "So what's up? You seem exceptionally pleased with yourself this morning."

Edmond glowed with the knowledge of some truly juicy gossip. "So you didn't hear then?"

"Hear what?"

Edmond leaned closer to Nancy and answered, "Lamar took a header out of the third story of his mansion Friday night. They think he jumped."

Nancy's expression changed to one of shock. "Oh, my God! Was he drunk?"

"I don't think so. They're calling it a suicide, but it just seems really weird. He always seemed so in control to me. Of course, you know what this means?"

"Gone is the heir apparent to Frederick. Everyone knows the board of directors is in Frederick's pocket so really the choice for the successor CEO of Pharmican is his. That means one of us has a shot at it."

"That's right. I assume I'll have your support."

Nancy threw her pen at Edmond with a smile. "I'll have your support is more like it."

Edmond snatched the pen out of the air and smiled. "We'll see. Let's just make sure it's one of us. We can start by undermining the others."

Nancy smiled a corrupt smile. "You are soooo evil. Let's get right on it."

The two shared a mirthless laugh.

***

Pendella sat on Aikeem's chest. Aikeem lay in his king-sized bed on top of the blankets fully clothed. He closed his eyes, and after a few moments, Pendella leaned forward and licked his nose.

Aikeem's eyes snapped open. "Thank you for the kiss, lady, but your sandpaper tongue has awakened me once again. How am I to train to be a dream warrior when you keep me awake?"

Pendella stood up and turned away from him. "Grab my tail so we may fly to the Dreamscape."

Aikeem sat up with a perplexed look. "Lady, I said you woke me. I think I'm a bit large for you to be dragging me about by your tail."

Pendella sighed. "My kiss was a blend. It was meant to commingle your conscious and your subconscious so that you might travel to the Dreamscape with me. Look behind you."

Aikeem was quite disturbed to find his corporeal self fast asleep beneath him. "My that's unnerving. I've heard of astral projection, but I've never tried it myself."

"That's different. You leave your body empty when you do that. This is dream walking. A subconscious ectoplasmic tendril always connects you to your body in this state so that your body is never in jeopardy of being taken over by a soulless being."

"Good, because I hate it when that happens," Aikeem said with a smile.

"Now grab my tail Aikeem."

Aikeem did as he was told and was jerked into the ether. He was awestruck as Pendella soared through the subquantum unreality that separated the real worlds from the Dreamscape. Fantastic, brilliant clouds of color soared by. They seemed to have a dull peculiar taste. Wild, but not very loud, cacophonous sounds played at the edge of Aikeem's hearing and smelled wonderfully. At first Aikeem was terrified by the speed, but as the cat jumped over the moon, he relaxed and enjoyed the ride.

Pendella momentarily joined a living bridge of thousands of cats who traversed the interreality. Out of respect for Pendella's rank they opened a path. Pendella very quickly veered off to the right and dropped into an exomorphic molecular glyph, which had a raspberry odor to it.

On the other side of the glyph, cat and human landed with a thump.

Aikeem picked himself up off the ground and dusted off his knees. "Really, lady, you could have landed a little softer."

"Your manna threw me off. I'm not used to such weight."

"Are you saying I have a fat spirit?"

Pendella shrugged. Aikeem looked up at her and was surprised to find that she wore her beast. She was triple her normal size, and her canines gave her the appearance of a mini saber tooth tiger. Her fur had a metallic sheen to it. Closer inspection revealed that her fur was razor sharp and was indeed made of an organic metal.

"You wear your beast, lady. I'm surprised. I thought you didn't like the potential loss of control in this form."

"Here on the Dreamscape, it is just another soma that I may adopt. It is no more real than the subconscious adoption of your own human form that you currently wear."

"You're saying that I can change my body?"

"To anything you can think," Pendella replied.

Aikeem mused on this. "How interesting. I shall have to play with that."

"A dream warrior must learn how to crawl before he learns how to walk."

Aikeem smiled a sarcastic smile. "Yes master. Your humble student awaits his instruction."

Pendella ignored Aikeem's sarcasm and began to circle him. "The Dreamscape is a place constructed of chaotic, but tenuous, energy. This entropic energy is so weak that even our subconscious thoughts can give it shape, as evidenced by our surroundings."

Pendella motioned at their current environment with her tail. Low mountains loomed off in a hazy horizon at the edge of the desert upon which they stood. A partly cloudy sky moved through a lazy afternoon in this silent place.

"This place is constructed from your subconscious, Aikeem. Do you recognize it?"

Aikeem looked around. "Not really. It could be any of a dozen places I've been to."

"It is probably all of them muddled together. Normally, when humans walk the Dreamscape, they only do so with their subconscious. Cats, and now you, have the ability to walk the Dreamscape with our consciousness intact. This gives us great ability in this place. We can direct our thoughts and manage this netherverse, but as with all things, there must be balance."

"And what is the nature of this balance, lady?"

"The Dreamscape wants to be chaotic. When you place order on it, you upset the balance."

"So by conjuring up this place, I've caused chaos somewhere else?"

"Yes, but it's not as bad as you may think. Your subconscious uses very little energy in here. This world you've created is probably only chaotic at its edges and is constrained to only your dreams. It is when you use your conscious in this place that you begin to stir things up."

"And why is that?"

"As you know conscious thought can be very powerful. In this place, where the energy flux is so low, conscious thought has absolute power. In here you can create worlds with a thought, but when you do the balance of this place is upset. Because of this, somewhere else on this plane an entropic tidal wave will roll over the Dreamscape and most likely it will roll back over you. The Dreamscape likes to be treated very gently otherwise…"

"Nightmares," Aikeem surmised.

"Nightmares and dream quakes." Pendella stopped in front of Aikeem. Her eyes glowed amber for effect. "You have heard that if you die in a dream, then you die back in reality?"

"Of course."

"Ninety percent of the time this is true. This is why nightmares are to be avoided; otherwise, you risk a problematic undershock, which translates back down your subconscious ectoplasmic tendril to the real worlds. This typically stops your heart."

"Oh, my. That is bad," Aikeem observed.

"Dream warriors must always be circumspect in the weapons they choose on the Dreamscape. Keep in mind that any imbalances you create affect broad areas around you. It is also possible for you to affect dreamers nearby."

Aikeem thought on this. "You're saying it is possible for me to cause others nightmares?"

"Deadly nightmares, if you're not careful. Children are especially vulnerable."

"Well, then, I shall be careful."

"Good. Now let us begin your training." Pendella looked at the ground under Aikeem's feet. Aikeem followed her gaze, and a six-foot hole opened up underneath him. He disappeared with a scream.

***

Frederick Silverman pored over the financial reports that Nancy Etherton had sent to him. He smiled with satisfaction as he reached a bottom line replete with even more juicy profits. Ten years of hard work were finally paying off in a big way, and he was becoming very rich. More importantly, he was becoming very powerful.

He sat back and reflected on his empire. He had been with Pharmican for twenty years and CEO for half that time. It was Morphicphan that made him and almost destroyed him. It was a miracle drug that was supposed to eliminate nightmares and bad dreams. It worked wonderfully during initial trials, and then nine months into testing, people started jumping out of windows and slitting their wrists. Frederick immediately moved to minimize the damage, and not a single lawsuit was filed. Lexington Abernathy, Frederick's predecessor at Pharmican, was so impressed by the way he handled the problem that he made him his successor.

And now he had it all. Pharmican was easily five times bigger than when Lex was CEO. Frederick had gobbled up half a dozen smaller biotech firms, creating the fourth largest pharmaceutical company in the world. His stockholders loved him, and the board of directors was in his pocket. The only fly in the ointment was Lamar's demise. He still had another ten years to go until retirement (at least!), but he wanted the firm left in good hands. What good is an empire if it crumbles in your absence?

Lamar was his handpicked successor. Initially he was just a research scientist, but Frederick soon came to realize the man was multidimensional. Lamar was also key in helping him to resolve the Morphicphan mess.

Frederick typically was unflappable, but Lamar's suicide had really unsettled him. There must have been a Lamar he didn't know. Typically, the man was a heartless rock, brilliant, but a rock nevertheless. His only weakness was classical music, and typically that did not cause one to leap out of a third story window.

Frederick sneezed and yanked a handkerchief out of his pocket. He shuddered. He hated germs. He blew his nose and prayed he wasn't coming down with a cold. He threw the cloth into a wastebasket when he was done.

Now Frederick was left with the task of picking a new successor. He had no choice; he had to pick from one of the four survivors of the Morphicphan project. They had all sworn to protect him as long as he took care of them and so far he had. They were all capable players, but Lamar was the best of the bunch.

He sighed. Life was so unfair.

***

Aikeem splashed into the blood red waters of a dream lake. He clawed to the surface and sputtered and spewed when he regained the air. He began to tread water and noticed the liquid tasted like strawberry punch. Pendella floated over to his position on an immense purple lily pad.

"Pendella, that was quite unnecessary!"

Pendella bore a Cheshire grin and replied, "It is all part of your training, Aikeem."

"Posh! You're just getting back at me for not changing the litter box."

"That sounds like a guilty conscious to me. It's important for you to understand that attacks can come from anywhere on the Dreamscape. You can be dropped from one world into another in a heartbeat. This required almost no energy on my part, and it effectively immobilized you. What do you think would have happened had I dropped you into a volcano?"

Aikeem frowned, but he remained silent.

"The most effective dream warrior attacks are those that require the least energy with maximum effect. The best way to do this is to draw on your enemy's subconscious fears. For instance, I know you fear sharks."

Aikeem stared in disbelief as a single gray fin rose from the depths of the blood red sea and headed straight for him.

"Pendella!"

"You must defend yourself."

"How?"

"Use your instincts. You must feel the Dreamscape flow through you. You must—"

Pendella did not get to finish her sentence because Aikeem spun in the water and began to swim like a mad man in the opposite direction from the shark.

"That's not really what I had in mind," Pendella said to herself.

The shark gained rapidly on Aikeem, but fortunately for him, he was only twenty yards from a sandy blue beach. The shark turned away in the shallow waters as Aikeem dragged himself out of the blood red lake. Pendella floated over on her lily pad.

"It would seem, lady, that I have out swum your shark."

Aikeem was unnerved by Pendella's newly expansive Cheshire grin. The shark came at the beach full speed. At the last second its tail fin morphed into legs and the creature ran up on the beach after Aikeem. Aikeem screamed and ran away.

"Land shark," Pendella observed.

"Laaaaaadddddddyyyyyyy!"

Pendella bounded off her lily pad on to the blue beach and chased after the two combatants. She didn't want her man getting killed his first time out.

Aikeem ran, but the fish ran faster. Its gapping jaws snapped at the air just behind him. The light of inspiration replaced Aikeem's mind-numbing haze of terror. He looked down at his empty hands. A metal cylinder filled with pure oxygen suddenly appeared there. Aikeem spun and jammed the cylinder in the shark's mouth. The creature clamped down on the tank and stumbled to the ground under the weight of it. Aikeem continued to run, gestured again, and turned with a saddle rifle in his hand. He fired at the cylinder's relief valve and blew the shark up.

"Thank God for the movies," he said to himself between ragged breaths.

Pendella stopped in front of her man. "That was interesting. Not how I would have done it, but it was quite effective."

"Lady... huff ... you're making me ... huff, huff ... very angry."

"Come, come, Aikeem, don't be such a child. We have much to learn in a very little time. I must use these methods to bring you up to speed."

Aikeem regained his composure and glared at his mistress. "What is the all-fired hurry, lady? Time is on our side."

"No, it isn't. There is a rogue Weaver on the Dreamscape."

"A Weaver?"

"A Dream Weaver, the most deadly of all dream warriors. They are able to manipulate the Dreamscape without obeying most of its rules. They may conjure at will causing nary a nightmare or dream quake."

With that the ground trembled momentarily under Aikeem and Pendella's feet.

"What was that?"

"A minor temblor set off by your indiscriminate conjuring of weapons," Pendella pointed at the gun with her tail.

"Somewhere a child has had a bad dream."

"Oh, my!" Aikeem was visibly upset.

"Don't be alarmed. It was a minor, forgive me, faux paw, and will probably only result in a restless night's sleep."

"And this does not happen to a Weaver?"

"Truth. It is what makes them so dangerous."

Pendella gestured with her tail, and the blood red sea and blue beach faded away to a realm of mist and cloud.

"Where are we now?"

"The same place. I have just converted your thoughts to the raw stuff of the Dreamscape. Look about you Aikeem. These white tendrils you see here are the stuff of which dreams are made. A Weaver has total control over this, often with devastating effect."

"So you need me to help you battle this rogue Dream Weaver?"

"Precisely."

Aikeem seemed to visibly relax. "Very well then lady. Lord knows you've helped me enough back on the real worlds, but can we please go just a little bit slower."

Pendella's heart softened. "As you know, I love you very much Aikeem, but... no."

With that Aikeem was blown back into the empty black void of space as a thousand comets chased him down. He screamed as he flew.

Pendella sighed, "We have so much to learn."

***

The Weaver reached through the mists until she found what she was looking for. Several denizens of the deep swam in a dream state back in the real world. She blew an apparition across their limited consciousness and directed them to a particular spot in the open sea. After a time, they reached that spot. She let them be for a while and began to think up the dream she would send them. It would have to do with feeding.

***

Aikeem was drawn to the photographs on the mantle of Celise's expansive West Side apartment. His lady had undeniable taste. Her apartment was a mixture of Caribbean, African, and European eclectic. The colors were subtle, and she was partial to a mixture of earth tones and gossamer whites. The veritable jungle of plants that adorned the place provided most of the color in the room.

Aikeem perused the pictures and stopped when he came to what was obviously an old photo of Celise's mother. She was perfection. Her complexion was a creamy brown with soft highlights. Her nose was petite, but not too small, and her cheekbones were high and proud. Her hair was unlike Celise's in that it was tight and curly, black as black, and cut short. It was just a still photo, but her perfect, ample and muscular body suggested subtle, seductive motion. Aikeem cleared his throat and placed the picture back on the mantle. This was no way to think about his paramour's mother.

"Wasn't she beautiful?" Celise entered from behind Aikeem and slipped a creamy, smooth arm around his waist.

"A goddess."

"She was so kind too. I miss her so much."

Aikeem studied the photo again. "I can't help but notice she seems a little sad in this picture."

"That's what killed her. She suffered from depression. Back then depression was easily misdiagnosed. She took her own life. I wasn't there when it happened. One day she was just gone… along with her smile."

Aikeem turned and embraced his lover. "I'm sorry, dear heart."

"As a little girl, I used to dream that she had never left me. We would have tea in the garden together, and she would tell me of all the wonderful places she'd been to."

Aikeem kissed Celise on the forehead. "She's always with you then."

"Lately I've been dreaming about her quite a bit. She comes and talks to me about how things are going in my life. I often tell her about you."

Aikeem smiled. "I hope I have her approval."

Celise returned a teasing smile. "Well, so far I've given you a good review, but she is very protective."

"Well, then, I'll just have to be sure to treat you in a fashion that wins her respect. What shall I call her if I meet her in my dreams?"

"Her maiden name was Marie Lavalle."

"Ah, another name like your own that surrounds itself with beauty."

Celise smiled again, which turned into a kiss. "I noticed you brought a package with you. Is it for me?"

Aikeem grinned and went to the antique coffee table to retrieve the gold wrapped gift he'd brought with him. "I had this made especially for you. This is no mass produced item. This is handcrafted by an old friend of mine."

Celise carefully unwrapped the package and found a black jewelry box underneath the gold paper. She carefully opened the box and smiled at its contents. "It's beautiful Aikeem. Will you put it on me?"

Aikeem took the black velvet choker and ivory cameo from the box, and Celise spun around so that he could place it on her neck.

"How did you get a cameo that looks like me?"

Aikeem delicately secured the choker with the silver clasp. "I drew a profile of you and my friend carved it from ivory."

"I didn't know you were an artist."

"I am many things, dear heart, and over the course of time, you will come to discover them all. Did I tell you I'm a bit of an oenophile?"

Aikeem grabbed a gold paper bag from the table and produced a bottle of white wine. "I hope it hasn't warmed up too much."

Celise smiled. "I'll go grab some glasses and a corkscrew."

Aikeem watched her go and turned his attentions to the bottle of wine. He held it outstretched in one hand, mumbled some words, and gestured with his free hand. A hint of frost formed on the bottle and quickly began to melt.

"That should be just about perfect," Aikeem mused to himself.

Celise returned with the glasses and corkscrew, and Aikeem set himself to opening the bottle. "This is Pouilly Fume, which is a cousin to the more well known Pouilly Fuissé. This is just as dry and sometimes not as overstated. Do you like your wine dry?"

Celise grabbed Aikeem's forearm and gave it a heartfelt squeeze. "Dry as the desert. I've become partial to the progeny of the desert."

Aikeem popped the cork and poured them both a glass. "Let's drink it on the balcony."

Celise took both glasses and headed for the double French doors that lead to a balcony that overlooked the city. Aikeem grabbed a CD off the coffee table and made his way to Celise's impressive entertainment center. He powered the system up, popped the CD in the player, and the lush full voice of Aretha washed over the room in surround sound.

Gotta find me an Angel, Aretha sang as Aikeem joined his ladylove on the balcony.

Celise handed Aikeem his wine, and they shared an unspoken toast to their love. After a few sips Aikeem took their glasses and set them down on a café table. He circled his arms about Celise's slender, firm waist and delicately placed a kiss upon her lips.

"It seems I've found my Angel."

***

Everett Winters emptied the bottle of shark repellent over the port side of his forty-five foot Wellcraft Excalibur. He hated sharks. In fact, he was terrified of them. He'd never really even seen a shark outside of an aquarium. Actually, he stayed away from them at the aquarium too. He really hated sharks.

He loved the ocean though. He could get away from Frederick and the company's crap and forget about Pharmican. He especially needed to get away now. With Lamar's suicide, the corporate sharks were beginning to circle. Nancy, Edmond, and Jack would do whatever it took to become the heir apparent to the top job at Pharmican.

Everett picked a Bass ale out of the cooler, popped the cap, and drank straight from the bottle. He shed his shirt, plumped up a pillow and lay down on the plush aft couch. He sighed in total contentment. He loved his boat. He loved the ocean. He loved being alone. He hated his job.

He had sent an email to the sharks before he left. He told them he had no interest in Lamar's position. He also hinted that if they tried to mess with him to further their own careers, he'd toss them off the top floor of Pharmican's home office building.

A seagull flew overhead and pondered landing on the bow of Everett's motor yacht. It decided better and flew on. A gentle warm breeze blew over the aft section, and Everett basked in the glow of the sun.

When he had started at Pharmican fifteen years ago, it was a great job. He was a biologist fresh out of graduate school with a PhD in molecular biology. All the big names courted him: Pfizer, Genetech, Centecor, and Merck. He ended up going with Pharmican because of Pierre. Pierre had been doing groundbreaking research on biotech and higher brain function, and that was the area of science that really fired Everett up.

Back then, he and Lamar just about worshipped Pierre. The man was a true genius. Whenever they stumbled on a problem, Pierre was there with the answer. Pierre would just take an afternoon off on his own boat and then come right back with an answer. It was like magic.

Those first two years were nirvana, and then Pierre's wife got sick. Up until that point Pierre had only a middling interest in sleep disorders, but it turned out that that was the nature of his wife's illness. He became obsessed, and the team became obsessed along with him.

Everett reflected on how they crammed ten years of work into one. The result was Morphicphan. It was an amazing product. Its primary purpose was to smooth out and reduce the sleep cycle. The final result was a capsule of three separate drugs each with a time release delivery system. Each component mastered a section of the subject's circadian rhythm, and allowed for a perfect night's sleep in half the normal time!

Pierre tried it on himself first. This was totally against laboratory protocol, but he was a man possessed. Everett and company kept silent. He took it for two weeks without incident, and everyone was jealous of how well rested he looked. The team termed the project a success and brought Frederick in to begin the product's life cycle.

Everett sipped from his beer and sighed. No one knew Pierre was giving it to his wife too. Frederick railroaded Morphicphan through the FDA and got clinical trials going in two months. That was absolutely unheard of at the time. Meanwhile, Everett's wife began to show signs of depression. Previously, her symptoms were lack of energy and occasional irritability, but now a darker cloud loomed over her.

Pierre monitored her, but Everett mused, in retrospect, he was probably in denial. Pierre found her in the pond behind his house floating face down. He was devastated. He lived for that lady, and the rest of the team was heartbroken too. They'd failed where they wanted to succeed most.

By that time Frederick had brought Edmond and Nancy in on the project, and they'd sold Morphicphan to Lexington Abernathy, the current CEO. By the time Pierre had recovered from his grief and went to Frederick to get him to pull the plug on the project, they were all well into it. Frederick was livid. He didn't give a damn about Pierre's wife or anyone else for that matter. He claimed there wasn't enough evidence to prove his wife's death was a suicide, never mind the result of Morphicphan.

Pierre was too weak with grief to put up much of a fight, and he relented. Everett recalled how Lamar seemed to lose all respect for Pierre at that point. Lamar could be a cold bastard. When things were going great, he was fun to be with, but when they turned sour he'd be the first to stab you in the back. Frederick put Lamar in charge of the lab and retired Pierre with an unheard of number of stock options. Frederick thought he was buying Pierre off. Everett knew Pierre could never be bought off.

Then it hit the fan. One year into the project, test participants started jumping in front of trains, off buildings, and into the deep blue sea. Everett smiled at the one time he truly saw fear in Frederick's eyes.

He called a damage control meeting and swore the team to secrecy. He promised he'd work things out and that the team would all be taken care of for their loyalty. Lamar pointed out that Pierre was no longer part of the team and that he might talk.

Everett frowned. He should have known something was up when Jack Lawless from the security department joined the team on its visit to Pierre's house. They all confronted him, and sure enough, he was putting the data together for submission to the FDA. Frederick pointed out that they could all lose everything, but Pierre was married to the truth.

Frederick, Nancy, Edmond, and Lamar badgered him for an hour. Everett remained locked in a guilty silence. In the end Frederick took Jack aside and gave him some instructions. Fifteen minutes later four monsters in suits and sunglasses showed up. Everett didn't want any part of that and ran out of the place. He waited in the limo.

It seemed like an hour before Frederick and the rest left Pierre's home. Everett didn't know what had taken them so long, but he feared the worse. He felt no better as he watched the suited monsters escort Pierre to another waiting limo. That was the last time he ever saw Pierre. A week later Everett read about Pierre's boating "accident" in the paper.

Frederick warned Everett that he was a co-conspirator in the whole affair. If he ever breached his silence, they'd all go to jail. Frederick bought Everett off over the years by giving him huge salary increases and promotions to ever-important jobs. His title was merely ceremonial at this point, and he was given only enough responsibility so that he couldn't screw things up.

Everett sighed. He was a coward. He never meant to be. He had only wanted to save some small part of the world, and in trying to do so, he had destroyed a bit of it. Pierre was the best of the whole team, and they'd destroyed him.

Everett closed his eyes to shut out the pain. In seconds he was asleep.

His eyes snapped open. From somewhere over the port side he could hear laughter and splashing about. He placed his beer in the holder and rose to inspect the commotion.

His jaw dropped when he spied three absolutely gorgeous blond, buxom beauties swimming off the port side of his yacht and not a single thread of clothing among them.

"Come on in Everett! Come on in and entertain us."

Everett didn't need a second request. Here was something to help him forget. He ripped off his bathing suit in a flash and leapt into the water.

Everett's eyes snapped open as the chill Atlantic waters hit his naked body. He tried to brush away the dust in his brain from a summer nap as he treaded water. He spun around to find his yacht behind him. The hairs on the back of his neck stood up. He could have sworn he spied a fin as he turned.

Everett began to swim to his boat and froze in abject terror. A foot and a half fin cut the water between him and his boat. He felt a sharp yank at his leg and mind-numbing pain flashed for an instant. He rose back to the surface of the water and watched dumbfounded as a shark swam off with his leg.

The water turned blood red and for some reason Everett's last thought was, "I guess the shark repellant doesn't work."

***

Aikeem left Celise's apartment early the next morning. He fairly glowed with satisfaction, having spent the evening with his ladylove. He meandered down the hall to the elevator with the air of someone who didn't have a care in the world. He popped the elevator button door with relish and entered the cab. He spun on a heel and froze.

Opposite him, standing outside of Celise's apartment, a black woman stared at him. The elevator doors closed and Aikeem dived at the door button. The doors reopened, but the woman was gone. Aikeem could have sworn it was Marie Lavalle.

***

Snapper-Cat was a super sleuth and a dream scout extraordinaire. His exploits across the Dreamscape were legendary, and few had traversed its lengths as often as he had. He'd even been to the Desolation Plains. They bordered the Darkling Space where the Scatter Clans lived alongside the refugees of nightmares. Some said the dark races plotted in these places, but not many cats had ever returned to tell this tale.

Today, he tracked a Weaver. A Weaver! He had heard of such creatures, but he'd never seen one before, never mind tracked it. He sniffed the dreams the Weaver wove and slid silently behind her cloud. It was definitely a she, he thought, and a human to boot.

He'd caught the scent earlier in the day when he spied dream stuff being dragged through the netherverse by some invisible force. He followed it for half a nap until he came upon a human female atop a mountain of clouds. Fascinated, he watched her weave a smallish dream and send it back to the real world. Then she flew off. He marked the spot with a bit of pee and lit off after the Weaver.

The Weaver stopped and so did he. In a flash she spun and locked Snapper-Cat with a gaze meant to ensnare. Snapper-Cat couldn't move. She was too powerful in this place, and all he could do was shake in fear.

The Weaver marched through the stuff of dreams as it wound about her ankles up to her knees. It wanted to be part of her. She stopped and looked down at the quaking cat. She reached down with one hand. Every fingertip was edged with a razor sharp nail.

The Weaver scratched the head of the quaking cat. "Pretty kitty."

Snapper-Cat opened his eyes and she was gone. He spun, but she was nowhere to be found, and no trail betrayed her path. Snapper-Cat shrugged and returned to the spot he had marked.

"Actually, she seemed very nice," Snapper-Cat mused.

***

Edmond cowered under a desk in the study. He shivered in terror. He looked at his tiny hands and the pretty pink dress he wore. He reached up and stroked his long dark brown hair. He really didn't understand why he was a little girl. He was sure he was something else.

He shivered again and stole deeper under the desk. The grownups were yelling again. They were yelling at his papa. They were mean. Some big men in suits came and took his papa away. He wanted to cry out, but he was afraid these men would come and take him. He felt a rough hand grab him.

"Jesus! Look what I found!" A pretty, but mean looking woman pulled him out from under the desk.

"Let me go!" Edmond tried to pull away from her, but she was much stronger.

The leader of the group frowned at him. "Christ it's his kid! What the hell do we do now?"

The dark woman said, "Send her off with her father."

"No!" a man with thick glasses exclaimed.

Their leader looked surprised and turned to him. "Why not, Lamar? You're not developing a conscience are you?"

"It's too risky. Remember this all has to look like an accident."

The dark woman held Edmond tighter. "What risk? He's going to have a boating accident. So he has it with his daughter on board. What's the big deal?"

The man with the thick glasses looked down at Edmond. "Pierre always boats alone. He'd never take her along."

Their leader frowned again. "Then what do we do?"

"Wait here," the man with the glasses said as he left the room.

Edmond began to cry. The dark woman spun Edmond around and got right in his/her face. "Be quiet, or I'll sew your mouth shut!"

Edmond hushed up. He spied another man in the corner of the room who was laughing at him. He didn't understand, because the man was him, but here he was in this pink dress and the dark woman—he felt sure he knew her name—was hurting his arm.

After several minutes, the man with the thick glasses returned, and he had one of Papa's big syringes in his hand. "Hold her still."

He began to kick and scream in earnest. It took everyone in the room to hold him down. Eventually, they secured a limb, and the man with the glasses drove the needle into his arm and emptied the syringe.

Just before he passed out, he heard the man in the glasses say, "No one has ever taken this large a dose. If she survives, she'll be a vegetable."

Edmond fell unconscious to the sound of mirthless laughter.

***

Pendella sniffed about the spot that Snapper-Cat had marked. Snapper-Cat watched Pendella with an approving eye. He had heard about her from the sayer stones on the Dreamscape and from the legends passed down by his ma—but to be in her presence!

Pendella turned to Snapper-Cat. "It is the Weaver all right. There are endomorphic refractions that could only be the work of a Weaver."

"Can you trace it back to the real worlds?"

Pendella studied the dream spore. "The trail is cold, but I think it is possible. I will need your help though."

Snapper-Cat swelled with pride. "I am at your service, Mistress Pendella."

Pendella began to scratch submaterial runes in the spot marked by Snapper-Cat. When she was done, she sat on her haunches and contemplated the circle of figures now surrounding the disturbance in the dream stuff. The runes began to glow a light turquoise blue.

"Join your spirit with mine."

Snapper-Cat did as he was told. He sat beside Pendella and concentrated on the power within. The runes burned. In an instant a vision back to the real worlds opened where the disturbance was. A hole that looked on to earth sprung open over the clear blue waters of the Atlantic ocean just off Long Island. Pendella studied the contents of the vision before it dissipated, and she noted the location in the real worlds.

Pendella turned to Snapper-Cat. "Thank you, sir cat. Your services will not go unnoticed by the Thirteen."

If Snapper-Cat could have flushed, he would have, but he simply bowed his head instead.

Pendella was gone in one quantum leap.

***

Edmond downed the last of his fourth coffee. He looked haggard. He was not his usual pretty-boy perfect. He'd even forgotten to shave, which is something he never did. Nancy entered his office with a single floppy disk clutched between thumb and forefinger.

"Here are the budgets we… What happened to you?"

Edmond looked up at his sometimes lover and attempted a smile. "It's my turn to have a bad dream."

"Really," an intrigued Nancy replied. "What was yours about?"

Edmond sank back into his chair and frowned. "You remember that day at Pierre's?"

Nancy instantly froze. She began to look around the room like some unseen presence might be about. "Shut up, Edmond! We're not supposed to even think about that."

"Tough! That's what my dream was about, except I was playing the part of Pierre's little girl."

"What are you talking about?"

"That's who I was in the dream. I was in her body… her clothes."

Nancy teased, "You must have looked adorable in that little pink dress."

"Ha, ha, ha. Laugh it up. It wasn't so funny when I got shot up with Morphicphan."

Nancy went cold again. "That's enough, Edmond. Just deal with it. I don't want to talk about this anymore."

Edmond sulked. "We talked about your dream."

"My dream couldn't get us arrested." Nancy threw the diskette on Edmond's desk. "Here are the budgets I customized. They go back five years. If Jack gives us any problems, we'll spring these on him."

Edmond cheered up a little with this news and smiled for the first time that day. "Good work. Now all we have to do is wait and see who Frederick selects. You got Everett's email? He's out of the picture."

"I was never really worried about Everett. He's always been weak. Jack's my only real concern... and you of course." Nancy smiled a wicked smile.

Edmond frowned. "I hope you haven't made up one of those budgets for my department."

Nancy feigned shock. "Edmond! How could you say such a thing! Don't you trust me?"

Nancy batted her eyes, and Edmond grimaced. "Give me a break. Remember our pact. We take care of each other."

Nancy sauntered around Edmond's desk and sat in his lap. She planted a red-hot kiss on his lips, and when she was done, she said, "I'll take care of you when I'm CEO, Edmond. Don't you worry."

Edmond held his tongue and simply smiled. He didn't trust her for a second.

***

Pendella stretched out in front of the front door to Aikeem's apartment. She heard the jingle of keys, and a second later Aikeem strolled through the door.

"Where have you been? We have work do."

Aikeem squatted down to address his mistress. "Lady, I just woke up from a glorious night's sleep. I can't train in the dream arts now."

Pendella stood up and rubbed against Aikeem's leg. "This work is in the real worlds. One of my scouts found something."

"And what is that, lady?"

"Pick me up, and take me to the small world in the room of books."

A confused Aikeem did as he was bid. "The small world? Oh, the globe."

Pendella rolled onto her back in Aikeem's arms and pawed his face. "You've been with Celise. Am I to lose you to her?"

Aikeem made his way to the library in his apartment and scratched Pendella's belly. "Never, lady! How could I live life without you?"

Pendella purred. "Precisely my point."

Aikeem rounded the corner through the open door and stopped in front of an antique globe that sat in the middle of the room.

"Hold me to it," Pendella directed.

Aikeem held his lady to the globe, and she began to spin it with one paw. She stopped when she spied the location she was looking for and pointed at it with one sharp claw.

"This is the spot."

"What spot is that, lady?"

"One of my scouts found the remains of a transport on the Dreamscape. The Weaver used this portal to send a dream back to someone in the real worlds. She has the ability to force a dream on the weary. I opened the transport to see where the dream was sent, and this is the spot."

Aikeem bent forward. "Let's see. It looks to be about ten miles off Long Island in the Atlantic Ocean. There's not much there but water, lady."

"Or perhaps a boat?"

Aikeem nodded. "That would be the obvious guess."

"Use your think box and see if there is any news of mishaps with boats in this part of the world."

"Good idea," Aikeem replied. He took Pendella over to the computer console and sat down. He placed his lady in his lap. Pendella immediately began to bat the computer's mouse around a bit.

Aikeem waited a moment until she was done. She looked at him sheepishly. "Well, it does look like a mouse!"

"May I continue, your Highness?"

Pendella ignored him and made herself comfortable in his lap. Aikeem began to click at the keyboard and jitter the mouse. In a few seconds an Internet browser came up and displayed a map of the world. Aikeem clicked again and zoomed into Long Island. A blinking icon indicated there was news in that part of the world, and Aikeem clicked on it.

Aikeem read the story and frowned at its conclusion.

"What does the think box say?"

"Your instincts were correct. There was a man's boat found at this spot, but he has disappeared. The coast guard found the craft adrift, but the owner was nowhere to be found."

"The Weaver took him."

"His name was Everett Winters. He was head of PR at Pharmican Global Pharmaceuticals."

"PR? He was in charge of purring? Humans don't do that very well."

Aikeem stifled a smile. "It means public relations. He's in charge of communicating the company news to the public."

"Oh. It's a human thing."

"Precisely. Now the question is: Why would the Weaver be interested in him?"

"What's a Pharmican? What's a Pharmaceuticals?" the curious feline queried.

"Pharmican is the name of a company. I've explained companies to you before."

Pendella sighed. "And I still don't understand it, but never mind."

"Pharmaceuticals are drugs, potions to heal us when we get sick."

"So this is a company that makes drugs."

"Precisely. You see, we humans aren't so mysterious after all."

"I would not go that far. The Weaver must be after a potion."

"Hmmm, that could be." Aikeem clicked about until he came upon Pharmican's home page. Pendella became bored and curled up in a ball on Aikeem's lap.

Aikeem meandered through the corporate home page, but he could find nothing that might interest a Weaver.

Aikeem sat back in his chair and contemplated the computer screen. He knew the answer was here somewhere, but where?

***

It was a grim foursome that sat in Frederick's office. Frederick glowered at the remaining Morphicphan conspirators from behind his pristine desk. Jack seemed bored, but Nancy and Edmond were obviously uncomfortable.

"I assume by now you all know that Everett has disappeared?"

No one answered, but it was obvious they knew.

"I promised you all during the incident that'd I take care of you, and I have. When Lamar exited this world, I wrote it off as a suicide, but now with Everett gone… It's too much of a coincidence, and my gut tells me someone's setting things up to take my place. One of you is messing with my finely made plans, and I want to know who it is."

Nancy and Edmond began to protest vehemently. Jack remained silent. Frederick turned to Jack.

"Quite frankly, Jack, I don't think either of these two are capable of pulling off a double murder."

Jack smiled an evil smile. The man was cut from stone. His closely cropped blonde hair crowned a rigidly structured face. His crystal blue eyes gave him the look of a Nazi commandant. He stood only five feet nine, but he was very wide. Muscle screamed for release from the tight fitting suit he wore. The head of security obviously took all aspects of his job very seriously.

"If I wanted your job, Frederick, you would have been the first one to disappear." Frederick frowned as Jack continued, "And these two idiots couldn't plot their way out of a bad mystery novel, as evidenced by the recent assaults on my department's financial statements."

Jack looked over at Nancy and Edmond. They exchanged brief looks of terror. Frederick scowled.

Jack smiled again and turned back to Frederick. "I've told you before, and now I'll let these morons know too, I have no use for your job Frederick. I'm quite happy in my current position. It affords me the luxury I've become accustomed to along with just the right amount of power. My needs have been met."

Jack turned to Nancy and Edmond. His face turned into a mask of menace. "So don't mess with me!"

Nancy and Edmond jumped. This actually brought a smile to Frederick's face. "Then you're saying this is an outside job."

Jack relaxed into his chair and ignored Nancy and Edmond. "It has to be. I've contacted my associates in law enforcement, and there is no evidence of foul play. Whoever did this is really good."

Frederick shifted nervously in his chair. "Coming from you that makes me uneasy. Do you have any idea as to whom it might be?"

Jack shrugged. "It could be any number of sources. We've had so many hostile takeovers. It could be a customer who was injured by a bad product, a disgruntled employee, an environmental nut who doesn't like biotech. The list goes on."

Frederick leaned over his desk and said, "Well, let's put our heads together and shorten the list. I don't like being a target."

"I think it's the Morphicphan thing."

All eyes turned to Edmond. Frederick squinted. "Why do you think that Edmond? That's a dead issue."

"I had a dream a couple of nights ago about it. It was so real."

Jack snickered, and Nancy shot Edmond a "You idiot" look. Frederick continued, "And based on this dream, you think someone from that era is attacking us? That sounds like a guilty conscience to me."

Edmond scowled. "That's something I don't possess. It's just my gut feeling is all. Why have that dream now when all this strangeness is happening? You can laugh all you want, but my instincts have served me well in the past."

Frederick sat back in his chair and contemplated Edmond. "There's no one left to attack us Edmond. They're all gone."

Nancy decided not to be left out. "What about one of the test subjects that survived the trials?"

Frederick turned to Jack who replied, "There were only half a dozen of them, and they were all well compensated. It seems highly unlikely."

Nancy continued, "How about the families of one of the subjects who didn't survive?"

Jack nodded. "That could be. It seems an awfully long time, though, to wait for vengeance."

Edmond blurted out, "What about Pierre's kid?"

After a pregnant pause Jack spoke, "She's a vegetable. I followed up after the incident. After you left her that day, the cops found her and took her to Bellevue. They couldn't revive her. The cops assumed Pierre pumped her up, and that's why he had the so-called accident. Of course, I helped with that theory."

"What happened to her after Bellevue?" Frederick asked.

"After Pierre's funeral I checked up on her, and she was sent to a home in upstate New York. As far as I know she's been there for fifteen years. Either that or she's dead."

"I want to know for sure. Find out."

Jack nodded and Frederick turned to Nancy. "You're a devious bitch. Your problem is you're always compensating for being a woman in a man's world."

Nancy started to protest, but Frederick cut her off. "Yes I know. I'm a chauvinist. Too bad. I'm not telling you this to cut you down. I'm telling you this so you can change and become stronger. I like deviousness, but smart is important too, and smart means losing all the excess baggage."

Nancy fell silent.

"You want my job? Good! Prove that you deserve it. Find out who is messing with us and eliminate them. Understood?"

Nancy nodded and fairly glowed with the knowledge that she had just been selected as Frederick's successor.

***

Aikeem walked in a dream. It was a funny thing. His conscious traveled with him, and yet he didn't feel as though he had control over this dream state. He seemed to direct his own actions in this unreality, but the environment was not of his imagination. This time he most assuredly did not walk the netherverse as a dream warrior.

He traveled down a dirt path behind a large gray house. Thick foliage bordered the path. In some places it was so thick that it was as if he traveled through a green tunnel. It was a beautiful sunny day, and he found the birds' songs uplifting. At the end of the dirt path was a small pond with an old gray weather-beaten dock stretching out into the water.

Aikeem walked to the end of the dock and stopped in horror. Laying face down in the water was a woman in a long white dress. Aikeem thought to jump in after her, but he could tell it was already too late. It occurred to him that even from this position she seemed familiar. He also noticed that the water around her was filled with floating flowers and candles in decorative little paper boats.

Aikeem looked down to find a bit of parchment at his feet. He bent over and picked it up. It was in a strange language, but he instinctively knew that it was a spell. He looked back at the woman and started. She rolled over in the water and sat up.

It was as if the water beneath her had become partially solid, and she stood upon it. Marie Lavalle walked across the water to a dumbfounded Aikeem. She reached up to Aikeem for assistance, and the flummoxed wizard helped her up onto the dock from the water.

"My apologies dear lady. I did not mean to be rude. It's just that I'm not used to seeing dead women rise up on the water."

Celise's mother smiled. "It happens around here all the time."

Aikeem was disarmed by the lady's smile and began to relax. "How is it that I am so privileged to meet you in my dreams?"

Marie took Aikeem's hand and led him off the dock. "I've come to ask a favor of you and to give you some information."

Marie led Aikeem to a small flowerbed. Fronting the bed was a bench, and she motioned Aikeem to sit there. "And what is that lady?"

Marie sat beside Aikeem. "I wish for you to protect my daughter."

"This is a request you need not make, for she is always under my protection."

Marie looked deep into Aikeem's eyes. "You say that now, but things may change."

Aikeem started to protest, but Marie held a finger up to his lips. "Hush sorcerer and listen to what I have to say." Aikeem held his tongue. "When I was a young girl I was cursed by a Caplata."

"Caplata?"

"A voudun evil priest. Americans call it voodoo."

"Oh, yes, I am somewhat familiar with this religion."

"My mother killed that vile creature. He took advantage of me."

Aikeem could see the pain in Marie's eyes, and he took her hand. "Before he died, Daagbo, that is his name, cursed my mother and her heirs with the dream death."

"What is that?"

"Daagbo has transformed himself into a malevolent spirit that walks the Dreamscape. From here," Marie gestured to the dream space around them, "he has harassed my family with nightmares… terrible nightmares that sometimes feel real. When I was young, my mother protected me, but when I married and moved away, she could no longer protect me. When I first moved to America, life was fine. Pierre and I made a wonderful home, and I bore Celise, but eventually Daagbo found me on the Dreamscape."

Aikeem felt a great sorrow for this woman. He could see that she'd been tortured. "That loathsome creature even struck at my infant, but my mother came to me in my dreams and taught me how to protect her. All this warring took its toll on me, and I sank into a deep depression. My husband tried to help me with his science, and at first it worked. I became stronger and held Daagbo off for a long time, but eventually even the drugs could not help me."

"So you committed suicide," Aikeem queried.

"No!"

Aikeem sat back from the ferocity of her reply. "I needed to protect my daughter and remain strong, and the only way I could do that was to make a pact with Oshun, the Goddess of Love. I sacrificed my body to her waters so that I might fight Daagbo on the Dreamscape. And so have I done for many years now. He spends most of his time off the Dreamscape now in the Darkling Space."

"Your battles must have been effective since Celise seems quite happy to me," Aikeem observed.

"Celise has not told you everything."

Aikeem's curiosity arose. "Really?"

"She has never been hurt by Daagbo; this is true. However, there are dangers that confront her, not only here, but in the real worlds too. That is why I selected you to guard her."

"Excuse me?"

Marie smiled and brushed a hand down the side of Aikeem's face. "Your chance meeting with my daughter was not just luck Wizard. Who better to guard my daughter than a student of the mystical arts and a warrior to boot? You're someone with the abilities to watch over her in all realms. I searched long and hard for one worthy of my daughter's love, and then I blew a kiss on both of you."

Aikeem stroked his goatee. "This is unprecedented. A mother who does not cease her matchmaking even after death."

Marie broke into a musical laughter. "Forgive me Aikeem, but I have only my daughter's best interest at heart."

"And what is the nature of these dangers back in the real worlds?"

"I told you my husband gave me a drug."

"To fight the voudun priest, you said."

Marie leaned forward and took Aikeem's hands in her own. "He thought he was combating my nightmares but no matter. After I died, I was so embroiled in my battles with Daagbo that I could not watch out for Celise back on the real worlds."

Marie's expression changed to one of pure hatred. "Some of my husband's associates killed him and filled poor Celise with Pierre's drug."

Aikeem shrank from the intensity of Marie's hate. "While I battled that bastard priest on the Dreamscape, they killed my husband and assaulted my beloved Celise back in the real worlds."

Aikeem tried to calm Marie. "But she is fine now. She's very happy."

Marie softened. "Now this is true. I tended to Celise for a long time after they almost killed her. I taught her things while I protected her from Daagbo."

"What kinds of things? Who must I protect her from in the real worlds?"

The skies instantly burned black. A startled Aikeem looked up to see a perfectly blue sky swirl into a dark cauldron of thunder and lightning. A terrific wind blew up and whipped the landscape about them. A face formed in one of the thunderclouds.

Marie hissed. "Daagbo!"

Marie jumped to the sky and feathered wings sprung from her back. Raven claws sprang from her fingertips and toes as she took flight. An awestruck Aikeem watched as the Daagbo cloud solidified and fell to meet her. A clash of thunder and a bolt of lightning blasted the landscape as they clashed.

"Wake up!"

Aikeem screamed as fifteen pounds of Pendella landed on his stomach and bounced him off the bed. Aikeem crawled to his hands and knees. He slowly managed to stand. Pendella licked one paw clean on the center of his bed.

"Lady! What are you doing?"

"I sensed you were having a nightmare. You may thank me for saving you."

"I was taking a meeting with Celise's dead mother on the Dreamscape, and she was about to tell me who her earthbound attackers might be!"

"I distinctly heard thunder and storm," an aloof Pendella replied.

"We were being attacked by an evil voodoo priest."

"So you see? I saved you. You may thank me now."

Aikeem started to protest but then decided it wasn't worth it. "Thank you," Aikeem grumbled as he stumbled off to the bathroom clutching his stomach.

***

Frederick walked through the halls of Lamar's mansion. It was empty, hollow and a little dark. Frederick didn't actually remember how he had gotten here or why he was here for that matter. He strolled down the main corridor admiring the artwork. He didn't much care for Lamar's tastes, but it wasn't bad for what it was.

Halfway down the hall stood an old grandfather clock that began to chime the hour. Frederick strolled over to the clock to admire its craftsmanship. Much to his surprise two eyes opened up on the face of the clock along with a mouth sporting a broad grin.

"Good day Silverman."

Frederick stumbled backwards and grabbed the wall for support. He was quite sure grandfather clocks were not supposed to talk; nevertheless, he replied, "Hello."

"What's a matter? You never seen a grandfather clock before?"

"Not one that talks."

"Happens all the time around here."

"At Lamar's house?"

"No you putz! On the Dreamscape. You're not very smart for a CEO are you?"

Frederick was taken aback. "Excuse me, I didn't know grandfather clocks were so rude."

The clock leaned forward. "Actually, I'm a bit more than just a clock. I'm a God. Well, actually the son of a God. I'm more of a Godling."

Knowing something of mythology, Frederick asked, "Do you have a specialty?"

"I bring dreams of inanimate things."

Frederick looked at the clock sideways. "You look pretty animate to me."

"Hey buddy, do I tell you how to do your job? How about a little respect?" demanded the clock.
"Do you have a name?"

"I'm the God Phantasus."

Realization lit Frederick's eyes. "Oh, yes, and from your name derived the word fantasy!"

"Yeah, yeah, yeah, Mr. Etymology."

"And to what do I owe the honor of your presence?"

"Today, I've come as a metaphor."

Frederick mused on the sly face of the godfather clock and replied, "For what?"

"Figure it out and don't take too long. I've got another gig to go to in a minute, and I'm not as omnipotent as I look. I suck at teleportation! Here's a hint. Look at my hands."

Frederick studied the clock's face. "It appears to be a quarter to midnight."

"Duh! So what's it mean."

Frederick was becoming aggravated by the clock's rudeness. "I'm sure I don't know, and I'm sure I don't care."

The clock began to laugh. "Oh, you will! You will! Talk to my brother Icelus. He'll tell you what happens at midnight! After midnight, we're gonna let it all hang out," and with that the clock popped out of sight.

"What a strange dream," Frederick mused to himself. Frederick stared in silence at the blank space for a minute, shrugged and then continued on down the hall.

Eventually he came to Lamar's library. The arched window at the end of the library was wide open. Frederick began to peruse the books when a large black raven flew in through the window and landed on the sofa next to him.

"Nevermore! Nevermore!" it squawked.

"That's rather trite, don't you think?" Frederick commented.

"Listen bud! I had Mexican road pizza last night, and I feel like a thousand la cucarachas are doing the tango across my insides. So guess when the next time I'll have Mexican road pizza again?"

"Nevermore," Frederick replied.

"You're not as dumb as you look."

"You must be Phantasus' brother, Icelus. The family attitude is unmistakable."

"That's me. Was he a metaphor too?"

"A grandfather clock metaphor."

"Right! The quarter to midnight thing. You must have it by now."

Frederick sighed. "I'm afraid you're all a little too subtle for me."

Icelus reared up and spread his wings. "Putz! How obvious do we have to be?"

Icelus took flight and headed for the window. "Don't strain your brain too much Frederick Silverman. The raven is the harbinger of death!"

The raven flew out the window, and the hairs stood up on the back of Frederick's neck. All of a sudden, his dream had taken a nasty turn. He didn't like the sound of Icelus' last observation.

Frederick looked about him, and Lamar's place seemed just a little darker. He spun to the sound of a whisper that called out his name. It was all about him, but it came from nowhere. It sounded like Lamar, but he couldn't be sure. At this point, he decided it was time to leave.

Frederick headed for the door and turned down the corridor. An impassable brick wall cut off his only exit. He thought for a second and decided he might be able to climb out of the library window. He turned to find the library door bricked shut. A mist gathered at Frederick's feet. He looked up, and it issued forth from the top of the stairs in front of him.

"FFFFrrrrrreeeeddddddddeeeeeeeerrrriiiiiiccccckk," whispered a voice from the top of the stairs.

Frederick frowned. "Oh, please! These Victorian attempts at horror are so boring!"

Frederick mounted the stairs and followed the mist into Lamar's bedroom. As he expected, Frederick found Lamar there. He sat opposite Frederick in a large overstuffed chair looking out the floor-to-ceiling arched window. Lamar turned and motioned Frederick to come closer.

"Hello, Lamar, you look pretty good for a guy who jumped out a window."

Lamar sneered and turned his head. The right side of his face was caved in and mangled. "That was my good side."

"That's truly disgusting Lamar. If this wasn't a dream, I'd be throwing up all over you."

"My name's not Lamar."

Frederick smiled. "Let me guess. You're Morpheus, bringer of humans to dreams."

"You're finally starting to catch on, eh Frederick?"

"I suddenly recalled where we got the name Morphicphan from. So what juicy gossip do you bring me from the land of the dead?"

Lamar rose and shambled on his broken limbs over to Frederick. "You're pretty relaxed for someone in the middle of a nightmare."

"Nightmare? Oh this is far too surreal to be a nightmare, and it's not nearly menacing enough," Frederick yawned in mock boredom. "Actually, the whole thing is rather blasé. Now the dreams I had about my ex-wife, those were nightmares!"

Lamar sneered an evil smile. "Well, maybe you should know that this whole affair is to inform you of your impending death. You're to end up like me, ah, I mean Lamar, Frederick."

Frederick sneered back. "Scary, scary, may I go now?"

Lamar grabbed Frederick in a fit of anger. "Mock me you little rodent?! See how you like this."

With that Lamar picked Frederick up and tossed him out the window. Frederick screamed as he felt the glass cut him. Blood and terror covered his face as he rocketed toward the pavement.

Frederick snapped awake. He grabbed his chest and felt his face. He gulped in great lungsful of air. After a few moments, he regained his composure. He looked around his large, empty office. He was alone. He looked behind him to find the sun had long ago set behind the cityscape.

A glass of water sat on his immaculate desk, and he grabbed it. He stopped drinking in horror. An eyeball at the bottom of the glass winked at him. He threw the glass away and two plastic, elastic arms stretched from out of the desk and grabbed him by the lapels. They jerked him down to the desktop.

Lamar's ravaged face formed on the computer monitor. "You didn't think you were getting away that easily did you?"

The desk hands threw Frederick backwards, and he crashed through the window into the night air. He screamed as he slowly rolled over and headed for the pavement. The city streets were barren this night as Frederick swan dived to give them a final kiss.

Frederick snapped awake. He clutched the sheets and skittered backwards up against the headboard. He wiped the sweat from his brow and breathed deeply. Terrified, he looked around his empty bedroom. He was alone. He concentrated. He was sure that he had gone to bed this evening in his home, and this was reality. He was pretty sure.

***

A somber Aikeem caressed the keys of his baby grand piano. Pendella sat in front of him and purred to the sampling of Mozart her man performed. Aikeem regaled Pendella with the story Marie had told him as he played. Aikeem finished both music and story with a flourish.

Pendella gave Aikeem kitty eyes and continued to purr. "That was beautiful Aikeem. Even my beast is soothed."

"I guess several centuries of practice have paid off."

Pendella spread out sphinx style before Aikeem. "This information from Celise's mother is most interesting."

"And there's more, lady."

Pendella began to clean one paw. "Do tell."

"After I awoke from my dream walk with Marie, I did some research on the computer. Celise's father, Pierre Bellamore, was a top research scientist at Pharmican Global Pharmaceuticals."

"That's one of those company things."

"Correct. The same company that Mr. Everett Winters worked at. Does that name ring a bell?"

"He's the one my scouts traced the Weaver to. The one missing from his boat."

"Correct. I also came to find out that just recently a Mr. Lamar Johnson, another high level employee at Pharmican Global Pharmaceuticals, committed suicide by jumping out a window."

"The work of the Weaver."

"My thoughts precisely. Marie said some of Pierre's associates killed him, so I looked up an old newspaper article that reported on his untimely death. The article claimed it was a suicide. Celise was discovered in a coma induced by a new drug Pierre had been working on. They thought he had accidentally given her an overdose and thus committed suicide out of guilt."

"But Marie said it was one of these associates," observed Pendella.

"I'm inclined to believe Marie, but one must wonder why anyone would commit such horrific crimes."

"Humans are like that," Pendella observed.

Aikeem frowned. "Not all of us, lady."

"Of course not. Well, it is obvious to me that Marie is the Weaver."

Aikeem was taken aback by this observation. "Why do you say that lady?"

"She was given great ability by this Goddess. She has no physical body to confine her, and she has great powers with which to combat this Daagbo. Obviously, she has begun to take vengeance on her family's attackers back in the real worlds."

"Then what does she need me for?"

"In her current state she can only get at her enemies through their dreams. Given all that you've told me, I do not believe she has the power to force a waking dream on her victims. Therefore, she would need you to protect Celise back in the real worlds."

Aikeem mulled this over. "You may be right. The question is: Who am I to protect her from?"

"Who killed Pierre and drugged poor Celise?"

Aikeem nodded. "Good point. Given that the Weaver has killed two people already, and Marie still needs me to protect Celise, there must be more than one person involved in this crime."

"She wants you to protect her daughter while she kills them all," Pendella surmised.

"Possibly."

"There is a danger that the conspirators may figure out that they are under attack. They may figure that it is because of Celise and hunt her down. She is the only victim left alive, and in their reality, the only one that could be doing them harm."

Aikeem didn't like Pendella's words, but he was afraid they might be true. "I must protect Celise."

"And in doing so you aid the Weaver. Old Grizzle-Whiskers isn't going to be too happy about that. Neither is the Administration, for that matter, for they ordered the Weaver's termination."

"I will not kill Marie. It's not her fault. She's just protecting her daughter."

"She's a non-sanctioned creature of power on a murder spree."

"Those are the Administration's words not mine!" Aikeem was adamant.

"But you are bound by their laws too, Aikeem. We are their servants."

Aikeem paused in reflection. "There is more than one way to skin a—"
Pendella's eyes opened in horror and Aikeem cleared his throat. "Rat."
Pendella relaxed and returned to cleaning her paw. "I think it is time for the next phase of your training."

"Oh, goody. Are you going to drop me into a sun this time?"

"That would be somewhat redundant," Pendella observed. "It is time for you to learn some of the more difficult techniques. We'll discuss it this evening."

With that Pendella jumped off the piano and headed for the kitchen and her bowl. Aikeem watched her go with no small amount of trepidation. Things were going badly, and he worried for his ladylove and her mother.

***

Jack hung up the phone with a grimace. He didn't like any of this business. Murder was a very risky enterprise, and he liked to use it only as a last resort. Frederick had just given him the order to have Celise Bellamore terminated.

He picked up a terrycloth towel and strolled out the open slider doors. He stepped onto the cream colored Italian tile that surrounded the Olympic-sized pool.

He swore to himself as he took his shirt off. He never would have left the little girl alive in the first place. He went with his men to take care of Pierre, so he never knew Frederick and company had left her drugged up. They'd expected her to die, but the little brat went into a coma instead. Frederick let slip about the girl a year after the incident, and that's when Jack followed up on her. He figured she was a non-threat tucked away in a coma. He'd only just discovered a few days ago that she'd come out of it three years after they'd juiced her up.

Jack had returned to the nursing home in upstate New York. The nurses who knew her said it was very strange. Her body hardly suffered any debilitation from the coma. It was as if she just woke up from a very long nap. The executors of her father's estate took care of her from there on in. She fairly raced through high school and then college. As near as he could tell, she had no job now but was living off of her father's ample trust.

Jack rubbed sun tan lotion over his perfectly molded body. He strolled over to a cell phone on a deck table and punched in some numbers. He loved technology. A PBX in a warehouse on the other side of the country automatically answered. Jack punched in a special code. The PBX would in turn send a preset code to a web server out on the Internet that would in turn grab some files from a PC he had set up just yesterday. After the transfer was done, this new PC would erase itself.

The files were being transferred to the same four men who had helped him terminate Pierre. It seemed only appropriate that they get this job too. Once they had those files, they would have everything they needed to eliminate Celise Bellamore. Everything complete with a single phone call and no traces back to him.

Jack smiled, returned the phone to the table, and jumped into the pool. He swam to the silver, floating water couch in the middle and splashed up onto the float. He basked in the sun and closed his eyes.

Bellamore was good. Jack didn't know how she managed the Johnson and Winters hits, but it was a professional job. Not a lick of evidence left to implicate her, or anyone else for that matter. He admired her for that. He wondered to himself if she had contracted the job, and if it was anyone he knew.

No matter, soon this Morphicphan thing would finally be done with, and he could turn his attentions to Etherton and Jeffries. Mess with his budgets! He was going to put a hurt on them they'd never forget. He couldn't wound Etherton too bad since she was now Frederick's successor, but Jeffries was fair game. Maybe he could figure out a way to slam Etherton through Jeffries. He knew the two were lovers. Yeah, that would be sweet.

Jack's float moved from the force of a small wave and he snapped open one eye. He squinted in the bright sunlight. He looked around the pool area, but no one was evident. The water seemed calm. He mentally shrugged and closed his eye.

The float bobbed again, and this time both eyes came open. Something was hovering in front of him in silhouette. Jack shielded his eyes with one hand. He screamed in terror as the massive tentacle came crashing down on him. Jack managed to heave in one massive gulp of air as the tentacle dragged him under water.

Jack fought to pry the beast's appendage off him, but it was too big and strong. He wanted to scream in terror when he saw the razor sharp beak he was being drawn to. In desperation, he grabbed a mouthful of the tentacle and ripped the flesh with his teeth. The creature immediately let go of him, and in two powerful strokes he broke the surface.

Jack gasped as he gulped in a huge lung full of air. The beast below grabbed him by the feet and yanked. Once again Jack was dragged under. He tried to swim away, but the beast would not let him go. Two more tentacles slithered in and wrapped around Jack. He was pinned by the creature. It slowly drew him down. Jack struggled in absolute desperation, but eventually his lungs burst and filled with water.

Jack's body slowly floated to the surface of the pool. The Weaver watched from her dream cloud that floated above one end of the pool. Satisfaction oozed from her pores. She wondered if anyone would get her little joke. Pierre had died in a boating accident. Jack Lawless had died in a floating accident.

With a snap of her fingers and a chuckle, the Weaver was gone.

***

Pendella spread out sphinx-style on Aikeem's chest and stared into his eyes.

"The next phase of your training will be in the art of dream intersection."

"And what is that lady?"

"I will teach you how to become part of others' dreams."

Aikeem shifted uncomfortably. "I'm a bit uneasy with that Pendella. It seems a bit like voyeurism to me."

"That is a human construct. What if a child is having a nightmare? Do you ignore the emergency out of concern for privacy?"

Aikeem mused on this. "Point well taken. So what do I do?"

"Close your eyes and open the dream state as I have taught you."

Aikeem did as he was bid and replied from the nether place, "I am there, lady. Now what?"

"Feel the dream stuff around you. Let it flow through your spirit, subconscious and conscious."

"Yes Yoda."

"Yoda? Why did you call me that?"

Aikeem smiled through his dream state. "Never mind."

"Now, do you feel the rhythm of the dream stuff?"

"Yes, lady."

"Good. Reach out around you. Do you feel a change in the rhythm?"

"Yes! Yes, I do."

"That is someone else's dream. Grab on to that rhythm with your mind, and let it drag you into their dream."

Aikeem concentrated, and in an instant, popped into an endless green field on the Dreamscape. Pendella popped in next to him.

"Aikeem! You popped into a dog's dream!"

Aikeem smiled as he watched a toy poodle play about the field.

Pendella was disgusted. "It's that idiot next door! Fifi! What kind of self-respecting animal goes by the name of Fifi! That's not a name! It's a curse!"

A bright blue Frisbee popped into existence and flew near the dog. Fifi jumped and snatched the Frisbee out of the air. A dozen more Frisbees popped into the Dreamscape, and Fifi caught everyone in a single leap.

"So that's what dogs dream about. I'm quite sure she can't do that in the real worlds."

"Who'd want to? It seems like a good excuse for a bonk on the head to me. She is soooooooo stupid."

A dozen red balls rolled into existence, and Fifi yipped in total delight as she chased them about.

This caught Pendella's interest. "The balls look fun though."

Fifi soon tired of the balls and turned around to a line of dogs a hundred strong that appeared behind her.

Pendella was shocked. "That's totally disgusting!"

Aikeem chuckled as Fifi went down the line of dogs and sniffed each of their butts.

"Let's get out of here before she decides to start marking her territory."

"Agreed," Aikeem replied and closed his eyes, which he thought was somewhat redundant given where he was. He concentrated.

Aikeem popped into a boudoir. Pendella popped in behind him. A woman in her late seventies stood before a four poster bed that was populated with four naked young men one-third the woman's age. Aikeem was shocked.

"That's Mrs. Henderson from across the hall!"

Mrs. Henderson turned when she heard Aikeem and smiled. She wore a long black diaphanous nightgown that revealed her slender, aged, and wrinkled body underneath. Her silver locks spilled over her shoulders, and she batted her eyes at Aikeem.

"Aikeem, you again?" Mrs. Henderson began to advance on Aikeem.

Aikeem stumbled backward and looked down at Pendella. "What does she mean <u>again</u>?"

Pendella mentally shrugged as Mrs. Henderson continued toward Aikeem. "The boys dropped over for tea, but I was going to teach them a new game. Wanna play?"

"Pendella!"

Aikeem awoke in his own bed. Pendella opened her eyes, and Aikeem just knew she was laughing on the inside. The lady bounded off his chest and strutted out of the room.

"That's enough for today."

Aikeem watched her go with a frown. What on earth was he going to say to Mrs. Henderson the next time he saw her in the hall?

***

Once again Nancy and Edmond squirmed under Frederick's stare. Frederick was obviously on edge. That made the two of them even more nervous. Nothing bothered Frederick. He was typically a rock, but now something was beginning to nibble at him at the edges.

"I recently had a very strange dream. It was not only disturbing, but very, very real. I'd never experienced anything like it in my life. Edmond, you told me that you too had a dream. Was it realistic?"

Edmond nodded in the affirmative.

Frederick turned to Nancy. "What about you? Have you had any strange dreams recently?"

Nancy wasn't used to having this kind of conversation with Frederick, and this added to her unease. She also nodded yes.

Frederick mused on this. "I've been thinking about my dream and Lamar's and Everett's deaths. Did you know that Lamar was deathly afraid of heights?"

The two shook their heads no.

"And Everett was terrified of sharks."

"They never found Everett," Edmond noted.

"My point precisely. Sharks wouldn't leave much would they? Do you know what Jack was afraid of?"

Nancy and Edmond froze. Their intuition warned them of what was coming.

"He was always afraid of drowning. That's why he spent an hour every day swimming. It was his way of conquering his fears. In the end they conquered him."

"Jack's dead?" Nancy asked haltingly.

"I got a call a half-hour ago from the police. They found him floating face down in his pool. There wasn't a mark on him."

"What is going on?" Nancy cried in desperation.

The light of realization lit Edmond's eyes. "It's Pierre's girl, isn't it?"

Frederick smiled a hollow smile. "Very good Edmond. I'm impressed."

"What? What are you talking about? She's alive?" Nancy was becoming tense from lack of information.

"Jack tracked her to a nursing home in upstate New York. She came out of her coma three years after the Morphicphan affair, and I believe she's the one attacking us."

Nancy looked at Frederick sideways. "How? In our dreams?"

"Think about it, Nancy. We pumped the girl full of a drug that manages circadian rhythms. Pierre told me he believed that the drug could even subdue nightmares. He believed this was possible by giving the subject some conscious control over his or her dream state."

"Oh, come on Frederick. This isn't like you. She's probably just hired some very good contractors."

Frederick spread his hands. "Contractors don't enter your dreams. I believe she told me in my dream what her intentions are. How about your dream Nancy? What did she tell you?"

Nancy shuddered and fell back into her seat. She didn't want to remember. "Let's just take the bitch out!"

"How? Jack's gone. He handled those kinds of projects, and he's the only one I'd trust to take care of this kind of business."

"Can't we just hire someone else?" Edmond pleaded.

"I don't think you ungrateful little bastards realize how good Jack was. He saved all of our asses after the Morphicphan thing, and no one suspected anything. He was the consummate professional. I don't know how I'm going to replace him. There is one hope though."

Nancy's eyes widened. "What's that?"

"He might have gotten the contract out before he died."

"Thank God," Edmond sighed.

"That's not who I'd be thanking. I confirmed the order to him at noon. If he followed his routine, he might have delivered the contract before he died."

Edmond leaned forward. "When will we know?"

"Jack was always quick about these kinds of things. If she's not gone in a week, then the contract didn't go out, and we'll have to think of something else. In the meantime, I've hired some other professionals to keep an eye on her so we'll know what's going on. I suggest that the both of you suppress your fears and watch your backs. We're up against our most powerful enemy yet. Understood?"

The two subordinates somberly nodded. Frederick didn't like the feeling of desperation in the room. He wasn't used to it. Control had always been the first order of business, and now that order had been changed to survival.

***

Celise sat in a cane chair with a broad fan back. She stroked the head of a bronze cat statue that stood next to one arm of the chair. Scratched out in blood on the floor in front of her was a large pentagram. A black candle burned at each point of the star in the pentagram. A bit of parchment engraved with strange glyphs was centered in the symbol.

A click sounded from the front door as the lock was picked. Celise waited. The four monsters in suits entered the room. The tallest one was a blonde, blue-eyed Nazi who was obviously their leader. He looked down at the symbol written on the floor.

"What's this?"

Celise smiled. "It's a spell."

The four men chuckled and the Nazi replied, "You're going to need more than a spell to protect yourself sweetheart."

The Nazi drew an automatic pistol from under one arm and began to fit it with a silencer. His partners followed suit.

The Nazi waved his pistol at Celise. "Let's go. It's time to have your accident."

Celise gestured and the four men screamed. Their weapons turned into tarantulas, and they threw them away in panic.

"Don't you hate it when that happens? What would the N.R.A. say?" Celise taunted.

After a second of disbelief, the Nazi advanced on Celise, but then he stopped dead in his tracks. The metal cat by her side stepped forward and leapt on him. He screamed in fear and then agony as the cat began to shred his chest. The Nazi fell over backwards from the metallic feline's assault.

One of the other monsters moved toward Celise. She gestured from her chair, and he exploded backwards, bouncing off a wall. Celise stood up. The assassin on her right snapped in with a kick to her midsection. She turned out of the way, caught his leg, and blew out the kneecap of his supporting leg with a kick of her own. The last thug threw a vicious roundhouse punch at her face. She simply caught his fist and twisted. He screamed in pain and dropped to the floor clutching his broken arm.

The metallic cat retreated from the quaking Nazi, and Celise advanced on the prone thug. She gestured and the magical façade that masked Celise and the cat fell away revealing Aikeem and Pendella. An infuriated Aikeem pointed at the Nazi. "Your litany of black deeds is written all over your transparent little minds like neon signs! Today you pay!"

Aikeem finished the spell he had prepared with a gesture, and the lines of the pentagram fired up and became laser red. They burned for a second. A silent implosion caused the floor to fall away, and a fiery red pit replaced the circle of the pentagram.

Aikeem turned back to the terrified Nazi and spoke again. "You asked what that is? It's a portal straight to the first ring of hell. They just love fresh meat down there, especially when it hasn't had the opportunity to die yet."

Aikeem grabbed the murderer's leg and began to drag the Nazi over to the pit.

"No!"

Aikeem froze. Hovering over the pit was the Weaver on her dream cloud. She was dressed from head to toe in black garb. A black ghutra concealed her features. Her eyes burned a hate filled, fierce red.

"These are mine! They destroyed my family!"

Aikeem was unsure of what to do when his decision was made for him. The Nazi kicked him in the rump, and Aikeem sailed into the pit. He screamed in horror. The Weaver and cloud dove to snatch Aikeem's arm. She floated back up with Aikeem in tow to hover a few feet above the pit. She turned her attentions to the assassins.

"I wanted your deaths to be slow and torturous, but I suppose this is better because it will last for eternity."

The four did their best to back away from the pit. "There is a pet near the top of the pit. I have sent it a daydream of a snack."

Four blood red tentacles covered in razor sharp barbs shot out of the pit and landed with a booming thump on the floor. The four men screamed and Pendella dove behind a couch. Eyestalks emerged from each tentacle, and in a second each man was dragged screaming into the hellhole. Aikeem waved a hand and the pit closed.

The Weaver dropped Aikeem, and he landed unceremoniously on his back. His eyes widened as he saw something revealed under the woman's ghutra. Part of her headpiece had fallen away when she had grabbed him, and what Aikeem saw froze his heart.

"Stay out of my business, Wizard. I'll have my revenge," and with that she winked out of the real worlds.

Pendella extricated herself from behind the couch and sauntered over to Aikeem. "Are you all right lover?"

Aikeem snapped out of his daze and stroked his lady's head. "Yes, dear heart."

"That didn't go exactly as we planned, but we were right about Celise being a target," Pendella pointed out.

"No, it didn't," replied a distracted Aikeem. "Come. We need to return to my sanctum. Things are coming to a head. I can feel it."

Pendella pranced over to Aikeem's knapsack that was propped up in one corner of the room and slid inside. Aikeem strapped the pack across his back and shook his head. He did not like the destiny he had been thrust into, and if he was not very careful, he knew he was headed down the path to damnation.

***

A tinny Musack version of "The Girl from Ipanema" played over the elevator speakers. The depths of Frederick's depravity were evidenced by his enjoyment of this music. The doors opened, and he made his way to the lobby of the Pharmican building. The security guard tipped his hat to him. Frederick acknowledged the man's presence and pushed through the revolving doors.

The door froze. Frederick jerked the door, but it would not continue its revolution. He swore and spun around to get the attention of the guard. The guard was gone. He swore again and spun to grab the attention of his limo driver who must be waiting nearby.

Frederick froze in horror. Someone dressed in black floated on a cloud just in front of the door. Frederick backed away as best he could; the hate in those eyes was blinding.

"I wanted to save you for last. I wanted your death to be oh so slow, but the fates have conspired against me."

The Weaver began to circle Frederick, who watched in amazement as she floated through solid matter. "Your greed and lust for power will be your damnation Frederick Silverman."

Frederick summoned up his courage. "I'm not afraid of you! This is just a dream!"

The Weaver's smile was evident through her ghutra. "Really? Your associates thought the same thing just before they died too."

Frederick's courage left him, and he began pounding on the glass doors. "Let me out! Let me out of here!"

The Weaver continued her circle. "I've been studying you for a while now. You were very difficult to figure out. What could his worst fear be, I wondered?"

Frederick started kicking the glass of his cage, but to no avail. "Finally, it occurred to me that a man who obviously views all humans as bugs must be afraid of the little things. And then it hit me! He's the President of a drug company! He's doing his best to wipe out his fears: Germs!"

Frederick began to pound the door in earnest. He didn't want to find out what this devious bitch had conjured up for him.

"I've conjured up some special ones for you Frederick Silverman. They're bigger than most."

Frederick screamed as gelatinous, one celled, green gobs oozed out of the tile around the revolving door. They squirmed from all directions toward his cage. Frederick pounded the door with tears in his eyes.

"Oh, Frederick. That's just the appetizer. Look behind you."

Frederick shrieked at the sight of the six foot, cilia-covered amoebae that slithered toward his cage. The germs oozed through the bottom of his cage, and he screamed as they began to ruin his shoes. He squished them as best he could, but some managed to climb up his socks.

"Can I get you a hanky?" the Weaver taunted.

The amoebae fell against the outside of Frederick's glass cage with a thump. He screamed and pushed back away from it. Several cilia slithered under the rubber apron of the revolving door and grabbed his feet. Frederick fairly frothed at the mouth as his feet were yanked out from under him. His cage began to fill with the Godzilla-sized germs. Intense pain racked his legs as the amoebae's cilia penetrated his flesh. Frederick tried to crawl up the glass, but he was yanked back down as his cage filled with bacteria. The last thing he saw was the Weaver's mirthless smile.

***

A weary Aikeem closed the door to his sorcerarium. Pendella awaited him.

"You prepare for battle," she stated.

"I have concocted a defensive spell that will serve me on the Dreamscape and in the real worlds."

"Very good. That seems a wise move to me."

"It is time to bring this matter to a close. I know who the remaining players are in this tragedy. When we met Celise's attackers in her apartment, I brought a mind see spell with me. I plucked the identities of our enemies from their minds. We must intersect their dreams and conclude this affair."

"Very good, beloved. Let's retire to your bedroom and take flight to the Dreamscape."

Aikeem nodded and turned down the hall to his bedroom. Pendella followed. Before she entered the bedroom, she looked back down the hall. She gave Snapper-Cat kitty eyes, and the dream scout bounded back to the Dreamscape. She would protect Aikeem, but she would not betray Grizzle-Whiskers.

***

Edmond followed Nancy through the revolving doors into the lobby of the Pharmican building. "I don't like this Nancy. We should just wait like Frederick said."

Nancy spun on Edmond and fairly spit. "I'm tired of waiting! I'm not going to be sitting around when that little bitch comes for me!"

Nancy reached into her purse and withdrew a handgun. Edmond's eyes went wide at the sight. "What! Are you crazy?"

Nancy smiled. "Yes!" She stormed past Edmond and headed for the elevators.

Edmond pleaded, "Well, what are we going to do anyway?"

Nancy punched the elevator button, and it immediately opened. They stepped inside. "I have a cousin who has a girlfriend whose brother is a limo driver for a Mafioso."

Edmond looked at her sideways. "You've got to be kidding me."

Nancy punched a button and folded her arms across her chest, the gun still in her right hand. "Do you have any better ideas?"

Edmond pouted and slunk to the back of the car. They rode the elevator in silence up to the top floor of the Pharmican building. Nancy led Edmond through the lobby to the CEO's office and burst through the doors. Frederick's chair was facing the window.

"Frederick! I'm sick of waiting! It's been a week, and it's time to do something!"

Edmond hesitantly followed Nancy into the office and was surprised that there was no resultant tirade from Frederick.

Nancy stormed over to Frederick's desk. "Don't ignore me! We need to take action now!"

Frederick did not reply. In a fit of anger, Nancy rounded Frederick's desk and spun the chair around. Both she and Edmond screamed at the sight of Frederick's dead body. His fingers were clawed into each arm of the chair. His face was gaunt and white, and the expression on his face was one of pure terror.

"Not very pretty is it?"

Nancy and Edmond spun around to find a tall, handsome man sitting off to one side. In his lap was a cat who eyed them warily.

"Who the hell are you?" Nancy demanded.

"I am Aikeem Abdul Jamal Yosaffa and this is my lady, Pendella Purrfect."

Nancy shook her head in disbelief. "What are you doing here?" She motioned at Frederick's corpse with the gun she still held. "Did you do this!?"

Aikeem smiled. "Actually, I think he did it to himself. It seems the fruits of your misdeeds have finally begun to ripen."

Nancy and Edmond shot each other nervous looks. Edmond pointed a finger at Aikeem, and shrieked, "I'm calling security!"

"They won't come," Aikeem pointed out.

Nancy scowled. "Why not?"

Pendella bounded out of Aikeem's lap and sauntered over to Nancy. She looked up into the woman's eyes and said, "Because they're not here."

Nancy screamed as did Edmond, and they both ran to the opposite wall. Nancy waved the handgun in Pendella's direction and stuttered, "The cat talked!"

Pendella began to lick a paw. "That's because we're on the Dreamscape. Here communication is possible beyond physical constructs."

"What?" an unraveled Nancy screamed.

Pendella turned to look at Aikeem. "She must have been a rat in a previous life. She's not too smart."

Aikeem smiled. "I would guess a jackal myself."

Pendella and Aikeem's attention was drawn upwards. With a flash of light and intense imaginary winds, Frederick's office blew apart around them. Nancy and Edmond clutched each other in terror as the fabric of their dream was torn asunder. When the Weaver was done, all that was left was a carpeted floor that seemed to stretch into forever and the chair that Aikeem sat in.

The Weaver floated on a cloud six feet off the ground and glowered at the shivering executives. Aikeem strolled over between the Weaver and the despicable couple. Pendella joined him.

The Weaver pointed at the two guilty executives. "They are the last. It is their turn to die."

Aikeem shook his head. "There has been enough killing. It is time to stop."

The Weaver spun on Aikeem. "I warned you before Wizard! Stay out of my business."

Aikeem seemed genuinely hurt. "Your harsh words wound me Celise. Why do you treat me like this?"

The Weaver's eyes went wide. Slowly Celise unwound the ghutra from around her head.

"How did you know it was me?"

"During our last interchange, your ghutra fell away, and I saw the cameo I gave you."

Celise's hand instinctively went to the jewelry on her neck. Nancy pointed the gun at her. "You know this bitch?"

Aikeem spun and glowered at Nancy. "I suggest you keep your mouth shut woman. If you insult my ladylove like that again, I'll let her have her way with you!"

Nancy's expression changed to one of shock, and Edmond clamped his hand over her mouth.

"Why do you protect these two Aikeem? Mother has spoken to me. I know you know my history. Do they not deserve to die?"

Aikeem turned back to Celise and sighed. "Probably, but not by your hand."

Celise was enraged. "Not by my hand! Not by my hand? Then whose? This one," Celise pointed a finger at Nancy, "injected me with a drug that left me in a coma for three years! And this one watched!" Celise jabbed an accusing finger at Edmond. "And they both participated in the murder of my father! And for what? To cover up their mistakes!"

Celise floated closer to the pair, but Aikeem kept himself between the duo and her. "But your foolish plan backfired, Nancy. The drug made me strong here." Celise swept an arm around her. "Here in the Dreamscape I am a goddess because of what you did to me. You brought me back to my mother who trained me how to use my new powers. How ironic! You attempted to kill me, but instead you made me the weapon of your own destruction."

"It shall not be done!" boomed a voice behind them.

Celise spun around at the sound of this new voice. Grizzle-Whiskers sat on his haunches surrounded by a dozen other cats of prodigious size. Cats by the thousands began to appear and surround the humans. Aikeem looked around desperately.

Aikeem addressed Grizzle-Whiskers. "I have things under control here, Lord Cat. I do not need your intervention."

Pendella was mortified that Aikeem spoke to her lord in this manner. Grizzle-Whiskers continued to stare at Celise, but addressed Aikeem. "We have been ordered to terminate this creature, Wizard. It is an order I intend to carry out."

Aikeem adopted a combative stance. "I know who you are sir, but if you touch one hair on the lady's head, I'll turn you into one incendiary feline."

Grizzle-Whiskers shot Pendella a dirty look. "Your human does not know his place, Pendella."

Pendella was too embarrassed to reply. Celise began to float higher. The place was thick with cats now, and they all eyed her with angry looks. Nancy and Edmond simply stood their ground and quivered.

"Who has ordered my execution?"

Grizzle-Whiskers looked up at her. "The Administration."

"What Administration?" asked a confused Celise.

"The Celestial Administration. They are the keepers of the Universe. You are an unsanctioned creature of power who has used her abilities to murder. For this reason you have been given the death mark."

Celise spun on the old cat and hissed at him. "They murdered my father and almost killed me!"

Grizzle-Whiskers shrugged his shoulders. "Certainly those are extenuating circumstances, but you should have filed the proper paperwork."

Celise was incredulous. "With whom?"

Grizzle-Whiskers sighed, "The Administration, of course."

"I didn't even know they existed until two seconds ago."

Grizzle-Whiskers shrugged again. "It's a strange universe, isn't it?"

Celise didn't know how to reply, and Aikeem spoke up. "You act more like a bureaucrat than the First of the Thirteen, Lord Grizzle-Whiskers."

Grizzle-Whiskers turned and glowered at Aikeem. "I grow tired of you human. Who are you to insult me? She's a rogue Weaver, and we are the Keepers of the Dreamscape. There is no more dangerous creature than this. We have been directed to terminate her, and so it shall be done!"

Grizzle-Whiskers stood and ten thousand cats began to move on Celise. Celise gestured, and a few hundred blew back away from her, but the hissing barrage began to attack from every possible angle in space. Claws of every description began to close and Celise looked around in panic from her cloud.

Aikeem screamed, "No!" He gestured outwards with both hands and a green fireball shot to a point just under Celise. There was a massive explosion as the ball connected with Celise's invisible, subconscious, ectoplasmic tendril. The tendril snapped, and the fireball followed one section to the dream Celise and the other to her physical self back in the real worlds. When the fireball slammed Celise's dream form, it encased her. She screamed in terror as it surrounded her, and she shot off at light speed into the nether regions of the Dreamscape.

Aikeem fell to his knees and screamed in agony, "No! Forgive me!"

Grizzle-Whiskers watched in silence and with a little bit of awe as Aikeem sobbed into his hands. Eventually he looked up and jabbed a finger at the old cat. "You forced me to do this!"

"You serve the Administration too, Wizard. You are bound by its laws also."

"And I do not need you to interfere with my execution of those laws." Aikeem practically spit, "Take your army and leave cat! You have made no friend here this day."

Grizzle-Whiskers studied the man for a second and then turned. The First of the Thirteen led his army away, and in a few seconds they had all winked out of existence. Pendella sat near her man, but she said naught. She knew he was greatly distressed, and she was at a loss as to what to do.

Aikeem spun on Nancy and Edmond who still clung to each other. Aikeem jabbed a shaking finger at them. "You are largely responsible for what has transpired here today. Do you think you have escaped?"

The two remained silent. "I have lost all that I hold dear, and so shall it be for you. Go back to the real worlds knowing you are cursed for the rest of your miserable lives."

With that Aikeem gestured, and both he and Pendella disappeared in a cloud of smoke and fire.

Nancy and Edmond would wake up later shivering in each other's arms. Theirs was the embrace of the damned.

***

Aikeem tucked the sheet in tightly around Celise's neck. He kissed her on the cheek and marveled at how beautiful she was. Her breathing was slow and steady, and she seemed to be fast asleep. A rack of nearby medical equipment monitored her progress.

Pendella sat on the end of the bed. She looked up at Aikeem. "Where is she?"

Aikeem turned to his lady. "What do you mean?"

Pendella gave Aikeem kitty eyes. "Aikeem, you could no more hurt Celise than I could hurt you. You may have fooled Grizzle-Whiskers but not me. I know you too well."

Aikeem smiled at Pendella. "Yet, you said nothing."

Pendella shrugged. "To what end? The Weaver was discovered. Her plans were foiled. The Administration is supposed to represent good. What good could come from Celise's demise? So where is she?"

A sad Aikeem turned back to his ladylove. "I do not know. I told you that I had prepared a spell of protection, but it was not for me, it was for her." Aikeem brushed a loving hand across Celise's cheek. "My spell separated her spirit from her body. It was meant to place a shield around both the physical and spiritual aspects of her, but I did not expect her spirit to shoot off into space like that. As you know, I'm new to the Dreamscape. I must have made the spell wrong."

Pendella walked over to Aikeem's side and rubbed his elbow. "I'm sure she's safe Aikeem, and I shall spend my every sleeping minute looking for her on the Dreamscape."

Aikeem smiled down at Pendella and rubbed her head. "Thank you lady. That means a lot to me."

The two returned their attentions to the sleeping beauty and dreamed of a time when body and spirit would be melded back into one.

And Then There Was Avalon

There are places of power that exist on the edges of unreality, realms that float in the chaotic mists between all domains. Sometimes they act as bridges between worlds and universes. These places may hold to a particular nature, that is to say, some lands may be steeped in evil while others glow with the forces of good. Some of these lands represent neither philosophy but are simply suffused with the raw energy of the multi-verse.

Avalon is such a place. It has merged with this world on several occasions. It brings with it mythic creatures that have chosen this place as their permanent home. It primarily consists of a long, broad hill overlooking a pleasant valley. On the far side of the valley is a long seemingly endless lake, and on the far side of the hill is a great wood that also extends into eternity.

Avalon has served as a final resting place for many a hero. Humankind has always worshipped this land for its serenity and, thus, has honored its heroes by burying them there. There have also been many creatures of power who've found peace in the greenery of Avalon and have chosen to make it their home.

And so Avalon floats between the realms, causing no hurt to the universe but giving it pause, for even the universe must breathe.

᷂ ᷂

I searched for a year on the Dreamscape, but I could catch no scent of Celise. During the first few months of her disappearance, Aikeem became more and more distraught. I feared for the well being of my man and did everything I could to aid in the return of his human ladylove, but our searches were fruitless.

Eventually, I think Aikeem resigned himself to the fact that Celise was lost to him forever. He did not give up his search, but his forays onto the Dreamscape became less frequent. It pained me to see him hurt so. He blamed himself entirely. I did my best to comfort him during this time, and thankfully, he did not withdraw from me. I think in some ways our relationship became even stronger.

In the real worlds Aikeem tended to Celise every day. During each visit he would talk to her, although he knew the vessel that was her body was vacant. When alone with her, he would lay magic on her that would protect her body from atrophy and disease. He always left her with a kiss.

I could not ask my fellow felines to search the Dreamscape for me; Celise had been ordered dead by decree. There might have been a few close friends I could have trusted, but I did not want to take the chance that the nature of Celise's semi-living state could get back to the Council of Thirteen. Grizzle-Whiskers would not have been pleased.

When not searching for Celise, I tried to keep Aikeem distracted, and we spent many hours training on the Dreamscape. I must admit that his talents began to rival even my own.

Neither of us had totally given up hope, but the Dreamscape was vast and we were but two.

᷂ ᷂

Blitherskites wore his human gangster façade. He sat in the dark corner of a sleazy bar in Durres, a city on the coast of Albania by the Adriatic Sea. He waited patiently for his contact and smiled when the crusty little Egyptian wearing a purple fez walked in. Farouk was a shifty character with a bushy mustache spread under an expansive nose. Short, cropped, coal black hair framed a laconic and timeworn face. His clothes were dingy and worn. Half of a hand-rolled Turkish cigarette hung from his slightly oversized lips. He nervously looked about the room and smiled when Blitherskites leaned out of the shadows.

Farouk tossed his cigarette aside and made his way over to Blitherskites's table. As he grabbed a seat he said, "Many greetings Monsieur Skites. My associates tell me you would like to do some business."

Blitherskites waved over the bartender. The dark, stout, older man reluctantly came over to the table and snarled in broken English, "Whata you want?"

Blitherskites looked at Farouk, and the Egyptian ordered an Ouzo. The bartender returned to the bar, and Farouk turned his attention to Blitherskites.

Blitherskites's eyes narrowed, and he leaned forward over the table. "I'm looking for guns, ya see, and ammunition… lots of guns and ammunition."

The dollar signs leapt into Farouk's eyes. "There is no shortage of weapons in this part of the world Monsieur. With that incident in Kosovo a few years ago, and now Afghanistan recently," Farouk shrugged, "there is a vast assortment to choose from. How many weapons do you require?"

The bartender returned with the Ouzo and plopped a bottle and shot glass in front of Farouk. The little man poured a glass as the bartender left.

Farouk took a sip from the glass. Blitherskites replied, "Twenty million."

Farouk sprayed the table with Ouzo.

Blitherskites frowned. "Is that some kind of Egyptian custom?"

Farouk choked a few more times, and then stared at Blitherskites. After a few seconds, he began to laugh. "You are playing with me, Monsieur!"

"No joke. I've got an army, ya see, that needs guns, lots of guns."

"There isn't an arms dealer in the world that could supply that many weapons. The Chinese don't have that many soldiers in their army, and they have the biggest in the world."

Blitherskites frowned. "I need guns, Farouk, ya see. Are you going to get them for me, or do I go elsewhere?" Blitherskites slammed a mottled hand on the table. When he removed it, a glowing pile of diamonds was left behind. Farouk's eyes grew wide.

Blitherskites's other hand plopped a large bulging cloth sack next to the pile. "Guess what that's filled with?"

Farouk's voiced wavered, "I could possibly pull together a half a million, maybe a million, but I will need a lot of time and," Farouk gingerly picked up a diamond between finger and thumb, "more of these."

"There's plenty more where this came from. These are your down payment. You've got six months. Can you do it?"

Farouk smiled. "Certainly Monsieur. How did you want delivery?"

"I'll get back to ya on that one, ya see?"

Farouk bowed his head in agreement and swept the diamonds into a pile on his side of the table. He withdrew a cloth pouch from a pocket and began to fill it.

Blitherskites smiled as he watched the greedy little man take ownership of the diamonds. He knew that in his heart Farouk was really a rat too.

***

Lord Dark Seer surveyed those before him from his throne of bones. The skull of a great cat crowned his royal seat; his vermin subjects reveled at this sight when they were allowed into the royal chamber. A low mist clung to the floor. Luminescent, amber glow stones were interspersed along the wall of this dark, moist room, and they cast a somber light. The walls and the high ceiling were made of organic bloodstone mined from the quarries of Alnarok, a place deep within the Darkling Space. Most of the furniture was merely functional, ugly and made of either stone or bone.

Rat guards of the First Order of Vile lined the chamber. They stood slightly hunched over and leaned on their long pikes ready to snap into action. The First Order of Vile was a berserker clan, and the mania that was barely held at bay was evident in their crazed, beady, red eyes.

Two lines of Plague Priests lined the rug that led to the dais upon which Dark Seer sat. The priests sat on their haunches and stared straight ahead in a mindless drug-induced haze, flush from the consumption of tatterweed. Every now and then a desperate titter would issue forth from under the cowls of their black cloaks. They dreamed black fantasies and transmuted them into even blacker magic.

Lord Dark Seer smoothed out the mottled gray cat fur of his floor length robe. He plucked a flea from his own fur and popped it in his mouth. Dark Seer placed a hand on the crown of a human skull and absent mindedly caressed it. The skull adorned the top of his staff of power, which leaned against his throne. He continued to stroke the skull and waited patiently.

Finally, he came. Skittermore was on the smallish side, but oversized thighs betrayed his natural speed. He walked upright in the manner of the high rats, but from his shambling gait it was obvious he preferred all fours. He was a brown rat from Greyskull's clan, which was rumored to be the fleetest of all the clans. That's why Dark Seer had chosen him. When one traverses the Darkling Space, one does it either very carefully or very quickly, preferably both.

Skittermore bowed down before the First of the Thirteen. "Lord Dark Seer, I bring a message from the one at the edge called Darkness."

Dark Seer studied Skittermore for a second before responding. He enjoyed watching the little rodent squirm under his gaze. "And what does Darkness say?"

"The Sloths have agreed to his terms. The troika is complete. The Axis of Evil is one. We may begin to unify and train as one army."

"And what of the various encumbrances?"

Skittermore wrung his claws as he spoke. "He has begun to address these issues, my lord. He says that he will soon send directives on how to deal with our enemies."

"And what of the bridge?"

"It is verified, my lord, but its location still eludes us. Darkness has his agents scouring the real worlds for the maps that will pinpoint its location and appearance."

Dark Seer stroked his chin and smiled a mirthless vermin smile. "Our time gathers with the dusk, Skittermore. Soon verminkind shall rule the real worlds!"

Dark Seer stamped his staff on the ground for effect, and the Plague Priests broke out into mindless applause and tittered excitedly. Skittermore bowed and exited the room. Dark Seer smiled as the small rat left. All was going as planned and he was pleased.

***

Only Sharpclaw O'Bannon had the nerve to travel the Darkling Space. Cats were reviled in these lands, for it was the cats that kept this place's inhabitants prisoners. Most creatures of this realm belonged to the black ways or were byproducts of vicious nightmares. Some were outcasts from the real worlds who had forfeited their corporeal form. Others were dark creatures of power who had escaped the Great Purge and chose to hide out in this place.

And, of course, there were the Scatter Clans. The Scatter Clans were the rodent armies of the high born rats that were blasted into the ether during the Great Purge. Most of the vermin were killed during the cataclysms, but some survived and thrived. After so many millennia, they reproduced to the point of becoming the undisputed masters of most of the dark realms.

The Darkling Space is infinite in dimension. It butts up against the Dreamscape at its most chaotic borders, and this is how its obscene denizens are able to cross over into nightmares. The Darkling Space is not a dreamland but a domain whose construct is somewhere between the real worlds and the Dreamscape. It is rumored that portions of it even touch against the various rings of hell, but this has never been verified.

The Darkling Space is as varied in its environments as any of the real worlds. Vast black jungles cover enormous swathes of land. Swamps the size of continents breed vile mutations that exist only to consume each other. Endless deserts burn from the heat of an invisible sun and are littered with the bleached bones of those who've attempted to cross them. Fantastically tall mountain ranges cut a large path across all the lands and hide monstrous denizens who tunnel into their very core.

Sharpclaw preferred to roam through the heat of the jungle. Here he always wore his beast. Sharpclaw was only fifth on the council, but his beast was by far the biggest. He stood as large as a Clydesdale horse, but his body was feline in confirmation and ability. His beast shed no fur, however, for he was scaled as a reptile. His coloration was mostly a dark green, but like a chameleon, he could change to the colors of the forest around him. Sharpclaw's head was low and long, like a panther's, and his canines jutted beyond his bottom lip. His eyes were long, narrow and a soft yellow. He had no tail in this form.

Sharpclaw stopped by a slow running river and selected a smooth rock. He padded over to the rock and extended one razor sharp claw. He held it up to inspect it and then began to stroke it back and forth across the stone, whetting it until its edge was to his liking. He wasn't called Sharpclaw for just any reason.

He wondered to himself where all the strange happenings of late would lead. He'd been spying on the Scatter Clans for several months now, and he was disturbed to find that they were not warring among themselves. Typically, the high rats spent their time slaughtering each other, but lately this had stopped.

Now their activity seemed even more sinister in nature. Some of the rats had even made forays back into the real worlds. His fellow council member Pendella Purrfect had foiled one such attempt only two years ago. Sharpclaw had discovered a plan to invoke a nameless one on earth proper, and Pendella had been dispatched to foil this conspiracy, which she did with aplomb.

Sharpclaw smiled as he moved on to the next claw. He liked that one Pendella. What she lacked in pure physical capability, she made up for in confidence and guile. They had fought side by side on a number of occasions, and it was her quick wit that saved them more than once.

"Yes," he thought, "she was a clever one."

Sharpclaw's frown returned. He worried that the rats were able to gain entry to earth. All of the paths from the Darkling Space back to the real worlds were supposed to have been blocked after the Great Purge. Obviously, some had been missed. Just how many there were concerned him. It was no secret that the high rats wished to return to earth and make it theirs. It absolutely galled them that their only representatives on the real worlds were their mindless cousins.

And now there was this thing with the Sloths. He'd followed a messenger from Lord Dark Seer's castle all the way to the sloth's domain. He rarely ventured into those jungles as he never really considered the Sloths a threat. Evidently, he was wrong. He'd heard from the Council that Pendella had foiled some plan of theirs recently, but what he saw in their realm chilled him to the bone.

The Sloths were exhibiting most unslothlike behavior. They'd been very busy building a vast and potent army. From what Sharpclaw had seen, he was sure they intended to align themselves with the rats. This was a disturbing turn of events; Sharpclaw wondered if the cats could stem an assault of this size on the Dreamscape.

He slid the last foreclaw across the rock and turned to go. Even now he was on his way out of the Darkling Space to report his findings to the Thirteen. His eyes narrowed. A strange telltale scent had briefly perfumed the air. He snorted and turned. It was hard to see through the dense brush that lined this place, but Sharpclaw knew he was being watched.

There! A pair of almond shaped, yellow green eyes peered out from under a tall fern. Beady red eyes began to appear among the green bush. A hundred pike bearing rats stepped out in the clearing to encircle him. Sharpclaw's eyes narrowed and he licked his lips. He did so love a challenge.

A black beast stepped out of the bush, and Sharpclaw's eyes went wide in surprise. This creature looked like one of the great cats! A feline of any sort in the company of rats! What vile conspiracy was this? It stood about four and a half feet at the shoulder, and its long black fur, glowed with a dark sheen. Its face was mostly flat and housed a broad flat nose and a mouth full of long sharp teeth. Its tail was covered in long matted black fur, and it lashed back and forth with an audible whoosh. Its limbs screamed power, and Sharpclaw doubted there was an ounce of fat on this creature's body.

"What manner of cat keeps the company of rats?" Sharpclaw fairly hissed.

One lip rolled back on the creature as it crouched low. "The kind that comes to rend you."

It screamed with an ear-splitting shriek and launched itself across the pebble beach. In time to its jump, the rats lowered their pikes and skittered about to create an inescapable wall of steel around the two cats. Sharpclaw leapt and the two crashed in midair.

Sharpclaw attempted to slash the beast in midair, but the creature put its head down and came in between his forelegs. It was fast, too fast. Before Sharpclaw could twist out of the way, it was up under him and on his neck. He screamed in agony as it sank its fangs into his neck. Where other creatures found his scale impenetrable, this beast found penetration. Sharpclaw rolled to his back dragging the beast with him. He attempted to get his rear legs under the belly of his attacker, but the beast slid to the side.

Sharpclaw was desperate. The beast's fangs sank deeper and searched for his jugular. He tried in vain to roll on top of the creature to crush it with his weight, but it managed to avoid this attack too. Still it held on. It twisted. It ripped and Sharpclaw screamed in agony.

The beast let go and backed away with a blood stained maw. Sharpclaw stumbled back in disbelief. How? He looked at the pool of blood at his feet. How could this happen to him? He was the greatest warrior of the Thirteen. His life's blood continued to leave him. He stumbled backwards. He began to feel woozy. His killer turned and dispassionately left the clearing. The rats moved in with their pikes.

***

Jackenstein Muddleboot carefully considered the five cards in his hand. The three other dwarves who sat at the beautifully carved marble table did likewise. A pile of exquisitely cut gems were centered on the table next to a beat up pile of cards. Jackenstein fingered a ruby and wondered if it was worth the attempt to fill a straight. He didn't give a damn about the gems. Down here, in the land they called Gullet, entertainment was more important than baubles.

How many thousands of years had it been since they'd been suckered into this place? Jackenstein guessed no one really knew for sure. After a while one lost any perspective of time.

When they first landed in this place they all thought they'd been killed. Back then there were a little over a quarter million dwarves. After a while they came to realize they'd been sent to some kind of prison by their tormenters. They decided to make the best of the situation and set about to what dwarves do best: They began to mine.

Gullet was actually pretty good land for mining. They'd found veins of various minerals, gems, and ores. They'd built quite a beautiful city that they called Mingle. It would have been the envy of any dwarf colony. Of course, it was still a prison. Every time they tried to mine up, they ran into an impenetrable wall made of some metal none of them had ever seen before.

Jackenstein threw in two cards and took two from the deck. He tried not to grin after filling the straight. 250,000 dwarves and only one deck of cards! Of course, who knew they'd be leaving home for good. He threw in his ruby and his mates matched him.

This was the first time in two hundred years he'd been able to play. You had to wait in line, and seeing as there was only one deck of cards, it was a really long line. Of course, the good thing was once your number came up, you could split work right away. Work was important, but poker was everything!

Diddle Buddlebut raised two emeralds and Jackenstein considered his straight again. He looked down at the dwindling pile of stones and frowned. You were allowed to play as long as you had a pot. Once it was gone, it was back to work. Jackenstein had only been playing a week, and he wanted more. Paduddle Gob-killer had set the record. A thousand years ago, he had played for a hundred years straight.

Jackenstein saw the emeralds and raised another ruby. Brakmeister and Hanslander folded their cards. Diddle saw Jackenstein's ruby and called. The two dwarves laid down their cards, and Jackenstein banged the table with an open hand and a yell.

"By the sacred layers of rock today is my day!" Jackenstein replenished his pile of gems with the ones from the center of the table. The other dwarves grinned. They could appreciate a good hand.

Jackenstein looked up above him into the Throat as Diddle shuffled the cards. A gentle warm breeze blew from the Gullet up into the Throat. The poker table was set up right underneath the massive tunnel that led into the heavens. No dwarf had ever been able to scale it. The Throat was lined with the same kind of metal that kept them from mining upwards. No dwarf pick could mar the impervious stuff. Jackenstein looked up from his cards. The Throat appeared to stretch at least a hundred miles overhead, but that was just a guess.

Jackenstein sighed as Diddle dealt the cards. One day they'd leave this place. He was sure of it.

High overhead in the mists of the Dreamscape, lost in thought, a caterpillar skated around the rim of the Throat.

***

Conniving Blitherskites slid the manhole cover back over the sewer hole with a groan. He stood and checked his suit to make sure it wasn't soiled by any sewage. Personally he liked the smell but it seemed to offend humans. He sniffed under his armpits to make sure they were not repugnant either.

He checked his hands to ensure that he looked human. He grunted with satisfaction that his spell was still intact, and he exited the alley. He passed a dumpster and nearly jumped out of his skin. A homeless man in a dirty, long woolen coat dropped out of the garbage bin.

"Hey buddy! What 'cha doin'? You scared the hell out of me."

The homeless man stared at him with red-rimmed bloodshot eyes. Dirty, unkempt hair flooded down over his face to merge with a scraggly blond beard. "Sorry. Just getting lunch."

The homeless man skittered off back down the alley, and Blitherskites licked his lips in envy. He wondered if the homeless guy found anything good. He shrugged and moved on.

The homeless man wound his way about the alleys avoiding contact with anyone who might be hunting in there. He clutched an oily brown paper bag to his breast. He'd found enough food for both himself and his mate that would fill their bellies for a change. Eventually, he came to a burrow primarily constructed of an old refrigerator box and discarded crates. He lifted a canvas flap and scurried inside.

A woman napped in there. She too wore a long woolen cloak. Her clothes were tattered and old, and she wore at least three pairs of socks on her feet. The homeless man grabbed a foot and shook it. The homeless woman spun instantaneously and whipped out a sharpened steak knife. She relaxed when she saw who it was and sat up.

"What did you find today?"

"Good stuff! None of it's moldy."

The homeless man slid next to his mate and pulled the contents out of the bag. He laid out stale bread, various meat scraps and vegetables between them. They attacked the food as though it were the finest banquet. When they were done, the woman leaned against the wall of their makeshift abode and began to sob.

"I can't believe how good that tasted," she said between tears.

"Then why are you crying?"

"Because it's someone else's garbage," the woman fairly spit. The homeless man reeled back from her venom.

"We had it all, and look at us now! Picking through the garbage!" The woman broke into tears again.

The homeless man took her hand and tried to calm her. "At least we're alive."

The woman rolled away from him and sobbed, "If you call this living."

Edmond Jeffries contemplated Nancy Etherton's back. He knew they were reaping just what they'd sown. He understood that expression now. He wondered what his mother would think. He sighed, sat back, and dreamed of dessert.

Blitherskites mounted the steps to the New York Public Library and made his way to the offices of Marlene Robbins. Blitherskites had called her a few days before and asked her about tracking down a book of maps in their rare books collection. The lady was positively ecstatic when Blitherskites told her what he was looking for. Evidently she'd been unaware that such a tome ever existed, never mind that it might be hidden in her library.

Blitherskites made his way to the back of the building. Lord Dark Seer himself had contacted Blitherskites about the map book. He was promised that if he could find the book, he would be brought back into the good graces of the council, and the death mark would be removed from his head. He especially liked that last bit.

Blitherskites turned a corridor and made his way through the stacks. He'd been searching for a week now and felt confident that this Ms. Robbins had what he was looking for. He wasn't sure what Dark Seer was up to, but he was sure humanity was going to regret it. He actually enjoyed the company of humans. At first, he found their furless ways disconcerting, but he found many among them who weren't that different from him, especially the lawyers.

"Oh, well… them's the breaks," he said to no one.

He found the woman's tiny office in the back of the building, and he rapped on the jamb of the open door. Ms. Robbins looked up over her bifocals and gave Blitherskites the once over. She was in her late forties and rail thin. Her thick glasses attested to many hours of reading and her graying hair, stacked up in a bun, gave her a distinguished look.

"May I help you?"

"I'm Connie Skites, ya see? I called you about that rare map book."

The woman became positively animated. "Oh, Mr. Skites! I found it! I'm simply at a loss. I mean such a find in our own library!"

The woman made Blitherskites nervous. "Yeah, yeah, it's a real doohicky. Can I see the book?"

Ms. Robbins clapped her hands together. "Of course. Come with me. We need to go to the rare books reading room. How did you ever even find out about such a book?"

Blitherskites followed the woman as she led him through the labyrinthine library. "A friend from another country asked me to look it up."

"And you say it's actually a copy of an original?"

"I'm told some guy named Dante Alighieri copied it as a favor for a business associate. It's a collection of maps from before the mid-twelve hundreds."

"Which is absolutely fascinating to me. You see Dante was a respected poet, and for him to undertake such a task, which would normally be the undertaking of a monk…"

"I guess he owed the guy a lot of money or something. Did ya look at it yet?"

Ms. Robbins eyes fairly glowed. "Oh, yes. There are several pages that document where the various maps came from, but what I find positively fascinating is that there are fantasy maps in this collection. This is unheard of! From that time period anyway."

Blitherskites shot the woman a sideways look. "Fantasy maps?"

"Why yes. I thought you knew. There is a copy of a map by Merlin. Merlin! To the land of Avalon where he buried King Arthur."

Blitherskites smiled. "Yeah, that's the one I'm looking for. Will I be able to get a copy of it?"

"Certainly Mr. Skites. That's the least I can do for you after you brought this exciting book to my attention."

"Yeah, yeah, no problem toots." Ms. Robbins giggled and Blitherskites wrung his hands together. Just a few more tasks to complete, and he could feel the death mark being lifted from his head.

***

I can not remember a time when I'd seen my lady so distressed. I walked into the great room to read the day's paper. I was used to her ignoring me on such occasions, so I thought nothing of her not stirring as I sat down next to her. After several minutes of this, I noticed a black cloud that seemed to hang over her. This was very unlike Pendella.

"What is wrong lady? You look as though you ate a rotten mouse?"

I was shocked when she replied with the most pitiful sounding rowl I'd ever heard in my life. "By the one God, lady! What is wrong? Shall I rush you to the vet?"

She looked up at me with tear-stained eyes, and through the mist of a great depression said, "Sharpclaw O'Bannon has been murdered."

I supposed I should have known who that was, but I asked nevertheless, "Who is Sharpclaw O'Bannon?"

"He was Fifth on the Council of Thirteen. He was the greatest warrior on the council and my friend."

I stroked my lady's head, and although I'm sure this made her feel better, she did not purr. "They found what was left of him in the Darkling Space."

"I'm sorry lady. Is there anything I can do?"

Pendella rose and ran a paw over the corner of one eye. "Thank you, lover, but no. I must go to Wo'Em to meet with the rest of the council. We will bury Sharpclaw there and consult on what course of action to take."

"Where is Wo'Em lady?"

"That is a secret meant only for cats, Aikeem. Suffice it to say it exists between the Dreamscape and the real worlds. It is a gift to us from the Administration for guarding the Dreamscape."

"And when will you return?"

"I can't say."

I rubbed my lady's head, and she smiled. "Take care Pendella. Sharpclaw's murderer may have a taste for other members of the Feline Council."

Pendella gave me kitty eyes in appreciation of my concern. She jumped off the couch, meowed a syllable of power, and walked through the wall. My eyes widened as her tail disappeared.

"She's never done that before," I said to myself.

That was a week ago, and I have heard nothing from my lady since. I have not felt so alone in a very long time. Both of my ladies are absent, and I have found myself becoming lethargic. I am a great warrior and a powerful sorcerer, but I am nothing without the company of my soul mates.

***

Xaviar Napman slowly made his way through the labyrinthine corridors of Darkness's castle. This place once belonged to an ogre by the name of Grimlot. Darkness tricked the ogre into going on to the Dreamscape, and he was never seen again. Whether or not Darkness killed him there was anyone's guess. Xaviar gathered his long gray robe more tightly about him; this place was cold. He held his staff of power more tightly. He expected he wouldn't have to use it, but it was better to be safe than sorry when traversing the Darkling Space.

Eventually, he came to the throne room that was guarded by two pike wielding snakemen. Xaviar was surprised to see such creatures; they typically inhabited a region that was much deeper in the Darkling Space. They opened the heavy metal doors for him, and he shambled in.

The throne room was immense. It was entirely constructed of blackstone. Torches were hung every few feet along the entire perimeter of the room, and they gave the place a smoky atmosphere. At the far end of the chamber on a raised dais sat Darkness. His royal seat was also made of blackstone, but it was molded to conform to his body.

Darkness wore a long black robe with a cowl. At first Xaviar wasn't sure if anyone was in there, but the blood red eyes that stared out from that cowl gave the man away. At least he thought it was a man. That was the rumor.

Xaviar looked up at the iron candelabra that hung from the ceiling as he walked under it. Each foot long candle was jammed into the skull of a different creature. At least one of the skulls belonged to a sloth, and he frowned. He stopped before Darkness and bowed his head out of respect.

Darkness's voice was a baritone blend of whispers and menace. "To what do I owe the honor of a visit by the First of the Sloth High Council?"

Xaviar leaned on his staff. "We have done our part Darkness. We await the fulfillment of your part of the bargain."

"The Chitin armies are ready then?"

"Yes. Each unit is slothed with one of my best officers. These mindless soldiers will bring untold slaughter to the real worlds."

Xaviar thought he could detect a smile under that cowl. "Very good Lord Napman. The Scatter Clans have upheld their part of the bargain also. Their wars have ceased, and they have gathered under Lord Dark Seer's banner. Between these two armies, the real worlds will not stand a chance."

Xaviar smiled. "You make it sound so easy, Darkness, but you forget that the Sloths have already tried to assault the real worlds, and we were foiled before we really got started. My predecessor Bennington Sloman built the Chitin armies, but he was never able to deliver them to the real worlds."

Darkness growled. "I will keep my part of the bargain, Xaviar. I said I shall provide a bridge, and so I shall."

Xaviar stroked his chin in thought. "Which brings us to another issue. The Sloths are providing an army over ten million strong as are the Scatter Clans. Your part in this affair, although very important, is relatively small. Why should Lord Dark Seer and I bow to your leadership in the new world order?"

Darkness frowned at Xaviar's challenge and made a furtive gesture with one hand. The sloth's eyes went wide with terror. The beast he had heard rumor of padded into the room from behind Darkness's throne. The creature was the size of a small pony and built for slaughter. Darkness lazily pointed to Sharpclaw's killer with one hand. "This is Legacy. You've heard of my assassin and right hand creature?"

Xaviar frowned. "Yes, but I still—"

Darkness leaned forward and fairly frothed. "You are aware of my abilities! Between the two of us, there is no entity in any realm that could keep us from consuming them! I calmed the Scatter Clans! I brought the armies together! I have formed this Axis! Do not betray me Xaviar Napman, or your head will grace my candelabra!"

Darkness jabbed one bony, black finger in the direction of the chandelier over the sloth's head. The sloth's grip on his staff tightened, but he took no action. He could hear Legacy's breaths in the silence of the throne room like some great bellows. No, he would not anger this one.

"I meant no disrespect Darkness. I only wished for an explanation."

"Well, now you've had it." Darkness said with some venom. He calmed himself and motioned again to Legacy. "We've all had concerns about the keepers of the Dreamscape. This one has killed their greatest warrior. This is merely a down payment on all that I have promised."

The sloth's eyes widened. The cats pretty much left the Sloths alone, but they would be a concern when it was time to move. Xaviar had heard of the cat that Darkness obviously spoke about. "The one called Sharpclaw is dead?"

Darkness nodded. "And soon we will have prisoners. I expect we will find this insurance most useful in the days to come."

Xaviar eyed Legacy warily. "Then I guess the only question left is when will the bridge be provided?"

"The required documents are being gathered for me even as we speak. Once in my possession, I will be more able to answer that question. Now return to your armies Lord Napman, and see that they train until it is time to take the real worlds."

Xaviar bowed, turned, and exited Darkness's throne room. He looked at his own three-fingered hand. Soon it would have the digits required to weave potent spells. All Sloths would be graced so, and then they'd see about who ruled whom.

***

On the edge of the Dreamscape lies the land Wo'Em. It is a green place of broad fields and everlasting sunshine. It is said that the one God created this place as repayment for the cat's tireless protection of the Dreamscape. Cats come here to rest, frolic, and associate. In the Palace of Trees at the center of Wo'Em, the council gathers to conduct its business.

But this time was a sad occasion for all felines. One of their best was gone. Gandabon, Whiskertysnips, and Drusillia Delicious pulled the bier on which Sharpclaw was laid. As the procession passed through the endless sea of felines, a great caterwauling went up to the heavens. Cats of every shape and confirmation joined in the cacophonous choir. This disharmonious rowl shook the heavens and even extended into the Dreamscape.

Gandabon and Drusillia stopped atop the hill of heroes and detached themselves from the stretcher. Grizzle-Whiskers made his way through the crowd and stopped before Sharpclaw's dead body. Sharpclaw's beast was gone now. Now he was a fine looking orange tabby of prodigious size and wide yellow eyes. Grizzle-Whiskers sat on his haunches and simply stared at Sharpclaw for a long time. Pendella soon arrived to sit next to him.

"I feel as though I have lost a son," Grizzle-Whiskers said softly to Pendella.

Pendella licked him behind the ear and replied, "All of our hearts are heavy, Lord Cat."

Grizzle-Whiskers motioned to a great black Manx named Cleftmore, and the feline began to scratch in the earth. After a minute of digging, he marched away and another cat began to dig. This went on for an hour until a suitable grave for Sharpclaw was dug. Drusillia grabbed Sharpclaw by the scruff of the neck and dragged him into the hole. A new procession of cats marched by. Each cat threw in a paw full of dirt and soon the grave was filled.

To a cat, the feline sea bowed their heads when this was done and fell silent. Eventually, Grizzle-Whiskers raised his head and left for the palace of trees. Soon the rest of the cats dispersed, and Sharpclaw was left alone to rest in his new home.

The palace of trees was a large circle of impossibly tall pine trees atop a small hill. At their upper reaches, the pine branches meshed to form a ceiling, except for one bare spot at the center. Pendella entered the palace to find Grizzle-Whiskers standing outside the sunspot that illuminated the center of the room.

The sunspot was ever present in the center of the palace due to Wo'Em's eternal sun. Cats very rarely tried to cross the spot lest they immediately become entranced into a long, but restful nap. It was silent within the palace, and Pendella softly made her way to sit next to her master.

"These are dangerous times Pendella. All manner of evil attempts to disrupt the universe, and the Administration is stretched beyond its means. We have no one to help us with the troubles that brew on the Dreamscape, Pendella."

"What troubles, my Lord?"

"Sharpclaw had been scouting the Darkling Space for quite some time. Recently, he discovered the Scatter Clans had ceased their warring. He believed there was a new force in the Darkling Space, one that is uniting the clans."

"What kind of force?"

"He died before he could tell me."

Pendella pondered Grizzle-Whiskers words. "Do you think the Scatter Clans mean to make war on the Dreamscape?"

Grizzle-Whiskers thought long before he answered. "I do."

"The last time they tried this, we slaughtered their armies before they even breached the Darkling Space. Why would they try it again?"

"I think it has something to do with this new force. We need to discover its nature. We need information."

"Then I shall go into the Darkling Space and get it," Pendella said with resolve.

Grizzle-Whiskers smiled. "You are brave Pendella, but you will not go alone. I want you to take your wizard with you. Do not tell him that this is my direction because methinks he does not have much use for me after that affair with his mate."

Pendella grimaced. "I'm afraid it's true. He holds no love for you Grizzle-Whiskers."

"No matter. He will do it for you. I've assigned two cohorts of cats to escort you back to the real world. Go there; collect your man; and prepare for an expedition into the Darkling Space. I need to know what is happening. In the mean time, I will increase the patrols along the Dreamscape and the Darkling Space."

"Why do I need an escort?"

"Sharpclaw's killer may have a taste for council members. All council members will have guards until I feel it is safe for them to be alone again. Of course, on the Darkling Space you and your man will be alone." Pendella frowned, but she did not argue.

Grizzle-Whiskers turned and licked Pendella behind the ear. "You be careful Pendella Purrfect. I could not stand to have my heart broken twice in so short a time."

Pendella smiled and returned the kiss. She spun and left the palace of trees. She stole one last look at the wonderful streaming sunlight that made the sun spot. She had a premonition that she would not see it again for some time.

***

Blitherskites placed his backpack down and put his furry butt on a rock. He absentmindedly wrapped his rattail about the rock and sniffed the air. He sighed with pleasure. Nothing like the fetid air of a decaying cesspool. He was deep within the bowels of the New York sewer system. This section had been built almost one hundred and fifty years ago and probably hadn't been visited by humans for at least fifty of those years.

Blitherskites checked the fastener on the top of his backpack again. He knew he was being compulsive, but he was taking no chances. The multiple copies of the maps in there were encased in five layers of plastic. If he had had access to Kevlar, he would have used that too. His future was tied up in those charts. He was tired of being an outcast from rat kind. He needed the company of rodents. Humans were all right, but all that furless skin got on his nerves.

He picked up his pack and resumed his trek. He'd discovered this place almost a hundred years ago by accident. Good thing too because without it he would have ended up on the wrong end of a pike. Back then Dark Seer wanted him dead—very dead. Blitherskites couldn't understand why the old rat was so upset. One had to expect a palace coup on occasion.

Blitherskites stopped at a dead end and cinched up the waist strap on his backpack. He set to removing rocks from the wall in front of him. This was a very old section of the sewer. Algae coated the slick, rounded rocks, and thick spider webs danced across large sections of the tunnel.

After a few minutes Blitherskites threw his backpack through the hole and scampered in after it. On the other side he resealed the hole with a nearby pile of rocks. He had done this many times before. Once the hole was closed up, he resumed his hike down an ancient tunnel.

It was very dark in here. Even his rodent eyes had trouble making out the surroundings. Eventually, the ancient rock became more illuminated and Blitherskites knew he was nearing the gate.

Finally, he rounded a corner and came upon the ancient artifact. He never ceased to marvel at the collection of arcane energies that danced before him. These silent forces sealed off the height and breadth of the tunnel. Colored bands of light interspersed a central glow globe that sat motionless. Occasionally blue lightning would play about the edges of the globe.

Currently the globe was a translucent blue. He learned long ago to enter the globe only when it was dark purple. He once entered it when it was red and ended up on a ledge over a boiling volcano instead of on the border of the Darkling Space. He landed one step away from being fried rat.

He waited patiently and after several minutes the gate began to glow the appropriate color. He smiled a yellow tooth-filled smile and picked up his backpack. Without hesitation he stepped into the globe and silent lightning danced all about him. He felt the same old tingly sensation as he traversed the arcane power flux and stepped between worlds. On the other side, all of his fur stood up on end from the energy of the gate.

On the opposite side was a tunnel that mirrored the one he had just exited. He began to travel down this passage too, although it was not nearly as long as the one he'd just came from, and it did not connect to any human sewer.

Blitherskites recalled his first terror-filled journey down this path which he had discovered by accident. He was trying to escape Dark Seer's pike men on the Desolation Plains. The Plains were the middle realm that filled the void between the Dreamscape and the Darkling Space. As he stumbled through a boulder-strewn field, he fell into a rock-lined pit. On one side of the pit was the opening to this tunnel. He heard the pike men passing overhead, and he dove into the tunnel. He ran and ran until he came to the gate. He didn't know what it was, but he was sure that pikes waited for him back in the pit. He was feeling depressed and despondent at that point in his life anyway, so he into the gate he went.

Many a creature in the Darkling Space would sell their souls to know about this gate, but Blitherskites kept it a secret. This was his gate and he wasn't sharing it with anyone. Besides, it gave him a certain notoriety. There were many that knew he traveled between worlds, and they were held in awe by this feat.

Blitherskites exited the tunnel into the bottom of the pit and began his climb up the rock wall. He scampered over the lip of the pit and made his way through the boulders. Eventually, the boulders gave way to the gray, dusty Desolation Plains. He unstrapped his backpack and looked out over the plains for a moment to watch the dust devils at play.

Out of his sight, just over the horizon lay the Darkling Space. Behind him was the Dreamscape. That was a place no corporeal being could go, well, except for the cats and certain creatures that had come from nightmares. Anyone else that went in there was lost forever or consumed or something worse. No one really knew for sure.

Blitherskites stayed far away from the border between the Dreamscape and the Desolation Plains. The Dreamscape had this nasty habit of constantly moving about like the tides on Earth. One day you might be on the Plains and the next, you might be surrounded by dream mist. If you stayed put you might be all right, but then again you might just disappear.

He bent over and reached into his backpack. He pulled out a combat ready Uzi with a folding stock and inspected the clip. He smiled a big, toothy, rodent smile. Oh yes, there were a lot of things about humans he liked. When he was a member of the Rodent Council of Thirteen he had great magical powers. Dark Seer had stripped him of those just before he escaped. Human weapons didn't require arcane knowledge; pull the trigger and watch 'em dance.

He reached in and pulled out two holstered .44 magnum Desert Eagle automatics. He strapped them around his waist and secured them to his thighs. One did not walk the Desolation Plains without being heavily armed. There were many hungry creatures in this place, and they all seemed to think rat was on the menu. The first time he crossed the Plains he made it by sheer luck. He liked luck, but firearms and lots of ammunition were better.

Blitherskites hauled his backpack into place and began the long trek to Sid's Desolation Bar and Grill. It was the only establishment on the Plains and the rendezvous point he had set up with Dark Seer. There was no way he was going into the Darkling Space to meet with the Seer's rats. He learned long ago, while sitting on the council, that you don't trust anyone.

After about two miles of walking, he passed the desiccated skeleton of a man-sized lizard. He smiled. The skull had five 9mm holes in its head. The toothy jump-a-lot had stalked him for ten miles last year. He was on his way back to the gate when it caught his scent and began to stalk him. It made the mistake of charging him dead on and he let a clip go across its head. There were a fair number of toothy jump-a-lots on the Plains, and one had to be constantly on the look out for them. The humans had another name for them. What was it? He saw them in a movie. Oh yeah, velocio-raptors.

Blitherskites sighed and marched on. The gray, cloud-covered sky cast its morbid pale over the Plains for as far as the eye could see. It was rumored that there was a sun behind those clouds, but they never went away so that couldn't be verified. It wouldn't be so bad if it rained once in a while, but the clouds never shed a tear. The Desolation Plains were doomed to an eternity of dry weather and lifeless sand, clay and rock.

He marched on for a few days and passed more than one skeleton. He was very careful with his water. After predators, lack of water was the second biggest danger on the Plains. He always brought plenty of food too.

Eventually, Sid's Desolation Bar and Grill began to take form on the horizon. Sid's had been here for as long as anyone could remember. It was rumored that Sid opened up just after the Great Purge, but Blitherskites didn't know anyone that old, making it hard to say if this were true or not. Blitherskites once met an old gnome who claimed Sid won the place from a wizard during a poker game. Of course, one could never be sure of gnomes. They talked a lot, but seldom really knew what they were talking about.

After an hour, Blitherskites was finally on the well-worn path to Sid's front door. The building was mostly just an immense three-story box with a stable hung off one side. It was made of clapboard and was painted a dark gray. Dust stained the shutters over the multitude of windows. They were always shut to keep the Plain's dust out. Two chimneys belched black smoke and the air smelled of fried food. The main entrance was a small, enclosed porch that was sealed with two oak doors.

Tethered to the rail that stretched the length of the building was a single packing heffalump that chewed its cud and swished its broad dusty tail. Blitherskites knew this wasn't necessarily evidence of the number of creatures inside. Most of the dwellers on the Plains got around by foot. All the really good pack animals had already been eaten.

Blitherskites mounted the steps to the front porch and hauled on the brass door handle. He stepped inside and brushed the dust off of his black long rider coat. The dust fell to the metal grating underneath his feet and into a pit below that. Sid liked to keep his bar clean and insisted patrons dust off before entering his domain.

Blitherskites paused before going through the saloon-style, double swinging doors. He drew in a deep breath and summoned up his most strident machismo. He slammed through the doors and stepped into the cavernous barroom beyond. In one swift motion, he brushed his long coat behind the holsters on his thighs. In a flash, he snapped the two automatics out and flicked off the safeties.

He squinted and let his eyes roam about the room. Sid looked up from his glass cleaning duties. When he saw who it was, he winked. Two cats lounged in one corner and glared at him with hungry eyes. Four goblins shared a beer at a side table, and two raggedy looking humans spoke in hushed tones off to his left.

Blitherskites sneered and pointed his weapons in the cat's direction. "Hear me titter. I am rat!"

One of the cats yawned, and Blitherskites was tempted to put a bullet in its brain, but he didn't want to anger Sid. Sid absolutely hated messes. He kept a bottle of bleach under the counter, and if you killed anyone you were required to clean up the blood afterwards. Blitherskites absolutely hated the smell of chlorine. Most of the Plain's creatures hated cleaning in general, so the law tended to keep the violence to a minimum. Of course, there was always Boris the bouncer, too.

Blitherskites holstered his weapons and turned to his right. An eight foot tall, battle-scarred ogre with long black hair sat on a rickety wooden stool. Boris smiled at Blitherskites. "Hi, Connie," he said in a bass voice but with the innocence of a child.

Blitherskites returned the smile. "Hello, Boris."

Blitherskites made his way around the tables and chairs until he stood in front of Sid at the bar. He unslung his backpack and placed it on the bar. He sighed. He was happy to be among friends again. Here he felt comfortable without his faux gangster persona. That was for the humans back in the real worlds.

"How's it going, Connie?"

Blitherskites opened the backpack and reached into its bottom. "All right, Sid. Smells pretty good outside. Whatcha cookin'?"

Sid smiled an evil smile. "Rat burgers. Want one."

Blitherskites frowned. "Vicious, Sid, vicious. Why you gotta tease me like that?"

"Because I can. So you bring me some goodies?"

Blitherskites withdrew six boxes of shotgun shells from the bottom of his pack. "Three boxes of buckshot, two boxes of twelve gauge slugs, and one box of specialty rounds, including armor piercing."

Sid sneered a loveless smile. "My main rat! I've been having a problem with dragons on the roof. Those armor piercers will come in handy."

Blitherskites resealed his backpack. "So this makes us even, right?"

Sid gathered up the ammunition and placed it on a shelf behind the bar. "And then some, Connie. Enjoy yourself on me today."

"Thanks, Sid." Blitherskites smiled at the thought of his debts being paid off and made his way to the back of the saloon. The cats watched him as he slid behind an abandoned table, placed his backpack next to his feet, and sat down.

"You lookin' at me? I don't see anyone else back here! You lookin' at me?"

The cats turned away from Blitherskites and returned to their bowls of beer. He hated cats. As far as he was concerned, they were all bullies. These two had obviously just come off the Dreamscape because they were as tall as men. They had this trick where they could make themselves bigger on the Dreamscape and then retain that material form on the Desolation Plains and the Darkling Space. They still walked on all fours though. Punks.

A snide, little blue gremlin by the name of Pissy hustled up next to Blitherskites. "What you want, Connie?"

"Got any skunky beer?"

Pissy wrung his warty little hands together. "Smells like horse crap. Got some that'll make a grown man puke his guts up."

Blitherskites grinned and slammed the table with an open hand. "By the horned one, life is good! Bring it on."

Pissy ran off. Blitherskites noticed that Boris seemed to be pouting, and he popped his head with an open hand. "Geez, I almost forgot."

Blitherskites dug into his backpack and came out with a long trail of cherry lollipops all strung together in cellophane. He smiled when he saw Boris's eyes widen with excitement. He motioned with one long rat finger for the ogre to come over. Boris jumped up, which shook the place, and rushed over to Blitherskites's side, rattling the tables and patrons as he ran through the place. Connie gave the ogre the entire band of confections. The ecstatic giant promptly unwrapped one and popped it in his mouth.

"Thank you, Connie."

"No problem, Boris," replied the smiling rat.

Boris skipped back over to his stool and happily sucked on the lollipop. Connie learned a long time ago that it was best to have the bouncers on your side, especially Boris. More than one fool had tried to wrest Sid's place from the owner. Boris made quick work of them. He'd heard a story about a young dragon that was bent on stealing Sid's establishment from him some ten years ago. Boris fought the creature barehanded for ten hours. They had dragon steaks for the next year.

Blitherskites leaned back into the shadows and waited. He looked over at Sid and pondered the man. No one really knew much about him, and Sid didn't share much. He was a six-footer and was rail thin. Thick, long black hair spilled about his broad shoulders, and it seemed like his craggy dark face always hid a sneer. As usual, he was cleaning the bar. It seemed like he was always cleaning, and if he wasn't his help was. Blitherskites was absolutely positive that Sid's bathrooms were the cleanest in the universe. It was depressing.

The saloon doors swung open and a twitchy little rat with huge legs shambled through. Four leather-clad, pike-wielding berserker rats followed him in. The two cats in the corner sat up, and the hair along their spines began to rise. Boris reached behind himself to grab the handle of a monstrous cudgel.

"Hey!" Sid pointed a finger at Skittermore. "If your rats go berserk in here you're cleanin' up the mess! Understand?"

Skittermore wrung his hands together and looked over at Sid. He looked back at his rodent escort and said something in a hushed voice. The pike rats exited the way they had come in. Sid returned to cleaning the shelf behind some bottles.

The rat runner looked around the room, his tail swishing back and forth the entire time. Blitherskites checked him out before leaning out of the shadows. Skittermore spied his fellow rat and skittered.

"Are you the once Lord Conniving Blitherskites?"

"Of course I am. Anyone else around here look like me?" Blitherskites jabbed a finger at the smallish rat for emphasis. Skittermore recoiled a bit, and Blitherskites motioned for him to sit down. Pissy showed up with the beer, and Blitherskites ordered another for his fellow rat.

"So, do you have it? My Lord Dark Seer is very impatient."

Blitherskites slurped the head off the rancid beer and reveled in its malodorous perfume. "Of course I have it. You got the proclamation?"

Skittermore reached within his cloak and pulled out a parchment composed of lizard's skin. He handed it over to Blitherskites who carefully unrolled it and began to read it. After he was done, he smiled a broad smile and slammed the table with an open rat claw. Skittermore jumped.

"Ha! Do you have any idea how long I've been waiting for this?"

Skittermore vigorously shook his head no. Pissy arrived with the second beer. Blitherskites dug into his backpack and came out with the plastic wrapped maps. He handed them over to Skittermore who immediately stowed them away in his cloak.

"Damned strange thing to ask for," Blitherskites observed. "What's Dark Seer want with these maps anyway?"

Skittermore took a huge slurp of beer and sighed with satisfaction. "I don't know. He was directed to obtain them by the one called Darkness. It has something to do with some kind of bridge."

Blitherskites leaned back into the shadows. "Who's Darkness?"

Skittermore shivered. "He's a creature that lives deep in the Darkling Space. No one knows where he came from. He stole Grimlot's castle from him a few years ago and has been organizing the clans ever since. That's all I know."

Blitherskites pondered this. "Interesting. What manner of creature is this Darkness?"

Skittermore shrugged. "No one knows, but he must be powerful to have beaten Grimlot."

Blitherskites nodded in agreement. He remembered Grimlot from when he was on the council. That ogre made Boris look like a puppy.

"And what of the weapons, once Lord? Will you be able to provide these too?"

Blitherskites's eyes narrowed. "Yeah, well, we never did settle on a price for that part of the bargain. What's Dark Seer got for me?"

"You will be given a realm on Earth to lord over. You will, of course, report to Lord Dark Seer, but your autonomy in the realm is guaranteed."

Blitherskites smiled and began to wring his hands together. "I like that. Which realm?"

Skittermore shrugged. "It's your choice."

Blitherskites smiled. He was very partial to North America. His expression changed to one of concern. "There's just one thing."

"What is that, once Lord?"

"The best I could do is a million guns. I couldn't get anymore without drawing a lot of attention to our plans."

Skittermore's expression did not change. "I will report this to Lord Dark Seer, and he will have to decide if that's satisfactory."

Blitherskites shrugged, and Skittermore finished his beer and stood up.

"I must go now, once Lord. I'm sure Lord Dark Seer will be very happy with your service to the Scatter Clans. Thank you for the beer," and with that Skittermore spun on a heel and rushed out of the place.

Blitherskites finished off a few more beers and after a while meandered upstairs to a room that Sid had reserved for him. He didn't see the two cats slip out of the bar into the ever-present twilight of the Desolation Plains.

***

Pendella was encircled by a pack of one hundred cats. They marched at a fairly brisk pace through the rocky canyons that bordered Wo'Em. Typically, a cat moves in silence, but that many felines caused an eerie hushed padding that echoed quietly off of the canyon walls. Snapper-Cat padded next to Pendella and was forever testing the air with his nose.

Pendella loathed having an escort of this size, but Grizzle-Whiskers was right. These were dark times, and caution was the order of the day. The mist of the Dreamscape began to permeate the canyon, but the cats did not slow their pace. To a cat there was a general sense of unease.

"I don't smell anything Mistress Pendella, but I feel as though we are being watched."

"I feel it too," Pendella confirmed.

The cats padded on for an hour, and the dream stuff floated in and out of the canyons. At times, it totally obscured their view, but the cats managed to maintain their formation. At the end of a particularly long gorge, the mist totally disappeared and Pendella called her two cohorts of cats to a halt.

"What is wrong, Mistress?"

Pendella sniffed the air. "I have paced the path to Wo'Em on many an occasion, and this place is not on that path."

Snapper-Cat looked around and realized what she said was true. "But how—"

Pendella and Snapper-Cat looked in awe as he padded onto an outcropping of rock that jutted from a low cliff in front of them. Pendella thought he might be one of the great cats, perhaps a lion or tiger. His fur was as black as night, and he was very large. From behind him four pike rats of the First Order of Vile appeared. The tops of the walls of the gorge around them filled with rodent archers.

Pendella screamed. "Run! It's a trap!"

The cats bounded as one furry mass, and the arrows began to fall among them. Pendella cursed herself for not summoning her beast, but it was too late now. Her fellow felines dropped around her, and more than one leapt to take an arrow meant for her. They were adept at dodging the arrows, but there were so many.

They ran as one unit in a stampede. The gorge thinned out before them, but its entire length was lined with rat archers. By the time they reached the end of the gorge, their numbers had been decimated. At the opposite end of the gorge, the rock narrowed such that they were forced to enter two by two.

The opposite end of the narrow gorge channeled into a small box canyon. They were trapped. No arrows fell among them now. The lip of this place was lined with berserker pike rats. Pendella spun and the great black beast dropped from above a few yards opposite her. She turned to Snapper-Cat.

"Run! Escape with your fellows and tell my man Aikeem what has happened!"

"Never, lady! We fight to the death!"

Pendella hissed and the smaller cat shrunk back. "That is an order foolish one. They mean to take me prisoner. Do you see any archers in this trap? Now run!"

Snapper-Cat realized she was right and with a few sharp spits directed the bodyguards to follow him. He rushed up a rough path cut in the side of the thirty-foot canyon walls and charged the pike rats waiting there. Pendella could not see if any of them made it to safety.

Legacy padded up to Pendella and stared at her. He was silent. Pendella was crouched low in a fighting stance, but she knew that without her beast she didn't stand a chance against this monster. She tried to read the intentions behind its almond-shaped, yellow-green eyes and felt an eerie sense of déjà vu. What nightmare of hers had this beast sprung from?

A litter carried by four monstrous high rats entered from the narrow opening. The conveyance was composed of wood and cat fur. Pendella hissed in hatred at its sight. The rats placed the litter down behind Legacy and one of them pulled back the fur curtain. Lord Dark Seer stepped out wearing a snide smile.

He walked up next to Legacy and grinned at Pendella. "Pendella Purrfect, long time no see. I believe it was New York. Wonderful town, nice sewers."

Pendella's loathing oozed from her voice. "Lord Dark Seer, I thought I recognized your foul stench when you entered the cavern."

"Flattery will get you nowhere Mistress Cat. You have boggled up my plans for the last time." Dark Seer held up one bony, furry, crusty finger and pointed it at Pendella. He spoke the words that powered up his spell, and his arm glowed blue to his fingertips. Pendella began to doubt her prisoner theory when a vicious bolt of lightning slammed her in the chest. She fell over backward with a scream and did not move.

***

A despondent Aikeem meandered down Fifth Avenue. He was oblivious to the sea of humanity around him. His thoughts were entirely tied up with Pendella and Celise. He hated not hearing anything, and this lack of information left him feeling helpless. An infant screamed, and he looked up. An embarrassed mother tended to her upset baby and replaced a lost pacifier.

Aikeem adjusted his wonderful backpack higher up on his shoulders and shot the infant a smile as he walked by. It immediately ceased its screams and returned the favor. Next to cats, children were Aikeem's favorite beings. He knew, as did all enlightened creatures, that children were the keepers of innocence. Without them, the world would be a far darker place.

He made his way to Times Square and soaked in the frenetic activity of the streets. All manner of automobiles clogged the roadway, and their horns created a dissonant symphony. The overcast sky shed a dark pallor about him that reflected his mood. This was his first day out since Pendella had gone off, and he was thankful for the fresh air. He figured moping about his apartment while waiting for some word about Pendella just contributed to his depressed state.

After an hour of walking, Aikeem was farther downtown and in a less affluent section. Brownstone apartment buildings were interspersed with small grocery stores and delicatessens. A rotund, dark man of Mediterranean descent hosed down the concrete apron in front of his building. Crates of vegetables and fruit fronted his store. The smell of the wet concrete and the produce tickled Aikeem's nose.

He idly watched the man pick up a push broom to begin sweeping the dirt in front of his store into the gutter. A beat up Toyota passed behind Aikeem and the chest pounding bass beat of a rap song blared from the open windows of the car. A young man in his late teens bounced his head up and down in time to the rhythmic song.

Aikeem strolled on and marveled at man's total ignorance of the subtle powers that were ever present in the background of reality. Science and technology were man's natural law, and nothing else remained possible in his philosophy. Aikeem smiled at this notion—if they only knew. Of course, that's the way the one God wanted it. That was what the Administration enforced and that was the way it had been ever since the Great Purge.

Aikeem sighed. Unlike some of his peers, he was not at odds with science and technology. Every time he flushed a toilet, he thanked the one God. But it held no romance. It had no passion, and logic dictated that the results would always be the same. Where was the fun in that?

Aikeem pulled up short when a smallish cat with black and white patches stopped right in front of him. It was obviously distraught.

"You're the human who answers to Mistress Pendella Purrfect?"

"Well, I wouldn't exactly put it like that. You have news?"

A young black man sitting on a stoop looked in wide-eyed shock at Aikeem as the mage conversed with the cat in underspeak.

"She has been taken prisoner by the high rats of the Darkling Space. She ordered me to find you so that we may free her."

Aikeem frowned, and the young man on the stoop slowly inched away from him. "This is terrible! Do you know where they have taken her?"

"I should be able to track them. The trail is not that cold, and if we hurry, I should be able to catch their scent."

Aikeem unslung his backpack and placed it on the ground in front of him. He unstrapped the cover and flipped it back. "Hop in here, sir cat. I need to return to my apartment to prepare for this journey. I have been to the edges of the Darkling Space, and I will not go in there unprepared."

Snapper-Cat jumped into Aikeem's backpack and disappeared inside. Aikeem secured the cover and slung the knapsack over one shoulder. The boy on the stairs stared at him with a look that was both fear and amazement.

Aikeem held up an arm. "Taxi!"

A yellow cab zoomed to his position, and Aikeem jumped in. His fears had been realized. He wanted news of his lady but not like this.

***

Darkness peeled the last layer of plastic off the maps that Skittermore had brought him. He frowned at the lifeless paper in front of him. He preferred skin parchment. He would have favored the original tome, but he was in no position to complain. Besides, it was the information he was after anyway, and that should be intact, even in a copy.

Legacy padded up behind him as he carefully inspected each page. The black beast spoke in a bass whisper that betrayed great power. "Is it what you expected?"

Darkness stopped on the page that was a copy of Merlin's map of Avalon. He smiled a broad toothy grin. "Yes! This is it."

Legacy watched in silence as Darkness bent over the document and ran his crooked fingers over the runes and ancient lettering inscribed on the map. After a few minutes he cursed and slammed the desk on which the map lay with an open hand.

"What's wrong?"

Darkness pointed to the image of a desert city on the map. "We need to know the location of this place back in the real worlds." Darkness pointed to the images of a jungle city and an island city on the map. "I know where and when these places are, but this one is unknown to me."

"Why must you know its location?"

"Avalon only appears at certain times and certain locations on earth. In order to discover when and where, I must triangulate its position with these other realms."

"Then we must find one who knows the secrets of this city."

Darkness frowned. "You are right my friend, but it is not that easy. I know of only one individual who knows where this place is. I was told of him by a fellow dark spirit, a ghost who was once a mighty sorcerer. This malevolent spirit once lived in this city."

"Why not just ask this dark spirit?"

"Because Farjule has passed on to the next realm. His enemy, and the one who knows the location of this city, was responsible for sending his spirit on to the next plane."

"And who is he?"

"His name is Aikeem, and only he knows the location of the city called Qar."

***

Lord Dark Seer shifted on his throne of bones and reveled in how well everything was going. He fairly glowed with self-satisfaction. Two gigantic pike rats entered the room. They threw their package before their sorcerer king.

"Do you have to be so bloody rough all the time?" Dark Seer screamed at the two crazed pike rats.

The dimmer of the two spoke up. "We're berserker rats, my lord. We're supposed to be rough."

Dark Seer scowled at the twit and turned his attention to the creature bent on its hands and knees on the floor. "It's a pretty little thing. Skittermore!"

The rodent runner zipped around from behind the dais that supported the throne of bones and kneeled before his lord. "Yes, my lord?"

Dark Seer pointed a bony gray finger at the quaking creature before him. "Is this the one Darkness seeks?"

Skittermore looked up to inspect the creature on the floor. He scampered over to the haggard thing and took its head by the chin. He stared at it for a good long time. "Well, my lord, they all look alike to me, but Darkness summoned a vision and made me study it in detail. He knows I travel much of the Darkling Space. This is indeed the creature he seeks."

Dark Seer clapped his hands in joy at his good luck. "Delicious! Absolutely perfect! Skittermore, if you even think of this creature in Darkness's presence, I'll cause your blood to boil away."

Skittermore squeaked in abject terror and shrunk to the floor. He'd seen Dark Seer do that before, and it was terrible. "Please, my lord! I would never disobey you!"

Dark Seer waved him off. "Just do as I say. I want this one well taken care of. Clean it up, and keep it dosed with tatterweed. I hear it has powers, and I don't want it escaping. Put it in my golden room. This one will prove to be insurance against any betrayal on Darkness's part."

Skittermore looked up at his king in shock. "You think Darkness will betray the Scatter Clans?"

Dark Seer scratched his chin in thought. "Let's just say that this creature will make him think twice, if he has any such plans."

"But if he doesn't know you have it prisoner, why should it deter him?"

"Don't you know what a trump is fool?" Dark Seer screamed at his messenger. Skittermore hid under his arms at his lord's blistering invective. The cowering rodent amused the dark lord and he smiled, "Of course you don't. You're only a runner."

"This is true, my lord. I'm only a lowly messenger."

"Which reminds me, how did Darkness receive his maps?"

"He was very happy, my lord. He studies them even now."

"And how did he receive the news of the weapons?"

"He was not pleased, my lord. He has suggested that our generals will have to align their strategies with the lack of the human weapons."

Dark Seer shrugged. "So be it. We will have magical constructs to aid us too. I'm sure that will more than make up for the shortage of guns. Now, take this one, and see that it is well taken care of."

With that Dark Seer waved Skittermore off. The runner motioned to the prisoner's guards. This time they carefully picked the poor creature up, and Skittermore led them out of the room.

***

Pendella's eyes slowly opened and she whimpered and twitched. After a few seconds, the fog left her mind and she snapped to her feet. Legacy stood outside her prison cell and stared. His breaths were deep and long and reminded her of a bull's. She stared back at him, and once again was moved by a sense of déjà vu. After a few minutes of this, he padded out of the prison.

"He's been doing that for over an hour."

Pendella whirled to the sound of the voice and found Drusillia Delicious in the cell next to her. Drusillia was a white Persian with broad blue eyes and an extremely fluffy white tail.

"Drusillia! They've captured you too?"

"And me," replied a solid black cat with expressive green eyes. This large, solid feline was locked away behind iron bars in the cell opposite Pendella's.

"You too Gandabon? What is to become of the council?"

"Grizzle-Whiskers must be in a quandary with his most important council members taken prisoner," Drusillia observed.

Pendella ignored Dru's ego and pushed her nose up to the bars on one side of her cage.

"Don't touch the bars!" Drusillia warned. "They're magically protected so we may not pass through them. Gandabon got quite a shock."

Drusillia got close to the bars, and the two cats sniffed each other in greeting. "You said that beast was staring at me for an hour?"

"It was most strange. He never said a word," Drusillia replied as she began to clean a paw.

Gandabon jumped in. "It wasn't a look of hunger either, Pendella. It almost seemed to be longing. Do you know this animal?"

"He seems familiar to me, but it is only a feeling. I've never seen such a beast before."

"Good thing because one of those snake guards bragged that this black beast was the one that killed Sharpclaw."

"What?" Pendella exclaimed.

"It's true," Gandabon confirmed. "That was Sharpclaw's killer."

Pendella frowned at the thought that this black monster should be staring at her in her sleep.

"How are we going to get out of here?" Drusillia asked.

Gandabon scowled. "That will be no easy task. That vermin Dark Seer has blocked my beast from me with his foul magic."

Pendella winced at this information and turned inside herself. She tried to plumb the depths of her personal power, but a wall of ectophasic energy blocked her way. "It is true! My beast is sealed from me too!"

Drusillia sighed. "Mine too. It's most annoying. When we finally catch Dark Seer, I claim his tail."

Pendella laughed for the first time in a while. Drusillia had that power over her. "Dru, I think we should attend to these bars before we start thinking of Lord Foul Rat. Do we have any idea where we are?"

Gandabon's expression drew grave. "We're deep in the heart of the Darkling Space. There are snakemen everywhere."

Pendella shivered at that information. "Then escape will be even more difficult. With this curse laid upon us that keeps us from our powers, we are in dire straits."

Drusillia padded over to the door made of iron bars that fronted her cage. "At least they didn't get all of the council. Maybe Grizzle-Whiskers can figure out where we are and free us."

Gandabon frowned. "Don't be too sure of that Dru. Sharpclaw was the only one who would venture into this foul place, and he's dead."

"There is another."

Drusillia and Gandabon turned to Pendella, and Drusillia asked. "Who?"

"My man Aikeem. Before I was taken, I dispatched Snapper-Cat to inform Aikeem of my plight. If Snapper-Cat escaped, then my man will come."

"If," Gandabon observed.

"Yes... if."

***

Aikeem pressed the Velcro strap down and his shotgun was secured across the left side of his back. He had already strapped on the scabbard for his blade Moonwind, which jutted over his opposite shoulder. He had dressed for combat and was obviously not taking any chances. His boots were knee high and made of a light fireproof material over leather. Black plastic shin pads protected his lower legs. He wore black combat fatigues, and the many pockets were full of various implements of destruction. He wore a black Spectraflex bulletproof vest over a Nomax long sleeve shirt, and over all of this he wore a long black Aussie style trench coat. Even though his intent was to make war, he had a mind to being stylish.

Snapper-Cat sat patiently nearby. With no small amount of curiosity he watched Aikeem as he made ready for their journey into the Darkling Space. "How many layers of fur do you wear?"

"Fur? Oh, my clothes. Usually just two, but today I wear four. One layer is armored."

"Then I shall be sure to hide behind you when the time comes for hiding."

Aikeem smiled. "Very good, sir cat, although I prefer not to get in a situation where that's necessary. If possible, I'd like to sneak in and get her out. If we don't have to engage any hell spawn, that would be fine with me."

"Agreed. You have told me that you've prepared spells?"

"That's true. I am a sorcerer of some ability."

"How many spells do you bring?"

"I've only had the time and energy enough to prepare five."

"Five? They say Elderond Bundermage could store twenty."

Aikeem frowned and turned to Snapper-Cat. "Elderond was a hack. He'd prepare tiny little spells, and that doesn't count, and I'll remind you that he's dead."

Snapper-Cat was a little taken aback by Aikeem's intensity. "Well, that's just what I was told."

Aikeem finished securing the top to his wonderful knapsack and slung it across his back and over his weapons. "And I didn't count the spell of transference that will take us to the Darkling Space, so that's six. Are you ready?"

"I've been ready for sometime, Aikeem," and with that the cat turned to go.

Aikeem followed the cat as it meowed the syllable of power. Aikeem did likewise, and cat and man walked through the far wall of the Room of See. As with most spells of transference, the actual time spent in the energy flux was very brief. Aikeem's black cloak and longish black hair whipped about him as he followed Snapper-Cat. Wildly colored lightning played all about them, ending in a flash of blinding white light.

Aikeem followed Snapper-Cat out of the side of a man-sized boulder. They stood on the edge of the Desolation Plains and stared out into the gray world. "Where to now Sir Snap?"

Snapper-Cat looked over one shoulder. He could see the forward mists of the Dreamscape undulating in the distance. "I was the lead cat in Pendella's escort. Somehow we were fooled into marching onto the edge of these plains. We had traveled the road to Wo'Em on many occasions, but someone or something twisted the dream mists about us so we took the wrong path. It was a day's march from here."

"Then we'd best be on our way. Would you like to ride on my shoulders?"

Snapper-Cat smiled, and Aikeem knew that was a yes. He held out his arms, and the feline jumped into them. Aikeem reached behind and placed the cat on the backpack behind him. Snapper-Cat settled in, and the two started off into the wastes of the Desolation Plains

***

Xaviar strolled out to the balcony of his cliffside castle and looked out over the grassy plains that his Chitin armies had carved out of the jungle. Even now, they marched and trained under the watchful eye of their Sloth officers. They were the perfect soldiers, mindless, fearless, and deadly. Individually, they were not effective, but as an army, they were devastating.

His predecessor, Bennington Sloman, had dreamed these creatures up. He observed their smaller cousins fighting a micro war on an anthill one day when it occurred to him that with the right magic, they could be transformed into a glorious army. His lead mage, Striped Seer, spent years perfecting the proper spells. Finally, he produced a man-sized breeding pair, and now they had their army of warrior cockroaches.

His own personal warrior stood on the balcony watching his fellows, its feelers twitching all the while. Their intellect was very limited. Their thoughts were mainly on the next meal and procreation. Striped Seer had wired their tiny brains such that properly trained, Sloths could direct them with a thought. The Sloths' thoughts became their thoughts and thus, they could be directed in battle.

Xaviar contemplated his own Chitin soldier. Its shiny black carapace was a wonder of forced evolution. Its exoskeleton was much thinner proportionally than that of its smaller brethren, but it was five times as strong. In addition, his soldier's body had four segments, allowing it to stand upright on its last four legs. This left its top two legs free for fighting. These legs, or arms, or whatever the occasion called for, held three, claw-like pinchers that reminded him of a maneuverable grapple. With these appendages they could pick things up and manipulate crude tools. In addition, the serrated edges and native power of these claws made them devastating weapons in their own right.

Their fairly large dark eyes were protected under the lip of their head's secondary carapace and had a range of vision in multiple spectrums. Two antennae that served to pick up the Sloths' thoughts crowned their heads. Their underbodies were entirely covered with a light layered chitin that was reminiscent of scale mail. Their only weakness was their lack of flexibility. They were mobile and quick in straight lines, but a skilled warrior could easily work around their limited range of motion.

He shot a thought at his bodyguard and directed it to leave. It walked off in its upright four-legged gait in silence. Xaviar returned his gaze to the armies below. There were a thousand such training camps throughout the Sloths' portion of the Darkling Space. At first, the training was more a matter of teaching the younger Sloths how to control their insect charges. As Bennington predicted, this was not beyond the Sloths' capability.

They had struggled for so long that when Bennington was defeated back on the real worlds, Xaviar was crushed. Bennington was his mentor and success was just within their grasp. He never was able to find out what had happened to him. Of course, he'd sent spies in, but the place was a mess and Bennington and his retainers were all dead. They found Striped Seer in the basement of the building. Xaviar shivered at the memory of the pictures he'd seen. Somewhere on the real worlds, there was a terrible enemy.

Xaviar turned and looked at the rest of the castle, which stretched off in either direction. It was mined into the sheer face of the cliff and was an impressive bit of engineering. The ramparts were sculpted at the front of the flat cliff face. Spires that served as supporting columns leapt from floor to ceiling and were as much a testament to sculpture as they were to function. Organically shaped buildings undulated among the spires and columns cut from the rock. The place was a marvel of rock-hard, smooth-edged beauty.

Of course, the Sloths did not build such a structure. This was the work of dwarves. Xaviar smiled at their memory. They had given the Sloths so much. They had shown the Sloths the way off the Dreamscape and into the Darkling Space.

That was a very, very long time ago. Before the dwarves the Sloths had spent their ample sleep time roaming the Dreamscape. Padafar Wannamore was the sloth who stumbled upon the dwarf Gunderbuss at the edge of the Dreamscape. Evidently, it had wandered across the Desolation Plains in search of some mythic mine (or some such nonsense). Padafar cornered the dwarf while wearing his dream beast. He ate the dwarf in one huge bite, and the most amazing thing happened. Padafar was able to leave the Dreamscape and walk the Plains. Eventually, he came to the Darkling Space and roamed freely there too.

It was the sloth epiphany. In the real worlds they were doomed to spend seventy-five percent of their lives asleep. But now they could exist as corporeal creatures in two realms! The commonly held belief was that this transformation was possible because the Dwarves were magical creatures. Padafar gathered the Sloths together and showed them his newfound powers, and they conspired to lure the Dwarves on to the Dreamscape.

Padafar wove a spell of deception and returned to the Dwarves as Gunderbuss. He told them he had found the mythical mine and that it overflowed with gems beyond compare. Blinded by their mine lust, they followed him on to the Dreamscape. The Sloths made them a mine all right, but it was woven from dream stuff. When the last of them walked onto the Dreamscape, the Sloths ate every last dwarf and so became creatures to be feared in the Darkling Space.

And now Xaviar was the first of the Sloths. Padafar had long since gone to dust. Legend had it that he morphed into a terrible prehistoric giant tree sloth and challenged a dragon. The dragon won. The Sloths would always owe him a great debt. He was the first sloth in all of their hearts, and they hoped one day to honor his memory by attaining the one thing Padafar was never able to have.

Xaviar held up his hand and looked at the spot where a thumb and pinky should be. It was part of the dwarf's magic he suspected. No matter how hard they tried, they could not grow extra digits. They'd tried every spell in the book, and nothing ever came of it. He frowned. Back in the real worlds, Gray Seer had done it, but it took the cooperation of a human. Humans would not give up their fingers so easily, but Xaviar was sure that his Chitin armies would remedy that problem.

He turned and strolled back into his chamber. The walls were covered with tapestries that chronicled great dwarfish battles. He would have preferred jungle scenes, but Sloths are not so good at weaving. Damned fingers.

All that was going to change soon. He didn't trust Darkness, but Xaviar knew he was very powerful. Darkness would summon the bridge. With the rats aligned with his Chitin armies, the real worlds would see a force beyond their wildest nightmares.

Avalon was absolutely vital if the plan was to work. The bridge had to be a magical one. Great energies were required to solve the paradox of multiple existences. Sloths could not exist in two worlds at the same time. This was against the fundamental laws of the universe. However, the power that coursed through Avalon resolved this issue. Both sloth physical somas would merge at Avalon's nexus during the crossing. Once in the real worlds they would house the powers of both realms in their new bodies. He held up his hand. The only thing missing would be a few digits, and thanks to Grey Seer, they knew how to take care of that problem.

Xaviar removed his robe and yawned. It was time to sleep and wake up in the real world. His life was much different back there. In the jungle he was weak, despised, and covered with algae. No matter, all that would change soon. He lay down on the large feather stuffed bed and placed his head on a pillow. He closed his eyes and awoke in a world that would soon be his for the taking.

***

Aikeem's long black cloak billowed out behind him as he strode across the dusty fields of the Desolation Plains. Snapper-Cat had dug his claws into the top of Aikeem's knapsack and napped. The Plains seemed to stretch on forever. Occasionally, they would seem to change off in the distance. Aikeem thought he spied rock formations there, but for the most part the Plains were a flat affair. The earth beneath his feet consisted of sparsely populated dead or dying grass, and of course, plenty of dust.

He had tied a black bandana over his mouth and nose to keep the dust out. This lent him the appearance of some Old West desperado, except that he was missing the horse. Aikeem mis-stepped and stumbled, but he did not fall.

Snapper-Cat instantly awoke and dug in his claws so as not to be hurled to the ground. "Do be careful, Aikeem."

Aikeem grumbled something about being a beast of burden when Snapper-Cat looked behind them. In a flash he leapt off the backpack and dashed away ahead of Aikeem. "Run!"

A dumbfounded Aikeem stopped and watched the cat take off. "What's wrong, Snapper-Cat?"

Aikeem barely heard the cat's reply as it sped off. "Toothy jump-a-lots!"

Aikeem scratched his head. "Toothy jump-a-whats? What on earth are they?"

Aikeem lazily turned around and spied a cloud of dust in the distance. Whatever they were, they were definitely headed in his direction. He reached into one of the many pockets of his trousers and withdrew a small but powerful pair of binoculars. He placed the optics to his eyes and focused in on them.

Aikeem screamed. He jammed the binoculars in his pocket and took off after Snapper-Cat. There must have been twenty of the monsters chasing them. He was sure that such creatures had been extinct for millions of years. The closest he had ever been to one was at the movies, and now an entire pack of them was on his heels. He unstrapped his shotgun on the run and pumped a round in the chamber.

After half a mile, he caught up with Snapper-Cat. He grabbed the cat by the scruff of the neck and threw him on his shoulders.

"Hey! Easy! I break you know?"

"Sorry, sir cat, but I don't have time to dawdle."

"We are close to where Pendella was taken. We probably would stand a better chance in there. They will be forced to come at us one by one, and you can take them out with your boom stick," Snapper-Cat said as he pointed into the distance with one paw.

Aikeem squinted and made out some large rock formations in the distance. He looked behind him and cursed when he saw how much closer the raptors were.

"I guess that's where the veloci part comes from," he said to himself.

Aikeem delved deep into his energy reserves and kicked in some more speed. He hated running. He always felt that was what horses were for. He was a stand and fight kind of man; however, he wasn't stupid either. One did not take on a plethora of pugnacious, prehistoric carnivores on the open plains by one's self.

Aikeem managed to huff out between breaths. "Snapper-Cat! You don't…perchance…conceal a beast?"

Snapper-Cat sighed. "I'm afraid not. I'm a young cat who is only just learning the ways of power. My mentor tells me to be patient, but sometimes it is so hard."

Aikeem frowned. "And inconvenient."

"Why don't you use one of your spells?"

"I will…if I have too…but I would rather…save them."

Aikeem made it to a field of boulders that lay before a steep rock formation just a hundred yards in front of the raptors. He weaved in between the great rocks and slid down a steep slope that led into a narrow canyon. At the end of that canyon was a constricted passage lined by two immense cliffs. Aikeem dashed for it.

"They're coming!"

They made it into the narrow passage and spun. A raptor leapt in an attempt to land on Aikeem's back, but he fired with a scream, and blew the creature over backwards. Aikeem ran backwards and pumped another round in the chamber. The next raptor leapt over its fellow, and Aikeem pulled the trigger. The creature's head exploded as a third stepped by it. Aikeem pumped again and shot this creature in the heart. It bounced off the cliff wall and fell on its brother.

The remaining beasts stopped and sniffed their dead comrades. Aikeem dashed back down the narrow strait with Snapper-Cat clinging onto his shoulders for dear life.

"Good job, Aikeem! They're not so anxious to give chase now. Uh-oh, here they come."

Aikeem exited the narrow and ran down a path into a new gorge. He turned and blasted two more of the creatures as they exited after him. Once again, their fellows hesitated when they saw their dead brothers.

Aikeem spied another narrow off to his left between two cliffs and sprinted for it. The remaining raptors flooded out of the passage and gave chase. They began to scream, a dreadful high-pitched chirping noise. He leapt over a small rock and into the narrow. He was halfway down the passage when the raptors entered the chasm.

"They've entered! Boom again!"

"I'm out of ammunition, sir cat, unless you can reach in my backpack and hand me some more."

Snapper-Cat looked at the backpack underneath him and suddenly wished he possessed hands. Aikeem dashed out of the narrow and ran into what was obviously a rocky dead end. He cursed and made for a group of boulders at the opposite end of the place.

"This does not look good," Snapper-Cat observed.

They dived behind some boulders just as the first raptor emerged from the narrow. Aikeem scrambled to open his pack when a most amazing thing happened. A man-sized rabbit bowled him over as he hopped by.

The rabbit turned and looked down at Aikeem. "I'm very sorry! But I'm late! I'm late for a very important date!"

With that the rabbit hopped off behind another group of boulders while a dumbfounded Aikeem looked on.

Aikeem turned to Snapper-Cat. "Did you see that, or am I hallucinating from lack of oxygen?"

Snapper-Cat sniffed the air. "That was the biggest rabbit I've ever seen. Even I wouldn't chase after that one."

One of the raptors screamed in frustration and sniffed the air. "Well, I'm going to. Maybe it knows a way out of here."

Aikeem grabbed the pack under one arm and Snapper-Cat under the other and took off after the rabbit. The remaining raptors screamed when they saw Aikeem and leapt after him. Aikeem rounded some boulders and spied the rabbit as it disappeared into a small hole in the side of a cliff. Aikeem made for the hole. He threw Snapper-Cat into it, followed by his pack, and then dived in headfirst himself.

Aikeem skittered forward on hands and knees while pushing the pack in front of him. Every now and then, he cursed when his sword jammed against the low ceiling. The raptors howled at the other end of the tunnel for their bodies' configuration would not allow them into such a low place.

After a hundred yards or so, the tunnel opened up into another small gorge. Snapper-Cat waited there for Aikeem. Aikeem caught his breath as he strapped his shotgun back across his shoulders, followed by the knapsack.

"Uh, what's up, Doc?"

Aikeem spun to find the prodigious rabbit perched on a large rock to his right.

Aikeem smiled. "What is this? Rabbit cliché day?"

The rabbit wrinkled its nose in a frown. "Hey! How about a little respect! I just saved both your butts!"

Aikeem bowed his head in deference. "My apologies, sir rabbit. We are truly grateful."

"I can't believe I saved a cat. I hate cats." The rabbit pointed a forepaw at Snapper-Cat. "You're lucky I'm a vegetarian, bud!"

Snapper-Cat eyed the rabbit warily but didn't say anything. Aikeem cleared his throat. "What is such a remarkable rabbit like you doing in such a dangerous place?"

The rabbit shrugged. "Dreaming, I guess. I never had a talking human in one of my dreams before. Well, at least one that speaks rabbit. You got any carrots? A salt block?"

Aikeem spread his arms. "I'm sorry. If I'd known you would be here, I would have brought some."

"Too bad. So what are you guys doing here?"

"We're looking for another cat. She was taken captive by a hoard of rats."

"Oh, yeah, I saw that. Damned funny business. These are some bizarre dreams that I've been having."

Aikeem became animated. "Did you see where she was taken? I would be forever grateful if you could take us there."

The rabbit hopped off the rock and started down a rocky path. "Sure, no problem. Right this way."

Aikeem clapped his hands and grabbed Snapper-Cat. He placed the feline on his backpack again and started off after the rabbit. "Are you sure of this, Aikeem? We don't know anything about this rabbit."

"Fear not Snapper-Cat. Our luck has changed. I'm sure our lepine friend has no ill intentions."

Snapper-Cat settled onto the top of the knapsack and frowned. "I hope you're right. I don't have much use for rabbits outside of a meal."

Aikeem followed the rabbit for the better part of a day, an earth day that is. The creature led him through a maze of small gorges, canyons, and fields of boulders. Eventually, they came out on the Desolation Plains again, but very close to the Dreamscape.

"You're sure this is the right way, sir rabbit?"

"Positive. Being a naturally curious rabbit, I followed them for a bit, at a distance of course!"

Aikeem resigned himself to follow the rabbit, but he was beginning to feel uneasy. He'd never been on the Dreamscape in corporeal form before. Pendella had taught him much about being a dream warrior, but that lesson had not been taught yet. Cats on occasion walked the Dreamscape as creatures of substance, but she had warned him the rules changed dramatically when one was physically substantive in an ethereal realm.

The rabbit stopped and turned to face Aikeem. It was wearing a smile that Aikeem found most disconcerting. It spoke in a vengeful tenor. "Payback's a bitch."

With that a tidal wave of dream stuff flowed about man and cat. Snapper-Cat leapt off the backpack, and Aikeem instinctively shielded his eyes. The dream wave totally engulfed him, and Snapper-Cat disappeared in its mists.

The rabbit's eyes began to glow a feral, burning red. "You probably don't remember me. My name is Warren. There's someone here who would like to talk to you."

A gigantic hand reached out of the mists and grabbed Aikeem by his lapels. He was jerked up high into the air and brought face to face with the visage of a fifty-foot woman.

"I'm going to take my time with you traitor! Yours will be a slow agonizing death!"

Aikeem could not swallow in the face of such terror. He shrunk from the hate filled mask in front of him. Marie Lavalle sneered at the little man dangling before her and then took him farther into the Dreamscape.

***

Pendella rested her head on her forepaws and stared out through the iron bars of her cage. She was feeling very agitated but refused to let it show. She wondered about her man and the Feline Council. She was very afraid that the foul rats might have killed even more cats. If only she could get out a warning, she would feel better.

There was a sonorous clang from the other end of the cellblock as a metal door was thrown open. Four tall, green-scaled snakemen dressed in fur loin cloths and sporting pikes escorted a lone dwarf into the dungeon. They stopped at the empty cell next to Pendella's and threw the dwarf inside. One of the snakemen threw the iron bar door shut and locked it. The foursome exited the prison.

The dwarf threw an obscene gesture after the snakemen. "Up yours lizard lips!"

The dwarf began to storm about his cell, occasionally grabbing the bars and testing them. Pendella watched him with no small amount of interest. Eventually, the dwarf sat down in the center of the cell cross-legged and placed his chin on his fists. He looked over at Pendella.

"So how long you been in here, babes?"

"My name is Pendella Purrfect, shorty, and it's been a few weeks," a disdainful Pendella replied.

The dwarf's eyes went wide and he sat up straight. "Orc Slayer! You're Pendella, the Orc Slayer?"

"Heard that story did you?"

"By the Rock Gods, every dwarf knows that story. We hates orcs."

"Thankfully, you don't see many around these days," Pendella observed.

"If you go deep enough into the Darkling Space you can find plenty of 'em. All kinds of nasty creatures in there. I'm Cragstein Muddleboot, but you can call me Craggy."

Pendella graced him with kitty eyes. "Pleased, I'm sure." Pendella turned her head toward Gandabon. "This is Gandabon Whiskertysnips." She turned to the other cage next to her. "And this is Drusillia Delicious, your fellow captives."

Both cats nodded at the dwarf and he waved back. "Damned glad to meet you, although I wish it were under better circumstances."

Drusillia looked the dwarf up and down. "I'm surprised to see a dwarf. We thought you had all but disappeared."

The dwarf became livid. "Damned Sloths! They all but finished my people off. They lured the entire city of Men'Grath on to the Dreamscape and consumed 'em all. Only a few of us what was left behind to guard the city escaped. A few others made it out of the Dreamscape and told us what happened."

Pendella sat up. "The Sloths? Really? I had a recent encounter with that bunch."

"Oh, this was a very long time ago. Probably a couple thousand years or so."

"Oh, that's not that long ago," Gandabon observed.

"Long enough. They've been hunting us down ever since. See, if a sloth eats a dwarf on the Dreamscape, they can move out into the Darkling Space. Bad bit of luck that."

"That's terrible!" Pendella was obviously sickened.

The dwarf conspiratorially looked around him. He moved to the bars that separated his cage from Pendella's and lowered his voice. "Turns out it ain't as bad as it seems."

Pendella moved closer. "How's that?"

"Us survivors got to thinking that our brothers was ate on the Dreamscape, right?"

"Yes."

"Well, how could a non-corporeal creature eat a corporeal one. It just don't make sense."

Pendella pondered this and could not deny the logic. "So, we're thinking that my clan are either still on the Dreamscape or they're being held captive some place."

Gandabon spoke up. "Or they could have been shunted to a closed realm. I've seen it happen before. I was once dispatched to resolve a terrifying recurring nightmare that a little girl was having. The creature in that dream was a chaotic contrivance that was beginning to take material form. I battled it for several days, and we fell into a pit of transference. I managed to hang on by one claw, but the creature fell into that other place. I notified Grizzle-Whiskers, and we sent a flying lizard in to check the place out. Sure enough, it was an entirely different zone that was connected to the Dreamscape by an interphasic transdimensional tunnel."

Craggy's expression changed to one of hope. "So you think my brothers and sisters could be locked away in another world hung off the Dreamscape?"

Gandabon replied, "It is very possible, but it bears further research."

"Which can't be done from here," Drusillia observed.

Pendella sniffed Craggy's hand and enjoyed his earthy smell. "How is it you find yourself captive, Craggy?"

Craggy sat down opposite Pendella and sighed. "This punk Darkness has his snakemen beating the bush for us survivors. I don't know what they're up to, but they're trying to recruit every sloth they can off the Dreamscape."

Pendella's eyes narrowed. "Interesting. Who is Darkness?"

Craggy was obviously surprised by this question. "He's the owner of this castle. It used to belong to an ogre by the name of Grimlot, but Darkness tricked him out of it. Too bad. Grimlot really wasn't a bad sort. He could drink like a team of horses. Darkness has been up to something with the rats too. I seen a mess 'o them in his throne room."

"Sloths and rats aligned?" Drusillia asked to no one in particular.

Gandabon sneered. "So it would seem, through this one called Darkness."

"These are disturbing facts. The Scatter Clans united alongside the sloths? The council needs to be warned," Pendella observed.

Silence replaced conversation as the dire nature of the situation sank in. Pendella's feeling of helplessness returned.

***

Aikeem hung in mid-air strapped spread eagle across two massive oak beams that were crossed to form a large X. Marie, bearing a most malicious smile, stood in her fifty-foot form in front of the levitated sorcerer. Aikeem had turned a distinct green color, and he bore a dazed expression.

"I've been watching you for some time, Aikeem. When I saw you march out into the Desolation Plains, I could not believe my good luck."

Aikeem summoned up what strength he could. "Please lady, if you would only listen to me."

"Why? So you can tell me more lies?"

Marie motioned with one tree sized finger, and Aikeem's levitating cross began to spin in place. Marie ceased her motion, and the cross came to a neck-breaking stop. Aikeem began to empty his stomach on the Dreamscape.

"You swore to protect Celise, and you killed her!"

Aikeem managed to stop gagging and pleaded. "I saved her!"

Marie was appalled. "What lies! Do you think me a fool, Wizard? I was there on the Dreamscape when you used your foul voudun! I was close by in the form of a cat. I know exactly what happened."

"You know only what it appeared to be. Celise is alive!"

Marie fairly spit. "You lie to save your own skin!"

"Do you not admit that the felines were about to tear her apart?"

"Yes! So?"

"I knew what we were walking into. Before we left for the Dreamscape, I prepared a spell that would protect her spirit and her body. Her body lays protected back in the real worlds."

Marie contemplated this and seemed to soften just a little. "And what of her spirit?"

Aikeem was obviously embarrassed even in his sickened state. "Well... I kind of bollixed that bit up. I don't know where her spirit is."

Marie swore and stamped the ground with her car-sized foot. "Then your incompetence has killed her!"

Aikeem became perturbed and sneered into one gigantic eye. "You don't know that! My spell was meant to protect her spirit too. Unfortunately, it seems to have thrown her somewhere else, but she should be safe."

Marie scowled. "Should be! Somewhere else! All half-truths to save your skin! You were sworn to protect her, Wizard. You failed, and now you shall pay."

Marie raised a gargantuan fist over Aikeem and he stared at her defiantly. "I go to my death with a clean conscience."

Marie screamed and fell over backwards. Two cohorts of cats attacked the woman's legs as if they were gigantic scratching posts. Aikeem screamed as his cross rocketed toward the misty Dreamscape's floor. A flying cat the size of a diesel engine grabbed the cross in its teeth before it crashed to the ground. The impossibly large feline landed on the run and laid the cross gently on the ground. It deftly severed Aikeem's bonds with a claw as large as a guillotine's blade.

Marie batted the cats as they attacked her, but she was overwhelmed by the flying felines. The train sized cat glowered at her. It was an awesome creature to behold. It was shaped like a panther, but its fur was snow white. Two feathered wings were folded along its massive back, and a tail that might have belonged on a snow dragon whipped back and forth. Its face was angular and powerful looking. It turned its broad green eyes, which looked very familiar to Aikeem, to focus on Marie Lavalle.

An intense ray of green light flooded out of its eyes and slammed Marie in the stomach. She began to shriek in terror as she also began to shrink. She managed to roll out of the path of those beams, and the cats about her jumped for their own safety. She leapt to her feet and in a mind numbing flash of arcane dream force, she blurred into the distance.

And then there was silence. The cats formed a circle around the gargantuan flying cat who stood guard over Aikeem. Snapper-Cat jumped out of their midst. The great beast looked down at him.

"You finish up here young one. I'm going to pursue that dream spirit and see if I can catch it."

Snapper-Cat bowed before the beast. "Yes, my lord."

The gargantuan cat unfolded its jumbo jet sized wings, and the dream mists swirled about. The magnificent creature flew off at an impossible speed to give chase to Marie Lavalle. Aikeem rose and immediately threw up again.

Snapper-Cat frowned. "Do you have a fur ball?"

"No. I have a very upset stomach. That woman has spent the last two hours using me as a gyroscope. If I ever hear 'Wizard's wobble, but they don't fall down' again, I'm sure I'll just puke." Whereupon Aikeem threw up.

Snapper-Cat gestured with a tail to one of his fellows, and a pack of cats escorted the man-sized rabbit over to Aikeem. Aikeem managed to collect himself and frowned at the rabbit.

"Treacherous rodent! You led us from the raptors just so I could become Marie's spinning top!"

Warren scowled. "Yeah, so what! You deserved it after what you did to me! I had it all until you and that cat showed up and messed up my plans!"

A look of recognition flooded Aikeem's face. "You're the bunny with the totem!"

Warren stuck out his chest. "Yeah that's me! Warren the Prolific! What about it?"

"What shall we do with this creature Aikeem? My fellows are fond of rabbit. I'm told it tastes just like chicken," Snapper-Cat observed. Warren's expression rapidly changed to one of terror.

Aikeem pondered the bunny as his color returned. "How is it you came into the company of Marie?"

"We met on the Dreamscape. She's all over the place in here. When she discovered I'd been 'enhanced' by the power of the fertility artifact, she showed me how to get around the Dreamscape. One day I stumbled out on to the Desolation Plains, and she freaked. She can't go there being a spirit and all, so she was really impressed when she found out I could. She's been watching you and that freakin' cat for a long time. She got real excited when she found out that I'd crossed paws with you guys before. So, we decided to join forces and take you out," Warren said pointing an accusing claw at Aikeem.

Snapper-Cat licked his lips. "What would you like to do with this one, Aikeem?"

Aikeem pondered the misguided cottontail and sighed. "Let him go."

Warren's eyes grew wide and Snapper-Cat was aghast. "What?"

Aikeem jerked a finger at Warren. "You and I are even now. I never meant you any harm back on the farm. We were sent there to retrieve the artifact of power, although I would have intervened on the part of the farmer anyway. I'm sparing your life, and I expect you to stay off the Dreamscape, or at least not to cause any trouble on it."

Warren was incredulous. "You're serious?"

Aikeem nodded. "I'm a warrior not a murderer. Many do not understand that distinction, but maybe now you do."

Warren's demeanor softened. "I dunno, but I'll stay out of your hare."

"See that you do. I'm sure that my fellows," Aikeem gestured to Snapper-Cat and company, "will be keeping an eye on you now that they know you exist."

Snapper-Cat gave Warren one last menacing glare and then gestured to his fellow felines. They opened a path for the rabbit, and in two lightning dream hops, the creature was gone.

Snapper-Cat turned to Aikeem. "Grizzle-Whiskers isn't going to like that much."

"Grizzle-Whiskers be damned. Where's my backpack?"

A pony-sized calico pranced out of the pack of cats and dropped Aikeem's knapsack and weapons at his feet. "Thank you," Aikeem responded.

The cat nodded and then leapt off. In a few seconds all of the cats had bounded away, and Aikeem stood alone with Snapper-Cat. "Thank you, Snapper-Cat. Marie was being most unreasonable."

"She is a powerful enemy here on the Dreamscape. We should get back to the Desolation Plains to pick up Pendella's trail as soon as possible."

"Agreed," and with that Aikeem strapped on all of his equipment and followed Snapper-Cat off the Dreamscape.

***

Farouk leaned on the balcony of his small rented apartment on the outskirts of Alexandria. He puffed on the remains of a hand-rolled Turkish cigarette, as he soaked in the ambience of his hometown. A sniff of late morning air produced a smile. He reveled in the pungent aroma that floated off the Mediterranean. Down below him, the bedlam of the late morning traffic ensued as cars and people commingled in frenetic activity.

There was a rapid knock at his door, and Farouk spun to answer it. He threw the smoldering cigarette into a brass spittoon as he passed by. Once at the entrance, he unlocked the heavy wooden door and smiled at the sight of his guest.

Resmije Fitaku, a broad, dark Albanian greeted him with an expansive smile. The two men embraced, and Farouk led the younger man into his apartment. The jean clad Resmije wore his hair shortly cropped. His dark brown eyes betrayed a war hardened youth, and a small scar across one cheek provided further testament to time spent on the battlefield.

"Resmije, you are looking well. How is your family?"

Resmije's smile faded a bit. "What is left of it is finally doing well."

Farouk motioned to a low table surrounded by plump, soft, embroidered pillows. "Come. Share some coffee with me, and let us talk of things."

Resmije sat opposite Farouk on one of the pillows. Farouk poured them both aromatic cups of coffee from a brass antique kettle. They raised their brass cups and saluted each other with an unspoken toast.

Resmije sighed at the fresh roast. "This is good. My family and I...no, my people and I can never thank you enough for your help, Farouk. Without your help, even more Albanians would have been slaughtered."

Farouk bowed his head. "Allah has taught us to protect our own. One can not rely on the whims of the infidel."

"Of course. However, in the end, N.A.T.O. did rescue us," Resmije pointed out.

Farouk shrugged. "Today it serves their interests. Tomorrow?"

Resmije obviously didn't agree, but he didn't say anything. "But you didn't call me here to discuss politics. How can I help you Farouk?"

"I'm told that N.A.T.O. did not gather up all of the weapons that were supplied to the K.L.A. I'm told that a group of young men hid the best ordinance away for the future."

Resmije grinned. "I can neither confirm nor deny that fact."

Farouk returned the grin. "I have a customer in great need of a large number of weapons. How would you like to unload your cache?"

Resmije's smile faded. "You know how grateful I am to you Farouk, but my people must remain safe in the face of any future Serb threat. Who knows if those dogs might decide to come back to Kosovo to finish their foul ethnic cleansing?"

Farouk waved a hand over the coffee table. In its wake was a small pile of brilliant, sparkling diamonds. Resmije's eyes widened.

Farouk smiled. "First, however, Kosovo must repair its economy. Then it will be able to buy even more modern and reliable weapons. Right now you have N.A.T.O. to protect you from the Serb aggressors. With these, and more to come, you will be able to build a solid economic foundation for Kosovo and, of course, yourself."

Resmije seemed hypnotized by the gems. He picked one up and rolled it over in his fingers. He held it up to the light streaming in from the balcony and gasped at the jewel's clarity.

"It's beautiful."

"I have a very generous buyer, and, as I said, he needs lots of weapons. Are you interested?"

Resmije placed the gem back in the pile. He grabbed the coffeepot and poured two more cups. The young man held up his brass cup with a smile. "To the secure economic future of Kosovo."

Farouk smiled as the two clinked cups. They downed their coffees in one gulp and shared a good laugh.

***

Alice Cranston pushed a cart of linens before her. She had one last room to take care of, and then she could take a break. The final room was easy because the patient was still there, and she didn't have to change the bottom sheets. She sighed. She felt so bad for that nice young lady. She was so beautiful, and to be locked up in a coma seemed like such a waste.

There was a very handsome gentleman who came to visit her every day, although he hadn't been around for at least a week. He seemed to be foreign; he had the hint of an accent. He could have been Spanish or maybe even Greek. It was hard for Alice to tell. He had those dark good looks that could have belonged to any of a dozen nationalities.

She stopped in front of the young woman's room and opened the door. She couldn't wait for her break. Her feet hurt. She'd been out dancing with her new boyfriend, Jake, last night, and she wasn't use to all that floor pounding. That was the nice thing about working at a nursing home. There was always a tub and pack of Epsom salts around to soak your feet in.

She pushed the cart into the room and froze. The bed was empty. The sheets had been thrown back as if the patient had gotten up and left. At first Alice thought maybe a miracle had happened and the young woman had come out of her long sleep. She rushed over to the private bath, but it was empty. She didn't understand. Alice grabbed the clipboard off the end of the bed and rushed out of the room to report Celise's disappearance.

***

Aikeem trudged through the dust of the Desolation Plains, always on the watch for toothy-jump-a-lots and whatever other horrors the plains might conceal. He now wore a bandoleer of shotgun shells across his chest. He was not going to be caught short again.

Behind him Snapper-Cat dozed on the top of his backpack. Aikeem never ceased to be amazed at the feline ability to sleep anywhere, anytime. He wondered if his new friend currently roamed the Dreamscape, or if the rules were different because they were so close to that strange place.

The constant breeze that blew across the plains was light now. This kept the dust to a minimum, although he still wore a bandana across his mouth. He'd passed a few abandoned sets of bones and was distressed to see more than one human skeleton. How humans came to this place was beyond him.

His thoughts roamed to the day just past. He pondered the magnificent animal that had helped save him and then took off after Marie. He wondered whose beast that was. He decided to ask Snapper-Cat when he awoke. Pendella had explained to him that many felines owned a beast, and it was a right of passage to becoming a creature of power.

She'd explained to him that all cats secretly desired to obtain their own beast. Among other things, it was a prerequisite to being elected to the Council of Thirteen, although, the council typically had a full compliment. There were only three ways to leave the council: retirement, death, or expulsion. To be expelled, one had to commit some act of ultimate treachery.

Aikeem sighed. It was too bad about Sharpclaw. Although he didn't know the cat, he felt badly when any feline was struck down. Pendella had openly wondered where Sharpclaw's soul had gone. When a cat died, its soul usually wandered the Dreamscape until a kitten was born. The cat would then return to earth to be reborn in this new vessel. This was probably where the concept of a cat having nine lives came from, although Aikeem was perplexed as to why that specific number was coined. He would ask Paul McCartney the next time he saw him. The musician seemed to have a connection with that particular number.

This rebirth arrangement was set up by the Administration. It seemed the most expedient way to keep the Dreamscape protected, never mind the fact that this was another species' afterlife that they didn't have to worry about managing. Their hands were quite full with humanity.

Council members, however, were a different story. Once on the council, a cat had pretty much reached the apex of feline evolution. When a member died, its soul went to the Administration. Where they would send it then was anybody's guess. Aikeem suspected they probably graduated the cat to human form. He would never tell Pendella that because most cats would consider that a demotion.

Aikeem stopped. He'd been following the well-worn trail that the rats had left behind. However, the farther he went the less obvious the trail became because the dust had covered large portions of it. The trail stopped in front of him, and he figured he'd better wake Snapper-Cat and have the feline use its talented nose to pick up the scent.

As he turned, his eyes went wide. There was a building off in the distance! It was hard to imagine that anyone could maintain any semblance of civilization in this place, what with toothy-jump-a-lots and all. Aikeem began to shrug his pack off and Snapper-Cat was lurched to consciousness.

"What! Where? Claw 'em up I will," the dazed cat exclaimed as it rode Aikeem's pack to the ground. The cat shook its head to rid it of sleep dust.

"Hello, sir cat. We've reached a break in the trail, and I need your expert nose to pick up the scent. In addition, I've discovered something most amazing." Aikeem pointed off into the distance. "There is a structure out in this wilderness!"

Snapper-Cat followed Aikeem's gesture and yawned. "Oh, that. That's Sid's Desolation Bar and Grill."

Aikeem's expression changed to one of bewilderment. "Bar and grill?"

"They serve a very nice rat burger."

Aikeem's nose wrinkled. "I think I'll pass, thank you. I think we should visit this place because Pendella's kidnappers passed nearby. They may have information."

Snapper-Cat seemed hesitant. "It's a very unsavory place."

Snapper-Cat leapt off Aikeem's backpack, and he hoisted it back in place. "I'll be careful Snap. Come."

Aikeem loosened the strap to his shotgun so that its pistol grip hung low and near his right hand. In an instant, he could snap it into position. He started off through the dead grass covering the Plains toward Sid's. Snapper-Cat led the way.

After a mile, Aikeem came to the front of the weather-beaten establishment and reveled in the smell of fried food. His stomach growled, despite what he guessed might be on the grill. The outside of the place was deserted, but he could hear the strains of light music coming from within. He mounted the well-worn steps to the enclosed front porch and entered through the scarred oak doors.

Aikeem discovered the metal grating in the floor on the other side of the door. He saw the pile of dust underneath and took the hint. He brushed the dust off himself and cautiously made his way through the double swinging doors. Snapper-Cat dashed in behind him and quickly disappeared under a nearby table.

Aikeem's eyes grew wide when he saw the gargantuan ogre sitting on a small stool next to the entrance. The creature nodded at him, and Aikeem returned the silent salutation. He resolved to stay out of trouble. This was one bouncer he didn't wish to tangle with.

The bar was mostly empty. A lone ferret in a beret strummed on a beat up old guitar in the back while puffing on a hand rolled cigarette. A tortoise with profane graffiti written all over its shell played poker with what looked like a jackal and a hyena off to one side. The three looked at him when he came in but soon went back to their game. Aikeem was amused to note that other than Snapper-Cat, all the animals in this place were the size of small men.

Aikeem spied a rough looking fellow behind the bar and guessed this would be Sid. He made his way around the tables to the bar and waited for Sid to turn his attention from glass cleaning to him.

Sid placed the sparkling glass down into a pile of immaculate barware and looked up with a smile. "What can I do you for, mate?"

Aikeem returned the smile. "A glass of beer and possibly some food would be wonderful, sir."

Sid's expression edged with suspicion. "What you got for payment? You look new so you might as well know printed currency don't hold no weight around here."

"What form of exchange do you prefer?"

Sid eyed Aikeem's bandoleer. "That there strap full of ammo would get what you want and then some. That buckshot?"

Aikeem looked down at his ammo belt. "Certainly is my friend, and you're in luck."

Aikeem unslung his backpack, placed it on the bar, opened it, felt around, and then withdrew another bandoleer. He placed it on the bar with a smile. Sid grinned and began to grab it, but Aikeem placed a hand on Sid's.

"Just exactly what do I get for my barter?"

Sid replied, "All you can eat, drink and shelter for a day."

Aikeem grinned. "Five days."

Sid was taken aback. "Five days! Do I look like a charity organization? Two days."

Aikeem frowned. "I would never excuse what you're offering as charity, sir. Four days."

"Four days! Is the concept of profit beyond you, mate? Three days and that's me final offer!"

"Done!" Aikeem fairly yelled, and the two men smiled with the satisfaction of a thoroughly enjoyable barter.

Sid began to pour a beer. "So wot would you like for eats, mate? Gots the best rat burgers on the Plains, I do."

Aikeem's nose wrinkled to Sid's amusement. "Actually, something along a bovine line would be more to my tastes."

"Well, there's not many beefs that wanders out into the Plains."

"How about chicken?"

Sid shook his head. "Nope, not much chickens either, but a rat friend of mine hauled in a big anaconda carcass a few days ago. I put it in the freezer. If you want I can make you some burgers out of that. It tastes like chicken."

Aikeem smiled and took the beer offered him. "Actually I'm quite fond of snake. That would be excellent, Sid. You are Sid?"

Sid reached over the bar and offered Aikeem a hand. "That's me name mate. Pleased to make your acquaintance."

"Aikeem Abdul Jamal Yosaffa, sir, and the pleasure is mine."

The two men exchanged a hearty handshake, and then Sid disappeared into the back to prepare Aikeem's meal. Aikeem unslung his shotgun and sword and placed them on the bar next to the backpack. He stripped off his coat and placed it on the pile. Aikeem spun and rested his elbows on the bar as he took in the ambience of the place. Snapper-Cat sat on a table near the poker game and watched the players. He smiled as he watched the giant Ogre pop a lollipop in his mouth.

Eventually, Sid returned with a plate containing two burgers, some pickles, potato salad and coleslaw. Aikeem rubbed his hands together in anticipation. "Do you have any ketchup?"

Sid wrinkled his nose. "On snake?"

Aikeem shrugged and Sid replied, "To each his own."

Sid disappeared and soon returned with a bottle of ketchup. Aikeem poured the red condiment while Sid poured him another beer. Aikeem began to dig in with relish and sighed. "Now that is excellent snake burger."

Sid smiled at the compliment. Aikeem looked down at the stool next to him. Snapper-Cat was looking up at him with a somewhat annoyed look. "Sorry Snap," Aikeem turned to Sid. "Would you have any more snake for my friend here?"

Sid smiled at Snapper-Cat. "How's it going Snap?"

Snapper-Cat shrugged. "As well as can be expected."

"I got an extra made up. You can have it."

"Thanks," Snapper-Cat replied and settled onto the barstool while Sid went off to get his burger. Snapper-Cat continued to give Aikeem an annoyed look.

"I'm sorry! You weren't over here, and I forgot."

"Good thing I didn't forget about you on the Dreamscape while Marie was making a meal of you."

Aikeem sighed and ignored the barb. Sid returned, and Snapper-Cat jumped up on the bar to indulge in his portion of snake. While the two ate, a dark figure dressed in a khaki shirt, worn jeans and a black, long rider style coat sat down at the bar two stools away from Aikeem.

Aikeem and Blitherskites turned to look at each other in the same instant. Aikeem dropped his sandwich and exclaimed. "Conniving Blitherskites!"

Blitherskites instantly bounced away from the bar and snapped out his two .44 magnums. Aikeem stepped away from the bar and scowled at the man-sized rodent.

Blitherskites jabbed his weapons in Aikeem's direction. "You're that human that belongs to the pathetic punk Pendella Purrfect!"

Aikeem's expression turned to one of pure rage. Before Blitherskites could react, Aikeem jumped and flashed out two knife edged hands. Blitherskites's arms jerked outward from the concussion of the double blow, and his weapons flew. Aikeem snatched the rat by the throat and hoisted him high into the air over his own head. Blitherskites dangled above the ground suspended by Aikeem's outstretched hands.

"You dare insult my lady, you rapacious rodent!"

Sid watched but did not intervene. It was his policy to not get involved with the affairs of his patrons, no matter how friendly he was toward them. Snapper-Cat smiled.

Blitherskites gargled something through his constricted throat. Aikeem fairly spit. "Why am I so sure that you had something to do with her abduction, worm? Tell me where she is, or I'll lay you out on this bar and make a purse out of your loathsome hide!"

Blitherskites's eyes began to bug out of his head, and he gargled again.

"He might be a bit more loquacious if you were to let him breathe, mate," Sid observed.

Aikeem dropped Blitherskites to the ground, and the rodent grasped his throat. He sucked in as much air as he could and looked up at the man-wizard in terror.

"I didn't have nothing to do with that! Ask Sid! I was here the entire time."

Aikeem sneered. "Then you do know of her abduction. Tell me what you know or die."

"Lord Dark Seer and some beast named Legacy set a trap for her just off the Dreamscape. That's all I know. They passed this way a week ago and were headed back to the Darkling Space."

Aikeem grabbed Blitherskites by the lapels and hoisted him up to his feet. "Where on the Darkling Space?"

"I imagine back to Lord Dark Seer's castle," a quaking Blitherskites responded.

Aikeem eyed the rodent suspiciously, and Sid spoke up. "I thinks he's tellin' the truth, mate. We all saw a huge regiment of rodents pass by here last week. They sent some runners here which this one met with."

Aikeem's eyes narrowed. "You said you weren't involved, rodent."

"I wasn't," Blitherskites squeaked. "I have other business with Lord Dark Seer. I'm doing some barter for him in the real worlds!"

Aikeem studied the terrified rodent and looked deep in his eyes. "I believe you, although it's hard to believe a rat can tell the truth." Aikeem turned to Snapper-Cat. "Do you know the way to Dark Seer's castle?"

"Nope. Sharpclaw was the only one who went into the Darkling Space. It's a very dangerous place."

Aikeem turned back to Blitherskites. "Pendella told me you were once on the High Council of Rats. You must know the way."

Blitherskites didn't reply, and Aikeem knew it to be the truth. He dragged the rodent with one hand over to his pack. With his free hand, he opened the knapsack and felt around inside. Aikeem withdrew a plain looking leather collar and strapped it around Blitherskites's neck.

"This is a magical artifact that I have constructed called a kabosh. In case you didn't know, I'm a sorcerer of no small talent. This device will cause your head to explode if you are more than a hundred feet from me. If you try to take it off, or if I say the appropriate word it will also explode. Do you understand?"

The timorous rodent shook his head vigorously. "You are going to take us through the Darkling Space to Lord Dark Seer's lair, and you will do it surreptitiously. If you betray us, I will give this some use," Aikeem said as he tugged at Blitherskites's new leather collar. "Do not underestimate me, rodent, for I have put the kabosh on you."

Blitherskites nodded vigorously and Aikeem returned to his meal. He noted, with some amusement, that Blitherskites now sat on the chair next to him. He obviously didn't want to get too far away. Sid returned to cleaning his glasses and quietly returned to the bar once more. Snapper-Cat eyed the rodent as he ate his meal; he was quite amused.

***

Lord Dark Seer's long, cat fur robe dragged behind him on the floor as he made his way to the Gilded Room. This was his special place for thinking about things to come. It was his sanctum sanctorum and it gave him great calm. Of course, it totally reviled his peers, which brought him no small measure of glee.

He'd decorated the room with all manner of pretty things. All of the finishes were done in gold and ivory. Sweet incense perfumed the air, and fresh flowers were brought in daily. The furniture was all finely sculpted and plush. It was any sane rat's ultimate nightmare, a place to be tortured.

Dark Seer leaned on the gold finished door that sealed his gilded room, and it slowly opened. A wash of light spilled out into the corridor behind him. He shielded his eyes from the glare and took a few seconds to let his eyes adjust. He didn't like that much light either, but he loved the expression of pure horror when other council members were exposed to it.

He strolled into the room and took in a great lungful of the heavily perfumed air. He sneezed and sprayed the floor with a mouthful of spittle. He meandered over to the over-sized golden birdcage in one corner of the room. In there was his newest prize. She was a lovely creature. Such beauty disgusted most rats, but Dark Seer could appreciate it from an artistic point of view.

The creature watched him from the back of the cage. The confusion that had previously clouded its eyes was gone. It drew the silk blanket draped over its legs up over its chest. It no longer seemed afraid.

Dark Seer attempted a calming smile, but it looked more like a leer. "Are you comfortable, my dear?"

"As a prisoner, I can never be comfortable."

Dark Seer's smile widened. "My apologies, pretty, but here in the Darkling Space this is for your protection. In these lands, humans are considered a delicacy."

She frowned with disgust. "I'm lost. I wish to be returned to my world."

"Ah, that would be a neat trick. It takes great magic to transport back to the real worlds. I'm assuming that's where you're from. I was there only a few years ago, and that trip drained me terribly."

"Then you have the power to send me back?"

"I have the knowledge, but alas, currently not the power."

She looked away with a sad expression. Lord Dark Seer liked that. "Never fear, my pretty. I'll take very good care of you."

She said nothing, and Dark Seer made his way to the café style table and chairs placed by one of the expansive windows. A cup of green tea awaited him. He preferred blood, but variety was the spice of life.

***

Aikeem stepped back from the bed after turning down the covers and almost tripped over Blitherskites. He shot the rodent an annoyed look. "Listen Blitherskites! I said you have to be within one hundred feet of me, not a hundredth of an inch! Now will you stay out from under my feet, please!"

Blitherskites began to wring his hands and skittered off to one corner of the room. Snapper-Cat chuckled from the end of the bed. Aikeem went and threw the bar on the heavy oak door. He gestured and spoke some arcane words that laid an alarm spell on the door. Aikeem yawned and began to undress. Sid had given them a small room for the night, or day, or whatever you called it under a perpetual gray sun.

Aikeem turned to Blitherskites. "It might occur to you to try and slit my throat in the middle of the night. Although I seriously doubt that you could get by Snapper-Cat, you should also know that if I die before I remove the kabosh, that too will make it explode."

Blitherskites began to wring his claws again, much to Aikeem's amusement. Aikeem pulled some woolen nightclothes from his magical backpack and slipped them on. He slid under the covers and laid his exhausted head on a plump feather pillow.

Aikeem offered up a small prayer with a smile. "If I die before I wake, I pray the lord my soul to take."

Blitherskites squeaked. "What do you mean by that?"

"Hush!" Aikeem admonished the rodent and in a few minutes was asleep.

Snapper-Cat circled the end of the bed until he was sure his position was just right and that he was at the most comfortable spot on the bed. He stared over at the jittery rodent in the corner.

"He talks in his sleep, you know."

Blitherskites wondered what the cat was getting at. "So?"

Snapper-Cat yawned and placed his head on his paws. "I hope he doesn't say the magic word that causes the kabosh to explode."

Blitherskites did not sleep all night long.

The next morning Aikeem had the luxury of a steaming hot bath in the private washroom that adjoined his bedroom. Blitherskites was thoroughly disgusted by all this washing nonsense, but he said naught. Once refreshed, Aikeem gathered his belongings and got his threesome down to the bar for some breakfast.

Sid graciously provided ham and eggs—Aikeem didn't want to know what kind of eggs—and some of the richest coffee he'd ever had. Snapper-Cat indulged in a plate of chopped snake and Blitherskites ate the same as Aikeem.

Aikeem noticed Blitherskites was fidgeting mercilessly and finally could take no more. "What is your problem rat? You act as though a thousand fire ants are pecking at your butt?"

"I need to relieve myself, but I'm afraid to go too far," Blitherskites whimpered.

Aikeem sighed. "I told you you've a radius of at least one hundred feet."

Sid grinned. "The lav ain't but ninety feet away mate."

"Ninety?" Blitherskites began to wring his hands.

Sid chuckled. "I'm just yankin' yer chain mate. Go take care of business before you explode."

"That's what I'm worried about!" Blitherskites hesitated but finally skittered off.

Aikeem returned to his meal, and after a minute, Sid leaned over the bar. "Hey Aikeem. I was wonderin' if you'd do me a favor."

Aikeem looked up from his meal. "What's that, Sid?"

Sid seemed embarrassed but went on. "Well, I actually has a soft spot in me heart for the little bloke." Sid jerked his thumb in Blitherskites's general direction. "And I would be most grateful if you could try to see that he makes it out o' the Darkling Space somewhat intact."

Aikeem was somewhat taken aback. "That is your friend?"

"Ah, he's not all that bad. He takes care o' me ogre friend over here without being asked, and he brings me trade as well. You know he was once on the Rodent Council o' Thirteen?"

"I'd heard that."

"Well, the way I hears it, he got himself in trouble because he was too trusting. Now trust ain't typically a very rat like behavior, but Blitherskites got it."

Aikeem pondered this. "I'll do my best Sidney to see that he comes to no harm."

Sid leaned back with a smile. "That's all I'm asking for, mate. And by the way, it's Siddartha, but I prefers Sid."

Aikeem gave him a funny look and then returned to his meal.

After breakfast, the trio left Sid's and headed out over the dusty plains to the Darkling Space. Snapper-Cat resumed his spot atop Aikeem's backpack, and Blitherskites remained just a few steps behind Aikeem.

Blitherskites kept a constant vigil. Aikeem had returned his .44s to him along with his Uzi and other accouterments. Aikeem explained to Blitherskites again about it being in the rodent's best interests that Aikeem stayed alive. Blitherskites was more than a little aggravated. Not only did he have to watch over his own skin, but this human's as well. The cat was on his own.

Blitherskites skittered up next to Aikeem. "You know the Darkling Space is a very dangerous place. In there they consider humans a tasty meal."

Aikeem smiled. "Really? I hope to disprove that theory."

"Even rats don't travel that place alone, except maybe the runners, and they stay to the roads."

"I have no intention of following any roads. The clans will have them watched. We need to approach Dark Seer's realm unnoticed. I trust you know a way to do this?"

Blitherskites's eyes narrowed. "I know a way, but it's even more dangerous."

"Well, then we'll have to be very careful."

Blitherskites grumbled and fell back a few paces. This human was totally unreasonable.

They traveled for the better part of three days, stopping only for an occasional rest and a meal. Finally, they began to spy the Darkling Space on the horizon. At first, it was just a subtle darkening of the clouds in the distance. Eventually, Aikeem could see a vast gray and brown mountain range looming above a never-ending forest. Here and there the infinite sun of this realm actually broke through the clouds and bathed some areas in light.

Aikeem also noticed the grass had begun to turn greener, and it was longer. Eventually, it became knee high at the edges of the well-worn path they traversed. The rat brigade that had preceded them had drifted onto what was obviously an often-used dirt road. After a half-hour, the massive black trees of the Darkling Space began to loom in the distance.

"Soon we will have to leave the road," Blitherskites observed. "Dark Seer's clan guards the entrance to the Darkling Space at the forest edge. If they see us, they will certainly arrest us."

Aikeem looked down at Blitherskites. "Feel free to take the lead at any time. Just don't get too far ahead of us, otherwise, kablooey!"

Blitherskites twitched at Aikeem's gesture. Snapper-Cat giggled from his perch behind Aikeem. Blitherskites didn't find anything at all funny about Aikeem's teasing. Eventually, he did lead them off the path and through the high grass. They paralleled the forest edge for half a day. The gargantuan conifers that made up this portion of the forest awed Aikeem. They were at least three hundred feet tall with a diameter of twenty feet at the base. Their needles were a very dark green, which gave the forest its almost black color. It was obvious that the light in this place would be minimal. He sniffed the air and sighed. The fresh forest smell was a happy departure from the artificial odor of the city.

Eventually, they came to a stop and Blitherskites demanded a full night's sleep. Aikeem offered no resistance in that he too was exhausted. They made camp and Snapper-Cat stood guard because he was already well rested. The light never changed as they slept. That was the way of the Desolation Plains and the Darkling Space.

In the morning, defined as the time after sleep, Aikeem pulled out a small camper's stove from his backpack, a large mess kit, and enough food for a very pleasant breakfast. Blitherskites watched Aikeem unload his backpack with no small amount of interest.

"How do you do that?"

Aikeem began setting up a small table, which was also from his backpack, for the food's preparation. "Do what?"

Blitherskites pointed at the pack. "Fit all that stuff in there?"

Aikeem smiled a knowing smile. "I'm a genius at packing algorithms."

Blitherskites held up his hands, looked through his fingers and framed them around the stove and table. "There is no way you could fit all of that stuff in there."

Snapper-Cat lay nearby in the grass. "That's nothing. You should see all of the rooms in there. Pendella's decorated one very nicely with her feline flair."

Blitherskites jaw dropped. "Rooms?"

Aikeem looked over at Snapper-Cat. "She has has she? She didn't leave any small dead animals in there did she? I've noticed an odor coming from my pack."

Snapper-Cat yawned. "Not that I saw."

"I shall have to talk to Pleep."

"Rooms? Who's Pleep?" Blitherskites asked again.

Aikeem ignored Blitherskites's query. "One egg or two?" Aikeem held up two eggs for Blitherskites inspection.

"Two."

"How about you, Snap?"

"I'd love some of that mix that cats call for by name."

Aikeem smiled, reached into his backpack and pulled out a box of the feline's requested fare. Aikeem filled a small bowl for Snapper-Cat and shoved the box back into his knapsack. After a few minutes, they were all busily engaged in a hearty morning meal.

"How much farther until we enter the wood?" Aikeem asked as he dabbed at the corners of his mouth with a linen napkin.

"Half a day's march. After that, it will be another half day until we reach the Murkies."

"The Murkies?"

Blitherskites sopped up the remaining yolk with a slab of bread. "It is a large swamp that covers the eastern border of Dark Seer's realm. It will probably take us a week to get through it."

"Swamp, eh? I'm not partial to them myself. They always seem to be filled with unspeakable horrors bent on doing terrible things to you," Aikeem observed.

"The Murkies ain't no exception," Blitherskites pointed out as he waved his bread around. "And Dark Seer's populated them with all kinds of mutations he's conjured up. He was always afraid one of the other clans might try a sneak attack across the swamp. Of course, no one ever has."

"And what awaits us after the Murkies?"

"The Nattering Forest. That's not so bad, except it's pretty populated, and we'll need to be extra careful in avoiding Dark Seer's clan rats."

Aikeem grinned. "That is something I'm prepared for. I've a camouflage spell that will keep us hidden."

Blitherskites pointed at an enormous mountain off in the distance. "That's Mt. Klegmore. Dark Seer's castle is cut into the side of that mountain. It protects his back. No one's ever crossed the top of the mountain, and the cliff behind his castle has a two thousand foot vertical."

"It seems the rodent king has chosen a fairly defensible position," Aikeem stated.

Blitherskites shrugged. "That's one of the reasons why he's first on the council."

Aikeem began to stow all of the camp gear back into his pack. He collected all of the dirty dishes and stuffed them in there also. Blitherskites seemed surprised by this.

"I thought you humans liked everything clean?"

"Excuse me?"

"You shoved those dirty dishes into your pack."

"Oh. Pleep will get them." Aikeem strapped on the scabbard to his blade Moonwind so that it was available over his right shoulder. He hoisted his pack over this and slung the shotgun strap over his right shoulder.

"Who's Pleep?"

Aikeem ignored the query. "Let us go, sir rat. We've more marching to do."

Blitherskites gathered up his pack and slung his Uzi over his right shoulder. Aikeem picked up Snapper-Cat and placed the feline on his perch behind him. The threesome headed out over the Desolation Plains toward the break in the forest that would lead them to the Murkies.

Their march was uneventful, although Aikeem began to see living things in the grass. Typically, they were small animals, mostly rodent species, but it was a welcome change from the morbid nature of the high plains. Aikeem even heard the cry of a bird of prey and noticed its smaller avian cousins flitting about the upper branches of the Darkling Forest.

They marched through the high grass without issue, occasionally taking a rest. Finally, almost half a day had passed. Blitherskites brought them up short and pointed at a massive rock ledge that cut into the forest at its border.

"That's where we go in. We head straight north through there until we hit the Murkies."

Aikeem motioned with an open hand. "Your lead, sir."

Blitherskites released the safety on his Uzi and tromped off toward the forest. Aikeem did not miss the rat's act of precaution and flipped off the safety on his shotgun. They entered the Darkling Forest between the rock and a massive pine. The rough bark of these trees was a deep rich brown. There were no branches for a least thirty feet up the trunk. This tended to create the atmosphere of some great natural cathedral as they walked under the trees.

The forest floor was littered with brown pine needles and bark scaled off the trees. There was the occasional cry of a bird, but for the most part, it was very quiet. They followed what must have been an animal path. It was very faint but traceable. Aikeem noted that Blitherskites's nose was constantly testing the air. He was glad for that because his own olfactory sensibilities were not so keen.

Neither rat, nor man, nor cat spoke as they passed through this quiet place. Aikeem was suffused with a sense of unease. He wasn't sure if it was out of reverence for this dark, but awesome environment, or if it was due to the possibility of profound menace lurking behind every tree. They rested several times, and on one occasion heard a dreadful scream from deep within the forest.

"My God, what was that?" an alarmed Aikeem asked.

Blitherskites smiled. He was happy to see something unnerve the human. "Tree harpy. Nothing for you to worry about. They like the little stuff, like him," Blitherskites jerked a thumb at Snapper-Cat who ignored him.

Aikeem frowned at the thought of some monstrosity snatching Snapper-Cat from his perch, although he suspected the cat could take care of himself. Eventually, the forest began to thin out and the brush on the forest floor became thicker. Aikeem also noticed there were more animals in this portion of the forest, and they spied several small herds of deer along the way.

Finally, they came to stop at the edge of the Murkies. The mist-enshrouded swamp stretched out before them into the distance. Green-brown clumps of rotterweed and jimspasm poked up through the moist earth. Cyprus-like Bellan trees were covered with grayman's moss. Here and there a massive pine still managed to survive. There were also more than a few trees' corpses. The gray, barkless wood jutted up from the swamp like the accusing fingers of some massive skeletal hand.

Aikeem decided to camp here for another night's rest before entering the swamp. He figured they'd need all of their energy to cross this place. Once again, Snapper-Cat kept guard.

"You seem to know your way around here pretty well, Blitherskites. Do you come this way often?"

There was more than a little pride in Blitherskites's voice. "I travel between the real worlds and this one at will. I've been to Dark Seer's castle many times, even though he had a death mark on my head."

Snapper-Cat snickered, "Oooohh, you so bad."

Blitherskites sneered at the cat. Aikeem smiled. "You speak of this death mark in the past tense. It has been removed?"

Blitherskites hesitantly replied, "I told you, I had business with Dark Seer. As a reward for my service to his clan, he removed the death mark."

"If he finds you helping me, he may put it back on."

"I'm fully aware of that, but I have no choice," the rat growled and tugged on the kabosh.

Aikeem laid his head down on a plump little pillow he'd propped against a tree. "Don't fret, sir rat. These things have a way of working themselves out."

Blitherskites frowned but didn't say anything. Humans were always so damned optimistic. It drove him nuts.

In the morning Aikeem fixed them a cold breakfast. They threw it down quickly and then proceeded into the swamp. Aikeem had switched to a waterproof pair of knee high boots. He was not sorry that he had because the swamp water was typically over his ankles for most of the trek. They were on a path of sorts, but at times it all but disappeared under the murky, brown water.

The swamp was the aural opposite of the forest. It was alive with the cries of birds and many animals that Aikeem had never heard before. They had to be very careful where they stepped; on more than one occasion, a long dark snake slithered out from the reeds in front of them.

"Are there any alligators or crocodiles in here, Blitherskites?"

"Of course, but there aren't many along this path."

"Why is that?"

"Because the swamp dragon has eaten them all."

"Swamp dragon!"

Blitherskites smiled. He loved it when the human became unnerved. "I've seen it a few times. It is bigger than a locomotive, and its head is the size of an automobile. It has no wings, and it has much softer, smoother scales than its airborne cousins. It typically doesn't bother with prey as small as me and the cat. You on the other hand—"

Aikeem frowned, but he ignored the rat's tease. He pumped a round into the chamber of his shotgun. He'd known a few dragons in his day. As with most creatures, not all of them were bad, but most tended to let their stomachs do their thinking for them.

After several hours and a few rest stops on soggy ground, they came upon what might have passed for a hill. It rose only three feet above the surrounding quagmire, but at least it was somewhat dry. Aikeem followed Blitherskites to the crest of this knoll and collapsed near a rotting log. He pulled off his boots and drained them on the ground. Snapper-Cat took a perch on the log, and Blitherskites curled up by a nearby stone.

For a brief instant the infinite sun blasted through the dark gray clouds and bathed them in sunlight. Aikeem closed his eyes and turned his face into the welcome warmth. He sighed with contentment. Blitherskites did his best to shield his night loving eyes from the blinding light. After a few seconds the clouds took over again, and Aikeem slumped against the log. He looked over at Blitherskites who tried to blink the light out of his eyes.

"It was good to see the sun again… whatever sun it was."

Blitherskites snorted in disgust and removed his holstered 44s. Aikeem watched as he lay down next to the rock and cradled the Uzi in his arms like a loving child.

Aikeem pointed at the rat's weapon. "Why don't you flip the safety on that thing? I don't want you jumping to some jungle sound and accidentally spraying me with your machine gun. That would be detrimental to both of us."

Blitherskites's eyes widened at the thought, and he took the wizard's advice. Rat and man laid their heads down and both were soon fast asleep.

The night passed by uneventfully, while Snapper-Cat kept his ever vigil watch. On one occasion he had the opportunity to pounce on a snake that was headed for Aikeem's bare feet. The wizard never even knew how close the reptile came. Snapper-Cat ate half of it and threw the rest into the murky brown water.

After a solid eight hours, man and rodent began to stir. Aikeem reached into his backpack and pulled out an oiled rag and went over his blade Moonwind with it. Another reason he didn't like swamps was they tended to rust one's metallic objects. After tending to his sword, he began to polish the barrel of his shotgun.

Blitherskites pulled some moldy cheese and crackers from his backpack and reveled in the rank taste. He liked human food well enough, but it never had enough fungus in it for his tastes. For the first time Blitherskites noticed that Snapper-Cat was frozen in place staring into the swamp.

"What are you looking at, cat?"

Snapper-Cat quizzically cocked his head to one side. "I'm quite sure that rock or log, or whatever it is, wasn't there a few hours ago. I'm trying to decide if it's moving."

Aikeem turned to see what the feline was looking at. True enough, a slimy green something, about the size of a Volkswagen Beetle, seemed to be floating between two dead trees fifty feet away.

Blitherskites stood to get a better view. "Where?"

Aikeem pointed. "Right there between those trees."

Blitherskites squinted. The rodent screamed in absolute terror and dove for his Uzi. A perplexed Aikeem watched as the rat fought for the safety but released the weapon's magazine instead. Aikeem chuckled as the ammo hit the ground.

"Is this some sort of comedy act?"

Snapper-Cat flashed by Aikeem's feet and dove behind a stone. Blitherskites looked past Aikeem and his eyes grew even wider. He spun and ran in the opposite direction. Aikeem turned and his jaw bounced off the ground.

The log/tree had opened its eyes and had reared up to its full sixty feet. It spread its great dripping arms as gobs of muck fell from its soggy limbs. It drew in a monstrous breath and its massive scaled chest filled with air creating a sound like that of a thousand bellows. Its enraged yellow serpentine eyes gleamed as it screamed an unholy tenor shriek that sounded like the wail of a dozen freight trains. The swamp dragon took one massive step toward the knoll and a wash of fetid water gushed up, displaced by its massive weight. It brought its treelike fore claws forward and its eyes narrowed in on Aikeem. It opened its maw and hissed at the wizard.

Aikeem raised his shotgun with one arm, aimed and fired. The dragon's head jerked back and a splash of green gore exited out the back of its head. It teetered for a moment and then fell over backward, causing a great wave of water that washed up almost to Aikeem's knees.

Aikeem turned and found an awed Blitherskites staring at him. "Twelve gauge armor piercing shells. I never leave home without them," Aikeem placed the gun down on one of the only dry spots and reached into his backpack to pull out a sandwich. Snapper-Cat came out from behind the stone and rubbed up against the man's leg. Aikeem smiled.

Blitherskites eventually waded out of the muck and returned to his pack on the knoll. He finished his cheese and crackers while studying the human. He had a much greater appreciation for this wizard and would make it a point to stay on his good side.

***

Derrick Anderson stopped at a small gas station ten miles south of Dickey, Maine. He stepped out of his Chevy van and stretched the tired muscles of his long lean body. He'd been on the road for several hours and hadn't taken a break once. That didn't used to bother him when he was in his twenties, but ever since hitting forty or so, it was getting harder to do.

It's not that he was that old. He looked into the long rear view mirror that hung off the side of the van. He rubbed the blond stubble of his tanned, angular face. His crisp blue eyes were stamped with crow's feet at the edges. He rubbed a hand over a shock of blond hair that looked like the hairline might be receding. He sighed with a smile. He might be getting older, but he was still a handsome devil.

Derrick rounded the car and tended to the gas pump. He swore under his breath as a bit of gas splashed onto his work jeans and his leather work boots. He placed the nozzle in the gas port of the van and looked around. An old timer in blue coveralls and a red flannel shirt sat on an ancient stool on the rickety porch of the antiquated gas station. He watched Derrick as he went about his business.

The place was the stereotypical lost gas station of Maine. A beat up old Coke machine that offered vertically stacked bottles sat off to one side. An assortment of logging and farm tools decorated the brown cedar shingles of the station. This must also be the ancient burial ground for beat up old cars because they ringed the place.

Derrick locked the pump in place and strolled over to the old timer. "Hi there." The seventyish man replied with a silent nod.

"Could you tell me how to get to Micmac Mills?"

The old man grinned and said with his thick Maine accent. "You can't get th'yer from h'yer."

Derrick frowned, and the old man smiled. "Sorry. Being a life-long resident of Maine, I'm obligated to say that."

Derrick smiled and made his way over to the soda machine. "Can I buy you a Coke?"

"That'd be right nice of you. You from the city?"

Derrick popped the appropriate change in the machine and yanked out two bottles. "Not really. I'm a field worker for the EPA. I take test samples all over the northeast to monitor things like acid rain, ozone depletion, and global warming."

The old man smiled his mischievous grin. Derrick made his way over to the porch and handed him a Coke. "I'm all for global warming myself. Fig'yar I'll end up with some nice beachfront property."

Derrick grinned. "Yeah, well you might be right. So am I even close to Micmac Mills?"

The old timer pointed up the road. "You head straight up 161 through Dickey until you come to Old Rapid Road. You take a right th'yer and go about twenty miles up the road until you hit Passamaquaddy Road, which is on your left. Take that left for five miles and you'll be in Micmac Mills."

The trigger on the pump handle popped. "Thank you, sir, I appreciate the help."

"Don't mention it, son, although you won't find much in Micmac Mills."

Derrick spoke over his shoulder as he headed for the pump. "Why's that?"

The old man leaned back in his chair, the grin fading. "Cause about sixty years ago everyone in the town up and disappeared."

Derrick returned the nozzle to the pump and resealed his gas tank. "Say what?"

"It only had a population of about sixty, but they was all gone. I was just a kid when it happened. Damned strange thing."

Derrick reached into his back pocket to pull out his wallet. He made his way back over to the old man. "The cops didn't find anything?"

"There was a trail out into Misty Valley, which is a mile outside of the town. Seems all the folks headed out there and never came back. The police didn't find any signs of mischief. Damned funny thing."

Derrick handed the old man his gas money. "Sure is. Thanks again. See you later."

Derrick returned to his van and rode off. The old timer watched him go. "Maybe, maybe not."

Derrick followed the old man's instructions and eventually ended up on the dirt road to Micmac Mills. When he finally drove into the center of the tiny town, he realized the old man had not been telling him a tall tale. There were only six log cabin-style buildings bordering the main dirt road. Brush had grown up around most of the place, and every building seemed to have its roof caved in

He exited his van and locked it up, although he felt really stupid about doing so. He'd spent one too many years living in New York City in his youth. He smiled at his ridiculous force of habit. He mounted the steps to what must have been the town's general store. The glass in all of the windows was gone, and the store had been emptied out long ago.

The place was absent of human sounds, but nature had not abandoned the place. The birds and insects kept up an aural presence that reassured him that this place was not cursed. He'd been to a few of those places in his day. One superfund site he had visited was so dead it made his skin crawl. The silence of the place was a reminder of how clever man was at screwing up the earth.

He poked around the various buildings out of sheer curiosity but found nothing. He returned to his van and decided to set up camp farther outside the town. It might be deserted, but he knew he'd get the creeps if he set up camp in there. As he drove out of Micmac Mills only the forest watched him go.

***

Aikeem and company exited the swamp after eight days. They collapsed at the border of the Murkies and the Nattering Forest in total exhaustion. Although they had come through the swamp unscathed, they'd had a run in with the tentacles of a ganderbaff tree, a herd of toothy-swim-a-lots, and the obligatory pool of quicksand. They were happy to be out of the swamp.

Aikeem looked over at the weary rat who leaned up against a small tree. "You do that often?"

"No. Only once before. My trips to the Darkling Space in the past weren't to visit Dark Seer. He did have a death mark on my head after all."

Snapper-Cat inspected the nearby surroundings to keep an eye out for Dark Seer's soldiers. Aikeem and Blitherskites were so tired that they fell asleep where they sat. Eventually, they awoke refreshed, and Aikeem even took the luxury of a bath from a fairly clean pool of water at the swamp's edge. He noted what a peculiar combination of odors his shampoo, cream rinse, and swamp gas made.

After another cold camp-side meal, they prepared to make the journey to Dark Seer's castle. Aikeem gathered his threesome together. "I will now activate my spell of concealment. You must stay within ten feet of me for it to be effective.'

"Does it mask smells too?" Blitherskites asked.

Aikeem was a little miffed. "Of course. I only weave quality enchantments."

"Good thing, because there are going to be hoards of Dark Seer's clan rats about, and they all have pretty good noses. And what if things go bad? I take it you've got some battle spells ready to go?"

Aikeem strapped on his backpack. "Of course. I have four prepared."

"Only four? They say Elderond Bundermage could store twenty."

Aikeem exploded. He grabbed Blitherskites by the lapels and hoisted the terrified rat up so that they were face to face. "Listen you snide little rodent. Elderon Bundermage couldn't get a simple fireball spell right if his life counted on it. So he could store twenty spells! Big deal! I could store twenty glow spells if I wanted to, but what the hell is anyone going to do with twenty bloody glow spells!" The terrified rat shook his head. "I'm tired of hearing how Elderon could do this, and Elderon could do that, so don't compare me to that buffoon ever again!"

"Okay! Okay! Sorry! Put me down!"

Aikeem's anger passed, and he set the quaking rodent back on the ground. Snapper-Cat snickered from behind Aikeem's feet, and Blitherskites shot him a dirty look. A disgusted Aikeem gestured and spoke the word that was the key to unleashing the spell. The threesome disappeared. Of course, they could see each other, but any outside observer would never know they were there.

Aikeem grabbed Snapper-Cat and placed him on his perch behind him. "You lead rat and stay just in front of me."

Blitherskites looked at his hand and was surprised by the lack of invisibility. "I don't mean no disrespect 'cause you're a MIGHTY wizard and all and can toast my furry ass, but are you sure it's working?"

Aikeem frowned but kept his temper at bay. "It wouldn't be a very good spell if we were tripping all over each other now would it? Look," Aikeem flipped on the safety to his shotgun. "See? Would I do that if it weren't working? Even a dragon couldn't spy us with this spell."

Blitherskites shrugged and turned to lead them through the Nattering Forest.

"How long until we reach Dark Seer's castle?"

"It's two days' march from here."

Aikeem frowned. "That's going to make escape difficult."

Blitherskites didn't like the sound of that. "Why's that?"

"Because the spell of concealment is only good for three days. We'll be spending at least a day without camouflage."

Blitherskites was impressed. "You can hold the spell for that long?"

Aikeem warmed a little bit to the rodent. "Certainly. As long as I'm not unduly distracted."

Blitherskites merely replied, "Then let's be off."

They walked for a few hours before they began to see any of Dark Seer's patrols. Aikeem was surprised by the size of the rats they avoided,; some were taller than he. He pointed this out to Blitherskites who informed him that the clan rats and berserker rats were bred for size.

After half a day's march, they came to the first rat village west of the Murkies. It lived up to Aikeem's expectations. Blitherskites sighed with fondness for the town odor. It almost caused the cat and man to retch. The dens were a wild architecture of stick, stone, mud, and thatch. All manner of wooden perches jutted out from the structures that lined the road. The rodents jumped from perch to perch and disappeared into rat holes that opened into the core of these block long habitats.

They went unnoticed as they marched down the central dirt road that was lined with the rodent's dwellings. They took great care not to bump into any of the manic rodents scurrying about them. There was a gutter of sorts on either side of the dirt road filled with all manner of garbage. Aikeem wasn't sure if it was for disposal or if it was a feeding trough.

Most of the rats in this place walked upright, but some kept to all fours. They all wore at least one article of clothing, even if it was only a scarf or a cap tied in place. The place was constantly active with rodents scurrying about, and Aikeem noticed a fair amount of trade going on.

After they left the place, Blitherskites turned to Aikeem and noted. "That was the village of Blight. Soon we'll come to Scar and then Rodopulous, which is the city where Dark Seer keeps his castle."

Aikeem wrinkled his nose. "They don't all smell so badly do they?"

Blitherskites frowned. "What do you mean badly? That was the most wonderful perfume I've smelled in quite a while. Almost as nice as the city sewers."

Aikeem rolled his eyes and was thankful for the bandana he had in one pocket. They marched on, resting a few times along the way. They came to the town of Scar, which was a much larger version of the village they'd already been through.

Aikeem noticed that as they went on through the rodents' realm, it did indeed become more populated. In addition, he noticed that the rats around here used pack animals. For the most part, these beasts of burden were reptilian in nature. These creatures did not look as though they'd ever been in Earth's fossil record. They were horse sized lumbering creatures that were used for either transportation or pulling a plow.

Aikeem was also surprised to find the high rats were fairly adept at farming; they passed many large fields of various grains. He found this amusing, knowing how their less intelligent earthbound cousins had ravaged many a farmer's silo. He wondered what kind of vermin attacked the rat's grain bins.

After a day's march, they stopped by a small wood and hid in there. They took only a few hours sleep while Snapper-Cat kept watch. Aikeem served them all a cold meal after their rest, and they were soon on their way again. The patrols were becoming more frequent, and they passed by several military outposts. Aikeem was distressed by the vast number of rat soldiers he saw in training. He was unsure of the number of cats prepared to defend the Dreamscape, but he was certain they'd be stressed by this many rodent warriors.

It wasn't too long before the massive silhouette of Mt. Klegmore began to dominate the horizon. It jutted far above the smaller mountains that spread out to either side of it. After a few more rest stops and a day's travel, they came to Rodopulous. Aikeem was very impressed with the place. It was more than an affair of stone, stick, and mud. He found the place grim overall, but it definitely demonstrated a complex knowledge of engineering.

The rats had a fondness for skulls and bones. Their multistoried stone architecture was flowing, organic and, typically, capped off with a skull of some kind. The supporting columns of the larger structures were usually carved in the fashion of some great femur. The streets were paved with great slabs of limestone, and a true gutter system lined the city streets. Torches burned in iron stands, and a general smoky pall hung over the place.

In many buildings, the images of rats in triumphant battle over various enemies were carved in bas-relief. There were also a fair number of bronze statues placed in various spots along the main roads commemorating rat heroes or monstrous rat gods.

The immense castle was placed securely against the base of Mt. Klegmore, which loomed up into the clouds behind it. It was an awesome structure carved of stone. In many strategic spots it was sheathed in iron. Seven towers rose from behind the walls, and many fires burned around the place giving it an evil light. A greenish glow emitted from the open window of one tower, and Aikeem wondered what dark magic was being tested there.

The city gates were made of iron too, and the rats had constructed a complex set of gears and levers that controlled the massive portal. Rodopulous was even more frenetic than the previous towns they had passed through as all manner of rodents went about their business. Their party had to wait for a few hours before they could enter the gates without fear of bumping into some crazed group of rats rushing into the city.

After a time, the way did clear, and they sneaked into the depths of Dark Seer's lair. Aikeem was forced to wear his bandana as Blitherskites led them through the insanely twisting alleys into the bowels of the malodorous city. They passed more than one patrol of berserker rats, but Aikeem's spell held, and they went unnoticed.

Finally, they ended up in a filthy alley behind the ramparts of the stone castle. It was dark, and Aikeem was more than a little hesitant when Blitherskites opened up a metal rat hole cover. A stench preceded a green cloud that almost caused the wizard to spill his guts.

"We're not going in there are we?"

The rodent pointed down into the hole. "If you want to get in the castle without being seen, that's where we need to go. The main gates are too busy, and we'll bump into someone for sure. They're sure to alert the guards. Remember, in this place magic is an everyday thing, and Dark Seer's subjects are always on the look out for magical intruders."

Snapper-Cat spoke up. "Can I go in the backpack?"

Aikeem frowned, but he couldn't blame the feline. He was jealous. After a few moments Snapper-Cat was secure in the pack. Aikeem grumbled and followed Blitherskites into the rat's sewer system. At this point, the bandana wasn't doing much good.

At the base of the badly rusting ladder was a tunnel that stretched off into the blackness. Aikeem murmured and a glow spell illuminated their path. Against one wall the wizard could see the opening to the main sewer that emptied from the castle. He caught a whiff of it and proceeded to throw up. Blitherskites found this very amusing.

"We need to go in there," said Blitherskites pointing to the source of Aikeem's odiferous discomfort.

"Ducky," a green-at-the-gills wizard replied.

Blitherskites disappeared into the dank tunnel. The wizard took a moment to stow his sword in the backpack. He didn't want it banging on the low ceiling of the place. He kept his shotgun slung off his shoulder though. You never could tell what things crept about in these subterranean places.

The wizard did his best to step around the muck that flowed from the sewer. They traveled for what must have been a hundred yards before they came to the base of another iron ladder. Blitherskites began to climb it, and Aikeem followed closely behind. The rat pushed aside the steel grating that was over his head and climbed into a little used storage room. Aikeem soon followed him into the place and thanked the lord for a fairly breathable atmosphere.

"Where are we?"

"This is a storage room in the very bottom of the castle. The dungeons are nearby. If they brought your cat here, that's where she'd be."

Aikeem motioned to the single, heavy wood door. "Then lead on rat."

Blitherskites pushed on the door, and they were out into a low ceilinged corridor. The walls were made of great blocks of brown stone, and at this level, they sweated from the humidity. Here and there, bits of rotting straw lay on the ground where it had been placed to sop up the water that pooled under the walls. Every twenty feet or so, a sputtering torch was placed in an iron bracket that was riveted to the wall.

After another fifty yards, the place began to open up some, and they came to the main gate of the prison block. A rail thin rat of six feet sat on a wooden stool, his pike nearby. He could not see Aikeem who slammed him across the jaw with a concussive right cross. The creature truly never knew what hit him.

Aikeem took the rat guard's keys and opened the gate to the cellblock. The threesome spent twenty minutes inspecting all of the cells, but Pendella was nowhere to be found.

"Well, this is just sweet," Blitherskites fumed. "She ain't here! What the hell are we supposed to do now?"

Aikeem pondered that rat for a few seconds and then said, "We find Dark Seer and make him tell us where she is. I can be quite convincing."

The rat's eyes went wide. "What! Are you out of your skull? Dark Seer is a death mage! His staff can shrivel your winky just by being in the same room!"

Aikeem leaned into Blitherskites's face. "And I am a light mage with a superior winky. We will catch him by surprise and relieve him of his staff. Now where will he be?"

Blitherskites obviously didn't care for this plan. He tugged on his kabosh and resigned himself to the fact that he didn't have any choice in the matter. "I don't know what time of day it is here. He usually hangs out in the throne room."

"Then lead on," Aikeem said as he physically shoved the rat toward the exit.

They traveled the labyrinthine corridors of the castle for the better part of half an hour. On more than one occasion, they had to take another route to bypass a rodent patrol or a busy room. They came to the throne room, which was guarded by two massive berserker rats. Blitherskites eyed them with no small amount of fear in his eyes.

Aikeem merely smiled. He flashed out a spinning hook kick that slammed across both rodents' jaws, and they collapsed on the floor. "It doesn't quite seem fair does it? Just open the doors a bit in case the room is full."

Blitherskites did as he was told and cracked the massive oak doors open to peek inside. He swore under his breath. "It's empty."

Aikeem frowned. "All right, then where is the next place he might be?"

Blitherskites placed a finger on his chin and seemed to be lost in thought. "My guess is he's either in his laboratory or the gilded room."

"What's the gilded room?"

The rat frowned. "It's this disgusting place of gold and light and pretty crap he keeps. That rat's a sicko."

Aikeem grinned. "Let's go there. From your tone, it sounds like a place where he may be alone. It might even be a good thing to wait there for him."

Blitherskites shrugged. At this point, all the options seemed bad to him. The rat led the wizard down a new set of twisting dark corridors. They came to a corridor that stretched to the east wing of the castle. They followed this until they came to a gold finished door.

Blitherskites pointed at the portal. "It's behind here."

Aikeem gently pushed the rodent aside and leaned on the heavy door. He peered inside and smiled at the obviously non-rat décor. There appeared to be a man-sized cage on the opposite end of the room and much to Aikeem's surprise, there was a woman in it. He couldn't make out who the prisoner was, but he was certainly not going to leave her in this place. He pushed the door open and entered.

Blitherskites followed silently after Aikeem. The wizard brushed a table, and a vase almost crashed to the ground. He grabbed it, but the slight noise caught the attention of the woman in the cage. Celise could not see Aikeem because of the spell, but when he saw her, his heart fairly exploded.

He rushed the cage and as he did so his spell of concealment dissipated. Needless to say he always found Celise distracting. At first, she cowered at the strange sight of her lover rushing toward her from nothingness to solidity. He waved a hand over the simple lock and it fell open. He threw the door open, and the two jumped into each other's arms.

"My God, Celise, I'd thought I'd lost you!"

They exchanged a passionate kiss that fairly glowed with longing. Then Celise pried herself from the wizard and whacked him across one cheek as hard as she could. "You tried to kill me!"

A shocked Aikeem stood back. "I never did, lady!"

"You shot some damn green stuff at me that split me from my body! Do you have any idea what I've been through for the past year!"

"But lady I—"

Aikeem jerked. Green particles of arcane energy flowed all about his body, and he was frozen in place. Dark Seer strolled over from his café table followed by Skittermore. The rat lord was absolutely astonished that a human spy had violated his sanctum sanctorum. He was doubly shocked when he spied his old rodent nemesis.

"Blitherskites!" Dark Seer exclaimed and pointed one black claw at the befuddled rodent. "What are you doing here?"

Blitherskites couldn't move. Dark Seer held his skull staff, and his claws caressed the rod ready to bring forth its morbid powers.

Blitherskites could feel the death mark returning to his head when Skittermore aimed a finger at Aikeem and exclaimed. "That's him!"

Dark Seer turned to the rat. "That's whom, runner?"

"That's the human Darkness seeks! That's the wizard Aikeem."

In a fit of genius and total desperation Blitherskites spoke up. "At your service Dark Seer. You weren't in your throne room so I brought him here"

Dark Seer's eyes narrowed. "You mean to tell me you brought me this one as a prisoner?"

Blitherskites puffed out his chest. "I expect a great reward, Dark Seer."

Dark Seer was not to be fooled so easily. "It has a weapon. How could it be a prisoner?"

Dark Seer pointed at the shotgun. Blitherskites smiled. "I've rendered it useless. Why should I carry his baggage? Go ahead. Try it."

The Dark Lord went over to Aikeem and took the shotgun off of his shoulder. "I've seen these boom sticks used before in vision quests I've had in the real worlds. They work like this."

Dark Seer held up the shotgun and aimed it at Blitherskites head. He pulled the trigger, but the safety held. Blitherskites was glad rats didn't sweat like humans. "You see?"

The Lord rat was still not convinced. "How could you know that we were looking for this one or what he looked like. Darkness has just recently gotten the word out."

Blitherskites sighed in frustration. "How do I traverse back and forth to the real worlds at will, eh Dark Seer? You thought you stripped me of all of my powers, but this one is proof that I'm more than you think!"

Blitherskites crossed his arms for effect, and Dark Seer began to relent. "Why did you let it in with this other one?"

Blitherskites opened his arms. "Humans! They're so impulsive!"

Dark Seer nodded in agreement, and with that he turned to Skittermore. "Go get the guards. They can take this one to the dungeon and hold him there until we're ready to transport him to Darkness."

"No!"

Dark Seer was taken aback by Blitherskites's vehement response. The rat fingered his collar as he spoke. "Ah… this is a dangerous wizard, my lord, and I want to make sure he doesn't escape. I'll take him down for you." He held up his Uzi. "As you can see I'm prepared for this one."

The rat lord stroked his chin in thought. "Very well, Blitherskites. You brought him this far, so you must know your business. I'm very impressed with you of late. You're not the bumbling fool you once were. As you know, I've removed the death mark from you, but bringing me this one is a special service that will not go unrewarded. I may indeed bring you back to the council, *but*," Blitherskites flinched at the emphasis on that word, "I will not restore your magical powers to you. You've proven in the past you can't be trusted with them."

Blitherskites bowed his head in acquiescence. Dark Seer turned to Aikeem and waved a gnarled claw. The particles disappeared, and Aikeem fell to his knees. "I find it very strange that you know my pretty. How is that?"

Celise bent to tend to her man. She looked up at the rat lord. "He was my mate."

"Mate? Was?" Dark Seer observed. "Very interesting. The rat God Bl'ken Ba'morre must be at work here weaving a humorous fate for you both. Take him Blitherskites."

Blitherskites grabbed Aikeem roughly and hoisted him to his feet. "Come on, you. It's into the dungeon for you!"

Blitherskites pulled a dazed Aikeem out of the place, and Dark Seer watched them go. Skittermore locked the doors to Celise's cage and turned to his lord. "We will have to give this one to Darkness now."

An unhappy Dark Seer turned to his runner. "What are you talking about? Give up my pretty?"

"That wizard is sure to tell Darkness you have her. If he finds out you're keeping her for yourself, he may become upset."

Dark Seer frowned. "Fi!" The lord rat stormed out of his room with Skittermore on his heels. "Take care of it, Skittermore! Assemble an escort and take this wizard and his mate to Darkness."

"Yes, my lord."

Dark Seer didn't like being forced into things, but his runner had told him the truth. He couldn't afford to anger Darkness; yet, there would come a time when rat would ascend triumphant.

***

Derrick planted the last of his ground level gas collectors and headed back to the van. He'd set up a small camp just off the dirt road that exited to the north side of Micmac Mills. Most of the day was spent collecting soil samples and taking a couple of quick water samples from a nearby brook in the hope they'd come up clean. He got a real kick out of drinking fresh water from a cool running stream.

After twenty minutes or so, he was back at the campsite he had built up near his parked vehicle. The back of his van had been converted into a mobile laboratory. He wasn't going to process any of the samples tonight, but he wanted to read up on one of the testing procedures for a particular soil alkalinity test. As he entered the back of the van he knocked over his environmental gamma monitor and swore as it crashed to the ground. The on/off switch was knocked on and the device began clicking.

This was a very expensive piece of equipment. It measured gamma radiation at various levels of emission but still was only the size of a lunch box. He checked the LED display, and it appeared to be working just fine.

He stepped out of the van and began taking some test measurements. He flipped through all of the various sensitivity bands. The associated readings seemed to be normal for background radiation until he got to the far side of the campsite. He pointed the radiometer toward where he set up most his sampling equipment and grimaced. The gamma reading was far too high. The machine had to be broken.

He went over to the path that led into the woods, and the level continued to rise. He swept through all of the other bands again, but they all seemed fine. It didn't make sense to him that only the low-level setting would be off. It also appeared that the radiation was coming from the ground. This made no sense in this area since there wasn't much in the way of radioactive material in the ground. He shrugged and returned to camp. He'd check it again in the morning.

***

Four berserker rats escorted Blitherskites and Aikeem into the dungeon. Blitherskites kept his Uzi pointed squarely in Aikeem's back the entire trip. No one knew the safety was on. For that matter, none of them even knew what a safety was.

After a few minutes, they were in the presence of the guard Aikeem had knocked out. Blitherskites grinned at the rat's swollen jaw.

"What's this?" The guard pointed at Aikeem. "Who sends this prisoner?"

Blitherskites came around from behind Aikeem. "This human is to be held per Lord Dark Seer's orders. I want the cleanest cell you have."

The guard looked at Blitherskites askew. "They're all fetid pits from hell, rat! And why would I want to give a clean one to this human?"

Blitherskites flipped off the safety and shot up a table in the corner. The berserker rats instantly crouched into a battle stance while the guard retreated to a corner and tried to hide under his arms.

"Because I'm going to have to stand guard over this human, and I want a dry cell with fresh straw, and if you don't have a clean one, then prepare one!"

The terrified guard ran to the main gate of the cellblock and scurried about to fulfill Blitherskites's orders. The berserker rats eyed the Uzi with newfound respect. After twenty minutes passed, the guard came back and escorted Aikeem and Blitherskites to the freshly prepared cell.

"Now lock us in until our escort arrives."

The guard gave Blitherskites a funny look, but he obeyed. Blitherskites went over to one corner in the rear of the cell while Aikeem went to the other.

"I thought you liked disgusting smells," Aikeem said to his captor.

Blitherskites grinned. "It weren't cleaned up for me, human. Now keep you mouth shut, or I'll perforate you with this," the rat lifted the barrel of his weapon in the wizard's direction. "You'll never escape this place. It's filled with my fellow rats and they're all listening in, so don't try any funny business."

Blitherskites winked at Aikeem, and the wizard realized the rat was sending him a message. He knew full well why Blitherskites was standing guard over him. The moment the rat got too far away, his head would blow off. Aikeem wasn't sure if he was playing this game to save his own skin or if he truly intended to help Aikeem. Only time would tell.

Lord Dark Seer took no chances. The next day he assigned four cohorts of berserker rats of the Order of Vile to escort Aikeem and Celise to Darkness's realm. The contingent was led by Gut-Taker, the mutant assassin. This was Lord Dark Seer's personal killer, which proved the rat king was not taking any chances. Skittermore was also commissioned to act as navigator because he had been to Darkness's realm so many times.

They formed up in the training field that bordered one side of Dark Seer's castle. Aikeem's hands were bound tightly behind his back and a leather gag was placed over his mouth. His sorcerous ways were not to be tolerated on this trip.

Blitherskites kept the Uzi trained on him at all times and pushed him about roughly so that the other rats left the wizard alone.

Blitherskites escorted Aikeem to the center of the group. Gut-Taker made his way over to the human to stand toe to toe with him. He was a dark creature, even for a rat. His eyes burned with malice from a longish rodent face. His black fur glowed with an oily sheen that covered his massive six foot body. Magic had been laid on this rodent so that it bore four arms. He was dressed entirely in black leather and steel. The hilts of two short bladed swords jutted over his shoulders, while two massive dirks hung from his waist. Aikeem was sure that in a fight, this creature would be deadly.

Gut-Taker leaned into Aikeem so that the wizard was subject to its rotten breath. "I have not killed a human in a long, long time. I'm ordered to take you to Darkness and so I shall, but..." the rat took one gray nail on a black finger and drew it down Aikeem's chest until he drew a trace of blood, "once you are there and have served your usefulness, maybe Darkness will give you to me."

Aikeem had several unflattering responses for the vile creature, but the gag prohibited him from expressing them. Gut-Taker spun on a heel and returned to the head of the column. A silk-covered litter that was borne on the shoulders of four pack rats passed Aikeem and Blitherskites. It took a position just in front of them. At first Aikeem's heart leapt because he spied Celise.

The pain from Aikeem's bonds was nothing compared to the agony in his heart when he saw the look that Celise gave him. She had peered out from the silk curtains of the litter, and her eyes were full of accusation. He would have killed every rodent in that troop just to be near her to tell her the truth.

Gut-Taker mounted one of the great rambling lizards they used as beasts of burden and led the troop out of the city. Skittermore was seated on a smaller beast behind Gut-Taker, but the rest of the contingent was on foot.

They traveled for the better part of a week to the north of Dark Seer's realm. They rested every few hours. Blitherskites demanded that Aikeem's bonds be released now and then. Gut-Taker was hesitant at first, but Blitherskites reminded the assassin that he was responsible for delivering Aikeem unharmed. Blitherskites pointed out that if the wizard lost his hands, Gut-Taker would be held responsible.

Aikeem was grateful to Blitherskites, but he was still unsure of his motives. Rats could be very duplicitous, and the wizard was uncertain if the rat was using him for his own motives.

Several times during their trip Aikeem was lashed with Celise's harsh looks. He tried to tell her with his eyes he was sorry and never meant her any harm, but always she turned away.

At the northern reaches of Dark Seer's realm, the road became wilder, but no creature dared approach such a large contingent of warrior rats. After another week, they were well into the black forests of Darkness's realm. The creatures Aikeem occasionally spotted through the trees seemed to be mostly predatory. Wolves, tree raptors, and various reptilian constrictors paced the company or hung from the trees. Aikeem suspected they hoped to pick off any stragglers.

The forest thinned out, and the ground became rockier as they began to ascend into some low foothills that lay before a great mountain range. The road led them higher up the side of a small mountain until they came to another stone castle that was built on a massive rock outcropping. This place was also easily defended in that its back was to a cliff, and a steep precipice protected either flank. The only way in was from the road leading up to the front portcullis. The main gate was a massive affair of oak and iron.

A platoon of pike wielding snakemen stood guard at either side of the entrance.

Gut-Taker brought his beast up and dismounted. The greenest of the snakemen separated from his comrades and met the assassin. After much hissing and squeaking, one of the cohorts escorted the prisoners through the main gate into the castle courtyard. Gut-Taker roughly grabbed Aikeem—much to Blitherskites's consternation—and took him to the litter. Blitherskites followed close behind. Skittermore gently led Celise down from her litter and directed Gut-Taker to follow them.

Aikeem noted that the castle was built to martial specifications, with no concern for artistry. The place was decidedly built for an ogre; the structural specifications were all made to suit a creature of large size. As they entered the interior of the castle, he noted weapons adorned every wall, and here and there a suit of armor stood ready. The armor seemed built for creatures of all sizes and shapes.

The stone used to build the castle was a lighter tan color than that used in Dark Seer's abode. Once again, the primary method of illumination was torches set in sconces on the wall. Aikeem noted that they were few and far between. Darkness was true to his name.

They were escorted into a massive throne room. Fifty-foot pillars bordered either side of the room, and they were carved as silent sentinels holding aloft the wooden ceiling above. The room was filled with snake soldiers who sat at low tables along either side of the hall. Their tongues constantly darted out into the air as they watched the newcomers with emotionless yellow eyes.

Darkness sat on his stone throne in the shadows. The rat contingent stopped before him at the base of the stairs that led up to the dais he sat upon. Skittermore rushed up the steps and knelt at Darkness's feet.

Aikeem couldn't see the creature who sat on that throne, but he was sure he was human. He wore a black cloak all about himself, and occasionally, the whites of his eyes were reflected in the sparse light.

Darkness motioned Skittermore to come closer. He whispered in Darkness's ear and soon there was a low bass chuckle that polluted the air.

"Delicious. The Weaver and the Wizard all in one package." Darkness pointed a long bony finger at Celise. "I have been looking for you for a very long time. I want your powers, girl!"

Celise shuddered at the thought of being at the mercy of this creature. Aikeem's eyes began to burn. He wanted very badly to see this creature so that he could know who it was he would destroy. He noted Darkness spoke with an accent, although he couldn't place it. The finger pointed at Celise definitely betrayed him as human.

Darkness turned to Aikeem. "And you, wizard. You have some knowledge that I would make mine. Come closer."

Gut-Taker grabbed Aikeem by the arm, but Blitherskites interjected himself between the two. The incredulous assassin started to protest with a fist until

Blitherskites pushed his Uzi into his gut. Dark Seer's killer had heard about this weapon, and he backed off. Blitherskites led Aikeem up the steps to Darkness, and they stood before him.

Darkness gestured to Blitherskites. "What's this?"

Skittermore spoke up. "This is Conniving Blitherskites, my lord. He was once a member of the Council of Thirteen. It was he who captured Aikeem back in the real worlds and brought him to Lord Dark Seer. He is also the one acquiring the firearms for our armies back in the real worlds."

Aikeem started and glared down at Blitherskites. The rodent ignored him. Aikeem still could not see Darkness's face, but he could hear the surprise in his voice. "Really? Back in the real worlds, you say? You've been of great service to me, Mr. Blitherskites. I take care of those who take care of me."

Blitherskites bowed his head, and Darkness said, "Remove the wizard's bonds. He is of no danger to me in here." Blitherskites did as he was bid.

Darkness turned to stare at Aikeem. "I'm aware of your affection for the Weaver, so I'll be brief. I need to know the exact location of Qar and the times of its materialization."

Aikeem was taken by surprise. He could feel Darkness smile at his confusion. "You will tell me these things, or I will horribly torture the Weaver every day until you do."

Darkness extended a bony black hand holding pen and paper and handed them to Aikeem. "If you lie to me I will know; the wizard Farjule has given me some information on these matters."

Aikeem froze again in surprise. This Darkness knew far too much about his past for his tastes. He took the pen and paper and wrote down what Darkness wanted to know. He couldn't see the harm in it, and he surely wasn't going to let his lady be tortured. He handed the paper back to Darkness who greedily took it.

"Very good, wizard. I would have your powers too, but I will need time to prepare. Sleeth!"

A tall green snakeman with tattoos of runes inscribed across his body came forward and bowed to Darkness. Darkness stood but managed to remain in the shadows. He motioned to Sleeth and then to the two rats next to him. "Sleeth, take them to the dungeons. You two come with me. I want to show you something that will make Dark Seer very happy."

Aikeem could see the desperation in Blitherskites's eyes. The wizard dived on the rat and began to scream. "Disgusting vermin! Foul rodent! I'll kill you for this treachery!"

Aikeem slammed Blitherskites to the ground and began choking him. Sleeth and Gut-Taker jumped on the wizard's back. Roughly, they pulled him off Blitherskites.

Darkness clicked his tongue. "Really, wizard, this is undignified behavior."

Blitherskites grabbed his throat in an effort to breathe. He looked up at Aikeem in shock. The smiling wizard held the kabosh in one hand. Sleeth grabbed the leather collar and slammed Aikeem across the face with an open hand.

Sleeth pushed the collar in Aikeem's face and leaned close. "You want this human? It's mine now!"

Sleeth put the collar around his neck and roughly hoisted the wizard to his feet. "Come!"

The snakeman hurled Aikeem down the stairs of Darkness's throne. He tumbled at Celise's feet. His body hurt, but his heart leapt. For a moment he saw concern in his lover's eyes, and he knew down to his soul that she wasn't totally lost to him.

Gut-Taker followed Sleeth, several guards and the prisoners into the dungeons.

***

Blitherskites and Skittermore walked hurriedly after Darkness. The dark human was only a head taller than either rat and was short for a human. The rodents were still required to move quickly because Darkness was obviously in a hurry.

"Where's he taking us?"

Skittermore pointed at a heavy iron bound door farther down the corridor. "To his laboratory. That's where he's been working on the maps you brought back from the real worlds."

Darkness led the two rodents into the large room that held his laboratory. The place was filled with tables bearing all manner of equipment. Some of it was obviously magical in nature, while much of it was of the mundane real world sort. Darkness stopped at a chair placed at the center of a workbench and pulled it back to sit at the table.

In front of him was a powerful PC. He jiggled the mouse and the screen came to life. A curious Blitherskites peered over his shoulder. "Is that Windows 98?"

Darkness was impressed with the rodent's technical knowledge. "Yes, it is."

"Hmmm, you really should upgrade to Windows XP."

"I know. I know. I hate being forced into these damn upgrades every couple of years. They think I'm an evil megalomaniac? I've got nothing on Bill Gates," Darkness grumbled as he brought up his spreadsheet. "Ah, there we go. I've plugged all of the formulas for the various hidden realms in here. Qar is the last one."

Darkness tapped on the keyboard and hit the enter key with a flourish. He cracked an evil grin when the solution cell filled with the answer to his question. "There and when! That is how Avalon will show up next on earth! That will be our bridge! This will be the doom of mankind!"

Darkness turned to the two rats and said with a smile. "The room's supposed to echo with my maniacal laughter at this point, but I do so hate clichés. Care for some tea?"

Skittermore and Blitherskites anxiously nodded yes and followed Darkness out of the room.

***

Aikeem's head was snapped back by Gut-Taker who had a fistful of the wizard's hair in his claw. "You embarrassed me in front of Darkness human. You shall pay for your indiscretion."

Aikeem's hands were once again bound behind him, and he figured that this was not a good time to aggravate the killer rat. Gut-Taker shoved him forward, and he stumbled down the stone corridor. Sleeth hissed with laughter. Four other snakemen joined their leader and the rodent assassin to escort Celise and Aikeem into the bowels of Darkness's castle.

They came to a set of iron bars that housed a steel mesh gate. A snakeman opened the portal with a key, and they entered single file. The group passed through a large guardroom with two long wooden tables sided by benches. Two-dozen snakemen lounged here and watched the prisoners as they were escorted to a heavy wooden door bound in iron bands. Beyond this door was a long room of prison cells.

Gut-Taker grabbed Aikeem by the hair again and pushed him to his knees. Sleeth strolled to a cell near the end of the block and opened it up. Gut-Taker dragged Aikeem by the hair to the cell and threw him in. Celise scowled at the rodent as she walked by him but said naught.

Gut-Taker slammed the door shut and spit on Aikeem. "Enjoy what time you have left, human."

Aikeem scowled and looked up at the rat assassin. "It is you who should be thinking of his last days, vermin. We'll see how brave you are when I'm free."

"Free!" Gut-Taker laughed uproarishly and was joined by Sleeth. The pack of killers exited the place laughing at the joke. Aikeem watched them go with venom in his eyes.

"Aikeem!"

Aikeem spun to the sound of a familiar voice and almost broke into tears as his ladylove bounded into his arms. "Pendella!"

Ms. Purrfect jammed her head into Aikeem's chin, and the pair enjoyed a nuzzle most sublime.

"Oh, my lady, I feared the worst," Aikeem said as he began to stroke the luxurious fur of his beloved cat.

"And I was becoming quite concerned. What took you so long?"

"I think I can say the same thing!" Celise stood opposite the pair, her arms folded across her chest. Her expression had changed from concern to anger.

"You found Celise! Truly, life is good," Pendella exclaimed.

Celise ignored Pendella's observations and pointed an accusing finger at Aikeem. "You tried to kill me! Do you have any idea what I've been through?"

"But beloved I…"

"I was fried with that green light! My brain was scrambled! I was tossed into a strange evil world far from this strange evil world, and everything was trying to eat me! Why did you do this Aikeem? I loved you!"

Celise seethed; Aikeem was too flustered to speak, so Pendella put things in proper perspective. "Celise, Aikeem could no more hurt you than cut off his own legs. Now come over here, and give us a family hug."

Celise was speechless! Pendella's matter-of-fact observation totally caught her by surprise so that she couldn't move. Then she broke down in tears and rushed over to Aikeem and Pendella for an embrace that Aikeem had been waiting for for a very long time.

"Careful! Careful! You're squishing me," Pendella cautioned.

Celise kissed Aikeem on the cheek and parted. "I'm sorry, Pendella. What's happened to me? How come I can talk to the cat?"

"Not just any cat," Pendella huffed. Aikeem smiled and placed Pendella on the floor.

"You're the Weaver, my beloved. Why does this surprise you, Celise?"

"That was on the Dreamscape. This is..." Celise looked around her in confusion. "I don't know where this is," and she began to cry again.

Aikeem gathered his lover into his arms and tried to soothe her. "It is a long story, my sweets. Let me give you a check-up, and I'll explain it all to you."

"Oh, so you're a doctor, too? And they called you a wizard?"

Aikeem escorted his sweet love to the back of the cell, and the two sat down on a small dry pile of straw. "Although I've done my share of doctoring, I'm not an M.D., but I truly am a wizard, sorcerer, mage, and a few other things."

Celise wiped away a tear. "You never told me you were a wizard."

"You never told me you were a weaver, lady. If you had, it would have saved us both a lot of heart ache."

BAANNNGGG!

The three lovers jumped. Pendella looked at Aikeem. "What was that?"

Aikeem smiled a knowing smile. "There's one less obnoxious snakeman in the world. His head has been separated from his body."

Pendella had no idea what her man was talking about. She joined the two humans and adopted a sphinx like position on the straw next to Celise. "I was too obsessed with revenge against those who had destroyed my family and hurt me."

Aikeem's eyes softened, and he kissed his lady on the forehead. "I know love. I do not fault you for this."

Celise looked down at Pendella who gave her kitty eyes. "How come I can understand Pendella? Where am I? Is this place real?"

Aikeem began to gesture around Celise. Her eyes widened as glowing runes sprung from her body and began to float about her in mid-air. "You are in a place called the Darkling Space, and it is every bit as real as the Earth we come from. It borders the Dreamscape where you reigned supreme, lady."

Celise looked down at Pendella. "Why did all of the cats turn against me? I never did them any harm."

Pendella licked one paw. "Not all of them turned against you, Celise. I knew Aikeem would save you."

Celise smiled and reached down to rub the purring feline's head. "All right then. Why did the rest of the cats turn against me?"

"Because you are a weaver, and you were using your powers for a personal vendetta. On the Dreamscape, this is forbidden."

"By whom?"

Aikeem extracted some red runes from Celise's ear. "By the Administration, my love. They've chartered the cats to protect that place. You violated their law, and thus, a termination order was cut."

Celise looked even more confused. "What Administration? I didn't know about any such laws."

Aikeem smiled and caressed her check with a free hand. "The Celestial Administration. They are the keepers of the universe… multiverse… whatever, and I am well aware you knew nothing of their laws. If they'd known that, they probably would have rescinded the order, but everything happened so fast that there was no time."

The light of realization sparked in Celise's eyes. "So you cast a spell to make it look like you killed me! To protect me from the cats and this Administration!"

"Precisely."

"Oh, Aikeem!" His heart swelled as his ladylove grabbed him and gave him a glowing embrace. The runes jumbled up and flitted away.

They parted and Aikeem glanced at the dissipating magic. "Unfortunately, I boggled up my spell. I'd never written anything for the Dreamscape before. The intention was to split your spirit from your body and to protect both. However, when I launched the spell, the division was far too violent and it hurled your spirit out of the Dreamscape and beyond even the Darkling Space."

"She went beyond the Darkling Space?" Pendella was incredulous.

Aikeem pointed at some fading runes. "Yes. My examination has proven this to be the case." Aikeem placed a loving hand on Celise's shoulder. "The reason you were so confused for such a time was due to my spell. You were launched into a terrible place. The spell protected your sanity by scrambling your wits."

"Spells have intelligence?"

Aikeem felt as if he were speaking to a pupil. "Not as such. You could compare them to an earthbound computer. You give them parameters and they operate within those parameters. What I find very interesting is how long this one lasted. It must have picked up energy as it traversed the various realms."

Celise took Aikeem's hand from her shoulder and kissed the back of it. "It tried to bring me home."

Aikeem shrugged. "I think so. It dragged you through the outlands that lie beyond the Darkling Space until it reached the border of this realm. It must have run out of energy there."

"It's a miracle she's still alive. The Darkling Space is no place for humans," Pendella observed.

Celise shuddered. "I spent a lot of time running, but I never gave up."

Aikeem smiled at the strength of his lady. "You are a wonder, Celise. And to answer an earlier question, you can understand Pendella and the rest of these creatures for that matter because my spell has changed you."

"How?"

"You came off the Dreamscape as a spirit, but the spell has formed up a transdimensional, submaterial manifestation throughout you. Here you are real. The process of materialization has entwined your abilities as a weaver in your new form. Obviously interspecies communication is one of those abilities."

Celise looked down at her hands. "What else can I do?"

"I don't know. Only time will tell."

A distressed Pendella looked up at Aikeem. "Tell her."

Aikeem frowned, and Celise looked concerned. "Tell me what?"

Aikeem sighed. "I assume Pendella is referring to the fact that it will be impossible for you to return to earth in this form."

"What!" a distressed Celise cried.

"You can not be material twice in the same world. It is an unacceptable paradox."

Tears began to well again. "Then what am I to do?"

Aikeem sat silently for a second and placed a finger on his chin. "There is a way, but it will be difficult."

"I don't want to stay here, Aikeem. I want to go home."

Aikeem smiled and took his ladylove close to him. "And so we shall, beloved, and so we shall."

Farouk fairly glowed with self-satisfaction as he was driven through the windy stone streets of old Algiers. His driver was totally focused on the streets before them, which were alive with the city's populace. They traveled in a refurbished WWII era jeep that had been painted a desert tan color.

They entered a street that paralleled the harbor in the old section of the city near the Casbah. They stopped in the parking lot of a large, fairly new warehouse. Farouk smiled when he saw it. He'd done it. Inside was just over one million weapons and associated ammunition. He'd had to use every resource at his disposal, but in the end he managed to pull together the greatest non-governmental arms deal in history.

He stepped out of the jeep to be greeted by two monstrous Arab guards dressed in the flowing white garb of the desert. Under those robes were a pair of Kalashnikovs ready to cut down any trespassers. They bowed to Farouk and then escorted him to the warehouse entrance.

Of all his contacts, the Chinese had been the biggest help. They'd managed to put together half the order. The new government in Beijing was anxious for the hard currency the diamonds would yield. Farouk loved this new Communism.

He entered the building through a side door and marveled at the crates that were stacked to the ceiling. Wooden, military green boxes formed up rows of deadly hardware. Two Chinese nationals sporting MP-7 auto-guns met him at the door and escorted him on his inspection. They were two of many on loan to him until the shipment was delivered.

Farouk's assistant, Pierre Bonguerre, soon joined him with a notebook computer clutched in his arms. The tiny Frenchman was even shorter than Farouk and was just as lean and wiry. His slender fingers banged out numbers in the inventory program on the computer as he joined his boss.

Pierre pushed his spectacles into place and smiled at Farouk. "You will be a legend for this."

Farouk smiled. "I must admit I'm more than happy with the way things have gone thus far. However, the trickiest part lies before us. Our activities have not gone unnoticed by various governmental organizations. The CIA and MI6 are almost at our heels. Getting all of this hardware into the target country will not be easy."

Pierre brushed back a black lock of his longish straight hair. "The longer the inventory sits here, the more exposed we are. When do we get a destination?"

Farouk shrugged. "Monsieur Skites is a mysterious man. He comes and goes with the wind, but he is reliable. We will have to wait until he shows up with the rest of the payment and his instructions. Until then, make sure these weapons are well guarded. We've come too far to have things spoiled now."

Pierre nodded in assent, and Farouk began to stroll down one of the aisles. He smiled as he read off the contents of each box. After this deal, he was determined to retire from the trade. He would raise many children, see them educated, and bask in the glow of a loving family.

"Life is good," he mused.

**

Soon after Aikeem's examination of Celise, Pendella introduced the wizard, through the bars of their cell, to Gandabon, Drusillia, and Cragstein Muddleboot the dwarf. The cats and the dwarf filled Celise and Aikeem in on their particular plights. In turn, Aikeem filled his comrades in with the information he had.

After some discussion it was obvious to the wizard that his friends all expected him to manufacture an escape. He spent over an hour examining the cage and finally plopped down in the straw at the rear of the cell.

"Well?" Pendella queried.

"This Darkness is no fool. These cells are protected by strong yet subtle energies that drain most nearby magical energy. I'm barely able to do my small magic. If I had my skeleton key, I could open the lock, but without it I'm afraid we're stuck in here."

"This is not good Aikeem. The Dreamscape is in jeopardy. Obviously, Lord Dark Seer and Darkness are marshaling their forces to attack our realm."

"Don't forget about the Sloths! They're in on this too," Cragstein pointed out.

Aikeem turned to Pendella and Cragstein who sat in the cell behind her. "I don't think so my friends. I think they mean to attack the real worlds."

"What!" Cragstein exclaimed.

"How is that possible? There is no path from the Darkling Space to the real worlds," Pendella pointed out.

"I know. It doesn't make sense, but Dark Seer said Blitherskites was buying weapons for them in the real worlds."

Pendella fairly spit. "Blitherskites! Foul rodent! I should have known."

Aikeem grinned. "Don't be too hard on that one, lady. I think he may be more of a friend to us than you think."

Pendella doubted this. "It doesn't make sense. How could they possibly make it to the real worlds?"

"I don't know, but in my gut I know this is what they intend to do. We need to escape to warn the Administration."

"You'll get no help there wizard. The Administration is stretched beyond its capacity. It'll be up to us to solve this crisis," Gandabon pointed out.

Aikeem sighed. The mysteries of the One God eluded him, but, for once, he would have liked some intervention on his (or her, he wasn't sure of that either) part.

The door to the prison banged open against one wall. Four snakemen preceded Blitherskites into the cellblock. Another four snakemen followed the rodent in. They marched with the rat until he stopped in front of Aikeem's cell.

Blitherskites grinned an evil smile as he removed the knapsack he was wearing. He placed the pack up against the bars of the empty cell opposite Aikeem's and his companions' cell. He went up close to Aikeem who stood at the front of the cage and expanded his evil grin.

"So Wizard, how does it feel to be a prisoner? Now the sandal is on the other paw ain't it?" Blitherskites fairly hissed. Aikeem remained silent.

"Now I go to return to the real worlds. I have great powers that allow me to do this."

Pendella yawned. "We're so impressed."

Blitherskites sneered. "Soon Darkness will lead the combined armies of the Sloth Empire and the Scatter Clans into the real worlds."

Blitherskites's eyes narrowed as he looked at Aikeem. "Even these dim snakemen can see that a military package of this size is unstoppable."

Aikeem's eyes went wide. He raised a hand and subtly gestured as Blitherskites went on. "Back in the real worlds, I will be waiting with a cache of your human firearms. Two million soldiers will sweep across humanity before they even know what hits them. Humans don't stand a chance against these armies with the combined magical powers of Lord Dark Seer, Darkness, and the mighty Sloth armies. In one month Earth will be ours."

Blitherskites broke out into maniacal laughter. "Good luck, wizard, although the next time I see you, I expect it will be your corpse."

Blitherskites laughed all the way to the exit. The snakemen accompanied him out and soon the place was held in a depressed quiet.

"How I would love to slowly gut the little bastard," Gandabon mused.

Aikeem smiled. "Why would you want to do that to our ally?"

"What!" Drusillia exclaimed. "Did you not hear what the little worm just told us!"

"He was telling us their plans, and he has given us a chance to escape," Aikeem said as he pointed at his wonderful knapsack that was propped up against the cell opposite him. "He gave me a signal, and I confounded the Snakemen with some small magic, despite these bloody bars I might add, so they would miss my military package. Now I only have to figure out how to get to it."

The knapsack began to wiggle and then fell over. The cover jittered and then it popped open.

"Snapper-Cat," the party exclaimed.

The slightly embarrassed feline sat on his haunches. "Although it is very nice in there I'm happy to be out."

Aikeem pointed at the pack. "Quickly, Snap! Go back and tell Pleep I need my skeleton key." Snapper-Cat darted back into the pack.

"Who's Pleep?" Cragstein asked.

"That's the caretaker gremlin who lives in Aikeem's knapsack," Pendella informed them.

"Oh, is that one of them there magical containers of infinite space?" Cragstein asked.

Aikeem watched his pack. "Yes, but it's only a quarter infinite. That's all I could afford a couple thousand years ago."

"A couple thousand years!" Celise exclaimed. Her expression was one of shock. "You told me you were older than me, but you never told me you were old enough to be my great, great, great, great..."

"Don't go there, beloved. Ah, my key."

Snapper-Cat exited the backpack with a device that was the size of a man's hand. The body was that of a human skeleton. The head was a brass key that continuously morphed into various configurations. Snapper-Cat dropped the key, and it ran over to Aikeem's waiting hand. Aikeem stuck it in the cell lock and after some metallic clicks, the door sprung open. He opened the doors to the other prisoner's cells, and soon everyone was gathered around his pack.

Aikeem reached into his pack and felt around. "We're going to have to fight our way out of here, but we need to do so as quietly as possible." Aikeem smiled. "Ah Blitherskites you are a friend. He packed away my weapons," Aikeem withdrew his shotgun and the blade Moonwind from the pack. He handed the firearm to Celise.

"I'd prefer, if at all possible, that you didn't use that, love. It will bring the palace guard down around our head."

"Do you have any other swords in there? Preferably a rapier?"

Aikeem looked at his lady in amazement. "What do you know of such things, Celise?"

Celise arched an eyebrow. "Don't underestimate me, Aikeem. Mother wanted to be sure that I could protect myself. I've studied in the dreams of all the world's great martial masters. Heir Von Hagenburg himself was my instructor."

Aikeem bowed. "My apologies, dear love." Aikeem reached deep into his pack and came up with a beautiful, slender rapier with an exquisitely crafted silver, wire basket hilt. He handed it across one forearm to his ladylove. Celise slung the shotgun across her back and withdrew the proffered weapon from its scabbard. With a smile she sliced the air.

"Got any battleaxes in there?" Cragstein queried.

Aikeem smiled and once again dug deep into the pack. "I haven't used this in quite a while. It was given to me by Nanoc the Cimmerian. It's wonderful for splitting apart orcs, trolls, and snakemen although not necessarily in that order."

Cragstein's eyes fairly glowed when Aikeem withdrew a three-foot long double bladed battleaxe. The Weapon was almost as tall as he was. A large spike centered the two blades that lined the hardwood haft. Cragstein took the weapon almost reverently and held it aloft.

"Now this is a thing of beauty! It's as light as a feather, but it feels as sturdy as me grandpa's rocklike spine."

Aikeem smiled. "I expect you'll put it to good use."

Aikeem handed Celise the backpack. "Forgive me, dear heart. This is not a very gentlemanly act, but I prefer unrestricted freedom of movement when I wield Moonwind."

Celise smiled at Aikeem's chivalrous discomfort. "I never said I wouldn't be your beast of burden." Celise replaced the shotgun with the backpack and slung the shotgun over one shoulder.

Aikeem drew Moonwind and went over to the door. He placed one hand on the portal and began to rub very slowly up and down the hard wood. His eyes went blank and unfocused as he extended his mind. After a few moments, he came back to the party.

"There are twenty guards just outside the door and to the right. Two more are guarding the other side of the iron bars beyond this door." Aikeem turned to Celise. "I want you and the cats to take out those two. They absolutely must not get away or they will alert the entire palace, and we'll never get out."

Aikeem turned to his feline friends. "I know your beasts are not available to you, but cats have a particular knack for tying up bipedal feet. You must slow them down so that Celise can get through the steel door." Aikeem handed his skeleton key to Celise. "This will work on the lock. Just stick it in and he, the key that is, will do the rest."

Lastly, Aikeem addressed Cragstein. "You and I will take out the rest. Are you up to that many? Most of them are currently unarmed, but their weapons are stacked nearby."

Cragstein grinned a malicious smile. "Just open the door, Wizard. I'll show you how ready I am."

Aikeem shared the dwarf's sneer and flipped his sword so that it ran back up along his forearm. He crouched down next to the door and placed his free hand against the wood. He closed his eyes to concentrate again. Every muscle in the wizard's body tensed as ethereal blue powers began to coalesce about him.

"Be ready," he whispered through an electric voice. The party crouched. Aikeem flipped a pinky. On the other side of the door, the heavy crossbeam popped out of the iron brackets that held it in place. Several incredulous snakemen looked over at the door.

Aikeem took a giant step back from the door, gestured with both hands, and screamed a word of power. The door exploded out and he rushed in. The snakemen froze in surprise as Aikeem leapt into their midst. He danced a deadly steel ballet that sliced across reptilian throats and limbs.

Cragstein followed him in with a mighty dwarfish battle cry. Before they knew what had happened, several snakemen were swimming in their own blood. Celise and the cats made for their target. The guards on the other side of the iron bars were so stymied that they hadn't even moved by the time Celise was at the door. One of them rushed the bars and jammed a spear through to impale Celise. The weaver easily sidestepped the thrust and returned the favor with her rapier. The snakeman twitched for a moment on the end of her blade.

Celise jammed the skeleton key into the door as the remaining guard tried to flee. Four cats jumbled up his feet and he crashed to the ground. Celise jumped high as he spun to his back. She drove her blade through his heart, and the creature hissed his last.

Twelve snakemen lay still on the ground as Aikeem and Cragstein attempted to finish off the rest. The remaining reptilians were now armed and not as easily dispatched as their fellows. Cragstein swung a mighty blow and knocked aside five spears. Aikeem leapt high into the opening and came down on the skull of one, pulled his blade free, spun and decapitated two more.

A shrill, spine-wrenching, battle scream echoed through the room as the weaver dived into the fray. With lithe, swift moves, three slow snakemen clutched their ruined stomachs. After twenty more seconds, the last of Darkness's guards fell into a pool of their own blood.

Silence filled the room. Humans and dwarf bent over to catch their breath. The four cats sat nearby on their haunches.

"Actually they fight quite well," Gandabon observed.

"The dwarf is also very talented," Drusillia noted.

"We need to leave this place as quietly as possible and get as far away as possible before they realize we're gone," Aikeem cautioned between breaths.

"But where shall we go?" a distressed Celise asked.

"Good point," Aikeem replied.

Cragstein stepped forward. "I'll lead you mates! Old Grimlot and the dwarves got along just fine a long time ago. I know this area, and I know some ways to elude these here snakemen. Get us out of the castle wizard, and I'll get us through the woods."

"Good enough. Pendella, you take the point with me. Gandabon, Drusillia and Snapper-Cat you guard our rear."

Aikeem rushed by Celise, and they formed in single file. The party followed the dank rock corridors always looking for a way up. A few times they came to a dead end, but eventually they made their way to the first floor.

At several intersections they encountered guards. Aikeem and Celise were on them before they could offer much resistance, and in seconds they were silent. The group found its way to a doorway to the main courtyard. The palace gate stood open opposite them. Unfortunately, a dozen guards lined the ramparts, and there was no way they could cross the courtyard without being seen.

Pendella looked up at Aikeem. "What shall we do, lover?"

Aikeem gestured for Celise to come forward. He motioned with a finger and she turned around so that Aikeem could get into the pack. He whispered inside. "Pleep, get me the sleep dragons."

After a few seconds a scaled, gnarled, leathery hand popped out with a cloth-wrapped package. Aikeem unfolded the package and turned back to the courtyard. A dozen emerald green insects that looked like dragonflies with long thin spikes on their foreheads lined the cloth.

Aikeem looked at the guards and then whispered to the flies. "Seeeeeekkkkk." The wizard blew across the bugs and they came to life. They shot across the courtyard and impaled each snakeman in the back of the neck. One by one, the reptile men fell over asleep.

"Let's go," Aikeem waved the party on. They ran across the courtyard, sprinted out of the gate, and down the road. They trotted for about another mile and then slowed to a walk.

"Where to, Cragstein?" Aikeem asked.

Cragstein strode to the front of the party. "Two leagues down this road, and then we cut off to the west. Another four leagues into the forest, and we should be home free."

They traveled until they hit the branch point, and then followed Cragstein into the woods. Aikeem laid magics down the road behind them to disguise their trail. After several hours of traveling through the woods, they stopped by a small rocky stream. They were all exhausted, except for the cats who had traveled inside Aikeem's knapsack.

The four cats took up guard duty while Aikeem and company rested. Aikeem dug into his backpack and pulled out some sandwiches. Celise and Cragstein gratefully took them.

"What's this?" Aikeem exclaimed while digging through his pack.

Pendella strolled over as he withdrew a plastic-wrapped package. He opened up the documents and exclaimed. "Blitherskites, you son of a gun!"

"Gun? I think that Blitherskites is something other than a son of a gun," Pendella observed.

"You have the rat all wrong, lady. This is a copy of the map of interphasic realms. Qar, once my home city, is such a place." Aikeem jabbed a finger at a location that was circled with yellow magic marker. "That is Avalon, and that's why Darkness needed me to tell him of Qar."

A confused Celise said, "I don't understand."

"Darkness needs to know which realm will merge with earth next. By knowing Qar's multidimensional position, he can triangulate the next merge point. It is Avalon! That is how they plan to assault earth. You see here? According to this map, Avalon will phase in from the Darkling Space across the Desolation Plains to the edge of the Dreamscape, and then into earth. It is a very rare occurrence that will bridge these realms. This happens maybe once every thousand years."

"Then we must stop it. Perhaps a magical blast of some sort," Gandabon observed.

"No!"

The party was taken aback by the vehemence of Aikeem's exclamation.

Pendella was more reasonable in her response. "Why not, Aikeem? Mustn't we stop Darkness and his hordes?"

"Of course, but not by destroying the bridge. It is the only way Celise can return to earth."

"Of course," Pendella observed.

"Fill me in 'cause I don't understand," Cragstein said.

Aikeem pointed at the map. "Avalon is a sacred realm of magic. In this land, Celise can exist as a paradox. There I can merge her back into her body that still exists in the real worlds."

Celise hesitantly said, "Earth is more important than my single life."

Aikeem smiled. "I would dispute that fact, love, but then I am prejudiced. But it is not as simple as that either. If we destroy the bridge, then Darkness will just turn his forces elsewhere. He might even figure out a way to assault the Dreamscape. If we catch his armies at Avalon, we have a chance to defeat them."

"Of course! If we hold them there long enough, Avalon will disappear and rematerialize somewhere else," Drusillia exclaimed.

Aikeem studied the map for a moment and smiled a wicked smile. "According to this, if we can hold them for three days, then they will be stuck in the Mists of Time for forty years after that."

"The Mists of Time?" Cragstein observed. "Never been there before meself."

"Neither have I, but I've observed the place during a few wizardly junkets, and it's not for the uninitiated. If you step in the wrong place, you can age a thousand years in an instant or vice versa."

Celise smiled. "They'll march right into it if we can hold them."

"I hate to put a stick in yer craw, but from what the felines here've been telling us, and what you've said, the Scatter Clans got a mighty big army at their disposal. What you got?"

"I think we can gather 250,000 felines on the battlefield. A quarter of those will house beasts," Gandabon stated.

"I have some very destructive battle spells already prepared. I'm sure I can take out a few thousand on my own," Aikeem said.

"If we can lure some of them onto the Dreamscape, then I can do some serious damage," Celise promised.

Cragstein frowned. "From what I've heard, you're still outnumbered pretty badly."

Aikeem sighed in frustration. "We'll do the best with what we have. We have no other choice."

Cragstein smiled. "But you do, mate. I know another quarter or so million stout warriors ready to die by yer side, and from what you've been saying, they need this Avalon too."

Aikeem was confused. "Who would that be?"

Gandabon chuckled. "The dwarves. If we can find them."

"Of course! If we could get the Sloths on the battlefield along with the dwarves, the dwarves could reclaim their material selves," Aikeem noted.

"Just what I was thinkin', Wizard."

"Then our plans are made for us. Snapper-Cat, you are the Dreamscape's greatest scout," The feline couldn't blush, but he was embarrassed. "You will take Cragstein and search for his people. Gandabon and Drusillia, you must return to Wo'Em and gather the cats for battle. I will go with Celise to the Desolation Plains where Avalon will appear."

"And what about me?" Pendella asked.

Aikeem rubbed the head of his feline beauty. "You, dearest, will go back to earth and fetch Celise's body for us."

"How will I do that Aikeem? She is a bit large."

Celise started to say something but thought better of it. Aikeem dug about in his knapsack and came up with a gold necklace with a bright ruby for a pendant.

Pendella's eyes widened as he began to loop it about her neck. "Oh, this is very nice!"

"I knew you'd like this bauble. Stop batting at it lady; it's not a toy."

"What is it?"

"It's the Gentleman's Gem. It's meant to control the weak-minded. If you place it around the neck of a dimwit you can control them with a thought."

"Hey!" Celise was obviously perturbed.

Aikeem smiled. "No offense, lady, but your body is mindless without your spirit. Pendella, you need to work this over Celise's head back on the real world. Then you must direct her with your thoughts back to Wo'Em and ultimately to Avalon."

Pendella began to lick one paw. "I can do that."

"What will you and I do on the Desolation Plains, Aikeem?" Celise asked.

"We will go to Avalon and see what traps we can lay for Darkness's unsuspecting armies."

Celise nodded in approval. Aikeem became very serious and jabbed at the map. "We must make haste. We only have a month until Avalon appears."

Cragstein frowned. "That's bad. I know some shortcuts through the wood, but it's still going to take us at least a week and a half to get back to the Dreamscape. How can we find my people in such a short amount of time?"

Snapper-Cat was matter-of-fact. "We have no choice."

Aikeem surveyed his grim friends and echoed the feline. "We have no choice."

***

A furious and driven Gut-Taker led a cohort of trotting snakemen down the road out of Darkness's castle. Legacy trotted beside the lizard stallion that Gut-Taker rode upon. Darkness was absolutely furious when he was informed of his captives' escape. He was equally as rabid about Sleeth's murder by Aikeem's kabosh. Darkness directed Gut-Taker to lead his troops after the company and to slaughter them all. Evidently, the wizard's and the weaver's powers were no longer of consequence to him.

The rat assassin took these orders with relish. As he rode on, he fantasized about the many different ways he was going to torture the human wizard. Their prey had escaped several hours before anyone realized that they'd gotten away. Gut-Taker was not too concerned, for he knew they were on foot, and his snakemen were known for their speedy marches.

The rat assassin watched Legacy peel off from his company and wondered what the peculiar beast was up to. He didn't like that one. He was too quiet for his tastes and too much like a cat. For obvious reasons, Gut-Taker hated cats.

Legacy sniffed about the road as the snakemen passed him by. When he next looked up, Gut-Taker's troop was far down the road. Legacy brought his massive head up and sniffed in the direction of the forest. He was not so easily fooled. He'd let Gut-Taker and company continue on their fool's chase. There was one he wished to attend to personally. Gut-Taker never saw Legacy bound into the forest where Cragstein had led Aikeem's company.

***

Blitherskites's trip back to the real worlds had been a quick one. Darkness gave him a toothy-run-a lot to hurry him back to the Desolation Plains and then on to the Dreamscape. Blitherskites didn't particularly care for this mode of transportation, having had more than one run in with the lizard's more violent cousins.

Toothy-run-a-lots were taller, longer, and leaner than the jump-a-lot sort. They were big enough to support a saddle and rider, and they were certainly more domesticated. Blitherskites was also happy to note that their heads were much smaller than their jumpy cousins. Their mouths were not big enough to eat much more than small furry animals and fish.

Blitherskites carried two backpacks now. One was filled to the top with cut diamonds. Evidently, Darkness had gotten the stones from the Sloths who, in turn, had stolen them from some Dwarves. The gems were the currency that would finance the armament of Darkness's armies.

Blitherskites was more than a little nervous about the way things were going. Originally, his thoughts were only about getting the death mark off his head and coming back into the good graces of Dark Seer and the Council. Things had changed. He'd spent too much time among the humans.

He didn't know what he wanted anymore. His aid to Aikeem and company was impulsive and very unratlike. When the wizard pulled the kabosh off and saved his life he was dumbfounded. The wizard didn't have to do that.

Blitherskites didn't have many friends, and he cherished everyone he had. That's why he traveled so often to visit at the bar and grill with Sid and Boris. What the wizard had done was an undeniable act of friendship. There was no way he was going to let Aikeem be tortured by Darkness. He sighed. This was very unratlike behavior also.

Of course, he didn't have to leave the wizard the maps and, basically, tell the other side all of Darkness's plans either, but he liked Earth. For all their problems and squabbles, the humans had built up quite a nice realm, and he didn't want to see it destroyed because of three megalomaniacal leaders. He didn't give a damn about Dark Seer, Darkness, and the Sloths. He liked humans.

Now, here he was headed back to the gate between the worlds, ready to do Dark Seer's and ultimately Darkness's business. He frowned. It wasn't his fault. He made the deal with Farouk before he knew what was up, and he was honor-bound to complete the transaction.

"Hmmmmm," he mused to himself. Honor bound isn't a particularly common rat trait either. "What's happening to me?" he moaned. Several hundred years ago things were so much easier. Treachery, betrayal, intrigue, and black politics were all his modus operandi. Now he was acting like a priest of the One God.

He stopped before the rim of the pit that concealed the entrance to the gate. He plopped his two backpacks on the ground and sat to catch his breath. The trek across the Plains had been brutal. He'd left his toothy-run-a-lot at Sid's. He didn't want the creature running back to Darkness and betraying the location of the gate. He had to walk the remaining distance from Sid's to here with two backpacks. He was happy there were no toothy-jump-a-lots evident.

Deep in thought, he stared down into the pit. Soon he'd be back in New York, and he'd have to contact Farouk. He had a little over three weeks to see that the weapons were delivered to the invasion zone. He knew that was a short time, but he was also sure that Farouk could fulfill the order.

He was torn. He wasn't sure if Darkness and his mad armies could enslave all of mankind, but they certainly could muck things up really good. Mankind had forgotten about magic, and the evil troika's powers were great. In addition, there were all the guns that Blitherskites was providing them. Technology and magic together? Yes, they could definitely muck things up.

He tossed his old backpack into the pit and strapped on the one filled with diamonds. He hoped to the One God that Aikeem and company would escape and come up with a plan, for at this point, there was nothing else he could do. He expected that by the time all was said and done, he'd be alive either way, but at what cost?

Xaviar looked out over the parade field and was almost moved to tears. It was without a doubt the most awesome sight he'd ever seen. The Chitin soldiers were lined up in rows of ten each with a Sloth officer in front of every fifty. Twenty thousand cohorts stretched out into the distance before him.

The infinite sun of the Darkling Space broke through the clouds for the moment and splashed down upon his warriors. The bright yellow light glinted off the steel shod claws of the warrior insects, their spears, swords, and battleaxes. The view took his breath away.

Darkness had issued the mobilization order two days ago, and now they were prepared to march to the Desolation Plains. Darkness's warriors had cut a road to the Plains many years ago. They would take this path due south and then head west until they reached the spot on the map he'd been given.

Avalon, the bridge to earth and the domination of humanity! Mankind would come to learn the true nature of things in one bold move by Darkness's armies. It would take them a little under three weeks to make the trip. In a month Xavier expected to be enjoying the conquest of the real worlds.

***

Cragstein had short legs but he was relentless. After the first day of marching, Aikeem and Celise traveled in a daze of exhaustion. The cats rode in the backpack and only came out to keep watch while the company slept. These stops were few and far between. Cragstein was determined to make the trip in record time.

Thankfully the trek was fairly uneventful. At one point, a tribe of lumbering forest trolls paced them. The ugly, warty creatures always stayed at the edge of their senses waiting for an opportunity. When they finally stopped for a rest, Aikeem could hear them making preparations for an attack. He unloaded his shotgun in their general direction. From the screams induced by the buckshot, he correctly deduced that they wouldn't attempt to bother them again.

On occasion, Aikeem thought he also noticed a shadow pacing them. Twice he brought the company up short to inspect the forest. The company was on edge each time he did this, and they stretched their senses to no avail. Whatever it was, it was an entirely elusive creature.

After a weeklong, grueling march, they exited the black forests of the Darkling Space onto the grassy border of the Desolation Plains. Cragstein was very proud that they'd made such good time, but he was too exhausted to celebrate. The company set up camp at the edge of the forest with a huge rock at their backs and slept for a full day.

The next day Aikeem pulled out his camp equipment, and the company had its first hot meal in weeks. After cleaning their dinnerware in a nearby stream and returning everything to Aikeem's pack, they gathered around the wizard for his counsel.

Aikeem laid the map out in front of them. "Where are we on this map Cragstein?"

The dwarf fingered a point on the map with one gnarly, rock hard finger. Aikeem nodded. "So then it will be another week before Celise and I can reach the spot where Avalon will merge with this space.

"That would be my guess," Cragstein replied.

Snapper-Cat looked up from the map. "It will take Cragstein and me one day to reach the Dreamscape from here. It is a straight march."

Aikeem pointed at the cats who all sat next to Celise. "I want you to go as a group. You will all need to go into the Dreamscape to get to Wo'Em anyway. Your beasts will not be available to you until you enter that place."

"You mean Dark Seer's curse will go away!" Drusillia exclaimed.

Aikeem smiled. "Yes, lady. I've divined the nature of his curse, and its construction only allows it to hold power while you're in the Darkling Space. Once you cross into the Dreamscape, his spell will shatter and your powers will once again be available to you."

Gandabon sighed. "Thank the One God."

"Once on the Dreamscape, you'll need to split up and attend to your designated missions. Time is of the essence my friends. I would expect that Darkness's armies are already on the march. The lives of many innocents and the future course of mankind are in our hands."

Grim but determined expressions rounded the company. Aikeem folded up the map and returned it to his backpack. They broke camp and traveled to the edge where the tall grass of the Darkling Space met the dust of the Desolation Plains.

Dwarf and humans exchanged heartfelt handshakes. Pendella bounded up into Aikeem's arms. Aikeem kissed his lady on the head, and Pendella playfully batted his chin with a paw. They said nothing to each other, but Celise could see the concern in their eyes.

"Take good care of my human, Weaver. He's talented, but he's still just a man."

Celise smiled, and Aikeem grinned at Pendella's tease. "I will, Pendella, and you take care of yourself."

With that the company split. Aikeem and Celise marched off to the west while the cats and the dwarf headed due south. The infinite sun of the Darkling Space had no place to poke through on the Desolation Plains. The gray light that did filter through the ever-present clouds served to echo the mood of the two groups as they marched on to their fates.

***

Farouk screamed in Turkish into his cellular phone. "I don't care what they're charging for diesel! Pay it! I'll pick up the difference. I need you in Algiers now, and if you're not here in two days, then I'm getting someone else. This is a very lucrative contract, and if you don't believe me, call Captain Drakopulous and ask him what I'm paying."

Farouk jabbed the power button and cut off the Turkish Captain on the other end. He looked out across the parking lot of his warehouse to the dock beyond. Even now, forklifts were streaming across the blacktop like busy bugs.

Mr. Skites had delivered the first half of the payment two days ago. They'd gone over the delivery plans in detail the day before. Farouk was delivering the weapons in three separate shipments to various ports along America's East Coast. The bill of landing listed the relabeled crates as machinery. Indeed, some of the crates were dummies that held tractor parts.

Farouk's eyes just about leapt from their sockets when he saw all the diamonds. He'd contacted a gemologist from South Africa who he knew to be one of the best in the world. The man had been trained by the DeBeers' people. The jeweler was profoundly impressed by the clarity of the diamonds presented to him.

He had just delivered an estimate of the diamonds' wholesale value to Farouk. The arms dealer fingered the piece of paper in one pocket with a glowing smile. He wondered if Mr. Skites knew that he'd given Farouk enough to cover all of his costs for the entire shipment of weapons. The final payment would be entirely profit.

The ship's cranes lifted palettes of crates up over the hold. Farouk idly watched the process with a knowing smile. He wondered what army he was feeding in North America. He found the entire project very mysterious. He wondered if it was America's turn to experience some of the internal turmoil that so many other nations of the world had experienced. He smiled at that thought because it appealed to him.

***

Snapper-Cat carefully led Cragstein through the dream mists. It was obvious to the feline that the little man was uncomfortable in the Dreamscape. They'd parted company with the three feline council members only a few hours before. Cragstein wore his battleaxe across his back now. His gaze was constantly focused on the "ground." He'd never walked on clouds before, and he found the entire affair quite disconcerting.

"Where're we goin', cat? Can't see a blasted thing in this soup."

"We're going to see Chryssie, a friend of mine. He's been all over the Dreamscape and knows some of its stranger spots. I'm hoping he might have an idea of where your people might have ended up."

"Is it much farther?"

"A few hours earth time, and we'll be there."

Cragstein grunted in acknowledgement. He trudged on behind the feline and grumbled at the tenuous footing. He hoped to the Rock God that this wasn't all a wild dream chase. He wanted his people back. Dwarves got lonely too.

***

They spit out onto the Desolation Plains from the woods of the Darkling Space like a great gray plague. Thousands upon thousands of high rats lumbered out onto the grasses and began to form up into their associated regiments. Their black pennants marked with horrific standards flapped in the breeze as the rat officers whipped their troops into line.

The berserker rats of the Orders of Vile, Plague, and Murder formed the forward regiments. They were followed by twenty cohorts of archer rats from Lord Grim Seer's clans. In turn they were followed by the pestilence slinging, death rats of Lord Hell Giver. Pike rat regiments piled in behind them and so on until a great column fifty rats wide stretched across the plains.

Finally, Lord Dark Seer emerged from the woods on the back of a great horned war-lizard the size of an elephant. A throne had been fitted on the back of the beast so that Dark Seer could cast his cataclysmic spells from this perch.

Once in position, he pointed forward with one black claw, and the greatest rat army ever assembled set off to a place called Avalon.

***

Pendella bounded through the mists with the grace of a unicorn. She froze. The mists swirled behind her as she tried to penetrate the veil with a focused gaze. Nothing stirred there. She'd thought she spied a shadow out of her periphery again. She sat on her haunches and waited but nothing came.

She decided to put the time to good use, and she reached within herself to touch her beast. She purred. Her old friend was there and waiting. In her mind, she whispered the words of preparation. She would not be caught without her beast again. The runes of power danced around in her mind's eye as she drank from her personal well of energy. There was a sub-aural, interphasic click as her spell came together. Now her beast was available to her with a thought.

She turned and continued her trek through the dreamscape. She jumped up onto a misty tendril and bounded into a sea of milky white stars. A comet burst into fragments as it always did in this spot, and she swam through its creamy pale tail. She came to the apex of a quasar and dove into the crux of the biscuit. At the bottom of the crux was an immaculately clean kitchen, and on the kitchen counter there was a hotdog that was plugged into a wall socket. She sniffed it three times and meowed the syllable of power.

An interphasic portal morphed into existence next to the toaster, and Pendella strolled through it. Just as she was about to walk through the wall back into the real worlds, she felt something jump over her. She caught an orange flash precede her through the wall.

She stopped on the other side of the wall. She was in a corridor in the Mercy Love Nursing home where Celise's physical body was cared for. Pendella sniffed the air and she definitely smelled another cat; however, there were no felines in evidence. Something, however, had definitely come through the portal with her. She found this very strange. Why wouldn't this cat simply ask her for assistance, and why would it be so secretive? At least it could have said thank you. This behavior was rude and unbecoming.

She shrugged and made her way to Celise's room. Along the way, she had to dodge behind a few carts and wheelchairs to avoid being spotted by any of the humans. She didn't have time for their affections.

"Posh!" She looked up at the tall wooden door that closed off Celise's room. Humans were always locking things. She hated that. Pendella pushed the door with her head. This typically didn't work, but it would if the lock was loose.

The door opened to her delight and Pendella slid into the room. She jumped up onto the bed and exclaimed, "Oh, my!"

Celise was gone! She sniffed about the bed and realized that the Weaver had been gone for some time. This was terrible! What to do? She knew Aikeem would be crushed. Celise wouldn't be overly thrilled either. Aikeem's spell was supposed to protect the body while Celise's spirit was away, but it looked like it had failed. Pendella prayed that some evil spirit hadn't gotten hold of it. Evil spirits were a devil to get rid of. They were worse than fleas.

Pendella sighed and jumped off the bed. She decided the best course of action was to return to Wo'Em to help assemble the feline armies. She'd figure out what to do about Aikeem and Celise there. Pendella strolled over to the rear wall of the room and meowed the syllable of power. The wall became translucent and immaterial. She stepped through the portal and once again someone or something jumped over her in a flash of orange.

This was most intolerable! You just did not go jumping through someone else's portal without so much as a how do you do! She hunkered down into a crouch on the other side of the portal. The mists of the Dreamscape slid about her as she tried to penetrate the immaterial haze. Her heart froze.

His eyes glowed red from powerful internal energies as he stared at her. His breath was deep, bass, and caused the mists to curl about his muzzle. He said nothing as he stared.

Pendella was at a loss. The portal behind her had closed, and she doubted if she could out run this one. Her beast was available to her with a thought, but this one had killed Sharpclaw. Could she defeat such an enemy?

Legacy's low, bass voice rumbled over Pendella. "You betrayed me."

Pendella was confounded by this remark. The red glow dissipated from the black beast's eyes, eyes that stirred something in Pendella. She was haunted by a feeling of familiarity. "I'm sure I don't know what you're talking about. I've never betrayed anyone in my life."

"My human is dead because of you. I was banished to the Outlands and then the Darkling Space for eons. Why did you betray me, Pendella Purrfect? I loved you more than life itself."

Pendella's heart was in turmoil as Legacy morphed out of his beast and into the beautiful orange cat he truly was.

"Thomas Wondermore!" Tears welled up in Pendella's eyes, and she ran over to her once upon a time lover.

Thomas recoiled from his old mate, which stung Pendella to the core. "Why did you betray me, Pendella Purrfect? Do you have any idea how long I've been banished to these dark places? My heart was broken twice! Once by your betrayal and once by the death of Shakar!"

Pendella frowned. "Thomas Wondermore! I could no more betray you than cut off my own paws. Lord Skaaaa was the betrayer. He tricked me into thinking he was helping me when all he really wanted was revenge on Shakar."

Thomas dived into the well of Pendella's eyes in an effort to divine the truth. His heart was overwhelmed with the realization that she spoke the truth. He could not move or speak. He began to shake with agitation. He had blamed her for so long. He had hated what she had done, or thought she had done, but he could never stop loving her and now!

Pendella could see the acute pain in his eyes. Her heart ached for her former mate. "Tell me what happened to you, Thomas."

Thomas calmed a tad and solemnly told his tale. "We fell into a chamber filled with the once men of Lampor. At one time they may have been human, but they had devolved into semi-intelligent beasts that worshipped nameless horrific gods. There were several wizards among them who were capable and still possessed intelligence. They were the ones that seduced Shakar.

"When we landed on the other side of the mirror, the beasts sought to rend us apart. Lord Skaaaa was grabbed by a dozen of them and ripped to shreds. Ironically, this shielded Shakar from certain death. Before Shakar could be torn apart, the wizards intervened and drove the beast men back. I managed to escape early on by darting through their feet.

"The black wizards took my wounded Shakar deep into their stone fortress and threw him into a prison at the very base of that place. When they left, I went to my man. I squeezed through the iron bars and leapt into his arms. He hugged me for a very long time, and I licked his face. He was broken and bloodied from the rough treatment of the beast men.

"Shakar confessed to me what he had been up to. He told me how these vile wizards had seduced him and made him their thrall. In the end, he was his own man. He placed me gently before him and apologized to me for dragging me into this hell. He had some magic left and he gave it to me. He spent his last hours on earth weaving a spell of great power. When he was done with his preparations, he cast his last spell on me and I was given a great beast.

"He told me that I was all he had left in the world, and that I should no longer be called Pumba. I was his legacy and, as such, that would become my name. Then he lay down and died. I sat by his side for a very long time and wept. My world had been rent apart by a cruel fate.

"After a while, wearing my beast, I moved to the back of the cell and waited. The vile wizards of Lampor eventually returned to the prison. I suppose they planned to torture Shakar for his failure. They did not see me in the dark at the rear of the cell. When they opened the door to dispose of Shakar, I rejoiced in their screams of terror and pain as I tore them apart.

"I made them all pay, Pendella. I spent what must have been hundreds of years hunting down every last vile creature of Lampor. They are now extinct.

"Revenge is a funny thing. During its execution I was driven and focused, but when the task was done, I was left feeling hollow. What should I do? What was my purpose? I roamed the Outlands for a good long time after that. I hunted and learned to survive. There were many times when I almost did not make it, but Shakar had made my beast well.

"After a time I came to the Great Divide that separates the Outlands from the Darkling Space. It is a strange place of twisted perspective, skewed time, floating mountains, and unpredictable energies. I'm told only a few have ever crossed it. I was one of them.

"I hunted the Darkling Space for millennia and made a name for myself in the northern reaches. Very recently I chanced upon Darkness. He was beset by a pack of Orcs who had a taste for humans. I dislike Orcs. Darkness took me to his side out of gratitude for rescuing him. He told me of his plans to return to Earth and make it his. The thought of returning to Earth appealed to me, and so I have assisted him in this task."

Pendella sat on her haunches amazed by Thomas's exploits. "Truly you are a feline beyond measure."

Thomas smiled. "Not in your presence, lady"

Pendella smiled, but then the smile faded. "You killed Sharpclaw O'Bannon, Thomas. Why?"

Thomas shrugged. "Darkness ordered it. I didn't even know he was a feline until recently, although that wouldn't have made a difference."

Pendella was taken aback. "Don't be shocked, Pendella. I have been Legacy for a very long time. This form you see me in now, I have not worn it since Shakar changed me. I am my beast. I have hunted and killed for millennia. Sharpclaw was a challenge for me, and challenges are something I live for."

"He was a member of the Feline Council of Thirteen. You have killed one of your own," Pendella grimly pointed out.

Thomas shrugged again. "What is done is done. I did not know."

Pendella remained silent for a few seconds. "What will you do now?"

Thomas's eyes glowed red for a second, and Pendella stepped back as he morphed into Legacy. "I do not know, lady. Recently, all I wanted was to return to Earth and my beloved jungle. Darkness requires power, but I have no use for such human obsessions. You have shown me how to return to Earth via the Dreamscape, and I no longer need Darkness's assistance."

"We need your help, Thomas. Darkness plans to ruin the earth."

"Darkness plans to ruin the human earth. He will leave my realms alone."

Pendella was desperate. "You don't know what the humans are capable of, Thomas. They will do anything to protect their realm. Any battle on earth will cause massive destruction."

Thomas shrugged. "I'm told time heals all wounds." Thomas looked deep into Pendella's eyes. "I'm still working on mine."

Legacy turned and slipped into the mist. "We shall meet again, lady. I need time to think."

Pendella watched as her ex-lover disappeared into the mists. Her heart was drowned in a sea of mixed emotions. She bounded off to Wo'Em and prayed that Thomas's heart had not gone stone cold over the millennia.

***

Cragstein screamed in absolute terror. He hung onto Snapper-Cat's tail for dear life as the crazed feline negotiated a hyperactive asteroid field. A star exploded nearby, and Cragstein's scream went into the soprano range.

Snapper-Cat landed on a floating mountain out of frustration. "Will you hush Cragstein? You're splitting my ears!"

Cragstein grabbed his heart and flopped down on the rock. "We're in the middle of a flying mountain fight! Worlds are exploding! You're taking me through the very heart of creation as it rips about us!"

"I told you Cragstein, it's random dream stuff. As long as you hold on to my tail, which you're crushing by the way, you'll be all right."

Cragstein loosened his grip on Snapper-Cat's tail and sighed. "How much farther do we have to go until we see this friend o' yours?"

"He's not far from here. He's just over that solar system," Snapper-Cat pointed with one paw.

Cragstein followed his gesture and swallowed down his fear. "Well, let's get it over with before me heart stops."

Snapper-Cat jumped, and Cragstein managed to hold on and keep his mouth shut. They jumped over the solar system and landed on a salt flat beyond the celestial playground. On the other side of the planetary system, the dream mists began to coalesce again.

Cragstein let go of the cat's tail and attempted to regain his composure. "I tell ya mate, I'd rather go toe to toe with a fire breathin' dragon than take that trip again."

Snapper-Cat grinned. "I hope we don't have to go back that way."

Cragstein grumbled and then said, "So do you think this friend of yours will know where my people are?"

"He may give us a clue. He likes the out-of-the-way places on the Dreamscape. He's told me stories of semi-material places that form out of the backwashes of chaos."

"And that would be one o' the places where my people could be?"

"That's what I'm thinking. My friend likes to talk, and he has a tendency to ramble, so be patient. Try not to make any disparaging remarks about the Dreamscape either. He's very sensitive to them," Snapper-Cat replied.

"Why's that?"

"He wasn't born like you or I. He's a figment of some human mathematician's imagination. Sometimes on the Dreamscape, when an idea is so profound or shared by so many, it becomes semi-material. Chryssie's a figment that's come to life."

"Bloody hell," Cragstein mumbled. "We're gettin' advice from an escapee from the dream factory."

Snapper-Cat ignored the remark and led on. The ground they were walking on began to change into a greener, lusher environment. It reminded Cragstein of some of the fairy woods he'd visited a very long time ago on Earth before the Purge. They walked into a wood that was sparsely populated with oaks. Flowers littered the forest floor and man-sized mushrooms grew here and there.

Snapper-Cat stopped before a low, couch-sized mushroom. Sitting on top of it was a hookah smoking character. "Hello, Chryssie!"

The prodigious caterpillar looked down at the pair and pulled the pipe stem from his thick green lips. "Snapper-Cat! How delightful! We've not had a chat in quite a while. And who is your diminutive friend?"

Cragstein wasn't too astounded by the oversized insect. He'd seen many strange things over his long life.

Snapper-Cat introduced the dwarf. "This is Cragstein Muddleboot. He's got some questions for you, if you don't mind."

The caterpillar took a long drag off of his pipe. "Well, then, you've certainly come to the right place. What is it you seek to know?"

"We're looking for me people," Cragstein blurted out.

The caterpillar gave the dwarf a long droll look. "On the Dreamscape?"

"They were eaten by Sloths in this realm, and we think they may have been shunted into a sub-material dream continuum," Snapper-Cat opined.

"Hmmmmm," the caterpillar pondered. "That could very well be. I've seen such things before."

"You have!" Cragstein was hopeful.

"Oh, yes. There was a most disagreeable dream dragon who ate many an unsuspecting dream walker. But those who survived the initial fright of being consumed whole by this lascivious lizard were pleased to find themselves deposited intact on a giant lily pad not far from here. Eventually, all of the victims banded together, and they tricked the dragon into flying into a black hole. You are familiar with black holes? They're quite interesting mathematically and not very hospitable with all that gravity and all."

Cragstein shrugged. "Heard 'bout 'em. So, you seen a city's worth of dwarves hangin' about?"

The caterpillar took another puff off his pipe. "Actually, I've been across many centebueles of the Dreamscape. A centebuele is a hundred times longer than an idgit by the way. I'm particularly fond of strapping on my seventy-five pairs of roller-blades and meandering about this realm. I find it relaxing."

"And?" Cragstein was becoming impatient.

"Indeed, on my travels I have been in the dreams of many humans. Because of this I have a unique perspective on their awkward state of mind. I remember one human in particular with whom I used to have many conversations. He claimed to be a master of dream analysis, and we discussed the issue at length. He never did mention me in his book. I was quite disappointed. He kept trying to get me to switch from my hookah to his brand of cigars. I pointed out to him that I was smoking an original, antique Turkish hookah with the most flavorful tobacco available. I mean really! I told him flat out that a cigar is just a cigar... most of the time."

"By the sacred layers of rock, 'pillar! What about me people?"

Chryssie smiled at the dwarf's impatience. "An interesting turn of phrase that. I heard it on occasion near the border of Neverwhen and Everalways. These are places where humans seldom dream."

"You heard someone say 'by the sacred layers of rock'?"

"Actually, I believe he said in a voice very similar to yours, 'By the sacred layers of rock today is my day.' Why any day should be more his day than any other is beyond me."

"Where worm? Where?"

Snapper-Cat was aghast. Chryssie's expression turned black. and he leaned down into the dwarf's face. "Worms don't have legs. Worms are a dreadful reddish-brown color and somewhat slimy. I am a beautiful jade green and have exactly one hundred legs. Having said that, do *not* confuse me with a centipede."

The sheepish dwarf backed away. "Sorry, mate. Me tongue got away from me."

"You may ask what kind of caterpillar has exactly one hundred legs? A superior kind is my reply."

Cragstein was fairly bursting at the seams. "Obviously, mate. Now, about the dwarves."

Chryssie smiled, having had his ego appeased. "I was skating on the border of Neverwhen and Everalways. A stone Chumawok sings an everlasting ballad there in three-part harmony. It's quite nice. There is a pit near the Chumawok that is lined with some kind of metal. It was from the depths of that pit that I heard the phrase of which we spoke."

"I know where that is," Snapper-Cat stated. "Thanks Chryssie!"

With that Cragstein grabbed the feline's tail, and the cat leapt to the sky. In a wink they were gone.

Chryssie sighed, "Everyone's always in such a hurry. I didn't even get to tell them about that poor lost Ogre I ran into. Nice fellow really."

Chryssie plopped the stem of the pipe back in his mouth and returned to the mathematical puzzle he was working out in his head.

***

It took Aikeem and Celise exactly a week to make it to a spot just a half mile from where Avalon would appear. Their trek was mostly uneventful, except for a run in with a six pack of toothy-jump-a-lots. Out on the open plains, the two of them found the jumpies much easier to deal with. Aikeem blasted the lot to bits with his shotgun before they were within thirty feet.

They picked a rocky area to make camp. A small cliff formed a wall at their back, and several boulders offered a semicircle of protection. Their first night alone, the couple took the opportunity to reaffirm their relationship and make the passionate love of lovers long separated.

The next day, a reenergized Aikeem adopted the lotus position and inspected the nature of the battle spells he'd been holding for so long. They'd begun to unravel a little at the edges, but he tweaked and poked until they were of a quality that he was satisfied with.

"What are you doing, lover?"

Celise drew on a pair of black jeans as she watched Aikeem. The wizard blinked as he came back from within himself. "I was attending to the battle spells I've been holding. They're very deadly and require maintenance when not being used."

Celise looked confused. "I don't understand such things. How many spells must you maintain?"

"I've four battle spells waiting in the wings, and I just wove a minor one for Pendella."

Celise was surprised. "Five! So many?"

Aikeem jumped from his sitting position, and lofted his ladylove into the air. As she began to laugh, he said, "You are a dear! What a profound love!"

Aikeem gathered his beauty in his arms, and they delved into a heartfelt kiss.

They parted and Celise returned to dressing herself. Aikeem turned to the camp stove and began to fix himself a cup of tea. Celise buttoned up her white silk blouse and idly strolled over to the boulders that protected their camp. She looked quizzically out over the horizon.

"Aikeem?"

"Yes, my love?"

Celise pointed to a dust cloud that had formed on the horizon. "What's that?"

Aikeem followed his ladylove's gesture. He opened his magical backpack, reached inside, and withdrew a pair of binoculars. He strolled over next to his lady and nonchalantly looked out over the Plains.

"By the One God!"

Aikeem dashed back to his backpack and opened it wide. "Pleep! Get the fifty caliber, and forget the tripod! We don't have time."

"What is it, love?"

Aikeem dove into the backpack up to his armpit and came up with a bandoleer full of shotgun shells. He threw it to Celise. "Gut-Taker and at least fifty snakemen. You can guess why they're trotting to our position!"

Celise's eyes went wide. She strapped on the bandoleer and snatched the shotgun out of the air that Aikeem threw to her. She pumped a round into the chamber as the wizard began to pull a fifty-caliber machine gun out of his backpack. He grunted with the weight of it.

"I'm surprised that bag is so light," an amazed Celise observed.

Aikeem plopped the gun next to the bag and reached back in. "It is a container of infinite space and mass, my love. It doesn't weigh a thing until Pendella gets into it, for some strange reason." .

A squeaky gravel filled voiced echoed out of the bag. "Quarter infinite! You were too cheap to get a whole infinite."

Aikeem plopped a canister of ammo next to his weapon and then peered into the bag. "Whatever. Get me another canister."

"Please."

"Please! Please hurry!"

Aikeem pointed to an outcropping of rock to one side of the cliff. "Celise, take a position up there."

Celise frowned. "Aikeem, if you're trying to protect me, I—"

"Lady, pleeeeassseeee. We need to set up a cross fire and from that elevated perch, you can pick them off."

"Oh."

"Remember, you'll only have an effective maximum range of twenty yards at best, so wait until they come in."

Celise ran off to take her position. "Yes, dear."

The backpack wiggled, and Aikeem reached in to withdraw another canister of ammo. He rushed to set up his weapon between two boulders. He yelped when he looked up and saw the monsters only a half-mile away.

"Please don't jam. Please don't jam. Please don't jam," Aikeem muttered to himself as he fed the belt into the receiver.

Aikeem slammed the metal cover down over the belt, snapped back the bolt, let it go, and open fired at the approaching snakemen. They were only fifty yards away when Aikeem began to rake them with his weapon. The snakemen had never been subjected to a firefight before, and they weren't too smart about it. Snakemen bits sprayed about the Plains as Aikeem mercilessly tore them apart.

Gut-Taker's great lizard mount screamed in anger at the sound of the machine gun as the rat assassin drove it to a run. Aikeem took aim and blew the beast's head from its long neck. The reptile crashed to the ground and launched Gut-Taker into the dirt. Dust, gun smoke and dirt began to fill the air, and the targets became harder to acquire. A dozen snakemen made it to within twenty yards of Aikeem's position. They were certain to breach the boulder wall.

Celise opened fire and took out the first six with a blistering fusillade of buckshot. Aikeem turned his weapon on the remaining six and tore them to bits.

The last of the ammo belt finished off to the sound of the metallic links clinking off the boulders.

Aikeem sighed when he saw the last snakeman fall. He turned to give Celise the thumbs up when Gut-Taker came over the wall. The assassin rat jumped the wizard and they both tumbled over backwards. Aikeem kicked the killer rodent off and dove for his blade Moonwind, which lay next to his backpack. In one fluid movement he rolled over his blade, snatched it, and drew it from its scabbard.

Gut-Taker held two serrated, curved, short swords in his top two hands and a pair of long dirks in the bottom pair. Aikeem held the tip of Moonwind before him at the ready as the assassin sneered, "I've been dreaming of this moment, Wizard. You've caused me a great deal of trouble, and I shall make you pay slowly. Come. Learn why they call me Gut-Taker."

The rat leapt high and came down with a four-way slash across Aikeem's body. Aikeem parried the swords as he jumped back, but he felt the dirks rip the cloth of his shirt. Gut-Taker's attack was fearless and quick. Aikeem parried furiously, but the dirks drew blood more than once. Dark Seer's assassin drove Aikeem back until he was against a boulder.

Gut-Taker raised his two blades high over his head but protected his midsection with the dirks. "Now you die."

Gut-Taker sprouted a steel blade from his chest as Celise leaned from behind him to whisper in his ear. "That's *MY* man you're assaulting, rat. I am the Weaver. Feel my sting."

Gut-Taker's eyes rolled back into his head as his heart stopped. A dumbfounded Aikeem watched as the dead assassin slid off Celise's rapier onto the ground in a spray of blood. "Well said, lady! Very dramatic!"

Celise swept the air with her blade and bowed. "Thank you, sir. I've always felt one should dispatch her enemies with an appropriate word or two."

The two exchanged a smile, an embrace, and a heated kiss.

They parted and Celise looked around at their handiwork. "Let's hope the battle with the rest of Darkness's armies goes as well."

Aikeem followed her gaze. "True words, dearest, true words."

***

Derrick took the reading from one of his remote monitors and nearly shouted out loud. The phenomenon, as he had come to call it, was still getting stronger and affecting an area much bigger than he ever dreamed possible. He placed the monitor back in the ground and headed back toward his camp.

He never thought he'd be in this place three weeks. His supervisor nearly flipped when he asked for the extra time. When he wouldn't give it to him, he took it as vacation time. This was a once in a lifetime experience, and he wanted all of the credit. He would be in all of the big periodicals: Science, Nature, and The Smithsonian.

After he inspected his meter that first day and discovered it was working properly, he started taking more measurements. At first, he was scared because the radiation jumped to levels that should have killed him. But the birds still sang, and the crickets still chirped. The only logical conclusion was that this area was being subjected to a form of energy that hadn't been discovered yet. Whatever it was, it mimicked some of the properties of gamma radiation but not its deadly consequences.

For the past three days, the meters had been going off the scale. He'd kept very exact notes and had decided it was about time to bring the press in. This was getting too big to keep to himself, and he already felt a little bit irresponsible.

He stopped at the edge of his campsite in shock. Four Middle Eastern looking guys were tearing apart his encampment. "Hey! What the hell are you doing?"

His arms shot up in the air when four MP5 submachine guns were pointed in his direction. He couldn't speak. The dark, hairy men ran over to him and frisked him. The largest of the four inspected his wallet and became alarmed when he found Derrick's Federal ID. He yelled over the campsite to a man who was standing by an eighteen-wheeler.

Derrick was shocked. A line of trucks stretched out of sight down the road. Where had they come from? The man by the truck placed a cell phone to his ear and barked something in a foreign language. They waited until a Mercedes limo negotiated the dirt road and drove up between the trucks.

A dark little man with a bushy mustache and short-cropped, coal black hair wearing a purple fez walked up. He took the ID from his larger subordinate and read it. He began to laugh out loud.

He held Derrick's ID up in the air and yelled to his men. "EPA!"

They all began to laugh uproariously as Farouk turned to a sheepish Derrick. "You are in the right organization my friend. Had you been an agent for the FBI or CIA, you would be dead right now."

Derrick began to sweat at the d-word. "I'm very happy with my career choice."

Farouk smiled. "And so you should be. There is far too much pollution in the world. Now what are you doing here?"

"Observing an interesting radiometric phenomenon."

Farouk yawned. "How scientific. Well, my friend, your observations are over. You will wait with us until our shipment is delivered, and then you may go free. You have no idea how lucky you are. My peers would bury you in these woods, but I'm a family man, or will be anyway."

"Shipment of what?"

Farouk studied the inquisitive young man and smiled. "Maybe I will tell you later, but for now, let us share some coffee."

Farouk clapped his hands and barked some orders at his men. Three of them ran toward the Mercedes. The rest of the men began unloading crates that were marked "machine parts" in different languages.

Farouk took a seat in one of the chairs that Derrick had set up around the campfire. The little man motioned Derrick to come sit on a nearby log. Soon a coffee set was brought over to the two men, and a servant began fixing them some very aromatic java. Derrick wondered if things could get any stranger.

***

Jackenstein fingered his cards with profound affection. The hand of a lifetime stared back at him. Four aces and a ten high smiled at him like an expectant lover. The beauty of it was, his partners must have all felt the same way about their cards. A pile of gems had accumulated in the center of the table that would have made a king jealous. Forty dwarves surrounded the foursome and looked on in awe. Never in the history of the game had a stake this large been played.

It was Jackenstein's turn, and he threw in his last ruby. He smiled with knowing anticipation and said the word as though it was the key to an epiphany. "Call!"

The pile of gems exploded in front of them, and the dwarves screamed in fury. A rugged looking dwarf with an ax strapped across his back and a cat slung across his shoulders dropped into the center of the table scattering the gems and cards everywhere.

Jackenstein looked in abject horror at the backside of this perverse interloper and screamed. "By the sacred layers of rock, dwarf! You scattered me pot to the winds."

The cat jumped off the dwarf's back, and the little man whirled around. Jackenstein's face went white when he saw the face of his long lost brother. "Cragstein?"

"Brother!" Cragstein jumped off the table and dove on his younger—only by a hundred years—brother. Jackenstein's cards flew away in chaos, but he didn't care. The two rolled over in a bear hug that ended up against the alloy wall of the Throat.

The two parted, and Jackenstein fairly yelled, "By the Rock Gods, Cragstein what are you doing here? Where've you been?"

A beaming Cragstein stood up and dragged his brother with him. He pointed to a spot twelve feet above the table. A knotted cable dangled. "I've come to rescue you all!"

The dwarves looked up in disbelief at something they'd all been waiting for for thousands of years. They were shocked into silence. Cragstein frowned when he saw the ruined poker game. "I'm sorry I wrecked your game, brother, but I was at the end of me rope."

The dwarves burst out in cheers and grabbed Cragstein and threw him onto their shoulders. They carried him down deeper into the gullet to their city of Mingle. Dwarves had a new hero to celebrate. Snapper-Cat managed to keep from getting stepped on. He hoped the celebration wouldn't go on too long. They had a war to fight.

***

Aikeem and Celise stood atop a rock outcropping that towered above the plains. A stiff breeze blew their long coats behind them. They seemed like the harlequin pair with Aikeem in his black coat and Celise in a long white duster. The mists of the Dreamscape roiled off to their left, while the rest of their view was filled with the Desolation Plains.

The awestruck pair stared at the vista. The dead lands glowed an ethereal blue. Thousands of dust devils sprang up and danced a brownish ballet. A dark layer of clouds formed up over the spinning winds, and lightning leapt from the busy sky to the ground.

A bass note rumbled across the Plains. The rock they stood upon vibrated ominously. Lush Avalon rose from beneath the plains and began to morph at the same time. A bright light snapped from the mountaintops that thrust through the plains, and the dark clouds scattered. A great wind blew across the dead grass, and the pair shielded their eyes as a gigantic cloud of dust and debris blew past them.

The rumbling ceased, and they were almost moved to tears at the sight of such a beautiful, green place. Even from this distance, they could see clear, running streams, sylvan glades, and crystal blue lakes. The infinite sun bathed this place in a glorious bright light.

Aikeem gathered up his backpack and took Celise by the hand. The pair climbed down from their perch and began the short trek to this place of wonder. Aikeem was saddened by the thought that such a place of beauty should be used as a battlefield. For that he would make Darkness pay.

***

Farouk took a drag from his cigarette and smiled. He was stretched out on a chaise-lounge next to Derrick. Thousands of wooden crates were littered about. Some were stacked thirty feet high and still the eighteen-wheelers came. Farouk's men were as busy as army ants unloading the deadly cargo.

Derrick sat in his camp chair and listened as the weapons dealer continued his bragging. "Of course, the most difficult part of the entire operation was infiltrating the American border. Your blasted spy satellites have made my occupation so much more difficult. They say this Y2K bug, whatever that is, will knock them out of the sky. I hope it is true. But I am clever and can work around even these annoyances. I have several dummy vessels that matched the courses of my other ships. When they put into port, the local authorities found the wrong ships, and of course, they were either empty or carrying cargo other than what was expected."

Derrick nodded, pretending to be interested. He really didn't give a damn what the little rat was saying. All he wanted to know was whether he was going to be shot or let go. He didn't like the fact that Farouk was telling him all of his plans. Dead men tell no tales.

"Once the inventory was unloaded at various ports, it was transported along very circuitous routes all over North America. Half the shipment went into Canada and then back down into Amer—"

Farouk's eyes bugged out of his head. Derrick turned in the direction he was looking and slowly stood in awe. The men about the camp froze in amazement. Some dropped to their knees and began to pray in a foreign tongue. The entire atmosphere above the valley before them began to glow an ethereal blue. Dark clouds formed and lightning began to dance from the sky to the ground.

A bass rumble echoed out of the valley, and the ground beneath their feet began to vibrate. Derrick smiled with the realization that the phenomenon had reached its climax. Avalon morphed from below and merged with the Maine forest. A great wind rushed through the valley. The mountaintops that pushed up through the earth sparked with a great white light and the clouds above blew away.

The sun splashed the dream place with its golden light as it completed its rise. The assembled company looked on Avalon with profound wonder. They knew what they had just seen was impossible; yet, they had witnessed it.

"I don't think Monsieur Skites gave me all of the details," Farouk observed. He was beginning to become nervous about the nature of the army he would be supplying.

***

Ten thousand snakemen loped into position at the rear of a column that stretched into the horizon. Darkness flew overhead on the back of the great war dragon Gaums. A massive wood and leather saddle was fitted between the beast's wings and forearms. Darkness sat there wrapped in a black cowled cloak, grinning at the massive army that stretched out before him.

Gaums lazily soared over the snakemen and was joined by two more battle dragons, one red and one blue. Darkness mumbled a spell. The dark wizard held out his hands and finished conjuring. Two transparent globes formed above his open palms and continued to float there when he removed his hands. Lord Dark Seer's image reflected in one globe, while Xavier's reflected in the other.

"Xaviar, has Avalon risen as promised?"

The Sloth beamed. "Of course. The Chitin armies are ready to advance."

Darkness pointed at Dark Seer. "Let Lord Dark Seer's scouts precede you. We want to make sure there is no opposition waiting for us. At the very least, we've a payment to make on some weapons."

Dark Seer smiled and hissed, "I shall see to it immediately."

Darkness turned back to Xaviar and asked, "Have you cast your spell of transference?"

Xavier smiled. "Yes, I am drained but we are safe now. The danger of existing in one realm as two physical beings is no more. As soon as my sloths step into the real worlds, our physical bodies that sleep in the jungle will instantly transfer and merge at the insertion point."

Darkness grinned. "Good. Give the scouts a two hour head start, and then begin the march through Avalon to Earth."

Xavier nodded. "It shall be done."

Darkness waved a hand, and the two Generals disappeared from within the orbs. He looked out over his armies and glowed with the feeling of absolute power.

***

They raced through the mists of the Dreamscape like a vast ocean of fur. The warriors of the feline army were of every color and configuration imaginable. A quarter of a million cats bounded into Avalon. Of these, almost 60,000 wore their beasts. These fantastic mythic creatures of power led the feline's charge through the mists.

They flew no pennants or flags. They bore no weapons. They sang no songs nor beat any drums. They simply ran on in deadly silence to a war that would shape the universe.

Aikeem stood atop a grassy knoll and looked through his binoculars down at a stretch of Avalon that he had come to call the channel. It was a broad grassy plain that meandered between two columns of low hills. He was positive that this would be the place where Darkness's armies would come through. It was the only path that was large enough to accommodate the number of soldiers Darkness had amassed.

Celise touched her lover's shoulder and pointed in the other direction. He smiled at the glorious sight. From the dream mists far off in the distance, there came a sea of cats. They came out of the mists the size of a man or bigger. Aikeem knew no human had ever witnessed such a sight.

He'd set up a foldable table on the knoll behind a single, large oak that was surrounded by shoulder high bushes. The maps of Avalon were spread out on the table along with a number of firearms that Aikeem had taken from his backpack. Aikeem had also set up his fifty-caliber machine gun and several boxes of ammunition behind the bush.

A gray monster cat the size of a small horse led a dozen felines up the hill. The gray creature's eyes burned blood red with internal energies. The forward half of its body was covered in feathers while the rear half was scaled. It reminded Aikeem of a griffin variant. A black and white striped beast, which was a bit shorter and bore long wicked saber teeth, walked next to the gray monster. On the striped one's back rode Pendella Purrfect. They stopped before Aikeem.

"Hello, lover. I've brought some friends with me."

Aikeem smiled and pointed at Pendella's escort. "I see, and who wears these beasts?"

The gray monster boomed. "It's Gandabon, wizard."

"And Drusillia," the striped creature added.

Aikeem noticed that the jewel he gave Pendella to use in the retrieval of Celise's body was gone, but no body was apparent. "Where's Celise's body, Pendella?"

Pendella hesitated. She wanted to tell her man the truth, but his attention to the coming battle was of utmost importance. So she did something she almost never did; she lied. "I left it at Wo'Em under the protection of Grizzle-Whiskers. I felt it would be safe there until the battle was over."

"Grizzle-Whiskers wants you to direct the battle, wizard. We cats are fearsome warriors in single combat, but the strategies of massive battles are beyond us," Gandabon said.

Aikeem looked up into the air and watched several hundred feline avian transmorphs soar about the heavens. "Why is Grizzle-Whiskers not here with his army?"

Drusillia spoke up. "He sees to the security of Wo'Em, just in case this is a diversion. He will join us shortly."

Aikeem looked back into his binoculars to check the channel once again. "I doubt very much that this is a diversion, but he's probably being prudent."

"What are your orders?" Gandabon demanded.

Aikeem pointed to the low hills opposite him. "Split your army in half. Hide one half behind those hills," Aikeem directed as he pointed to the hills that stretched along the knoll he stood upon, "and hide the other half behind these hills. Have the fliers come down from the skies, too. Darkness is sure to send scouts through here, and we must catch them by surprise. There must be no hint of our presence."

Drusillia shouted, "Let's get to it!"

The two beasts took their brethren down the hill and spread the orders among the army. Pendella stayed by Aikeem's side. The wizard turned to Celise. "It is time, beloved. Snatch as many as you can but please be careful."

The two clutched each other in a soul-sharing embrace. They kissed and parted silently. Celise headed down the knoll to the dream mists in the distance.

"Where's she going?"

Aikeem turned to Pendella. "To the Dreamscape. Darkness's armies must pass very close to it. She's going to attempt to extend the Dreamscape and suck some of them in. It is within her power to drop them into some terrible nightmare from there."

Aikeem was more than a little worried as he watched his ladylove go.

"Have faith, Aikeem. She can take care of herself. You must attend to the matter at hand," Pendella directed.

Aikeem sighed; he knew his lady was right. After an hour, the skies and ground were cleared of felines of any form. Once the field was clear, Aikeem met with the ten members of the Council of Thirteen that were available to him. He gave them their orders, and they raced off to manage their particular segments of the feline army. Pendella remained at Aikeem's side.

A short time later, Aikeem squatted down below the bushes and pried them apart with his hands. Several hundred lizards that reminded him of a cross between an ostrich and a toothy-jump-a-lot raced by in the small valley below. Each lizard wore a saddle that held a man-sized rat.

Aikeem watched them go by and whispered to Pendella, "One of them carries a backpack. It's the same rat that escorted us to Darkness Castle."

Pendella spit. "That must be payment for Blitherskites."

Aikeem chuckled. "He deserves it, lady. He may have saved earth."

Pendella begrudgingly swallowed her anger. Aikeem turned to her. "Go and tell Gandabon to send a contingent after them. Let them cross over to the real worlds, but don't let them make it back into Avalon."

"Won't that make Darkness suspicious?"

Aikeem returned to his binoculars. "He's already committed. Those scouts are only being sent in for reconnaissance. If the fury of God were on the other side of Avalon he would still attack."

"The fury of God is in Avalon, lover," and with that Pendella slunk down the hill to deliver the orders Aikeem had given her.

***

Derrick, Farouk, and his men watched the phenomenon for a couple of hours before they returned to what they were doing. Derrick was going absolutely nuts in that he wasn't being allowed to record this event or alert the media. Farouk had a deal to close and that was that.

Farouk had returned to his chaise-lounge and was sipping yet another cup of coffee. Derrick couldn't contain himself anymore. "Please, Mr. Farouk, at least just let me videotape the valley!"

Farouk waved off Derrick. "No, no, no. Not until my business is concluded here, and I am far away. I will not risk upsetting my contact, whomever he may be. I know this is a very strange thing, but I'm sure it's something Mr. Skites was expecting."

Derrick was crestfallen. "I can't believe that he would mind if—"

Derrick's eyes popped out of his head. A man-sized rat rode up on what looked like a dinosaur. The rodent waved a heavy pack at Farouk. "I am Skittermore, human! I was directed by Once Lord Blitherskites to give this to a human with a purple hat. You are him?"

A dumbfounded Farouk vigorously nodded his head as dozens of these rat riders began to fill the woods about them.

Skittermore threw the pack at Farouk's feet. "Here is your payment, human."

Farouk smiled at the bag of diamonds. "Will you be needing instructions on the use of these weapons?"

Skittermore grinned. "My Lord Dark Seer has cast a spell of knowing on the Scatter Clans. We need no instruction."

Farouk shrugged. He had no idea what that meant.

Dark Seer's servant pointed at Farouk. "You have your baubles, human. I suggest you leave. The armies of Darkness come to reclaim what was once theirs."

Skittermore pulled on his reins and raced back to Avalon to report to his master. Several of the rodents dismounted and began to inspect the crates. Dozens more inspected the road and the surrounding wood.

Farouk spun and took Derrick's hand. "Well, it was very nice meeting you, Mr. Anderson, but I have to get very far away now."

Farouk clapped his hands and barked more orders at his men. They followed him out of the campsite and back to the road where his Mercedes and the trucks awaited. In a few moments they were gone. Several of the rats watched Derrick, but they did not bother with him. They were much too involved in uncrating the weapons.

Derrick was unsure of what to do. He didn't like the sound of that bit about the armies of Darkness. The scientist in him said it was all hogwash. Of course, he had just seen a large rat on a dinosaur drop off a suitcase of diamonds, and he was currently surrounded by a group of man-sized talking rodents.

He was trying to decide if he'd accidentally eaten some of the wrong kind of mushrooms when the cats showed up.

"Of course," he said to himself, "you've got to have man-sized cats to kill the man-sized rats."

A great screaming rose as the cats poured out of the valley and jumped the rats. Most of the rats bore swords or spears, but the cats were much better fighters. Typically they went for the throat or a deadly embrace where they raked their opponent's guts with their hindclaws.

Several of the rodents brought the machine guns to bear, and Derrick hit the dirt. They weren't very good shots, and the cats tag teamed them and took them

---

down quickly. After ten minutes of profound screams of rage and the tumultuous sounds of battle, it was quiet.

Derrick pulled his head out from under his arms and looked up. Standing over him was a creature the size of a small horse that resembled a saber-tooth tiger. "Do you conspire with Lord Dark Seer, human?"

Derrick managed to squeak out, "No."

A prodigious calico cat rushed up to the saber-tooth. "It is done. Maybe a dozen or so made it into the wood. Our runners are giving chase."

The saber-tooth snorted. "Set up a skirmish line along the border of Avalon. I don't want any of them getting back through to Darkness. I return to assist the wizard"

The calico ran off to execute its orders. Derrick watched as the saber-tooth bounded away.

"I'm positive none of those mushrooms had that little purple ring on the stalk," Derrick said to himself as he questioned his sanity.

***

Aikeem's arm fell limply to his side, the binoculars loosely held in his hand. His face fell, and dazed, he dropped back a step from the shrubs. Gandabon looked at Pendella as though she would understand the nature of his strange behavior.

Pendella addressed her man. "What's wrong, Aikeem?"

"We are doomed," the wizard barely whispered.

Gandabon became agitated. "Tell us what is wrong!"

Drusilla joined the ground, having returned from the border of Avalon and the real worlds. "Is there a problem?"

Aikeem turned to address the felines behind him. "The Sloths! They're leading an army of insect soldiers. There must be a million of them! If the rats have similar forces, then we're outnumbered at least eight to one!"

The cats were staggered. Gandabon peered through the bushes and gazed at the scene in the distance. Pendella stared deep into her man's eyes and shared the truth there. They were doomed.

"It makes no difference. We must hold them for three days," she stated.

Aikeem walked over to his map table and dropped his binoculars. "You're right, but I don't see how we can."

"I will help."

Aikeem's head snapped up and he gasped at the sight of Legacy. Gandabon and Drusilla hissed. They crouched down to leap on their enemy.

"Hold!" Pendella cried.

"This one murdered Sharpclaw," Drusilla hissed.

"It consorts with rats," Gandabon spit.

Legacy said nothing and addressed Pendella. "This is your man?"

Pendella nodded. Aikeem bore a quizzical expression. "You know this one, Pendella?"

Pendella didn't often cry, but she was very close to tears. "This is my most beloved, once mate, Thomas Wondermore."

Gandabon and Drusillia were obviously bewildered but relaxed their position.

Aikeem smiled. "Thomas Wondermore! Now I have heard of you! I am Aikeem Abdul Jamal Yosaffa." The wizard bowed to the large cat.

"I don't understand. Why did he kill Sharpclaw?" Drusillia asked.

Pendella turned on her comrades from the council. "We don't have the time now, Dru! We have an army of bugs about to give us a go, and we now have one more ally! Let us attend to the matter at hand!"

Aikeem strapped on Moonwind. "The lady is right. If she vouches for Thomas, then I would have him by my side."

Gandabon and Drusillia backed down. They weren't given to questioning Pendella's word. Aikeem belted on his shotgun and a double holster that housed two 10mm automatics.

The wizard turned to his lady and smiled. He bent down and caressed her behind one ear. "I've woven a small spell for you, lady; something to inspire us in the coming battle. Keep your ears perked."

Pendella gave her man kitty eyes. "I will, lover."

Aikeem turned to Drusillia and Gandabon. "Go to your columns behind the hills and wait. When you hear my signal, attack."

The two beasts nodded and sprinted off to their positions followed by the rest of the Council. The Wizard parted the bushes and started down the hill. Legacy followed close behind. Pendella remained at the tree.

She watched her two favorite males descend into the maw of the battlefield as the Chitin armies approached from the distance.

***

Guams soared above the rear quarter of Darkness's armies. They were still pouring into Avalon. Things were not going as quickly as Darkness would have liked, but at least they were moving. Dark Seer's scouts had not reported back yet, and this was making him nervous. He hoped to the very nature and core of his evil that Avalon hadn't merged with earth in the middle of one of its great oceans.

One of the globes of communication flashed red, and Xavier's image sprang into view. "Darkness!"

"What is it?"

"Someone has appeared in our path."

Darkness frowned. "Someone? We are two million strong. Who cares."

"So thought I, but there are magical cross currents emanating from this one. I swear he must be a mage."

"Show me!"

Xavier's image disappeared, and the plain before him was revealed. Darkness leaned forward to inspect the figure of a man in the distance. A large cat stood next to whomever it was. Legacy! What was he doing there? It seemed as though the man was chanting as he stood up and raised his hands.

A look of horror painted Darkness's face. "Aikeem! Raise your defenses! Raise your defenses!"

***

Aikeem cast out and two fireballs the size of massive haystacks rolled away from him. The Chitin warriors could not scream for they had no voices. Pops echoed as their bodies exploded in the intense heat. The sloths on the other hand were quite vocal as their fur caught on fire.

The fireballs raked down the ranks of insects and sloths alike. They went on for two miles before extinguishing. The front lines of the Chitin armies were in a shambles as the insects ran about in a daze of confusion. The sloths tried to regain control of their charges, and the column slowed to a halt.

"That went well," Legacy observed.

Aikeem raised his arms again and screamed. "And here comes steeeeerrrriiiiiiikkkkkeeee two!"

He gestured out and two gargantuan balls of lightning followed a similar course down the center of the column. More sloths screamed as the electrical arcs punctured them. Hundreds of insect warriors exploded in time to the touch of the deadly tendrils of power.

The entire first quarter of the Chitin armies ran about in chaos. Hundreds of sloth officers lay dead or dying. The leaderless soldiers scurried about looking for something to attack, but they only found each other.

Aikeem smiled at his handiwork. He gathered his strength and gestured again. "Are you ready! Here is steeeeerrrriiiiiiikkkkkeeee three!"

Random explosions shot up from the ground in a spray of earth and fire. The explosions extended for a mile and a half through the ranks of his enemies. Once again the enemy was thrown into turmoil.

***

Darkness screamed at the globe that housed Xaviar's image. "Run them over! Get your troops moving!"

"What about Legacy?"

"He has betrayed us! Kill them both!"

***

Horns sounded at the rear of the bug column, and it began to move forward again. If a leaderless battle roach got in the way, it was cut down. The living column of insect warriors rolled over its own as it moved toward Aikeem and Legacy.

Legacy observed nonchalantly, "I'm not sure, Wizard, but we may be outnumbered."

Aikeem smiled as the army drew closer. "Do you think so? Maybe we should call for reinforcements?"

The sloths began to scream their battle cries, and the insects moved from a march to a run, or skitter as the case may be.

Legacy replied, "If you must."

Aikeem spread his arms wide in a great sweeping gesture. Drums echoed across the valley. Trumpets followed and up on the hill Pendella smiled at her lover's choice of music. A great feline roar/scream filled in behind the music as

Emerson, Lake, and Palmer's version of Aaron Copeland's "Fanfare for the Common Man" resonated between the hills.

The sloths' battle cry turned into a battle squeak as they watched the 60,000 beasts at the front of the feline army slam into their flanks.

***

"Cats! Thousands and thousands of cats attack us," a frantic Xaviar screamed from his translucent globe.

"What! They're supposed to be on the Dreamscape!"

Darkness reflexively turned to look at the dream realm. His expression turned to one of horror. The mists had rolled over an eighth of his army.

"What! The weaver!"

He jumped up with a scream of rage and extended both arms out. Dark light leapt from his fingertips and beat the mists back, but where it had been was now empty space. Darkness's soldiers had been dragged to a screaming nightmarish death.

Darkness screamed into Lord Dark Seer's globe. "Dark Seer! Attend to your left flank! The weaver steals our soldiers!"

Dark Seer's image twisted to his left within the globe and cursed. The high rat rose and gestured with his skull staff. Green light shot forth from the eyes of the skull.

Darkness fell back into his seat and slammed the arm of his chair. He addressed both generals. "Drive on! Drive on! We must get our soldiers into Avalon now!"

***

A feline beast jumps, claws extended, into a troika of bugs. The target leans back, metal shod claws extended. They clash. Hindclaws rake down bug metal claws. Feline foreclaws eviscerate. The cat rolls away, springs under the other bug's defense. He bites and a head comes off in his maw. He jumps high as the third insect comes in behind him. He spins in midair and comes down on the bug's back. His weight collapses its spindly legs, and he crushes its head from behind with dripping fangs.

***

The bugs were no match for the feline warriors. The cats moved too fast. The weapons the insects held were wielded poorly. The sloths weren't much better, but occasionally they managed to take down a cat.

The feline avian transmorphs flew in from above to snatch wriggling bugs from the melee. They took them up high and dropped them back down on their fellows in the rear of the lines.

Aikeem noticed very quickly that the insect soldiers became confused as soon as their sloth officers were killed or distracted. Aikeem wove a quick spell of communication and sent a thought to all of the cats. "Strike down the sloths first if you can! They direct the bugs!"

The cats began to focus their attacks on the sloths, and the tide of battle fell even more into their favor.

***

Celise fell to the ground in absolute agony. Arcane energies crackled about her and her skin began to smoke. Instinctively, she knew she must leave the Dreamscape and with a thought she leapt into the mists at the speed of light.

She ejected out of the Dreamscape into Avalon where the two realms temporarily joined. She lay on her back gasping for air. She had no idea what caused such a reaction, but she was sure it had nothing to do with her enemies. She could not know that her physical self had entered the Dreamscape.

"Why now?" she cried in frustration to the heavens.

The screams of battle echoed from behind her. She spied the grassy knoll. She had taken many of their enemies out on the Dreamscape, but she was not done. She sprinted for the small hill.

Once atop the perch, she looked out onto the battlefield. It was an awesome sight. The cats decisively commanded the field. She was surprised to see Aikeem in the center of the valley with Legacy at his side. Apparently the beast had switched sides.

"It goes well." Celise started at Pendella's words. The feline came around from behind the bush.

"Why aren't you on the Dreamscape, Celise?"

"I don't know. I started to… cook."

Celise spied the fifty-caliber and smiled. "Now it is time for a different kind of attack."

Celise dragged the weapon from behind the bushes. She loaded the ammo into the gun as she'd seen Aikeem do and echoed his magical chant. "Please don't jam. Please don't jam. Please don't jam."

She snapped back the bolt and fired into the rear of the Chitin armies. They fell like dark weeds before her lead sickle.

***

Aikeem waded into the chitinous warriors swinging Moonwind. Legacy pounced on a bug to his left and crushed the creature. The wizard's first attacker swung a broadsword. He easily sidestepped it and relieved the creature of its arm. He dove high and came down to split the bug in two. Legacy raked the next bug with a roar, and it sprayed green bug juice as it fell apart.

Aikeem danced. Legacy bounded. Bugs died.

Aikeem stopped at the sound of machine gunfire. He looked back up the hill and smiled at the destruction his ladylove was inflicting at the rear of their enemy.

He screamed in pain as a metal claw pierced his right bicep. He dropped Moonwind. A claw came for his throat. He ducked, drew quickly, and placed his automatic in the creature's face. He fired and blew its tiny brain out.

More bugs skittered in, and Aikeem blasted them until a circle was cleared. Legacy bounded into the free space and Aikeem holstered his weapon. He waved his hand over his wounds to make them disappear. The energy drain made him stagger for a second. He was plumbing the depths of his personal power. He retrieved Moonwind and dived in beside Legacy as the beast ripped a channel between the bugs.

***

"My armies! My armies! They're slaughtering them. It's not fair!" Xaviar screamed hysterically into the globe.

Darkness stomped Guams' back in fury. "Get a hold of yourself sloth!"

Xaviar's head exploded in a font of red spray. The Weaver had found her mark.

Darkness stared in disbelief at the blank globe. "Guams! To the front! It is time to end this!"

The war dragon screamed a bloody roar, and his two fellows joined him on his trek to the front.

***

Gandabon leapt and crushed the back of the last bug. Its legs twitched and then fell limp. Aikeem picked his way through the wreckage to stand next to the council member. The battlefield was littered with insects, sloths, and the occasional feline corpse. They'd done well, but Aikeem was pained by the loss of so much life. At least a quarter of his army was gone.

A great, hate-filled scream rolled over the now bloody plain. The high rats of the Scatter Clans readied their pikes. Gandabon turned to Aikeem and spoke in ragged breaths. "These will not be so easy. Dark Seer's rats know how to fight."

Aikeem screamed at the cats around him. "Form up a skirmish line! Quickly!"

The cats lined up beside and behind him. Dark Seer rose from his throne on the back of the war lizard and pointed his skull staff in their direction. Aikeem hastily muttered and waved his arms. The staff spit death but fell short. The ground before the cats erupted in flame. Dark Seer raised his staff again; its beam slammed into their front lines.

Aikeem waved. The explosive rays that Dark Seer sent were deflected harmlessly off the translucent blue shield of power he raised. Dark Seer fell back onto his throne in a fit of anger.

Aikeem fell to his knees. Legacy licked his face out of concern. "I don't have much left. Another bolt like that and my shields will fail."

Lord Dark Seer screamed the death knell, and the Order of Vile led the charge. A picket of pikes rushed across the battlefield toward the feline front line.

Aikeem lurched to his feet and screamed. "Tough skins to the front!"

A flash of amber raced past Aikeem to the front of the line, and the wizard swelled with pride at the sight of his metallic Pendella. She was joined by a line of beasts whose skin was metallic, stone, or thick-scaled leather.

The pikes came in with a terrific clash, but the front line held. The cats waded into the rats with terrible consequence. Aikeem screamed and jumped into the fray. The bloody first engagement lasted for twenty minutes before the rats fell back.

Aikeem bore more than one open, red wound. He didn't have enough power left to fix them. He was dismayed when he saw the number of feline dead among the rodent carcasses. His eyes expanded with terror when he looked up into the sky.

Three dragons bore down on the feline hoards.

"DDDDuuuuuuuucccekkkkkkk!"

Aikeem dove to the ground and felines bounded in all directions as a trio of flame jets burst into their ranks. Those who were too slow screamed in rage and pain. The rats charged again.

"Form up! Form up!" The wizard cried desperately.

***

"You're sure you have one?" Celise screamed into Aikeem's pack.

"Damn sure," came a voice from the pack.

"Well, then get it!" Celise turned back to the sky and grimaced at the sight of the dragons. They were spinning to come in for another attack on the felines' rear. She could see Darkness on the back of one of the beasts.

The feline avian transmorphs dove on the dragons and began to harry them. Guams and one of his fellows were distracted such that they broke off their strafing run.

"Here you go! There's only one so make it count. The instructions are on the side."

Celise dove into the pack up to her elbow and came up with a shoulder-launched surface to air missile. She bore an evil grin as she read the instructions. She hastily unlocked the various safeties, threw the weapon into position, took aim and fired.

***

Aikeem split the skull of the rodent in front of him and kicked it over backwards. He stuck Moonwind in the blood soaked ground, quick-drew his automatics, and blasted twenty rodents back to the hell from whence they had come.

A dragon's roar issued from behind him, and he turned. His face fell as he saw a fire breather streaking toward their rear. A smoke trail tracked the creature's maw just as it was about to let loose. The lizard's head exploded in a bout of flame, and the dragon crashed into the ground in a spray of blood and earth.

Aikeem spun back in time to see a charge by a fresh group of warrior rats. Gandabon dove in front of him and slashed wildly. Aikeem watched in dismay as the rats swarmed the council member and took him down. A berserker rat with a battleaxe dove in.

"No!" Aikeem screamed in frustration as the axe was buried in Gandabon's chest. Aikeem holstered his weapons, reached behind, drew his shotgun, and blew the rat bastard away. He emptied his shotgun and cleared a new path.

The rats fell back again. Aikeem looked around desperately. They were down to fewer than half their numbers.

"Form up again! Form up again!"

Aikeem was relieved to find Pendella by his side. She gave him kitty eyes, but they faded when she spied Gandabon's corpse. Drusillia rushed by and sniffed her dead comrade. She placed her forepaws on his still chest and screamed to the heavens. The rest of the surviving feline army joined her in this roar of rage and sorrow.

The cats turned their attentions once again to the enemy. Aikeem watched them regroup their front line. His expression turned to dismay. He could see thousands of rat archers running through their ranks to take up position.

***

Celise gathered up the weapons from the table and went to join her lover.

"Celise."

Celise froze at the sound of her own voice. At first she was terrified to see the mirror image of herself. Her doppelganger was walking hand in hand with a ten-foot man-beast sporting ram's horns from the side of his head and carrying a massive battleaxe. Her doppelganger's eyes glowed a peculiar red as she led the monster over to Celise.

The Weaver aimed a mini-Uzi in their direction. "Stay back!"

The doppelganger smiled. "That's no way to talk to your mother, young lady."

The light of realization illuminated and Celise rushed to embrace herself. They parted. "I found your body back on earth. I've brought it back to you."

Marie continued, "I also found this one a while ago." Marie pointed to the ogre next to her. He bowed. "His name is Grimlot. He has a score to settle with that one called Darkness. Darkness stole Grimlot's castle from him and then banished him with evil magic to the Dreamscape. You and I know Darkness by another name."

Celise was puzzled. "Who is he mother?"

Marie fairly spit. "He is the vile voodun shaman who cursed our family! It is Daagbo! He's spent all these years conspiring with the sloths to return to Earth. We must end this. Now come child, take your body. There's a war to be fought. I must return to the Dreamscape for I have no form here."

Celise watched as the ghostly apparition of her mother departed the physical shell of her body. Instinctively Celise embraced the empty shell, and with a glow of white light she morphed back into one.

A bass voice rumbled from above. "I wish to do the same as you have just done with a treacherous little shaman who has stolen my body from me. I would have my physical form back from the one who took it from me. I'm told that in this place that is possible."

Celise smiled at Grimlot. "It is true. Come with me, sir. I'll reintroduce you."

The ogre chuckled, and he followed the Weaver down the hill into battle.

***

The wizard felt a hand on his shoulder. He turned to find his lady love. When he saw the monstrous beast next to Celise he exclaimed. "Who—"

"He's on our side," Celise stated simply.

Aikeem shrugged. He was grateful for whatever help he could get. The wizard turned back to the rat lines. His heart fell when he saw so many arrows nocked and ready to be launched.

A great battle cry rose up. On the hill along the rat's right flank were thousands upon thousands of heavily armed dwarves.

"Snapper-Cat!" The wizard spied the scout cat nearby and almost broke into tears.

They streamed down the hill and crashed into the unsuspecting rats. Dark Seer jumped up and fired from his skull staff again. Aikeem laughed as the beam bounced harmlessly off the little men. He'd heard they were magically resistant.

"Chargggggggeeeeeee!" the wizard screamed, and he led the remnants of the feline armies into the rats' front line.

The rat archers were confused and were unable to get off a solid volley. The rats broke. The rodents outnumbered their enemy, but with their right flank compromised, they floundered and ran. The dwarves and cats were merciless. They would take no prisoners.

Celise looked up and screamed with glee as Daagbo was plucked from his throne by the great white flying cat that had saved Aikeem from Marie so long ago. The creature turned its massive head as it flew opposite Guams. Two jade beams of energy punctured the dragon, causing its stomach to explode. The dead lizard crashed into the fleeing rodents below.

Daagbo tried desperately to fight the great white cat that held him in its claws. The shaman shot bolts of dark lightning into his captor, but the creature merely shrugged off the attack. It dropped Daagbo to the earth below. The shaman had no more magic to save himself, and he crashed with a sickening crunch onto a pile of dead rats.

Aikeem fell to his knees. Celise came to his side and he waved her off. "I'm fine, lady, just exhausted."

Celise helped her man up, and they stood to watch the dwarves and the feline warriors chase off the once great army of the Scatter Clans.

Aikeem turned and gently kissed Celise on the temple. "We did it, love. We won."

The pair watched the high rats flee. Aikeem smiled at the sight of Dark Seer's war beast. He could only see its tail end. He felt that was the best way to view it.

* * *

Hours later a broken Daagbo was brought in by an escort of angry felines. Pendella had returned to her normal feline form, unlike the council members around her. Cragstein and a contingent of dwarves were idly chatting with Aikeem and Celise when the prisoner arrived. Drusillia knocked the shaman down at the wizard's feet.

Daagbo, recently called Darkness, spit when he spied Legacy standing next to Aikeem.

"You betrayed me!"

Legacy shrugged. "I had to choose. It was either you or my own kind. I chose well."

Aikeem grabbed the small man by the breast of his cloak and hauled him up. "Many a fine creature has died because of you, little man. It is time for you to pay for your misdeeds and your lack of humility."

Aikeem released the man and stepped out of the way to reveal a grinning Ogre. Daagbo screamed and turned to run, but Grimlot grabbed him by the back of the neck.

"You ate me whole on the Dreamscape, shaman. That was a most unpleasant experience. It's also not my style."

Grimlot sucked the wizard in close and embraced him in a bone crushing hug. The humans winced at the sound of breaking bones and the shaman's scream. Daagbo flashed out of existence in a burst of black light.

Grimlot smiled, turned to his comrades and said, "Magically delicious."

The crowd could not help itself from laughing at the black humor.

The train-sized flying cat screamed a resonant roar over the battlefield, and the surviving cats sprang to attention at the soaring creature's call. The felines streamed off the battlefield to follow the great beast back into the Dreamscape. Groups of dwarves carried the feline dead on hastily built litters after the retreating cats.

Pendella looked up at Aikeem. "He calls us back to Wo'Em to bury our dead. Cragstein's people have graciously offered to carry our fallen for us."

Cragstein bowed. "We owe these here cats a lot," the dwarf winked at Snapper-Cat. "They rescued me people."

Aikeem watched the monstrous, flying cat beast sail off. "Who is that great flying creature?"

Pendella smiled. "It's Grizzle-Whiskers, of course. I'll see you back in the real worlds soon, lover," and with that Pendella took off after her fellows. A chagrined Aikeem smiled as Grizzle-Whiskers disappeared into the mists of the Dreamscape.

Aikeem and Celise exchanged goodbyes with Grimlot and the dwarves before they headed back to earth via Avalon.

After a few hours, the battlefield was devoid of life. In two more days Avalon slipped off into the Mists of Time and the Dreamscape once more bordered the Desolation Plains. Earth never knew of the brave heroes who died to protect her. She turned as she always did, home to a race who was secure in the knowledge that the universe was just so and always would be, regardless of what really was.

The Nature of Things

Farouk stretched out on a chaise lounge on a private beach on the Mediterranean. His new wife frolicked in the water, and he watched her with a profound sense of love and devotion. He needed someone that would keep a good home for him, and he was sure he'd found her. He was sure a son would be arriving in nine months time, too.

After he left America, he distributed the wealth he had brought back with him and closed up shop. He was generous to his employees, and he could afford to be. He was very rich now.

After settling his investments, he opened a theological school for children in the heart of Alexandria. Farouk had seen much of the world and had deep insights into the nature of men. After the business in America, he was sure he had no idea about the nature of Allah, but now there was no question that he existed.

Farouk took a sip of his aromatic coffee and sighed as he watched his beauty. Life was good.

***

Derrick Anderson took a moment to stop outside the office building where he worked and took in a great breath of air. He coughed from the carbon monoxide and various other pollutants. He smiled and sighed. The horns of New York City blared, and his grin spread even wider. He flagged down a taxi and hopped inside.

He adjusted the tie of his brand new suit and directed the driver to his new apartment on the Upper West Side. A few weeks after the phenomenon, he had quit the EPA and come to New York City to become an investment banker. They liked scientists these days for designing derivatives, and he found it an easy and lucrative job shift.

He swore after the incident in Maine that he was never leaving the city again. Here was logic, technology, and the bosom of mankind. There were no dinosaur rider rats in this place. He decided he might even take up smoking. He looked out the window into the artificial canyons of glass and steel and sighed. Life was good.

***

Blitherskites pounded another beer and slammed the mug on the bar. "Give me another!"

Sid gave him a sideways look, and a sheepish Blitherskites said softly, "Please."

Sid smiled and poured the rodent another brew. "Why'd you do it, mate? You coulda been a king on earth."

Blitherskites frowned. He was trying to forget all of that. This was his first trip back to the Darkling Space after the Avalon thing, and he was making it a point to get sloshed in an effort to forget.

Blitherskites was lucky in that the death mark was still removed. Dark Seer never knew of Blitherskites's complicity in the failure of the rat armies. After the battle, Dark Seer returned to his black kingdom with his tail between his legs. He had lost face on the Council of Thirteen, and the Scatter Clans had gone back to killing each other. Sid was the only one outside of those involved who knew the truth. Blitherskites had to tell someone whom he could trust.

"I don't know, Sid. That wizard was nice to me. Not too many people are nice to me. I think… I think he really, really liked me, Sid."

Sid placed the beer in front of the slurring rodent with a smile. "Friends is important, mate."

"Humans always treated me better than my own people. No human ever put a death mark on me. How could I let them destroy Earth, Sid? How could I—" hiccup.

"Well, in me humble opinion, Connie, you did the right thing."

Blitherskites felt a monstrous hand on his shoulder. He turned to find Boris smiling a broad grin with a lollipop stick dangling from one corner of his mouth. "I really, really like you too, Connie."

Blitherskites smiled and patted his friend on the shoulder.

"Me too, mate. Yer one o' a kind," Sid offered with a smile.

It was very unratlike behavior, but a few tears welled up in Blitherskites's eyes. He was suddenly overcome with the knowledge that it was friends like these that kept him going and that made life worth living. He sighed secure in the knowledge that in the end, life was good.

***

Aikeem, Celise, and Pendella shared a good laugh. They'd just watched a nature special on television about a strange phenomenon in South America. A couple of months ago thousands of three toed sloths started falling dead from the trees above. It was becoming hazardous to walk through the jungle. The scientists had concluded that this event must be the result of global warming. This was very humorous to the threesome.

Aikeem hit the power button on the remote, and the big screen TV winked out. Celise leaned over Pendella, who stretched out sphinx style between the pair, and kissed her man. Pendella gave her humans kitty eyes as they shared a bit of love.

Celise parted, rose, and stretched with a yawn. "I'm going to bed, my love."

Aikeem grinned a knowing smile. "You mean you're going to visit your mother."

Celise smiled. "That too. Good night."

Aikeem watched her leave the room, a slave to her seductive walk. Pendella leapt into her man's lap and rolled over on her back. Aikeem turned to her and smiled. He began to rub her belly.

He sighed to himself. In the end, not a soul on Earth knew what they'd done for them. Of course, that's the way the Administration liked things done, but a little recognition would have been nice.

When Aikeem and Celise left Avalon they found the massive cache of weapons abandoned in the Maine woods. Darkness's armies had never made it to Earth to use them. Aikeem had one spell left that he'd never gotten an opportunity to cast because he had run out of magical power. They stayed in that wood for about a week, and he powered the defensive spell up well beyond its original design.

Celise was brought to tears when she saw the spell cast. After Aikeem spoke the words of power and his great magic was released, a million weapons were turned into butterflies. Great clouds of living artwork filled the woods, and for a moment, it was as if they were in a heaven of color.

Aikeem smiled down at Pendella. She had come home from Wo'Em just the previous week. The cats had buried their dead. The council tried Legacy/Thomas for the murder of Sharpclaw and ultimately found him innocent due to extenuating circumstances. Grizzle-Whiskers proclaimed that he must serve penance, however, and made him the Fifth on the Council. There were no complaints, and Pendella was very proud.

Grizzle-Whiskers also consulted with the Administration, and Marie and Celise were given special status as weaver guardians. Grizzle-Whiskers was not about to condemn the Lavalles after the service they had performed for all of man and feline kind.

Pendella reached up, pawed Aikeem's chin, and gave him kitty eyes. "What are you thinking about, lover?"

Aikeem smiled. "Recent events, lady, and how well everything turned out."

Pendella rolled back on her stomach and stretched out sphinx style along her man's legs.

Aikeem picked up the nearby remote and turned on the CD player. One of Mozart's concertos filled the room. Aikeem stroked Pendella's back, and her sonorous purr reverberated around the concerto. Aikeem sighed. Although he was very wise about the way of things, he was humble enough to know that there was a great deal he didn't understand.

He was pretty sure about one thing though. He mused that the sum total of anyone's life was measured by the nature of one's relationships. He was sure that in order to reach a state of perfection, one must have some number of perfect relationships. He knew in his heart, as he stroked his lady's back, that this goal was most easily achieved by associating with a cat.

Aikeem and Pendella basked in the glow of their companionship, secure in the knowledge that life was indeed good.